MARKER

ALSO BY ROBIN COOK

Seizure
Shock
Abduction
Vector
Toxin
Invasion
Chromosome 6
Contagion
Acceptable Risk
Fatal Cure
Terminal
Blindsight
Vital Signs
Harmful Intent
Mutation
Mortal Fear
Outbreak
Mindbend
Godplayer
Fever
Brain
Sphinx
Coma
The Year of the Intern

MARKER

Robin Cook

DOUBLEDAY LARGE PRINT HOME LIBRARY EDITION

G. P. PUTNAM'S SONS NEW YORK

This Large Print Edition, prepared especially for Doubleday Large Print Home Library, contains the complete, unabridged text of the original Publisher's Edition.

G. P. PUTNAM'S SONS
Publishers Since 1838
Published by the Penguin Group
Penguin Group (USA) Inc., 375 Hudson Street, New York, New York 10014, USA • Penguin Group (Canada), 10 Alcorn Avenue, Toronto, Ontario M4V 3B2, Canada (a division of Pearson Penguin Canada Inc.) • Penguin Books Ltd, 80 Strand, London WC2R 0RL, England • Penguin Ireland, 25 St Stephen's Green, Dublin 2, Ireland (a division of Penguin Books Ltd) • Penguin Group (Australia), 250 Camberwell Road, Camberwell, Victoria 3124, Australia (a division of Pearson Australia Group Pty Ltd) • Penguin Books India Pvt Ltd, 11 Community Centre, Panchsheel Park, New Delhi–110 017, India • Penguin Group (NZ), Cnr Airborne and Rosedale Roads, Albany, Auckland 1310, New Zealand (a division of Pearson New Zealand Ltd.) • Penguin Books (South Africa) (Pty) Ltd, 24 Sturdee Avenue, Rosebank, Johannesburg 2196, South Africa

Penguin Books Ltd, Registered Offices:
80 Strand, London WC2R 0RL, England

ISBN 0-7394-5458-7

Printed in the United States of America

For Jean and Cameron
and all they mean to me

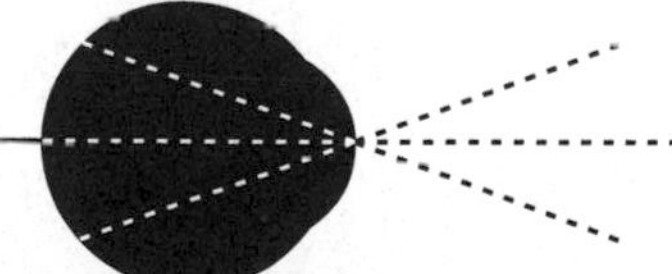

I would like to acknowledge my medical school, The College of Physicians and Surgeons at Columbia University in New York. It was an honor and a privilege to have attended. Both my professional life and writing career have depended heavily on the foundation of knowledge and experience I learned and enjoyed at that fine institution.

—R. C.

prologue

In the wee hours of February 2, a cold, steady drizzle drenched the concrete spires of New York City, shrouding them in a dense swirl of purplish-pink fog. Save for a few muted sirens, the city that never sleeps was at a relative standstill. Yet at exactly three-seventeen A.M., two nearly simultaneous, unrelated but basically similar, microcosmic events occurred on opposite sides of Central Park that would prove to be fatefully connected. One was on a cellular level, the other on a molecular level. Although the biological consequences of these two events were opposite, the events themselves were destined to cause the perpetrators—all strangers—to violently collide in less than two months.

The cellular event occurred in a moment of intense bliss and involved the forcible injection of slightly more than two hundred and fifty million sperm into a vaginal vault. Like a group of anxious marathoners, the sperm mobilized quickly, tapped into their selfcontained energy stores, and began a truly Herculean race against death: a remarkably arduous and perilous race that only one could win, relegating the others to short and frustratingly futile lives.

The first task was to penetrate the mucous plug obstructing the collapsed uterine cavity. Despite this formidable barrier, the sperm rapidly triumphed as a group, although it was a Pyrrhic victory. Tens of millions of the initial wave of gametes were lost in a form of self-sacrifice required to release their contained enzymes to make the passage possible for others.

The next ordeal for this horde of minute living entities was to traverse the relatively enormous uterine expanse, almost equivalent in distance and danger to a small fish swimming the length of the Great Barrier Reef. But even this seemingly insurmountable impediment was overcome as a few thousand lucky and robust individual sperm made it to the openings of the two oviducts, leaving behind hundreds of millions of unlucky casualties.

Still, the travail was not over. Once within the undulating folds of the oviducts, the fortunate ones who'd entered the correct tube were now spurred on by the chemotaxis of the descending fluid from a burst ovarian follicle. Somewhere ahead, beyond a tortuous and treacherous twelve centimeters, lay the sperm's Holy Grail, a recently released ovum crowned with a cloud of supporting cumulous cells.

Progressively goaded by the irresistible chemical attraction, a contingent of the male gametes accomplished the ostensibly impossible and closed in on their target. Nearly exhausted from the long swim and from avoiding predatory macrophages who'd engulfed many of their brethren, the number was now less than one hundred and falling rapidly. Neck and neck, the survivors bore down on the hapless haploid egg in a race to the wire.

After an astonishingly short one hour and twenty-five minutes, the winning sperm gave a final desperate beat of his flagellum and collided head-on with the egg's surrounding cumulous cells. Frantically, he burrowed between the cells to bring his caplike acrosome into direct contact with the egg's heavy protein coat to form a bond. At that instant, the race was over. As his last mortal act, the winning sperm then injected his contained nuclear material into the egg to form the male pronucleus.

The other sixteen sperm that had managed to reach the egg seconds behind the winner found themselves unable to adhere to the egg's altered protein coat. With their energy stores exhausted, their flagella soon fell silent. There was no second place, and all the losers were soon swept up, engulfed, and carried off by the deadly maternal macrophages.

Inside the now-fertilized ovum, the female pronucleus and the male pronucleus migrated toward each other. After the dissolution of their envelopes, their nuclear material fused to form the required forty-six chromosomes of a human somatic cell. The ovum had metamorphosed into a zygote. Within twenty-four hours, it divided in a process called *cleavage,* the first step in a programmed sequence of events that would in twenty days begin to form an embryo. A life had begun.

The nearly simultaneous molecular event also involved a forcible injection. On this occasion a bolus of more than a trillion molecules of a simple salt called potassium chloride dissolved in a shotglass volume of sterile water was injected into a peripheral arm vein. The effect was almost instantaneous. Cells lining the vein experienced a rapid passive diffusion of the potassium ions into their interiors, upsetting their electrostatic charge necessary for life and function. Delicate nerve endings among the cells quickly sent urgent messages of pain to the brain as a warning of imminent catastrophe.

Within seconds, the rest of the potassium ions were streaming through the great veins and into the heart, where they were propelled with each beat out into the vast arterial tree. Although progressive dilution occurred within the plasma, the concentration was still incompatible with cellular function. Of particular concern were the specialized cells of the heart responsible for initiating the heartbeat, those of the brainstem responsible for the urge to breathe, and the nerves and muscle spindles that carried the messages. All were quickly adversely affected. The heart rate rapidly slowed, and the heartbeats grew weaker. Breathing became shallow, and oxygenation inadequate. Moments later, the heart stopped altogether, initiating progressive bodywide cellular death as well as clinical death. A life had been lost. As a final blow, the dying cells leaked their store of potassium into the stagnant circulatory system, effectively masking the original lethal bolus.

one

The sound of the dripping was metronomic. Somewhere out on the fire escape, drops of water, fueled by the incessant rain, splattered against a metallic surface. To Laurie Montgomery, the noise seemed almost as loud as a kettledrum in Jack Stapleton's otherwise silent apartment, making her wince as she anticipated each splat. The only competition over the long hours had been the refrigerator's compressor cycling on and off, the hiss and thump of the radiator as heat rose, and an occasional distant siren or horn, sounds so typical in New York that people's minds instinctively ignored them. But Laurie was not so lucky. After tossing and turning for three hours, she'd become hypersensitive to every sound around her.

Laurie rolled over again and opened her eyes. Anemic fingers of light reached around the window shade's edges, allowing her a better view of Jack's barren and otherwise drab apartment. The reason she and Jack were there instead of at her apartment was the size of her bedroom: It was so small that the largest bed it could accommodate was a twin, which made communal sleeping problematic. And then there was also Jack's desire to be near to his beloved neighborhood basketball court.

Laurie glanced over to the radio alarm clock. As its digital readout relentlessly advanced, Laurie became progressively angry. Without much sleep, she knew from sore experience she'd be a basket case at the medical examiner's office that day. She wondered how in God's name she had made it through medical school and her residency, where sleep deprivation had been the name of the game. Yet Laurie sensed that her current inability to fall asleep wasn't the only thing making her angry. In fact, her anger was probably why she couldn't sleep in the first place.

It had been the middle of the night when Jack had inadvertently reminded her of her upcoming birthday, asking her if she wanted to do something special to celebrate. Laurie knew it had been an innocent question, coming as it did in the afterglow of lovemaking, but it had shattered her elaborate defense of taking each day at a time to avoid thinking about the future. It seemed impossible, but she was soon to be forty-three years old. Somewhere around age thirty-five the cliché about the ticking reproductive clock had become true for her—and now hers was sending out the alarm.

Laurie let out an involuntary sigh. In her loneliness as the hours had slid by, she'd fretted over the social quagmire in which she found herself ensnared. When it came to her personal life, things hadn't gone right since middle school. Jack was content with the status quo, as evidenced by his relaxed silhouette and the sounds of his blissful sleep, which only made things worse for Laurie. She wanted a family. She'd always assumed she'd have one, even during her comparatively wild twenties and early thirties, yet here she was, almost forty-three, living in a crummy apartment in a fringe New York neighborhood, sleeping with a man who couldn't make up his mind about marriage or children.

She sighed again. Earlier, she'd consciously tried to avoid disturbing Jack, but now she didn't care. She had decided she was going to try to talk with him again, even though she knew that the issue was something he studiously preferred to ignore. But this time, she was going to demand some change. After all, why should she settle for a miserable life in an apartment more suited to a couple of penurious graduate students than board-certified forensic pathologists, as she and Jack were, in a relationship where discussions of marriage and children were unilaterally verboten?

Yet things weren't all bad. On the career side, it couldn't be better. She loved her job as a medical examiner at the Office of the Chief Medical Examiner of New York, where she'd been working for thirteen years, and she felt lucky she had a coworker like Jack with whom she could share the experience. Both of them were awed by the intellectual stimulation that forensic pathology offered; each day they learned something new. And they saw eye to eye on a lot of issues: Both had little tolerance for mediocrity, and both were turned off by the political necessities of being part of a bureaucracy. Yet as compatible as they were work-wise, it did not make up for her burgeoning desire to have a family.

Jack suddenly stirred and rolled over onto his back, his fingers intertwined and hands clasped on his chest. Laurie looked at his sleeping profile. In her eyes, he was a handsome man, with closely cropped, gray-streaked light brown hair, bushy eyebrows, and strong, sharp features, usually sporting a wry smile, even in repose. She found him aggressive yet friendly, bold yet modest, challenging yet generous, and, most often, playful and fun. With his quick wit, life was never dull, especially with his adolescent penchant for risk-taking. On the negative side he could be aggravatingly stubborn, especially about marriage and children.

Laurie leaned toward Jack and looked more closely. He was definitely smiling, which aggravated her irritation. It didn't seem fair that he was satisfied with the status quo. Although she was reasonably sure she loved him and believed he loved her, his inability to make a commitment was literally driving her to distraction. He said it wasn't a fear of marriage or parenthood per se, but rather the vulnerability that such commitment created. At first, Laurie had been understanding: Jack had suffered the tragedy of losing his first wife and two young daughters in a commuter plane crash. She knew that he carried both the grief and the responsibility, since the accident had occurred after a family visit while he was retraining in pathology in another city. She also knew that after the accident, he had struggled with severe reactive depression. But now the tragedy was almost thirteen years in the past. Laurie felt that she'd been sensitive to his needs and had been patient when they finally did start dating seriously. But now, almost four years later, Laurie felt that she'd reached her limit. After all, she had needs, too.

The buzz of Jack's alarm shattered the

silence. Jack's arm shot out and swatted the snooze button, then retracted back into the warmth of the covers. For five minutes, peacefulness returned to the room, and Jack's breathing regained its slow, deep, sleeping rhythm. This was part of the morning routine that Laurie never saw, because Jack invariably was up before she was. Laurie was a night person who loved to read before turning out the light, often staying up longer than she should. Almost from day one of their cohabitation, Laurie had learned to sleep through the alarm, knowing Jack would get it.

When the alarm went off the second time, Jack turned it off, threw back the covers, sat up, and put his feet on the floor, facing away from Laurie. She watched him stretch and could hear him yawn as he rubbed his eyes. He stood up and padded into the bathroom, heedless of his nakedness. Laurie put her hands behind her head and watched him, and despite her aggravation, it was a pleasant sight. She could hear him use the toilet and then flush. When he reappeared, he was again rubbing his eyes as he came around to Laurie's side of the bed to wake her.

Jack reached out to give Laurie's shoulder a shake as per usual, and then gave a start when he saw her eyes open, trained on him, her mouth set in an expression of irritated determination.

"You're awake!" Jack said, his eyebrows arching questioningly. He knew instantly that something was amiss.

"I haven't been back to sleep since our middle-of-the-night tryst."

"It was that good, huh?" Jack said, in hopes that humor could defuse her apparent pique.

"Jack, we have to talk," Laurie said flatly, sitting up and clutching the blanket to her chest. Defiantly she locked eyes with him.

"Isn't that what we're already doing?" Jack questioned. He immediately guessed where Laurie was coming from, and he couldn't keep sarcasm out of his voice. Although he knew his tone was counterproductive, he couldn't help himself. Sarcasm was a protective mannerism he'd developed over the last decade.

Laurie started to respond, but Jack held up his hand. "I'm sorry. I don't mean to sound insensitive, but I have a sneaking suspicion where this conversation is headed, and it's not the time. I'm sorry, Laurie, but we have to be at the morgue in an hour, and neither of us has showered, dressed, or eaten."

"Jack, it's never the time."

"Well, then let's put it this way: This might be the worst possible time for some kind of serious, emotional discussion. It's six-thirty on a Monday morning after a great weekend, and we have to get to work. If it had been on your mind, there'd have been a dozen other times during the last couple of days when you could have brought it up, and I would have been happy to discuss it."

"Oh, bull! Let's face it, you never want to talk about it. Jack, I'm going to be forty-three on Thursday. Forty-three! I don't have the luxury of being patient. I can't wait for you to decide what you want to do. I'll be postmenopausal."

For several beats, Jack stared into Laurie's blue-green eyes. It was clear that she wasn't going to be placated easily. "All right," he said, exhaling noisily as if he was conceding. He averted his gaze down to his bare feet. "We'll talk about it tonight over dinner."

"I need to talk about it now!" Laurie said emphatically. She reached out and lifted Jack's chin to lock eyes again. "I've been agonizing over our situation while you've been sleeping. Putting it off is not an option."

"Laurie, I'm going to go in and take a shower. I'm telling you, there's no time for this at the moment."

"I love you, Jack," Laurie said after grabbing his arm to restrain him. "But I need more. I want to be married and have a family. I want to live someplace better than this." She let go of Jack's arm and swept her hand around the room to point out the peeling paint, the bare lightbulb, the bed with no headboard, the two night tables that were empty wooden wine cases set on end, and the single bureau. "It doesn't have to be the Taj Mahal, but this is ridiculous."

"All this time, I thought four stars was adequate for you."

"Save the sarcasm," Laurie snapped. "A little luxury wouldn't hurt for as hard as we work. But that's not the issue. It's the relationship, which seems fine for you but isn't enough for me. That's the bottom line."

"I'm taking a shower," Jack said.

Laurie gave him a crooked half-smile. "Fine. You take a shower."

Jack nodded and started to say something, then changed his mind. He turned and disappeared into the bathroom, leaving the door ajar. A moment later, Laurie heard the shower start and the sound of the shower curtain rings scraping across the shower rod.

Laurie exhaled. She was trembling from a combination of fatigue and emotional stress, but she was proud of herself for not shedding any tears. She hated when she cried in emotional situations. How she had avoided it at the moment she had no idea, but she was pleased. Tears never helped, and frequently put her at a disadvantage.

After slipping on her robe, Laurie went into the closet for her suitcase. The confrontation with Jack actually made her feel relieved. By responding just as she'd anticipated, Jack justified what she had decided to do even before he had awakened. Opening up her allotted bureau drawers, she took out her things and began packing. With the task almost complete, she heard the shower stop, and a minute later Jack appeared in the doorway, briskly toweling off his head. When he caught sight of Laurie and the suitcase, he stopped abruptly.

"What the hell are you doing?"

"I think it's perfectly clear what I'm doing," Laurie answered.

For a minute Jack didn't say anything, merely watching as Laurie continued her packing. "You're carrying this too far," he said finally. "You don't have to leave."

"I think I do," Laurie responded without looking up.

"Fine!" Jack said after a beat, an edge to his voice. He ducked back through the door to finish toweling off.

When Jack came out of the bathroom, Laurie went in, carrying the day's outfit. She made a point of closing the door, although on normal mornings, it remained open. By the time Laurie emerged, fully dressed, Jack was in the kitchen. Laurie joined him for a breakfast of cold cereal and fruit. Neither took the time to sit at the tiny vinyl dinette set. Both were polite, and the only conversation was "excuse me" or "sorry" as they danced around each other to get in and out of the refrigerator. Thanks to the narrowness of the room, it was impossible to move without touching.

By seven, they were ready to leave. Laurie squeezed her cosmetics into her suitcase and closed the lid. When she rolled it out into the living room, she saw Jack lifting his mountain bike from its wall rack.

"You're not riding that thing to work, are you?" Laurie asked. Prior to their living together, Jack had used the bike to commute, as well as to run errands around the city. It had always terrified Laurie, who constantly worried that he was going to arrive one day at the morgue "feet first." When they had begun to commute together, Jack had given up riding the bike, since there was no way Laurie would consent to doing the same.

"Well, it looks like I'll be on my own coming back to my palace."

"It's raining, for God's sake!"

"Rain makes it more interesting."

"You know, Jack, since I'm being honest this morning, I think I should tell you that I find this kind of juvenile risk-taking of yours is not only inappropriate but also selfish, like you're thumbing your nose at my feelings."

"That's interesting," Jack said with a smirk. "Well, let me tell you something: Riding my bike has nothing to do with your feelings. And to be honest with you, your feeling that it does seems pretty selfish to me."

Outside on 106th Street, Laurie walked west to Columbus Avenue to catch a cab. Jack pedaled east toward Central Park. Neither turned to wave at the other.

two

Jack had forgotten the exhilaration of riding his dark purple Cannondale mountain bike, but it came back to him in a rush as he coasted down one of the hills after entering Central Park near 106th Street. Since the park was nearly deserted save for the rare jogger, Jack had let himself go, and both the city and his suppressed anxieties miraculously disappeared in the misty city-bound forest. With the wind whistling in his ears, he could remember as if it were yesterday sailing down Dead Man's Hill in South Bend, Indiana, on his beloved red-and-gold, wide-tired Schwinn. He'd gotten the bike on his tenth birthday after having seen it advertised on the back of a comic book. Mythologized as a symbol of his happy and carefree childhood, he'd convinced his mother to save it, and it continued to gather dust back in the garage of his family's home.

Rain was still falling, but not hard enough to dampen Jack's experience, despite his hearing droplets splattering against the brow of his bicycle helmet. His biggest problem was trying to see through the moisture-streaked lenses of his aerodynamic bicycling sunglasses. To keep the rest of himself reasonably dry, he wore his waterproof bicycle poncho, which featured ingenious little hooks for his thumbs. When he learned forward with his hands grasping the handlebars, the poncho created a tent-like covering. For the most part, he avoided puddles, and when he couldn't, he lifted his feet off the pedals to coast until he reached drier pavement.

At the southeast corner of Central Park, Jack entered the Midtown city streets, already clogged with morning rush-hour traffic. There had been a time when he loved to challenge the traffic, but that was when he was, in his words, a bit crazier. It was also when he was in significantly better shape. Since he hadn't been riding much over the last few years, he didn't have nearly the same stamina anymore. His frequent basketball playing helped, but basketball didn't involve quite the same sustained aerobics that bicycling demanded. Yet he didn't slow down, and by the time he coasted down the ramp into the 30th Street receiving dock at the medical examiner's office, his quadriceps were complaining. After dismounting, he stood for a moment, leaning onto his handlebars to let his circulation catch up with the oxygen demand in his leg muscles.

When the hypoxic aching of his thighs had been mollified, Jack hefted his bike on his shoulder and started up the steps to the receiving dock. His legs were still rubbery, but he was eager to find out what was going on at the morgue. When he'd passed the front of the building, he'd seen a number of TV satellite trucks parked at the curb with their generators cranking and their antennae extended. He also had caught sight of a press of people within the reception area just beyond the front doors. Something was brewing.

Jack waved a greeting to Robert Harper through the window of the security office. The uniformed officer popped out of his chair and stuck his head around the jamb of the open door.

"Back to your old tricks, Dr. Stapleton?" Robert called out. "I haven't seen that bike of yours for years."

Jack waved over his shoulder as he carried his bike into the depths of the morgue's basement. He passed the small autopsy room used for examining decomposing corpses and turned left just before the central mass of drawer-shaped refrigerated compartments where bodies were stored prior to being autopsied. He had to clear a space for his bike in the area reserved for the Potter's Field pine coffins, used for the unidentified and unwanted dead. After stowing his coat and bicycle paraphernalia in his locker in the changing room, Jack headed for the stairs. He passed Mike Passano, the graveyard-shift mortuary tech, who was busy finishing up his paperwork in the mortuary office. Jack waved, but Mike was too engrossed to notice him.

As Jack emerged into the central corridor on the first floor, he caught another glimpse of the crowded front reception area. Even from the back of the building, he could hear the murmur of excited conversation. Something was up, and his curiosity was piqued. One of the most exciting aspects of being a medical examiner was that he never knew from one day to the next what was in store. Coming to work was stimulating, even exciting, which was a far cry from how Jack had felt in his former life as an ophthalmologist, when each day had been comfortable but utterly predictable.

Jack's ophthalmology career had ended abruptly in 1990, when his practice had been gobbled up by the aggressively expanding managed-care giant AmeriCare. AmeriCare's offer to hire Jack as an employee was another slap in the face. The experience forced Jack to recognize that old-school, fee-for-service medicine based on close doctor-patient relationships, where decisions were based solely on patients' needs, was rapidly disappearing. That epiphany led to his decision to retrain as a forensic pathologist, hopefully freeing himself from managed care, which he felt was more of a euphemism for "denial of care." The final irony was that AmeriCare had resurfaced to haunt Jack despite his efforts to distance himself. Thanks to a low bid for its premiums, AmeriCare had recently won a competitive contract for city employees. Jack and his colleagues now had to look to AmeriCare for their own healthcare needs.

Wishing to avoid the throng of media, Jack set off on the back route to the ID office, where the morgue's workday began. On a rotating basis, one of the more senior medical examiners arrived early to review the cases that had come in during the night, decide which ones needed to be autopsied, and make the assignments. It was Jack's habit to get to work early as well, even if it wasn't his turn to be the scheduler, so he could snoop through the cases and get the most challenging ones assigned to him. Jack had always wondered why other docs didn't do the same thing until he realized that the majority of the others were more interested in avoidance. Jack's curiosity invariably caused him to end up with the largest caseload. But he didn't mind;

work was Jack's opiate for taming his demons. While he and Laurie had been practically living together, he'd gotten her to come in early with him, which had been no mean feat, considering how hard it was for her to get up in the morning. The thought made Jack smile. It also made him wonder if she had already arrived.

Jack suddenly stopped in his tracks. Until now, he had deliberately kept the morning's confrontation from his mind. Thoughts of his relationship with Laurie as well as memories of horrific events of his own past flooded into his consciousness. Irritably, he wondered why she had felt compelled to end a beautiful weekend on such a downer note, especially since things had been going so well between them. In general, he almost felt content, a remarkable state of mind, considering he didn't feel he deserved to be alive, much less happy.

A wave of anger spread through him. The last thing he needed was to be reminded of his smoldering grief and guilt about his late wife and daughters, which happened with any talk of marriage or children. The idea of commitment and the vulnerability it entailed, especially starting another family, was terrifying.

"Get a grip," Jack murmured to himself under his breath. He closed his eyes and roughly massaged his face with both hands. Behind his irritation and frustration with Laurie, he felt the stirrings of melancholy, an unwelcome reminder of his past struggles with depression. The problem was, he truly cared for her. Things were great, except for the gnawing issue of children.

"Dr. Stapleton, are you all right?" a woman's voice asked.

Jack peeked out through his fingers. Janice Jaeger, the petite night-shift forensic investigator, was staring up at him while pulling on her coat, on her way home and apparently exhausted. Her legendary dark circles made Jack wonder if she ever slept.

"I'm fine," Jack said. He took his hands away from his face and shrugged self-consciously. "Why do you ask?"

"I don't think I've ever seen you standing still, especially in the middle of the corridor."

Jack tried to think of a witty retort, but nothing came to mind. Instead, he changed the subject by lamely asking if she had had an interesting night.

"It was wild around here!" Janice said. "More so for the tour doctor and even Dr. Fontworth than me. Dr. Bingham and Dr. Washington are already here doing a post, with Fontworth assisting."

"No kidding!" Jack said. "What kind of case?" Harold Bingham was the chief, and Calvin Washington was the deputy chief. Generally, neither appeared until well after eight in the morning, and it was rare for them to do an autopsy before the normal day began. There had to be political ramifications, which explained the media presence. Fontworth was one of Jack's colleagues, and had been on call for the weekend. Medical examiners didn't come in at night unless there was a problem. Pathology residents were hired as "tour doctors" to cover routine calls requiring a physician.

"It's a gunshot wound, but it's a police case, which is why Fontworth had to take it. As I understand it, the police had surrounded a suspect in his girlfriend's care. When they tried to arrest him, a barrage of shots was fired. There's the question of unreasonable force. You might find it interesting."

Jack inwardly winced. GSW cases could be tricky with multiple shots. Although Dr. George Fontworth was Jack's senior by eight years at the Office of the Chief Medical Examiner, or OCME, he was, in Jack's opinion, perfunctory. "I think I'll stay clear with the chief involved," Jack said. "What'd you handle? Anything of note?"

"The usual, but there was one at the Manhattan General that stood out. A young man who'd just been operated on yesterday morning for a compound fracture after a fall while in-line skating on Saturday in Central Park."

Jack winced anew. With his sensitivities aroused, thanks to Laurie, he had a negative response at the mere mention of the Manhattan General Hospital. Once an acclaimed academic center, it was now an AmeriCare flagship hospital after having been targeted and taken over by the cash-rich managed-care giant. Although he knew that the overall level of medicine practiced at the institution was good, such that if he took a bad flop on his bike and ended up in their trauma unit, which is where they would probably take him with the new city contract, he'd be well taken care of. At the same time it was still a managed-care establishment run by AmeriCare, and he had a visceral hatred for the company.

"What made the case stand out?" Jack asked, trying to conceal the emotion he felt. Reverting to sarcasm, he added: "Was it a diagnostic conundrum, or was there some sort of scurrilous hanky-panky involved?"

"Neither!" Janice sighed. "It was just the way the case struck me. It was just . . . rather sad."

"Sad?" Jack questioned. He was taken aback. Janice had been working as a forensic investigator for more than twenty years and had seen death in all its inglorious permutations. "For you to say it's sad, it's got to be really sad. What's the scoop in a nutshell?"

"He was only in his late twenties and had no medical history—specifically, no heart trouble. The narrative I got was that he'd rung his call button, but by the time the nurses got around to him five to ten minutes later—that's according to the nurses—he was dead. So it must have been cardiac."

"There was no resuscitation attempt?"

"Oh, they definitely tried to resuscitate him, but with no success whatsoever. They never even got a blip on the EKG."

"What made it so sad? The man's age?"

"The age was one factor, but it wasn't the whole story. Actually, I don't know why it bothered me so much. Maybe it has something to do with the nurses not responding quickly enough and my thinking the poor guy knew he was in trouble but couldn't get help. We can all relate to that kind of a hospital nightmare. Or maybe it has something to do with the patient's parents, who are very sympathetic. They came in from Westchester to go to the hospital, then came over here to stay near the body. They're really broken up. I get the impression their son was their whole life. I think they're still here."

"Where? I hope they're not stuck out there in that mob of reporters?"

"Last thing I knew, they were in the ID room, insisting on another ID even though it had already been established. To be considerate, the tour doctor told Mike to go ahead and do another set of Polaroids, but that was when I was called back to the

General for another case. When I got back here, Mike happened to mention the couple was still spaced out in the ID room, sort of emotionally adrift, while clutching the Polaroids. And, as if still hoping the whole affair was a mistake, they insisted on viewing the body itself."

Jack felt his pulse quicken. He knew all too well the emotional devastation of losing a child. "That case can't be what has the media people all stirred up."

"Heavens, no. The kind of case I'm talking about never reaches the public. That's part of the reason it's so sad. A life wasted."

"Is it the police case that's brought in the media?"

"It's what brought them originally. Bingham announced he would make a statement after the autopsy. The tour doctor told me the Spanish Harlem community is up in arms about the incident. Apparently, there were something like fifty shots fired by the police. Echoes of the Diallo case in the South Bronx some years back. But to tell you the truth, I think what the media is now mostly interested in is the Sara Cromwell case, which came in after they were already here."

"Sara Cromwell, the syndicated psychologist in the *Daily News*?"

"Yeah, the advice diva, capable of telling anyone and everyone how to get his or her life back on track. She was also a TV personality, you know. She hit most of the talk shows, including *Oprah.* She was pretty darn famous."

"Was it an accident? Why the fuss?"

"No accident. She was apparently brutally murdered in her Park Avenue apartment. I don't know the details, but it was on the gory side, according to Dr. Fontworth, who had to handle that case as well. I tell you, he and the tour doctor were out all night. After Cromwell, there was a double suicide in a mansion on Eighty-fourth Street, then a nightclub homicide. After that, the tour doctor had to go out for a hit-and-run on Park Avenue and two overdoses."

"What about the double suicide? Old or young?"

"Middle-aged. Carbon monoxide. They had their Escalade running with the garage door closed and a couple of vacuum hoses from the exhausts into the cab."

"Hmmm," Jack murmured. "Any suicide notes?"

"Hey, no fair," Janice complained. "You're grilling me about cases I didn't handle. But as far as I know there was only one note, from the woman."

"Interesting," Jack commented. "Well, I better get down to the ID room. Sounds like it's going to be a busy day. And you better get home to get some sleep."

Jack was pleased. The anticipation of an interesting day swept away some of the irritation that had resurfaced about the morning. If Laurie wanted to go back to her own apartment for a few days, it was fine with him! He'd just bide his time, because he wasn't going to be emotionally extorted.

Jack sped by the forensic investigators' office, cut through the clerical room with its banks of file cabinets, and entered the communications room just beyond. He smiled at the day-shift telephone operators but got no response. They were preoccupied with getting themselves organized. He waved to Sergeant Murphy when he passed the NYPD detective room, but Murphy was on the phone and didn't respond, either. Some welcome, Jack mused.

Entering the ID office, Jack got the same treatment. There were three people in the room, and all three ignored him. Two were hidden behind their morning papers while Dr. Riva Mehta, Laurie's office mate, was busy going over the sizable stack of potential cases to make up the autopsy schedule. Jack got a cup of coffee from the communal pot, then bent down the edge of Vinnie Amendola's paper. Vinnie was one of the mortuary techs and Jack's frequent partner in the autopsy room. Vinnie's regular and early presence meant Jack could start in the autopsy room well before anyone else.

"How come you're not down in the pit with Bingham and Washington?" Jack asked.

"Beats me," Vinnie said, pulling his paper free. "Apparently, they called Sal. They were already going at it when I got here."

"Jack! How ya doin'?"

A third person emerged from behind his paper, but the accent gave him away. It was Detective Lieutenant Lou Soldano, from Homicide. Jack had met him years ago when he had first joined the Office of the Chief Medical Examiner. Convinced of the enormous contributions of forensic pathology to his line of work, Lou was a frequent visitor to the OCME. He was also a friend.

With a bit of effort, the stocky detective heaved himself out of the vinyl club chair, clutching his paper in his beefy hand. With his aged trench coat, his tie loosened and the top button of his shirt open, he appeared like a rumpled character out of an old film noir. His broad face sported what could have been a two-day growth of beard, although from experience, Jack knew it was only one.

They greeted each other with a slapping, modified high-five, which Jack had learned out on the neighborhood basketball court and had jokingly taught Lou. It made both of them feel more hip.

"What's got you up this early?" Jack asked.

"Up? I haven't been to bed yet," Lou scoffed. "It's been that kind of night. My captain is worried sick about this supposed police brutality case, since the department is going to feel real heat if the involved officers' story doesn't hold up. I'm hoping to get an early scoop, but that's not looking good with Bingham doing the case. He'll probably be in there screwing around for most of the day."

"What about Sara Cromwell's case? Are you interested in that, too?"

"Yeah! Of course! As if I had any choice! Did you see all the media out in reception?"

"They would have been hard to miss," Jack responded.

"Unfortunately, they were already here on the police shooting. Guaranteed there's going to be a lot of newspaper and TV hype for that skinny psychologist, probably more than she would have gotten had they not been hanging around. And whenever a murder gets a high profile in the media, I know I'll be getting lots of pressure from above to come up with a suspect. So, with that said, do me a favor and do the case."

"Are you serious?"

"Of course I'm serious. You're fast and you're thorough, both of which fulfill my needs. Also, you're okay with me watching, which I can't say about everybody around here. But if you're not interested, maybe I can get Laurie to do it, although knowing her GSW bent, she'll probably want to get involved in the police case."

"She's also interested in one of the Manhattan General cases," Riva said in silky, British-accented voice, which was in sharp contrast to Lou's New York twang. "She's already taken the folder and said she wants to do that one first."

"Did you see Laurie this morning?" Jack asked Lou. He and Lou shared an appreciation of Laurie Montgomery. Jack knew that Lou had even once briefly dated Laurie, but it hadn't worked out. From Lou's own admission, the problem had been Lou's lack of social confidence. Graciously, Lou had become a strong advocate for Jack and Laurie as a couple.

"Yeah, about fifteen or twenty minutes ago."

"Did you talk to her?"

"Of course. What kind of a question is that?"

"Did she seem normal? What did she say?"

"Hey! Why the third degree? I don't remember what she said; it was something like "Hi, Lou, wassup?" or something to that effect. And as far as her mental state was concerned, she was normal, even bubbly." Lou glanced over at Riva. "Was that your take, Dr. Mehta?"

Riva nodded. "I'd say she was fine, maybe a little excited about all the fuss around here. She'd apparently had a conversation with Janice about the Manhattan General case. That's why she wanted it."

"Did she say anything about me?" Jack asked Lou, leaning forward and lowering his voice.

"What's with you today?" Lou asked. "Is everything copacetic with you guys?"

"Oh, there's always a few bumps in the road," Jack said vaguely. Laurie being "bubbly" added insult to injury, under the circumstance.

"How about assigning me the Cromwell case!" Jack called over to Riva.

"Be my guest," Riva said. "Calvin left a note saying he wanted it done ASAP." She took the folder from the "to be autopsied" pile and put it on the corner of the desk. Jack grabbed it and opened it, revealing a case worksheet, a partially filled-out death certificate, an inventory of medical-legal case records, two sheets for autopsy notes, a telephone notice of death as received by communications, a completed identification sheet, an investigator's report dictated by Fontworth, a sheet for the autopsy report, a lab slip for HIV analysis, and an indication that the body had been x-rayed and photographed when it had arrived at the OCME. Jack pulled out Fontworth's report and read it. Lou did the same over Jack's shoulder.

"Were you at the scene?" Jack asked Lou.

"No, I was still up in Harlem when this was called in. The precinct boys handled it initially, but when they recognized the victim, they called in my colleague, Detective Lieutenant Harvey Lawson. I've since talked with all of them. Everyone said it was a mess. Blood all over the kitchen."

"What was their take?"

"Considering she was seminude, with the apparent murder weapon sticking out of her thigh just below her private parts, they thought it was a fatal sexual assault."

"Private parts! So restrained."

"That's not quite how they described it to me. I'm translating."

"Thank you for being so considerate. Did they mention the blood on the front of the refrigerator?"

"They said there was blood all over."

"Did they mention blood being inside the

refrigerator, particularly on the wedge of cheese as described here in Fontworth's report?" Jack poked the paper with his index finger. Jack was impressed. Despite his previous experience with Fontworth's desultory work, the report was thorough.

"Like I said, they reported blood was all over the place."

"But inside the refrigerator with the door closed. That's a bit odd."

"Maybe the door was open when she was attacked?"

"So then she carefully put the cheese away? That's more than odd in the middle of a homicide. Tell me this: Did they mention footprints in the blood besides those of the victim?"

"No, they didn't."

"Fontworth's report specifically says there were none, but quite a few of the victim's. That's odder still."

Lou spread his hands and shrugged his shoulders. "So, what's your take?"

"My take is that in this case, the autopsy is going to be significant, so let's get the ball rolling."

Jack walked over to Vinnie and slapped

the back of his paper, making the tech jump.

"Let's go, Vinnie, old boy," Jack said happily. "We've got work to do."

Vinnie grumbled under his breath but stood upand stretched.

At the door into the communications room, Jack hesitated, looked back at Riva, and called out: "If you don't mind, I'd like to do that double suicide as well."

"I'll put your name on them," Riva promised.

three

"How about this," Laurie suggested. "I'll call you just as soon as I finish and let you know what I found. I know it won't bring your son back, but perhaps knowing what happened will be some comfort, especially if we're able to learn from this tragedy, to keep it from happening to someone else. If by some slim chance we still don't have any answers after the autopsy, I'll call you after I've had a chance to look at the microscopic and give you the definitive answers."

Laurie knew what she was suggesting was out of the ordinary and that skirting Mrs. Donnatello in the public relations office and giving out preliminary information would annoy Bingham and Calvin, both of whom were sticklers for rules, if they got wind. But Laurie felt the McGillin case warranted this change of protocol. After talking with them for only a short time, she'd learned that Sean McGillin Sr. was a retired physician who'd had a large internal-medicine practice in Westchester County. He and his wife, Judith, who'd been his office nurse, were not only fellow medical professionals but also extremely simpatico. The McGillins projected a salt-of-the-earth honesty and graciousness that made Laurie like them instantly; it also made it impossible for her not to feel their pain.

"I promise to keep you in the loop," Laurie continued, hoping her reassurances would allow the McGillins to go home. They'd been at the ME's office for hours, and it was obvious that they were both exhausted. "I'll personally watch over your son." Laurie had to glance away after her last comment, knowing it was deliberately misleading. She again caught sight of the crush of reporters in the reception area, even though she was trying to ignore them, and heard muffled cheering as coffee and donuts arrived. Laurie winced. It was unfortunate that as the McGillins were suffering their private grief, a media circus was going on in the next room. It had to make it harder for the McGillins, hearing banter and laughter.

"It just isn't fair that it isn't me who is lying downstairs in that refrigerated compartment," Dr. McGillin said with a sad shake of his head. "I've had a good run at life. I'm nearly seventy. I've had two bypass procedures, and my cholesterol's too high. Why am I still here, and Sean Jr. is down there? It doesn't make sense; he's always been a healthy, active boy, and he's not even thirty."

"Was your son's LDH high as well?" Laurie asked. Janice hadn't included anything about that in her forensic investigator's report.

"Not in the slightest," Dr. McGillin said. "In the past, I made sure he had it checked once a year. And now that his law firm contracted with AmeriCare, which requires yearly physicals, I know he'd continue to be checked."

After a quick glance at her watch, Laurie made direct eye contact with the McGillins, looking from one to the other. They were sitting bolt upright on the brown vinyl couch, their hands folded in their laps, clutching the identification Polaroids of their dead son. Rain spattered intermittently against the glass. The couple reminded her of the man and woman in the painting "American Gothic." They radiated the same resoluteness and moral virtue along with a hint of Puritanical narrowness.

The problem for Laurie was that she was organizationally shielded from the emotional side of death, and consequently had limited experience with it. Dealing with the grieving families, as well as helping them through the identification process, was done by others. She was also sheltered by a kind of academic distance. As a forensic pathologist, she saw death as a puzzle to be solved to help the living. There was also the acclimatization factor: Although death was a rare event for the general public, she saw it every day.

"Our son was to be married in the

spring," Mrs. McGillin said suddenly. She hadn't spoken since Laurie had introduced herself forty minutes earlier. "We were hoping for grandchildren."

Laurie nodded. The reference to children touched a tender chord in her own psyche. She tried to think of something to say but was saved when Dr. McGillin suddenly stood up. He took his wife's hand and pulled her to her feet.

"I'm sure Dr. Montgomery has to get to work," Dr. McGillin said. He nodded as if agreeing with himself while collecting all the Polaroids and pocketing them. "It's best if we go home. We'll leave Sean in her care." He then took out a small pad of paper and a pen from his inside jacket pocket. After writing on it, he tore off the top sheet and extended it to Laurie. "This is my personal phone line. I'll be awaiting your call. I will look forward to it sometime before noon."

Surprised and relieved at this sudden change of events, Laurie stood up. She took the paper and glanced at the number to be sure it was legible. It was a 914 area code. "I'll call as soon as I can."

Dr. McGillin helped his wife with her coat before putting on his own. He extended his hand toward Laurie. She shook it and noticed that it was cold.

"Take good care of our boy," Dr. McGillin said. "He's our only child." With that, he turned, opened the door to the reception area, and urged his wife forward into the press of reporters.

Desperate for news, the reporters instantly fell into an expectant silence the moment the McGillins appeared. Anticipating a news conference, all eyes followed their progress. The couple had advanced halfway across the reception area on their way to the main door when someone broke the silence by yelling out: "Are you part of the Cromwell family?" Dr. McGillin merely shook his head without slowing his progress. "Are you related to the police custody case?" someone else demanded. Dr. McGillin shook his head again. With that, the reporters switched their attention to Laurie. Apparently recognizing her as one of the medical examiners, a number even spilled into the ID room. An avalanche of questions followed.

Initially ignoring the reporters, Laurie went up on her tiptoes to see the McGillins exit the OCME. Only then did she look at the people pressed around her. "Sorry," she said, pushing microphones away. "I know nothing of those cases. You'll have to wait for the chief." Luckily, one of the OCME security personnel had materialized from within the reception area, and he managed to herd the reporters back to where they'd come from.

Relative silence returned to the ID room once the connecting door had been closed. For a moment, Laurie stood with her arms hanging limply at her sides. She had Sean McGillin Jr.'s folder in one hand and his father's scribbled phone number in other. Dealing with the grieving couple had been trying, especially since she was feeling psychologically fragile herself. But there was a positive side. Knowing herself as well as she did, she knew it was helpful to be involved in an emotionally wrenching situation, because it put her own problems in perspective. Keeping her mind occupied was a good hedge against backsliding into what she'd come to recognize as an unacceptable status quo.

Fortified to a degree, Laurie headed into the ID office while pocketing Dr. McGillin's phone number. "Where's everybody?" she asked Riva, who was still busy with the scheduling process.

"You and Jack are the only ones here so far, besides Bingham, Washington, and Fontworth."

"What I meant was, where are Detective Soldano and Vinnie?"

"Jack came in and took them both down to the pit. The detective asked Jack to do the Cromwell case."

"That's curious," Laurie remarked. Jack usually shied away from cases that attracted a lot of media attention, and the Cromwell case certainly fell into that category.

"He seemed genuinely interested in it," Riva said, as if reading Laurie's mind. "He also asked for the double suicide, which I didn't expect. I had a feeling he had an ulterior motive, but I have no idea what it could have been."

"Do you happen to know if any of the other techs are here yet? I'd like to get started myself with McGillin."

"I saw Marvin a few minutes ago. He got coffee and went downstairs."

"Perfect," Laurie said. She enjoyed working with Marvin. He'd been on evenings but had recently been switched to days. "I'll be in the pit if you need me."

"I'm going to have to assign you at least one more case. It's an overdose. I'm sorry. I know you said you had a bad night, but we've got a full schedule today."

"That's fine," Laurie assured her. She walked over to get the overdose folder. "Work's a good way to keep my mind off my problems."

"Problems? What kind of problems?"

"Don't ask!" Laurie said with a dismissive wave. "It's the same old, same old with Jack, but this morning I laid it on the line. I know I sound like a broken record, but this time I mean it. I'm moving back to my own apartment. He's going to have to make a decision one way or the other."

"Good for you," Riva responded. "Maybe it will give me strength."

Along with sharing office space, Laurie and Riva had become good friends. Riva's boyfriend was as resistant to commitment as Jack, but for different reasons, so she and Laurie had a lot to talk about.

After momentarily debating whether or not to have coffee and deciding not to, for fear that it would give her a tremor, Laurie started off to find Marvin. Although she was going only one floor down, she headed toward the elevator. She was exhausted from lack of sleep, just as she knew she would be when she had been unable to fall back asleep that morning. But instead of feeling irritated with herself, she was content. She certainly wasn't happy, because of her feelings for Jack, and she knew she was going to be lonely, yet she felt she'd done what she had to do, and in that way, she was satisfied.

When Laurie passed the forensic investigators' office, she leaned in and asked if Janice had left. Bart Arnold, the chief investigator, told her she had but asked if he could help. Laurie said she'd talk to her some other time and continued on her way. She had only wanted to fill Janice in about the conversation she'd had with the McGillins. She thought Janice would be interested. The fact that the case had penetrated Janice's usually thick emotional skin was what had intrigued Laurie in the first place.

Marvin was in the mortuary office, attending to his portion of the never-ending paperwork that engulfed the OCME. He had already changed into green scrubs in anticipation of getting down to work in the "pit," the term everyone fondly used in referring to the main autopsy room. He glanced up when Laurie appeared in the doorway. He was an athletic-looking African-American with the most flawless skin Laurie had ever seen. Laurie had been instantly jealous the first time she met Marvin.

Laurie was sensitive about her complexion. Along with her blond coloring, she had a spattering of freckles over the bridge of her nose as well as a scattering of other imperfections that only she could see. Although Laurie had gotten brown hair with auburn highlights from her father, her almost transparent skin and blue-green eyes came from her mother.

"Are you ready to rock and roll?" Laurie asked playfully. She knew from experience that she'd feel better if she didn't act tired.

"You're on, sister!" Marvin responded.

Laurie handed over the folders. "I want to do McGillin first."

"No problem," Marvin said, consulting the ledger for the location of the body.

Laurie first went into the locker room to change into scrubs, then went over to the storage room to don a "moon suit." "Moon suit" was the term used by the staff to describe the protective gear required while doing autopsies. They were fashioned of completely impervious material, with attached hoods and full-face masks. Air was brought into the suit through a HEPA filter by a self-contained fan, powered by a battery that had to be charged each night. The suits were not popular, since they made working more difficult, but everyone accepted the handicap for peace of mind, except Jack. She knew that when Jack was on call on weekends, he frequently dispensed with the moon suit on certain cases where he felt the risk of an infectious agent was low. In those circumstances, he reverted back to the traditional goggles and surgical facemask. The techs seemed content to keep his secret. If Calvin found out, there would be hell to pay.

After climbing into her gear, Laurie retraced her steps to the central corridor, then walked down to the door of the anteroom, where she washed and gloved. Thus prepared, she pushed into the autopsy room.

Even after working at the OCME for thirteen years, Laurie still savored the tingle of excitement she felt as she entered what she considered to be the center of action. It certainly wasn't the visual experience, for in that regard, the tiled, windowless room with its blue-white fluorescent lighting was cheerless. The eight stainless-steel tables were dented and stained from countless postmortems. Over each hung an antiquated spring-loaded scale. Along the walls were exposed piping, dated X-ray view boxes, old-fashioned glass-fronted cabinets containing an array of grisly instruments, and chipped soapstone sinks. More than a half century ago, it had been a state-of-the-art facility and the pride of the OCME, but now it suffered from lack of funds for both modernization and appropriate upkeep. Yet the physical plant didn't faze Laurie. The setting didn't even register in her mind. Her response was based on knowing that she would see or learn something new every time she entered the room.

Of the eight tables, three were occupied. One supported the corpse of Sean McGillin, or so Laurie surmised, since Marvin was scurrying around it in his final preparations. The other two, closest to where Laurie was standing, contained bodies in the middle of their procedures. Directly in front of her lay a large, dark-skinned man. Four people attired in moon suits identical to Laurie's were working over him. Although reflections off the curved plastic full-face masks made identification difficult, Laurie recognized Calvin Washington. His six-foot, seven-inch, two-hundred-fifty-pound frame was hard to conceal. The other one she thought was Harold Bingham because of his contrasting short, stocky stature. The last two had to be George Fontworth and the mortuary tech, Sal D'Ambrosio, but because they were about the same size, she couldn't tell them apart.

Laurie stepped over to the foot of the table. Just in front of her was a drain emitting a rude sucking sound. Water continuously ran down the surface of the table beneath the corpse to carry away body fluids.

"Fontworth, where the hell did you learn to use a scalpel?" Bingham growled.

It was now obvious which one of the suited figures was George. He was on the patient's right with his hands somewhere down in the deceased's retroperitoneal space, apparently trying to trace the track of a bullet. Laurie couldn't help but feel a stab of sympathy for George. Whenever Bingham came into the autopsy room, he liked to assume the professor role, but he invariably became impatient and annoyed. Even though Laurie knew she could always learn from him, she disliked the aggravation of working with him. It was too stressful.

Sensing that the atmosphere around table one was too charged to ask any questions, Laurie moved down toward table two. There she had no trouble recognizing Jack, Lou, and Vinnie. Immediately, she sensed the atmosphere was the opposite, with some semi-suppressed laughter dying away as she arrived. Laurie was not surprised. Jack was famous for his black humor. The corpse was that of a thin, almost emaciated, middle-aged female with brittle, bleach-blond hair. Laurie assumed it was Sara Cromwell. Of particular note was the handle of a kitchen knife protruding at an acute, cephalad angle from the upper, outer, anterior surface of her right thigh. Laurie wasn't surprised to see the utensil still in place. In such cases, medical examiners preferred that such objects be left in situ.

"I hope you are showing reasonable respect for the dead," Laurie gibed.

"Never a dull moment," Lou responded.

"And I don't know why I keep laughing at the same jokes," Vinnie complained.

"Tell me, Doctor Montgomery!" Jack said in an exaggerated professorial tone. "In your professional opinion, would you guess this penetrating entry into the thigh was a mortal wound?"

Bending over slightly so she could better access the point of entry, Laurie looked more closely at the knife. It appeared to be a small kitchen paring knife, which she guessed had a blade about four inches long, which had penetrated to the haft lateral to the femur. More important, the entrance was inferior to the anterior iliac spine but in line with it.

"I'd have to say it was not fatal," Laurie responded. "Its location suggests the femoral vessels surely would have been spared, so bleeding would have been minimal."

"And Dr. Montgomery, what does the angle of entry of the weapon suggest?"

"I'd have to say it's a rather unorthodox way for someone to stab their victim."

"There you go, gentlemen," Jack commented smugly. "We have confirmation of my assessment by the eminent Dr. Montgomery."

"But there was blood all over the place," Lou whined. "Where the hell did it come from? There are no other wounds."

"Ah-ha!" Jack said switching to an exaggerated French accent, finger raised in the air. "I believe we shall see in a few moments. Monsieur Amendola, *le couteau, s'il vous plaît!*"

Despite the glare of the overhead fluorescent lights off Vinnie's face mask, Laurie caught him rolling his eyes as he passed a scalpel into Jack's waiting hand. He and Jack had a curious relationship. Although it was based on mutual respect, they pretended it was the opposite.

Leaving the three to their own devices, Laurie moved on. She felt a mild disappointment that Jack could be so offhand and flippant. She couldn't help but think it wasn't a particularly good sign, as if he didn't care.

Laurie made an effort to put the problems with Jack out of her mind as she approached the next table. Stretched out on its slightly angled surface was the body of a well-muscled male in his mid-twenties, his head propped up on a wooden block. By reflex, she immediately began the external exam. The individual appeared healthy. His visible skin, although marble-white in death, was lesion-free.

His hair was thick and dark, and his eyes were closed as if in repose. The only visible anomalies were a sutured incision with a retained drain on his lower right leg, the capped-off end of an intravenous line running into his left arm, and an endotracheal tube protruding from his mouth, left over from the resuscitation attempt.

With Marvin still busy putting labels on specimen jars, Laurie checked the body's accession number and name. Confident that she was dealing with Sean McGillin, she continued the external exam, inspecting the IV site carefully. It looked entirely normal, with no swelling or other evidence of extravasation of blood or IV fluid. She looked more closely at the sutured wound on the leg, the site of the operation on the fractured tibia and fibula. There was no swelling or discoloration there, either, suggesting that there was no infection. The drain was sutured in place with a single loose loop of black silk, and there was evidence of a minimal discharge of serous fluid. The leg itself looked like the other leg, without any outward signs of venous thrombosis or clotting.

"I didn't see anything of note externally," Marvin said when he returned with a handful of sterile syringes and specimen jars, some containing preservatives and some without. He placed them all on the edge of the table to have them immediately available.

"So far, I'd have to agree," Laurie responded. There was a lot of give-and-take between the techs and the doctors, although it varied, depending on the personalities. Laurie always encouraged comments and suggestions, especially from Marvin. As far as she was concerned, the techs were a rich source of experience.

Marvin went over to the glass-fronted cabinets to get the required instruments. Despite the hum of her ventilation fan, Laurie could hear whistling. He was always cheerful, which was another thing she liked about him.

After checking for signs of intravenous

drug use and not finding any, Laurie used a nasal speculum to look inside Sean's nose. There was no suggestion of cocaine use. With a mysterious death, drugs had to be considered, despite what his parents had said to the contrary. Next, she opened the eyelids to examine the eyes. They appeared normal, with no hemorrhages on the sclera. Opening the mouth, she made sure the endotracheal tube was in the trachea and not the esophagus. Laurie had seen that on a few occasions with the predictable disastrous results.

With all his preparations complete, Marvin came back to the side of the table opposite Laurie and stood expectantly, waiting for the internal part of the autopsy to begin.

"All right! Let's do it!" Laurie said, reaching out with her hand as Marvin handed her a scalpel.

Although Laurie had done thousands of postmortems, each time she started another, it gave her a tingle of excitement. Starting the actual autopsy was akin to opening a sacred book, the mysteries of which she was about to discover. With her index finger pressing down on the top of the scalpel, Laurie expertly made the usual Y-shaped incision, starting from the points of the shoulders, meeting mid-sternum, and then continuing down to the pubis. With Marvin's help, she quickly reflected skin and muscle before removing the breastbone with bone cutters.

"Looks like a broken rib," Marvin commented, pointing to a defect on the right side of the chest.

"No hemorrhage, so it was postmortem, probably from the resuscitation attempt. Some people go overboard with the chest compressions."

"Ouch!" Marvin said sympathetically.

Expecting blood clots or other emboli, Laurie was eager to examine the great veins leading to the heart, the heart itself, and the pulmonary arteries, where fatal clots would usually be found. But she resisted the temptation. She knew that it was best to follow a normal protocol, lest something be forgotten. Carefully, she examined all the internal organs in situ, then used the syringes Marvin had laid out to take fluid samples for toxicological testing. A fatal reaction to a drug, toxin, or even an anesthetic agent had to be considered. Less than twenty-four hours had elapsed since the deceased had undergone anesthesia.

Laurie and Marvin worked together in silence, making certain that each sample was put into the correctly labeled specimen container. Once the fluid samples had been obtained, she began to remove the internal organs. Diligently, she maintained the normal sequence, and it wasn't until a bit later that she finally turned her attention to the heart.

"Here comes the money!" Marvin quipped.

Laurie smiled. The heart was indeed where she expected to find the pathology. With a few deft strokes, the heart came out. She peered into the cut end of the vena cava, but there was no clot. She was disappointed, since she had already noted that the pulmonary arteries had been clear when she'd removed the lungs.

Laurie weighed the heart, then with a long bladed knife, began an internal examination. To her chagrin, there was nothing amiss. There was no clot, and even the coronary arteries appeared entirely normal.

Laurie and Marvin's eyes met across the opened corpse.

"Damn!" Marvin exhaled.

"I'm surprised," Laurie said. She took a deep breath. "Well, you see to the gut and I'll take my micro samples, then we'll check the brain."

"You got it," Marvin said. He took the stomach and the intestines over to the sink to wash them out.

Laurie took multiple tissue samples for microscopic study, particularly from the heart and the lungs.

Marvin returned the cleaned gut to Laurie, who went through it carefully, taking samples as she proceeded. Meanwhile, Marvin started on the head by reflecting the scalp. By the time Laurie was finished with the stomach and intestines, Marvin was ready for her to inspect the skull. She gave him a thumbs-up when she was through, and he hefted the power-vibrating saw to cut through the bone just above the ears.

While Marvin was busy with the skull, Laurie took a scissors and opened the sutured wound on the lower leg. All looked fine within the surgical site. She then opened the long veins of the legs, tracing them from the ankles all the way up into the abdomen. There were no clots.

"The brain looks normal to me," Marvin commented.

Laurie nodded. There was no swelling and no hemorrhage, and the color was normal. She felt it with her practiced finger. It felt normal as well.

A few minutes later, Laurie had the brain out, and she dropped it into a pan that Marvin held. She checked the cut ends of the carotid arteries. Like everything else, they were normal. She weighed the brain. Its weight was within the normal limits.

"We're not finding anything," she said.

"I'm sorry," Marvin said.

Laurie smiled. On top of his other good qualities, he was empathetic. "You don't need to apologize. It's not your fault."

"It would have been nice to find something. What are you thinking now? It doesn't look like he should have died."

"I haven't the slightest idea. I'll hope the microscopic can shed some light, but I'm not optimistic. Everything looks and feels so normal. Why don't you start winding things up while I section the brain. I can't think of anything else to do."

"You got it," Marvin said cheerfully.

As Laurie anticipated, the interior of the

brain looked like its exterior. She took the appropriate samples, then joined Marvin to suture up the body. With both of them working, it took only a few minutes.

"I'd like to get my next case up as soon as possible," Laurie said. "I hope you don't mind." She was afraid that once she sat down, her fatigue would return with a vengeance. At the moment, she was feeling better than expected.

"Not at all," Marvin said. He was already straightening up.

Laurie looked around the pit. She'd been so engrossed that she hadn't seen all the activity. At that point, all eight tables were in use, with at least two and sometimes more people clustered about each. She glanced toward Jack's table. He was bent over the head of another woman's body. Apparently, he'd finished with Sara Cromwell, and Lou had left. Beyond Jack's table, Calvin was still at work with Fontworth on the same body they were working on before. Bingham had apparently left to give his news conference.

"How long will the turnaround take?" Laurie asked Marvin as he carried the specimen bottles away.

"Not long at all."

Laurie wandered toward Jack with mixed feelings. She was not prepared for more of his levity, but after the earlier tease about Cromwell, she was curious about what he'd discovered. Laurie stopped at the foot of the table. Jack was concentrating intently on making a mold of a lesion on the woman's forehead, just within the hairline. Laurie stood for a moment, waiting for him to acknowledge her presence. Vinnie had looked up immediately and had at least given a restrained wave.

"What did you find on your first case?" Laurie asked finally. It seemed unlikely that he hadn't seen her, but it had to have been the case. She didn't want to think otherwise.

Another few minutes went by without Jack responding. She glanced back at Vinnie, who spread his hands out, palms up, and shrugged his shoulders as if to indicate that there was no accounting for Jack's behavior. Laurie stood for another beat, uncertain of what to do before moving on. Although she was aware that Jack could become so engrossed as to be oblivious of his surroundings, it was demeaning for her to stand there.

Things were not much better at Fontworth's table. Even though Bingham had left, Calvin was riding poor Fontworth with equivalent venom as the case dragged on interminably. After a quick glance at the other five tables, Laurie gave up on socializing and returned to lend Marvin a hand.

"I can get one of the other techs to help," Marvin said. He'd brought in a gurney and positioned it next to the table.

"I don't mind," Laurie said. There had been a time not too long ago that between cases, the examiners would go upstairs either to the ID room or the lunchroom for a quick coffee and impromptu discussions. But with the more elaborate protection apparatus they were required to wear, it was too much effort.

Once Sean McGillin's remains had been placed in the walk-in cooler, Marvin led Laurie to the appropriate compartment for the next case, a man named David Ellroy. The moment Marvin pulled out the drawer to reveal the body of thin, undernourished, middle-aged African-American, Laurie remembered that it was a presumed overdose. Her trained eye immediately took in the scars and tracks on the man's arms and legs from his intravenous habit. Although Laurie was accustomed to overdose cases, they still had the power to evoke an emotional reaction. With less than the usual control over her thoughts, her mind yanked her back to a crisp, clear, flag-snapping October day in 1975 when she'd rushed home from her high school, the Langley School for Girls. She lived with her parents in a large, prewar flat on Park Avenue. It was the Friday before the long Columbus Day weekend, and she was excited because her brother, Shelly, her only sibling, had come home the night before from Yale, where he was a freshman.

As Laurie had gotten off the elevator in their private lobby, she sensed a disturbing stillness. None of the usual sounds issued forth from the laundry room door vent. Entering the apartment proper, she called Shelly's name while she stashed her books on the console table in the foyer before cutting through the kitchen. When she didn't see Holly, she was momentarily relieved, remembering it was their maid's day off. Yelling out Shelly's name again, she glanced in the den beyond the family room. The TV was on without sound, which heightened her uneasiness. For a moment, she watched the antics of a midday game show, wondering why the TV would be on without sound. Resuming her tour of the apartment, she called out Shelly's name yet again, convinced that someone had to be home. As she passed the formal living room, she began to move faster, sensing a secret urgency.

Shelly's door was closed. She knocked, but there was no answer. She knocked again before trying the door. It was unlocked. She pushed it open only to see her beloved brother stretched out on the carpet, clad in only his briefs. To her horror, bloody froth oozed from his mouth, and his overall color was as pale as the bone china in the dining-room breakfront. A tourniquet was loosely looped about his upper arm. Near his half-open hand was a syringe. On the desk was a glassine envelope, which Laurie guessed contained the speedball, a mixture of heroin and cocaine he'd bragged about the night before. Laurie had taken it all in instantly before dropping to her knees to try to help.

With some difficulty, Laurie pulled herself back to the present. She didn't want to think about her vain attempt to resuscitate her brother. She didn't want to remember how cold and lifeless his lips felt when she touched them with her own.

"Can you help move him over onto the gurney?" Marvin asked. "He's not very heavy."

"Certainly," Laurie said, glad to be of use. She put down David's folder and lent a hand. A few minutes later, they were on their way back to the autopsy room. Inside, when Marvin maneuvered the gurney next to the table, one of the other techs helped Marvin get the body onto the table. Laurie could see the dried remains of a bloody froth that had issued from David's mouth, and the image drew her back into her disturbing reverie. It wasn't her failed attempt to resuscitate her brother that occupied her thoughts, but rather the confrontation she had to endure with her parents a number of hours later.

"Did you know your brother was using drugs?" her father had demanded. His face was purple with rage and was mere inches away from Laurie's face. His thumbs dug into her skin where he held her upper arms. "Answer me!"

"Yes," Laurie blurted through tears. "Yes, yes."

"Are you using drugs, too?"

"No!"

"How did you know he was?"

"By accident: I found a syringe he'd gotten from your office in his shaving bag."

There was a momentary silence as her father's eyes narrowed and his lips stretched out in a thin, cruel line. "Why didn't you tell us," he growled. "If you told us, he'd be alive."

"I couldn't," Laurie sobbed.

"Why?" he shouted. "Tell me why!"

"Because . . ." Laurie cried. She paused, then added: "Because he told me not to. He made me promise. He said he'd never talk to me again if I did."

"Well, that promise killed him," her father hissed. "It killed him just as much as the damn drug."

A hand gripped Laurie's arm and she jumped. She turned to look at Marvin.

"Anything special you want for this case," Marvin asked, motioning toward David's corpse. "It looks pretty straightforward to me."

"Just the usual," Laurie said. As Marvin went to get the necessary supplies, Laurie took a deep breath to get herself under control. Intuitively, she knew she had to keep her mind busy to keep it from dredging up other bad memories. Opening the folder she had in her hand, she searched through the papers to find Janice's forensic investigator report and began reading. The body had been found along with drug paraphernalia in a Dumpster, suggesting that David had died at a crack house and had been thrown out with the rest of the trash. Laurie sighed. Dealing with such a case was the negative side of her job.

An hour later and back in her street clothes, Laurie stepped into the back elevator. The overdose case had been routine. There had been no surprises; David Ellroy had shown the usual signs of asphyxial death with a frothy pulmonary edema. The only mildly interesting finds were multiple, tiny, discrete lesions in various organs, suggesting that he had suffered numerous episodes of infection from his habit.

As the antiquated elevator clunked upward toward the fifth floor, Laurie thought about Jack. When she'd finished with David Ellroy, he had already started his third case. Between his second and third, he'd gone out of the room, pushing the gurney with Vinnie steering. Even from where she was standing, Laurie could hear the usual banter. Five minutes later, they'd both reappeared, bringing in the new case while carrying on with the same wisecracking behavior. They then proceeded to transfer the body to the table and go through the setup before starting the post. At no time through any of this did Jack make an attempt to come over to Laurie's table, engage her in conversation in any way, or even look in her direction. Laurie shrugged. Whether she wanted to admit it or not, it was becoming obvious that he was actively ignoring her. Such behavior was uncharacteristic. For the nine years she'd known him, he'd never been passive-aggressive.

Before Laurie went to her office, she stopped in the histology lab. In addition to the case folders, she was carrying a brown paper bag containing the tissue and toxicology samples from McGillin. It didn't take her long to locate the supervisor, Maureen

O'Conner. The full-bodied, busty redhead was sitting at a microscope, checking a tray of slides. She looked up as Laurie approached. A knowing smile spread across her heavily freckled face.

"Now, what have we here?" Maureen questioned with her heavy brogue. She looked from Laurie to the bag Laurie was carrying. "Let me guess: tissue samples whose slides you desperately need yesterday."

Laurie smiled guiltily. "Am I really that predictable?"

"With you and Dr. Stapleton, it's always the same story. Whenever you two come in here, you've got to have the slides immediately. But let me remind you of something, sister: Your patients are already dead." Maureen laughed heartily, and a few of the other histology techs who'd overheard joined in.

Laurie found herself chuckling as well. Maureen's ebullience was infectious, and it never varied, despite the lab being chronically understaffed due to OCME budgetary restraints. Laurie opened the bag, took out the tissue samples, and lined them up on the counter next to Maureen's microscope.

"Maybe if I told you why I'd like these sooner rather than later, it might help."

"As busy as we are around here, a few extra hands would be more helpful than talk, but fire away."

Laurie pulled out all the stops, knowing there was no professional reason for what she was asking. She started by describing how sympathetic Dr. and Mrs. McGillin were, and how their deceased son seemed to have been their whole life. She even mentioned the son's imminent marriage and the parents' hope for grandchildren. She then admitted that she had promised to provide the couple the cause of their son's death that morning to help their grieving. The problem was that the autopsy had failed to confirm her clinical impression. Thus, she needed the slides in hopes the answers would be forthcoming. What she didn't explain were her personal reasons for taking on this mini-crusade.

"Well, that's quite a touching story," Maureen said softly. She took a deep breath and then gathered up the samples. "We'll see what we can do. I promise you we'll give it a go."

Laurie thanked her and hurried out of

histology. She glanced at her watch. It was already after eleven, and she wanted to call Dr. McGillin before noon. Taking the stairs, she descended a floor and walked into the toxicology lab. Here, the atmosphere was different than in the histology lab. Instead of a babble of voices, there was the continual hum of the sophisticated and mostly automated equipment. It took Laurie a few moments to locate anyone. To her relief, she saw Peter Letterman, the assistant director. If it had been the lab director, John DeVries, Laurie would have walked out. She and John had gotten off on the wrong foot back when Laurie desperately needed quicker results on a series of cocaine overdose cases and had badgered the man. That was thirteen years earlier, when Laurie had first started at the OCME, and John had held on to his animosity like a dog with a bone. Laurie had long ago given up trying to make amends.

"My favorite ME," Peter said happily, catching sight of Laurie. He was a thin, blond man with androgynous features and almost no beard. He wore his long hair in a ponytail, and although he was pushing forty, he could still pass as a teenager. In contrast to John, he and Laurie got along famously. "You have something for me?"

"Indeed I do," Laurie said. She handed over the bag while warily looking around for John.

"The Führer is down in the general lab, so you can relax."

"It's my lucky day," Laurie commented.

Peter glanced in at the sample bottles. "What's the scoop? What am I looking for and why?"

Laurie told a shorter version of the same story she'd related to Maureen. At the end, she added: "I don't really expect you to find anything, but I've got to be complete, especially if the microscopic doesn't show anything."

"I'll see what I can do," Peter said.

"I appreciate it," Laurie responded.

After climbing back up the single flight of stairs, Laurie walked down the corridor toward her office. She passed Jack's office, with its door ajar, but neither Jack nor his officemate, Chet McGovern, were inside. Laurie assumed that they were both still down in the pit. Coming into her own office, she immediately caught sight of her suitcase that she'd brought from Jack's. Although she hadn't forgotten the morning's confrontation, seeing the suitcase brought it back with unpleasant clarity. It also didn't help that she felt let down by not finding a smoking gun during Sean McGillin's autopsy. The more she thought about it, the more surprising it was. How could an ostensibly healthy twenty-eight-year-old man die and the cause not be apparent from a combination of a detailed history and the autopsy? In some respects, the case was mildly shaking her belief in forensic pathology.

"That microscopic better come through!" Laurie voiced out loud as she sat down at her desk. She was emphatic but didn't quite know how she would act on the threat if the microscopic failed to live up to her expectations. Leaning over, she added the folders from the morning's cases to her sizable unfinished pile. It was Laurie's job on each case to collate all the material from the autopsy, from the forensic investigators, from the laboratories, and from any other source she needed to come up with a cause and manner of death. The meaning of "cause" was obvious, whereas "manner" referred to whether the death was natural, accidental, suicidal, or homicidal, each with specific legal ramifications. Sometimes it took weeks for all the material to be available. When it was, Laurie had to make her decision about the cause and manner on a preponderance of evidence, meaning she had to be at least fifty-one percent certain. Of course, in the vast majority of cases, she was close to or at one hundred percent certain.

Laurie took the sheet of paper containing Dr. McGillin's phone number from her pocket and smoothed it out on the blotter in front of her. Although she was reluctant to call him, she knew she had to make good on her promise. The problem was, Laurie was not good at any type of confrontation. It was a given that he was going to be even more let down, as there was, as of yet, no ostensible cause for his son's untimely death.

With her elbows on her desk, she leaned forward to massage her forehead while staring at the Westchester number. She tried to think of what to say in hopes of mitigating the impact. For a fleeting moment, she considered handing the situation over to the public relations department as she was supposed to do, but she quickly ruled that out, since she had specifically offered to make the call herself. While her mind was struggling over her prospective wording, she found herself thinking about the victim's first name, Sean, since it was the name of a college boyfriend.

Sean Mackenzie had been a colorful fellow Wesleyan University student who'd appealed to Laurie's rebellious side. Although he wasn't exactly a hoodlum, he'd been a bit over the edge with his motorcycle, artistic craziness, and outlaw behavior, including mild drug use. At the time the whole package had excited Laurie and driven her parents to distraction, which was part of the attraction. But the on-again, off-again relationship had been unhealthily mercurial from the start, and Laurie had finally put an end to it just before joining the OCME. Now, with her relationship with Jack in question, she vaguely thought about calling Sean, since she knew he was living in the city and had become a rather successful artist. But she quickly nixed the idea. There was no way she wanted to reopen that Pandora's box.

"A penny for your thoughts?" a voice asked.

Laurie's head popped up. Filling her doorway was Jack's athletic, six-foot frame. He was the picture of relaxed informality in his lived-in chambray shirt, knitted tie, and faded jeans.

"Let's up that to a quarter," he added. "There's been significant inflation since I learned that phrase, and I know how valuable your thoughts are." An impish smirk dimpled his cheeks. His lips were pressed together into a thin line.

Laurie regarded her friend of at least a decade and lover of nearly four years. His irreverent gaiety and sarcasm could at times be wearing, and this was one of them. "So you're deigning to speak with me now?" she questioned with an equally affected tone.

Jack's smile faltered. "Of course I'm going to talk with you. What kind of question is that?"

"Except for that brief professorial game when I first came into the autopsy room, you've been ignoring me all morning."

"Ignoring you?" Jack questioned with knitted brows. "I think I should remind you we came to work separately, which was more your decision than mine, arrived at different times, and since then, we've been working on our own cases."

"We work most days, and most days we communicate almost continuously, particularly when we are in the same room. I even went over to your table during your second case and asked you a direct question."

"I didn't see or hear you. Scout's honor." Jack held up his index and middle finger in the form of a V. His smile returned.

Laurie arched her eyebrows and shrugged. She was being provocative by suggesting that she didn't believe him, but she didn't care. "Fine and dandy, and now I have more work to do." She turned her attention back to the sheet with the Westchester phone number.

"No doubt," Jack said, refusing to rise to the bait or be dismissed. "How were your cases this morning?"

Laurie looked up but not at Jack. "One was routine and rather uninteresting. The other was disappointing."

"In what regard?"

"I'd promised a couple whose son died at the Manhattan General to find out what killed him and let them know immediately, but the autopsy was clean; there was no gross pathology whatsoever. Now I've got to call and say we have to wait for the microscopic to be available. I know they are going to be disappointed, and I am, too."

"Janice briefed me on that case," Jack said. "You didn't find any emboli?"

"Nothing!"

"And the heart?"

Laurie looked back at Jack. "The heart, the lungs, and the great vessels were all completely normal."

"I'll wager you find something with the heart's conduction system or maybe micro emboli in the brainstem. You took adequate samples for toxicology? That would be my second thought."

"I did," Laurie said. "I'd also kept in mind he'd had anesthesia less than twenty-four hours ago."

"Well, sorry your cases were a letdown. Mine were the opposite. In fact, I'd have to say they were fun."

"Fun?"

"Truly! Both turned out to be the absolute opposite of what everybody thought."

"How so?"

"The first case was this well-known psychologist."

"Sara Cromwell."

"Supposedly, it was a brutal murder during a sexual assault."

"I saw the knife, remember?"

"That was what threw everybody for a loop. You see there was no other wound, and she hadn't been raped."

"How could all the blood that was described come from that single, nonfatal stab wound?"

"It didn't."

Jack stared at Laurie with a slight smile of anticipation. Laurie stared back. She was in no mood to play games. "So where did it come from?"

"Any ideas?"

"Why don't you just tell me?"

"I think you'd be able to guess if you thought about it for a minute. I mean, you did look at how gaunt she was, didn't you?"

"Jack, if you want to tell me, tell me. Otherwise, I have to make my call."

"The blood was from her stomach. It turns out there was a fatal engorgement of food, causing a rupture of her stomach and the lower part of her esophagus. Obviously, the woman had bulimia, and pushed herself over the edge. Can you believe it? Everybody was convinced it was homicide and it turns out to be accidental."

"What about the knife sticking out of her thigh?"

"That was the real teaser. It was self-inflicted, but not on purpose. In her final moments, while she was puking blood and putting away the cheese, she slipped on her own blood and fell on the knife she was holding. Isn't it too much? I tell you: This is going to be a good case to present at our Thursday conference."

For a moment, Laurie stared at Jack's satisfied face. The story had touched a chord in her inner life. There had been a time when she'd had self-esteem problems after her brother's death, causing her to have a brush with anorexia and bulimia. It was a secret she hadn't shared with anyone.

"And my next two cases were equally intriguing. It was a double suicide. Did you hear about it?"

"Vaguely," Laurie responded. She was still thinking about bulimia.

"I tell you, I have to give old Fontworth

credit," Jack said. "I'd always considered him less than meticulous, but last night he seemed to have done a bang-up job. With the double suicide, he found a heavy Mag-Lite flashlight on the front seat of the SUV along with the victims and was smart enough to bring it with the bodies. He also noted the driver's-side door was ajar."

"What was important about the flashlight?" Laurie asked.

"Plenty," Jack replied. "First of all, let me say I was a bit suspicious when there was only one suicide note. In double suicides, it's usual to have two notes or one that is written by both parties. I mean, it makes sense, since they are doing it together. Anyway, that put up a red flag. Since the note was presumably from the woman, I elected to autopsy her first. What I expected to find after the fact was something toxicological, like a knock-out drug or the like. I didn't expect to find anything on gross, but I did. She had a literal indentation on her forehead just above the hairline that was curiously curved."

Jack paused. His smile returned.

"Don't tell me the flashlight and the indentation matched."

"You got it! A perfect match! It seems that the whole affair was an elaborate setup by the husband, who had prepared the scene and probably even wrote the note. After he knocked out his wife, got her into the passenger seat of the SUV, and started the engine, he probably went back in the house to wait. When he thought enough time had passed, he returned to check that his wife was dead, but didn't realize how quickly one can succumb to carbon monoxide if the level is high enough. Climbing behind the wheel, he rapidly fell unconscious and ended up joining his wife."

"What a story!" Laurie commented.

"Isn't it ironic? I mean, it was supposed to be a double suicide, and instead the manner of death turns out to be homicidal for the wife and accidental for the husband. Forensic pathology certainly can surprise."

Laurie nodded. She distinctly remembered having the same thought before she started her overdose case.

"Even the police case is turning out to be opposite of what was expected."

"How so?" Laurie asked.

"Everybody has been assuming it was a case of justifiable homicide by the police, since the police acknowledged shooting him a number of times, but Calvin just told me that as near as they can determine, it was suicide. They've been able to ascertain that the victim shot himself through the heart before he was hit by any of the police rounds."

"That should help quiet the neighborhood."

"We should hope," Jack said. "Anyway, it was an interesting morning, to say the least, and I just thought you'd like to hear that we've had a rash of cases this morning where the manner of death was the opposite of what was expected. With that said, are you going to pop down for some lunch soon?"

"I don't know. I'm not terribly hungry, and I've got a lot to do."

"Well, maybe I'll catch you down there. If not, I'll see you later."

Laurie waved at Jack as he disappeared down the hall. She turned her attention back to Sean McGillin Sr.'s phone number. She thought about what Jack had said about forensic surprises and considered what that could mean for Sean McGillin Jr. She'd expected his manner of death to be natural, a fatal clot or fat emboli or even a congenital anomaly. Since she'd not found anything of the kind, at least so far, she was now entertaining the idea that the cause of death could've been accidental, such as an unexpected late complication with anesthesia. But if the cause of death were to be truly opposite, like the cases Jack had just described, it would have to have been homicidal.

Laurie mulled the idea. It seemed far-fetched, but then she thought about Sara Cromwell and how only minutes earlier, she would have thought it totally far-fetched that her manner of death was accidental. Sean Jr.'s autopsy had already surprised her with its lack of findings. Could the case surprise her once more? She doubted it, but then again, she couldn't rule it out completely.

four

Despite Laurie's concerns to the contrary, the phone conversation with Dr. McGillin turned out be surprisingly civil. He had accepted that the autopsy had failed to show any pathology with unexpected equanimity. It was as if he had taken the information as a compliment about his adored son, corroborating the idea that the boy was indeed perfect, inside and out.

Having expected to be angrily chastised for not delivering on her promise, or at the very least anticipating having to weather passive-aggressive disappointment, Laurie felt even more beholden to the man when he maintained his composure. He had even gone to the extent of thanking her for her efforts on his son's behalf and for spending time with them in their hour of need. If she had been willing before to bend the rules by providing the man with the cause of his son's demise, she'd now become determined to get him that information.

After hanging up the phone with Sean Sr., Laurie spent some time pondering the case while staring blankly ahead at her corkboard with its various notes, reminders, and business cards. She tried to think of a way to speed up the process, but her hands were tied. She had to wait for Maureen and Peter, and hope that they would respond to her appeal.

Time melted away effortlessly. Riva came in and said hello as she dumped folders on her desk and took her seat. Laurie returned the greeting by reflex without turning around. Her mind by then had switched to Jack and his irritatingly insouciant joviality, and what that meant about their relationship. Although she hated to admit it, it was becoming progressively apparent that he was happy she'd decided to leave.

In a circular fashion, thoughts of Jack brought her back to Sean Jr.'s case as she recalled Jack's comments about forensics occasionally revealing that the causation and manner of death were the opposite of what was assumed. Laurie again considered the possibility that Sean's death could have been a homicide. She couldn't help but remember several infamous episodes of serial homicides that had occurred in healthcare institutions, particularly one rather recently that had continued undetected for an unconscionably long time. Such a scenario had to be considered, although she recognized that all the involved patients in those series were aged, chronically ill individuals and that there was an inkling of an imaginable, albeit sick motive. Not one of the victims had been a vigorous, healthy twenty-eight-year-old whose whole life was still ahead of him.

Laurie was certain that homicide was extremely implausible, and she wasn't going to worry about it, especially since Peter's toxicology screen would pick up an overdose of insulin or digoxin or another potentially lethal drug akin to those implicated in the previous institutional murders. After all, that was what the toxicology screen was all about. In her mind, Sean Jr.'s death had to be either natural, which was most probable, or accidental. Yet what was she going to do if the microscopic and the toxicological turned out to be negative? Such a concern seemed reasonable, considering the autopsy itself had been so surprisingly clean. From her experience, it was rare not to find some pathology, even in a twenty-eight-year-old, and even if the abnormalities were not associated with the demise.

To prepare for such an eventuality, Laurie needed as much information as possible. Although the usual course of action in such a case would be to wait for the microscopic and the toxicological to come back, she decided to be proactive to save time. Impulsively, she snatched the receiver and called down to the forensic investigator's office. Bart Arnold picked up on the second ring.

"I posted a Sean McGillin this morning," Laurie said. "He was an inpatient over at the Manhattan General. I'd like to get a copy of his hospital chart."

"I'm aware of the case. Did we not get what you need?"

"The forensic investigator's report is fine. To be honest, I'm on a fishing expedition. The post was negative, and I'm a little desperate. There's kind of a time constraint."

"I'll put the request in immediately."

Laurie replaced the receiver while racking her brain in hopes of coming up with something else that would be useful if everything turned out to be negative.

"What's wrong?" Riva asked. She had swung around in her desk chair after overhearing Laurie's conversation with Bart. "Knowing how tired you are, I thought I'd given you straightforward cases. I'm sorry."

Laurie assured her officemate that she needn't apologize. Laurie admitted that she was creating a problem when there really wasn't one, probably to keep from obsessing about her social life.

"Do you want to talk about it?"

"You mean my social life?"

"I mean Jack and what you did this morning."

"Not particularly," Laurie responded. She waved a hand as if swatting a nonexistent fly. "There's not much to say that you and I haven't hashed over before ad nauseam. The reality is that I don't want to be stuck in a never-never-land relationship, which is what I've been settling for over the last couple of years. I want a family. It's that simple. I guess what's really irking me is that Jack is being such an ass by acting so blasted cheerful."

"I've noticed," Riva agreed. "I think it is an act."

"Who's to know," Laurie responded. She laughed at herself. "I'm pathetic! Anyway, let me tell you about the McGillin case." Quickly, Laurie related the whole story, including the details of the conversations she'd had with the parents and then subsequently with Jack.

"It's not going to be a homicide," Riva said emphatically.

"I know!" Laurie agreed. "What's bothering me at this point is not being able to live up to the promise I made to the parents. I was so sure I'd be able to tell them today what killed their boy, and now I have to sit on my hands and wait for Maureen and Peter. My compulsiveness is driving me batty."

"If it's any consolation, my opinion is that

Jack was right about the microscopic being the key. I think you'll find the pathology in the heart, especially with a strong family history of elevated LDH and heart disease."

Laurie started to concur, but her phone rang. Twisting around, she answered it, expecting some quick tidbit of information on one of her cases, which is what the vast majority of her calls were about. Instead, her eyebrows arched in surprise. Covering the mouthpiece, she looked back at Riva and whispered. "You're not going to believe it! It's my father!"

Riva's face reflected equal disbelief. She hastily motioned for Laurie to find out the occasion for the call. Phone contact was restricted to Laurie's mother, and that was rarely at work.

"I'm sorry to disturb you," Dr. Sheldon Montgomery said. He spoke in a resonant voice with a hint of an English accent, despite his never having lived in Great Britain.

"You're not disturbing me," Laurie answered. "I'm sitting here at my desk." She was intensely curious why her father was calling, but resisted the temptation to ask directly, fearful such a question would sound too unfriendly. Their relationship had never been anything special. As a self-absorbed, workaholic cardiac surgeon who'd demanded perfection from everyone, including himself, he'd been emotionally distant and generally unavailable. Laurie had tried vainly to break through to him, constantly pushing herself to excel at school and in other activities, which is what she thought he wanted. Unfortunately, it never worked. Then came her brother's untimely death, which Sheldon blamed on her. What little relationship they'd had deteriorated even further.

"I'm at the hospital," he said. His tone was matter-of-fact, as if he was telling her the weather. "I'm here with your mother."

"What is Mother doing at the hospital?" Laurie asked. For Sheldon to be at the hospital was not out of the ordinary. Although he was retired from private practice now that he was in his early eighties, he still frequently went to the hospital. Laurie had no idea what he did. Her mother, Dorothy, never went to the hospital despite being active in various hospital fund-raising activities. The last time Laurie remembered her mother being in the hospital was for her second facelift fifteen years earlier, and even then, Laurie had learned of the admission after the fact.

"She had surgery this morning," Sheldon said. "She is doing fine. In fact, she is rather chipper."

Laurie sat up a bit straighter. "Surgery? What happened? Was it an emergency?"

"No. It was a scheduled procedure. Unfortunately, your mother had a mastectomy for breast cancer."

"My word!" Laurie managed. "I had no idea. I just spoke with her on Saturday. She didn't mention anything about surgery or cancer."

"You know your mother, and how she likes to ignore unpleasant issues. She was particularly insistent on shielding you from unnecessary concern until this was behind her."

Laurie looked at Riva with disbelief. As close as their desks were in the small office, Riva could hear both sides. Riva rolled her dark eyes and shook her head.

"What stage was the cancer?" Laurie asked solicitously.

"A very early stage with no apparent nodal involvement," Sheldon said. "Things are going to be fine. The prognosis is excellent, although she'll have to undergo further treatment."

"And you say she is doing well?"

"Very well indeed. She's already taken some nourishment orally, and she's back to her old self by being genuinely demanding."

"Can I speak with her?"

"Unfortunately, that would be rather difficult. You see, I'm not in the room at the moment. I'm at the nurses' station. I was hoping you'd be able to come over here to see her this afternoon. There is an associated aspect to all this that I would like to discuss with you."

"I will be right over," Laurie said. She hung up the phone before turning back to Riva.

"Is it true you had no idea about any of this?" Riva asked.

"Not a clue. There wasn't even the slightest hint. I don't know whether to be angry, hurt, or sad. Actually, it's pathetic. What a dysfunctional family! I can't believe it. I'm almost forty-three and a doctor, and my mother still treats me like a child about illness. Can you imagine, she wanted to shield me from unnecessary concern?"

"Our family is just the opposite. Everybody knows everything about everybody. It's the opposite extreme, but I don't advocate it, either. I think the best is somewhere in between."

Laurie got up and stretched. She waited for a moment of dizziness to pass. Her fatigue had come back with a vengeance after sitting at her desk. She then got her coat from behind the door. When she considered the differences between her family and Riva's, she thought she would pick Riva's, although she certainly wouldn't choose to live at home like Riva did. She and Riva were the same age.

"Want me to answer your phone?" Riva asked.

"If you won't mind, especially if it's either Maureen or Peter. Leave any messages on my corkboard." Laurie got out a package of Post-its and plopped them on her blotter. "I've got to come back here. I'm not going to take my suitcase with me."

Laurie stepped into the hall and briefly considered going down to Jack's office to tell him about her mother, then decided to skip it. Even though she was certain he'd ultimately be sympathetic, she had

had quite enough of his levity and didn't want to risk having to deal with anymore.

On the first floor, Laurie took a quick detour into the administration office. Calvin's door was ajar. Unchallenged by the two busy secretaries, Laurie glanced in to see the deputy chief hunched over his desk. A standard-sized pen looked like a miniature in his huge hand. She knocked on the open door, and Calvin raised his intimidating face and drilled Laurie with his coal-black eyes. There had been times when Laurie had clashed with the deputy chief, since he was both a stickler for rules and a politically savvy individual willing to bend those rules on occasion. From Laurie's perspective, it was an untenable combination. The occasional political demands of being a medical examiner were the only part of the job Laurie didn't like.

Laurie mentioned that she was leaving early to visit her mom in the hospital. Calvin waved her away without a question. Laurie didn't have to clear such a thing with him, but she had been trying of late to be a little more politically sensitive herself, at least on a personal level.

Outside, the rain had finally stopped,

making it easier to hail a taxi. The ride uptown went quickly, and in less than a half hour she was deposited at the front steps of the University Hospital. During the drive, she had tried to imagine what her father had meant by "an associated aspect" of her mother's illness that he wished to discuss. She truly had no idea. It was such an oblique statement, but she assumed he meant some limitations of her mother's activity.

The hospital's lobby was in its usual afternoon uproar with visiting hours in full swing. Laurie had to wait in line at the information booth to find out her mother's room number, castigating herself for failing to get it earlier. Armed with the information, she took the proper elevators up to the proper floor and walked past the nurses' station, where a number of people were busy at work. No one looked up at her. It was the VIP wing, which meant the corridor was carpeted and the walls were hung with original, donated oil paintings. Laurie found herself glancing into the rooms as she passed like a voyeur, reminding her of her first year of clinical residency.

Her mother's door was ajar like most of

the others, and Laurie walked right in. Her mother was in a typical hospital bed with the guardrails up, an intravenous running slowly into her left arm. Instead of the usual hospital garb, she was wearing a pink silk robe. She was sitting up with a number of pillows behind her. Her medium-length, silver-gray hair, which normally billowed on top of her head, was pressed down like an old-fashioned bathing cap. Her color was gray without her makeup, and her skin seemed to be pulled tighter than usual over her facial bones, and her eyes had retracted as if she was slightly dehydrated. She appeared fragile and vulnerable, and although Laurie knew she was petite, she looked particularly tiny in the large bed. She also looked older than she did less than a week before, when Laurie had seen her for lunch. There had been no conversation about cancer or imminent hospitalization.

"Come in, my dear," Dorothy said, waving with her free hand. "Pull a chair over. Sheldon told me he had called you. I wasn't going to bother you until I was home. This is all very silly. It's just not worth getting all upset over."

Laurie glanced over at her father, who

was reading *The Wall Street Journal* in a club chair by the window. He glanced up, gave a little wave and a wan smile, and then went back to his paper.

Advancing to the side of the bed, Laurie took her mother's free hand and gave it a squeeze. The bones felt delicate and the skin cool. "How are you, Mother?"

"I'm just fine. Give me a kiss and then sit down."

Laurie touched her cheek to her mother's. Then she pulled a chair over to the side of the bed. With the hospital bed raised, she had to look up at her mother. "I'm so sorry this has happened to you."

"It's nothing. The doctor has already been in, and he said things are just fine, which is more than I can say about your hair."

Laurie had to suppress a smile. Her mother's ploy was transparent. Whenever she didn't want to talk about herself, she went on the offensive. Laurie used both hands to sweep her highlighted auburn hair back away from her face. It was shoulder-length, and although she usually wore it up with a clip or a comb, she'd taken it down to brush it out after her morning's stint in the "moon suit" and hadn't put it back up. Unfortunately, her hair had been a frequent target for her mother ever since Laurie's teenage years.

After the conversation about her hair and a short pause in which Laurie tried to ask a question about her mother's surgery, Dorothy switched to another convenient target by saying that Laurie's outfit was much too feminine for working in a morgue. With some difficulty, Laurie restrained herself in response to this new criticism. She made it a point to wear such clothing. It was part of her identity, and she saw no conflict with her place of employment. Laurie also knew that part of her mother's response was derived from her distaste for Laurie's career choice. Although both her parents had mellowed to a degree and had even grudgingly come to recognize the merits of forensics subsequent to Laurie's work, they had been disappointed from the moment she had announced her decision to become a medical examiner. At one point, Dorothy had actually told Laurie that she had no idea what to say when her friends asked what kind of a doctor Laurie was.

“And how is Jack?” Dorothy inquired.

“He’s just fine,” Laurie said, not wishing to open that can of worms.

Dorothy then went on to describe some upcoming social events that she hoped Laurie and Jack would attend.

Laurie listened with half an ear while glancing over at her father, who’d finished with *The Wall Street Journal.* He had a large stack of newspapers and magazines. He stood up and stretched. Although he was in his eighties, he was still a commanding figure, well over six feet tall with an acquired aristocratic air. His silver hair knew its place. As usual, he had on a carefully pressed, conservatively cut, glen plaid suit with matching tie and pocket square. He walked over to the opposite side of the bed from Laurie and waited for Dorothy to pause.

“Laurie, would you mind if we stepped out in the hall for a moment?”

“Not at all,” Laurie said. She stood and gave her mother’s hand a squeeze through the bed’s guardrail. “I’ll be right back.”

“Now don’t you go worrying her about me,” Dorothy scolded her husband.

Sheldon didn't respond but rather pointed with an open palm toward the door.

Outside in the hall, Laurie had to step out of the way of a passing gurney carrying a postoperative patient back to her room. Her father came up behind her. Since he was almost a foot taller, she had to look up into his face. His skin was tan from a January trip to the Caribbean and surprisingly devoid of wrinkles, considering his age. Laurie didn't harbor any ill feelings toward the man, since she had long ago overcome her anger and frustration about his emotional distance. Her eventual maturation had made her realize that it was his problem, not hers. At the same time, there was no sense of love. It was as if he were someone else's father.

"Thank you for coming over so quickly," Sheldon said.

"There's no need to thank me. There's no question I'd come over immediately."

"I was afraid you might be more upset with the news coming out of the blue. I want to assure you that it was your mother's insistence that you not be informed of her condition."

"I gathered that from what you said on

the phone," Laurie said. She was tempted to say how ridiculous it was to keep such information from her, but she didn't. There wasn't any point. Her mother and father were not going to change.

"She didn't even want me to call you this afternoon, wishing to wait until she got home either tomorrow or the next day, but I had to insist. I had respected her wishes up until today, but I didn't feel comfortable putting it off any longer."

"Putting off what? What are you talking about?" Laurie couldn't help but notice her father looking up and down the hall as if concerned that they might be overheard.

"I'm sorry to have to tell you this, but your mother has a marker for a specific mutation of the BRCA1 gene."

Laurie felt her face flush with heat. Although she knew people were supposed to blanch with disturbing news, she always did the opposite. As a physician, Laurie was aware of the BRCA1 gene, which in its mutated form was associated with breast cancer. More disturbing, she knew that such mutations were inherited in a dominant fashion with high penetrance, meaning there was probably a fifty percent chance that she carried the same genotype!

"It is important for you to have this information, for obvious reasons," Sheldon continued. "If I had thought the three-week delay would have had any significance for you, I would have told you immediately. Now that you know, I must say that my professional opinion is that you should be tested. The presence of such a mutation raises the probability of developing breast cancer sometime prior to your eightieth year." Sheldon paused and again glanced up and down the corridor. He seemed to be genuinely uncomfortable about revealing a family secret in public.

Laurie touched her cheek with the back of her hand. As she feared, her skin was hot to the touch. With her father showing no emotion as usual, she was embarrassed that she was being so demonstrative.

"Of course, it is up to you," Sheldon recommenced. "But I should remind you that if you are found to be positive, there are things you can do to lower probabilities of developing a tumor as much as ninety percent, such as prophylactic bilateral mastectomies. Thankfully, the implications of a BRCA1 mutation are not the same as with Huntington's chorea gene or some other untreatable illness."

Despite her obvious embarrassment, Laurie stared back into the dark eyes of her father. She even found herself imperceptively shaking her head. Even if their relationship was strained, particularly after her brother's death, even if he didn't act like her father, she couldn't believe he could be saying what he was saying without more human warmth. In the past, she'd attributed his general detachment to a need for a defense mechanism against the stress of literally holding his patients' beating hearts, and hence their lives, in his hands on a daily basis. Having assisted at surgery as a first-year resident, she knew something of what such stress was like. She also was aware that his patients had ostensibly appreciated his detachment, seemingly interpreting it as supreme confidence rather than a narcissistic personality flaw. But Laurie hated it.

"Thank you for this most helpful sidewalk consult," Laurie managed, unable to keep the sarcasm from her voice. She forced herself to smile before breaking off from her father and returning back to claim her seat at her mother's bedside.

"Has he upset you, dear?" Dorothy questioned after taking one look at Laurie. "Your face is as red as a beet."

Laurie didn't answer for a moment. She had her mouth clamped shut to stop her lower jaw from quivering. Her emotions were threatening to surface, a weakness she had always despised, especially in the presence of her emotionless father.

"Sheldon!" Dorothy called out as he reclaimed his chair by the window. "What did you say to Laurie? I told you not to upset her about me."

"I wasn't talking to her about you," Sheldon said as he picked up *The New York Times.* "I was talking about her."

Jack put down his pen and turned to look at Chet McGovern's back hunched over his desk. Chet was a medical examiner colleague and Jack's officemate. Although he was five years Jack's junior, they had started at the OCME at almost the same time and got along famously. Although Jack appreciated sharing space with Chet for the companionship, he still thought it was ridiculous that the city didn't provide them with private offices. The problem was a continuous budgetary constraint that precluded updating the facility; the OCME was an easy target for politicians in a city strapped for funds. The building had been adequate when it had opened almost a half a century ago but was now something of a dinosaur, with space at a premium. Since Jack was aware that dinosaurs had lived on Earth for some hundred and sixty million years, he hoped the building in its present configuration wasn't expected to last quite that long.

"I can't believe it," Jack called out. "I'm finished. I've never been finished."

Chet swung around. He had a boyish face capped by a shock of blond hair that was considerably longer than Jack's but worn in a similar unkempt style. Like Jack, he also gave the impression of being athletic, but it was from almost daily visits to the gym, not from street basketball. He was in his mid-forties but looked considerably younger.

"What do you mean you're finished? Finished what?"

With his hands clasped into fists, Jack stretched his arms over his head. "All my cases. I'm completely caught up."

"Then what are all those folders doing in your inbox?" Chet used his index finger to point at the sizable stack threatening to spill out.

"Those are just the cases waiting for material to come back from the lab."

"Big deal!" Chet scoffed with a dismissive laugh before returning to his work.

"Hey, it's big for me," Jack said. He stood up and touched his palms to the floor and held them there for a beat. After the unaccustomed bike ride to work that morning, his hamstrings felt tight. After straightening back up, he glanced at his watch. "Good grief! It's only three-thirty. Will wonders never cease? I might make it for the first run on the court."

"If it's dry," Chet said without looking up. "Why don't you come over to Sports Club L.A. The court will be dry there. If you were smart, you'd tag along with me to body-sculpting class. I tried it last Friday, and I'm telling you, the chicks are incredible. There was this one that was something else. She had on a full-body, black, skin-tight body-suit that left nothing to the imagination."

"Ogling chicks!" Jack mocked. "One of these days, you'll wake up and be able to look back on these difficult years of puberty and laugh at yourself."

"The day I stop checking out the women will be when I'm ready for one of those pine boxes downstairs."

"I've never been much for spectator sports," Jack quipped. "I'll leave that up to you wimps."

Jack took his jacket from the back of the chair and headed out of the office, whistling as he went. It had been an interesting and stimulating day. When he reached Laurie's office, he poked his head in, wondering if she was inclined to change her mind about not coming back to his place that evening. The office was empty, though he noticed an open folder on Laurie's desk.

Jack sauntered in and checked the name. As he'd guessed, it was Sean McGillin. He was curious why Laurie and Janice seemed so engrossed in what sounded to him like a routine case. Generally, he wasn't one to stereotype women, but he thought it odd that they had both displayed what he thought was rather unprofessional emotion. He flipped open the folder and shuffled through it until he found Janice's report. He read it quickly. Nothing jumped out. Other than the victim being only twenty-eight, the circumstances weren't particularly noteworthy. It might have been sad and a tragedy for the victim's family and friends, but it wasn't sad for mankind or the city or even the borough, for that matter. There were a lot of individual tragedies in a metropolis the size of New York.

Jack quickly closed the folder and beat it out of the office as if he'd been engaged in something surreptitious and was fearful about being caught. All at once, he was less inclined to see if Laurie wanted to reconsider her decision to move back to her own apartment for fear of having to deal with too much emotion. Thinking about family tragedies was not a pastime he wanted to indulge in. He'd had too much personal experience.

Down on the first level, Jack retrieved his biking paraphernalia as well as the bike itself. He waved to the evening security man, Mike Laster, as he carried his bicycle out onto the receiving dock and then down onto the pavement. The rain had stopped, and it was significantly colder than it had been when he'd arrived that morning. He was thankful for his gloves as he climbed on the bike and pedaled across 30th Street to First Avenue.

In contrast to his morning ride, Jack enjoyed the afternoon slalom among the cars, taxicabs, and buses as he streaked northward, racing the traffic in daredevil fashion. Eventually, he cut over to Madison Avenue, using the brief crosstown traverse as a time to allow his circulation to relieve his aching quadriceps. Heading north again, he regained his speed. At the rare times he had to stop for traffic lights, he briefly questioned between breaths why he was enjoying challenging the traffic when he hadn't that morning. Sensing it had something to do with things he didn't want to think about, he gave up trying to understand and just savored the experience.

At the Grand Army Plaza, with the Plaza Hotel on one side and the Sherry-Netherland Hotel on the other, Jack entered Central Park. This was always his favorite part of his commute. With the temperature continuing to plummet, it was now cold enough for his breath to form a cloud of vapor with each exhale. Overhead, the sky had darkened into a deep purple, except to his left, in the direction of the setting sun. There it was still a rich but rapidly fading scarlet that formed a striking, blood-red backdrop for the sawtoothed spires of the buildings lining Central Park West.

The street lamps had come on in the park, and Jack rode between spheres of light and their intersecting penumbras. There were more joggers than there had been in the morning, and Jack kept his speed down. Above 80th Street, the number of joggers began to fall precipitously. By then, night had taken full command of the sky. To make things worse, it seemed to Jack that the distance between the street lamps had grown. As dark as it was, he occasionally had to slow down to walking speed between illuminated areas, since he could not see the ground and had to proceed on faith that there were no obstacles in his path.

When he passed 90th Street, it got even darker, particularly in the hilly section where he had felt such exhilaration that morning.

In contrast, now he felt the stirrings of foreboding. The leafless trees crowded the pathway. He could no longer see the buildings along Central Park West, and except for an occasional distant beep of a taxi horn, he could have been biking out in some vast, isolated forest. When he did approach a street lamp, it made the intervening, leafless branches appear like giant spider webs.

Exiting the park at 106th Street, Jack felt relief. As he hit the button for the traffic light, he had to laugh at his imagination and wonder what had stimulated it. Although he had not been riding in the park at night for months, he'd done it a considerable number of times over the years. He could not remember it having affected him in such a fashion. Even he recognized the absurdity of his having had no fear earlier in traffic, where it was truly dangerous, while getting the heebie-jeebies riding through the deserted park. He felt like an impressionable ten-year-old walking through a cemetery on Halloween.

Once the light had changed, Jack crossed Central Park West and rode along 106th Street. As he came abreast of the neighborhood playground, he stopped. Without taking his toes from his toe clips, he grasped the high chain-link fence and looked out onto the basketball court. It was illuminated by a series of mercury vapor lamps that he had paid for. In fact, Jack had paid to have the entire playground rehabbed. Originally, Jack had only offered to redo the basketball court, thinking the neighborhood would be overjoyed. To his surprise, he was forced by an ad hoc neighborhood committee into considering doing the whole park, including toddler area, if he was to be granted the privilege of upgrading the basketball section. It took Jack just overnight to decide to do the whole schmear. After all, what else was he going to do with his cash? That had been six years ago, and Jack had more than gotten his money's worth.

"You coming out and run, doc?" one of the players called out.

There were only five men, all African-American, casually warming up at the distant basket. In deference to the cold, they were all dressed in multiple layers of trendy hip-hop gear. One of them had stopped when he'd caught sight of Jack. From his voice, Jack knew it was Warren, a man with whom Jack had become close over the years. Warren was a powerfully built, gifted athlete as well as the de facto leader of the local gang. He and Jack had come to share a great mutual respect. In fact, Jack even gave Warren credit for having saved his life.

"That's my intention," Jack yelled back. "Anybody else coming out, or is it going to be three-on-three?"

"We got rained out last night, so the whole gang's going to show up. So get your kicks and get that white ass of yours out here on the double. Otherwise, you'll be standing around holding your dick. Catch my drift?"

Jack flashed back a thumbs-up. He'd caught the drift all right. There would be a lot more than ten guys, meaning the first ten would get to play while the others would be forced to jockey to get into subsequent games. It was a complicated system that had taken Jack a couple of years to comprehend. By most people's standards, it wasn't democratic or fair. Winners was taken by the eleventh guy to show up, who then chose the other four he wanted on his team. At that point, the order people arrived didn't matter. In fact, sometimes one of the members of the losing team would get selected because he was a particularly good player. Back when Jack had just moved to the neighborhood, it had taken him months to get into his first game, and that was because he finally realized he had to get out there early.

Motivated by not wanting to stand around on the sidelines in the cold, Jack quickly pedaled across the street, snatched up his bike on his shoulder, and ran up the steps leading to his building's front door. Skirting some large, green trash bags, Jack pushed open the inner door. Just inside were two derelicts sharing a bottle of cheap wine. They got out of the way as Jack charged up the stairs. He was careful because of the debris that sprinkled the steps.

Jack lived in the rear unit on the fourth floor. He had to put his bike down while he struggled with his keys.

Without even bothering to close his apartment door, Jack stashed his bike against the wall in the living room, then kicked off his shoes and stripped off his jacket, tie, and shirt, and tossed them over the back of his sofa. Clad only in his boxer shorts, he ducked into the bathroom to get his basketball gear, which normally hung over the shower curtain.

Jack stopped in his tracks. Instead of his shorts and sweatpants, he was looking at a pair of Laurie's pantyhose. He had forgotten that he had not played the previous night, and Laurie had folded his gear and put it in the closet.

Jack snatched the pantyhose off the curtain rod and held them in his hand. Slowly, his eyes rose to look at himself in the mirror. He was alone, and his slack face reflected the reality he'd been actively avoiding all day: Laurie wouldn't be there when he'd finished his basketball game. There wouldn't be the usual intelligent banter. There wouldn't be the inevitable laughter. They wouldn't be heading down Columbus Avenue for a bite to eat at one of the many Upper West Side restaurants. Instead, he would be coming back to an empty apartment just like he had for all those years after he'd first arrived in the city. It was depressing then, and it was depressing now.

"You basket case," he voiced with derision. He looked back down at the pantyhose, feeling a mixture of emotion that included anger at himself and at Laurie. At times, life seemed too complicated.

With unnecessary care, he folded the pantyhose and carried them into the bedroom. He opened one of the now-empty drawers that Laurie had been using and carefully put the lingerie inside. He closed the drawer and felt a modicum of relief with the painful reminder out of sight. He then ran to the closet to get his athletic gear.

To Jack's relief, he got back out onto the court before ten people had arrived, and Warren selected him to be on his team. Jack warmed up by shooting a series of perimeter jump shots. He felt ready when the game began a few minutes later, but unfortunately, he wasn't. He played poorly, and he was a significant factor in the loss. With another team ready to run, Warren and Jack and the rest of Warren's team were relegated to standing on the sideline, shivering in the cold. None of them were happy.

"Man, you were shit," Warren said to Jack. "You were killing us. Wassup?"

Jack shook his head. "I'm distracted, I guess. Laurie wants to get married and have a kid."

Warren knew Laurie. Over the previous

several years, he and his girlfriend, Natalie, double-dated with Jack and Laurie almost once a week. They had even gone on a wild trip to Africa together seven years ago.

"So your shortie wants to get hitched and have a kid?" Warren said derisively. "Hey, man, what else is new? I got the same problem, but you didn't see me throwing the damn ball away or letting a perfectly good pass bounce off my forehead. You got to pull yourself together; otherwise, you're not going to be running with me. I mean, there's a question of getting your priorities straight, you know what I'm saying?"

Jack nodded. Warren was right, but not quite the way he was implying. The trouble was, Jack didn't know if he was capable of getting his priorities straight, since he wasn't quite sure what they were.

With her ankle holding the insistent elevator door open, Laurie managed to get her suitcase onto the fifth-floor landing. It was a bit of an effort, since the floor level was a few inches higher than the elevator's cab. She then stepped out herself and let the door close. She could hear the whine of the elevator machinery on the roof as the cab immediately descended. Someone had obviously been pressing the call button.

Taking advantage of the suitcase's wheels, she got it over to her door without having to lift it again. The more she had struggled with it, the heavier it seemed to have become. She knew the culprit was the stash of cosmetics, shampoo, conditioner, and detergent she'd had to bring over to Jack's. None of it was travel-size. Of course, the iron didn't help, either. She went back to get the bag of groceries.

As she fumbled to extract her keys from her shoulder bag, she heard the door to the front apartment open as its securing chain reached its limit with a definite clank. Laurie lived in a building on 19th Street that had two apartments per floor. While she occupied the rear apartment that looked out onto a warren of postage-stamp-sized backyards, a recluse by the name of Debra Engler resided in the front. Her habit was to open her door a crack and peer out every time Laurie was in the hall. Most of the time, her nosiness had irritated Laurie as an intrusion on her privacy, but at the moment, she didn't mind. It was a reassuring familiarity welcoming her home.

Once inside, Laurie activated every one of the locks, bolts, and chains that the previous tenant had installed. Then she looked around. She hadn't been there for over a month and couldn't remember the last time she'd slept there. The entire apartment needed a good cleaning, and the air smelled slightly stale. It was smaller than Jack's but a quantum leap more cozy and comfortable, with real furniture, including a TV. The colors of the fabrics and paint were warm and inviting. A group of framed Gustav Klimt prints from the Met hung on the walls. The only thing missing was her cat, Tom 2, whom she had boarded a year ago with a friend who lived out on Shelter Island. She wondered if she'd have the nerve to ask for her pet back after such a long time.

Laurie dragged her suitcase into her tiny bedroom and spent a half hour organizing things. After a quick shower, she donned her robe before making herself a simple salad. Although she hadn't had any lunch, she still wasn't particularly hungry. She brought the salad and a glass of wine out to her desk in the living room and turned on her laptop. While she waited for it to boot up, she finally allowed herself to think about what she had learned from her father. It had taken effort to avoid thinking about the issue, but she had wanted to be by herself and have access to the Internet as well as be more in control of her emotions. She knew she didn't know enough to be able to think clearly.

The problem was that medical science was racing ahead at breakneck speed. Laurie had been to medical school in the mid-eighties and had learned a significant amount about genetics, since that was the time of the heady breakthroughs in recombinant DNA. But since then, the field had mushroomed geometrically, climaxing in the sequencing of the 3.2 billion base pairs of the human genome as announced with great fanfare in 2000.

Laurie had made it a point to stay reasonably current with her genetic knowledge, particularly as related to her specialty of forensics. But forensics was only interested in DNA as a method of identification. It had been discovered that certain noncoding areas, or areas not containing genes, showed dramatic individual specificity such that even close relatives had differing sequences. Tests taking advantage of the specificity are called "DNA fingerprinting." Laurie was well aware of this and appreciated it as a powerful forensic tool.

But the structure and function of genes were other issues entirely, an area where Laurie felt unprepared. Two new sciences had been born: medical genomics, which dealt with the enormously complex flow of information within a cell; and bioinformatics, which was an application of computers to such information.

Laurie took a sip of her wine. It was a daunting process to try to make sense of what she learned from her father; namely, that her mother carried the marker for the BRCA1 gene and that Laurie had a fifty percent chance of having the same marker. She shuddered. There was something unsettlingly perverse about knowing that she might have something potentially lethal hiding out in the core of her body. Throughout her life, she'd always felt that information was good in and of itself. Now she wasn't so sure. Maybe there were some things that were better not to know.

As soon as Laurie was connected to the Internet, she googled "BRCA1 gene" and got five hundred and twelve sites. She took a bite of her salad, clicked on the first site, and started reading.

five

"Whoa!" Chet McGovern murmured in appreciative homage to the female form he was watching out of the corner of his eye. It was the woman he'd mentioned to Jack that afternoon, and she was dressed in the black bodysuit he'd described. He guessed she was in her late twenties, but he couldn't be sure. What he was sure about was that she had one of the best figures he'd ever seen. At the moment, she was lying prone on a bench, using a machine to work her hamstrings and buttocks. The accentuated curve of the small of her back and the rhythmical rippling of her butt as she did her repetitions gave Chet a shiver of delight.

Chet was about twenty feet away, craftily using free weights in front of a mirrored wall so that he could get close without arousing suspicions. He'd seen her in body-sculpting class, as he had on Friday, but this time, spurred on after having mentioned her to Jack, he'd followed her into the weight room, where there was still a handful of people even though it was after nine P.M. It was Chet's intention to connect with her and ask her to have a drink in the hope that he could get her phone number. Most of Chet's dates were women he'd met at one of the multiple health clubs he frequented. For him, ogling women was not just a spectator sport.

The woman finished with the machine she'd been using. Wasting no time, she got up, glanced up at the wall clock, and then hustled down to the next machine to work the pectorals. Seemingly in a hurry, she started right in. Chet had watched her in the mirror, and in the background, he caught sight of one of the club's employees entering the room. Chet knew him reasonably well from pick-up basketball and sensed that he was a savvy dude, especially since he had some kind of supervisory role. His name was Chuck Horner. Stepping up to the free-weight rack, Chet deposited the weights he had been using and walked over to the employee.

"Hey, Chuck," Chet said sotto voce, "do you know that chick using the pectoral machine?"

Chuck craned his neck to see around Chet. "The looker? The one with the pixie face and a body to beat the band?"

"That's the one."

"Yeah, I know her. I mean, I know her name, since she comes in here all the time, and I happened to sign her up for membership."

"What's her name?"

"Jasmine Rakoczi, but she goes by Jazz. Quite a body, wouldn't you say?"

"One of the best," Chet admitted. "What kind of name is 'Rakoczi'?"

"It's funny you should ask, because I asked the same thing when she joined. She said it was Hungarian."

"Is she tight with anybody that you know?"

"I've no idea. But I can tell you she's a pistol. She drives around in a black Hummer. I should warn you: She doesn't do much socializing, at least not around here. Are you thinking of trying to make a move?"

"I'm thinking about it," Chet offered casually. He turned around to look at Jazz working her pectorals. She wasn't fooling around. Perspiration glistened like little diamonds on her tanned forehead.

"Five bucks says you can't get to first base."

Chet turned around to look back at Chuck. A wry smile appeared on Chet's face. Getting paid for what he wanted to do was a good incentive to overcome his hesitation. "You're on!"

Back at the free-weight rack, Chet lifted off several more weights. He was now committed to approach Jazz, but it wasn't without a certain amount of anxiety, especially with the daunting tidbits he'd learned from Chuck. In truth, Chet was not quite as bold as he liked to portray himself.

While standing in front of the mirror, doing curls with the free weights, Chet tried to think of some way to approach the woman that would leave him an out if he needed it. Unfortunately, he couldn't think of anything clever, and fearing she might suddenly finish and disappear into the women's locker room, he made his move.

In reality, it wasn't much of a "move" at all. He merely walked over when he thought she was almost done with her current machine. By now, his mouth was dry and his heart was thumping in his chest. Encouragingly, he managed to time his approach just about right. As he stepped in front of her, she stopped her repetitions and took her arms off the machine's grips. Taking the towel from around her neck, she wiped off her forehead using both hands, covering her face and breathing deeply from exertion.

"Hi, Jazz!" Chet said cheerfully, trusting she'd be instantly curious how he knew her name.

Jazz didn't respond except to slowly lower the towel to progressively reveal her features. She skewered Chet with her burnt umber, deeply set eyes. Up close, she wasn't pixie-like. Beneath a helmet of dark hair that was damp from her workout, her features had a hint of the exotic. What Chet had thought was tan was naturally dark skin that made her teeth appear particularly white. Her eyes were slightly almond-shaped, and her nose had an almost imperceptible aquiline bend. All this would have been acceptable to Chet, except for the mildly hollow cheeks and her expression. Those cheeks made her look mean, while her expression was intimidatingly brazen, like those he'd seen in photographic portraits of marine recruits.

Chet wasn't encouraged, especially when Jazz didn't respond.

"I thought maybe I'd introduce myself," Chet said, trying to maintain nonchalance, which was difficult, considering her stare. The free weights were also bothering him, dragging down his shoulders. Chet had taken some heavy ones in the hope of impressing this well-muscled woman. Besides her nipples, he could even see her well-defined abs beneath her spandex.

Jazz still did not respond. She didn't even blink.

"I'm Dr. Chet McGovern," Chet added. He used his doctor status as a trump card in his approach to meeting women, although he never mentioned what kind of doctor unless pressed. In his dating experience, the medical-examiner role didn't have the same cachet as that of a clinical physician.

The situation was quickly becoming critical. Not only hadn't Jazz said anything about his being a doctor, but also her expression had morphed from brazen to contemptuous. Chet tried to shrug but found it difficult with the free weights in his hands. Feeling desperate, he said: "I was hoping maybe, if you're not too busy, we could have a drink or something at the bar when you're finished with your workout." Unfortunately, the pitch of his voice came out higher than even he expected.

"Do me a favor, dickhead," Jazz said venomously. "Buzz off!"

What an ass!" Jazz thought as she watched Chet's face fall after she cut him off at the knees with her acerbic remark. He then slunk away like a dog with his tail between his legs. She'd seen him in the body-sculpting class on Friday and again today. On both occasions, he had acted as if he thought he was being slick with his furtive glances in her direction. As if that wasn't bad enough, today he'd followed her into the weight room, pestering her to death by watching her either in the mirror or out of the corner of his eye as she went through her routine, all the time pretending he was using the free weights so he could stay in relative proximity. He was such a pervert, and a dork to boot. She couldn't believe anyone in his right mind would prostitute himself by wearing trendy workout clothes with designers' names emblazoned across them. Polo! Good grief! In her mind, it was so tacky that it was gross.

Jazz stood up and headed for the inclined plane to do her sit-ups. She didn't know where Chet had gone and was glad to be away from his lecherous gaze. She hated Ivy League types, and Chet had certainly been one of those. She could recognize them a mile away. They strutted around with their fancy degrees and didn't know crap. The fact that Chet entertained even for a minute the idea that she'd want to have a drink with him was a slap in the face.

After another quick glance at the clock to

be sure she had enough time, Jazz did her hundred sit-ups, making sure her breathing was in sync. The only problem with the health-club scene—or so she had convinced herself without explaining why she liked to wear her suggestive outfit—was that she had to put up with men like Chet on a daily basis. Most of them said they wanted to buy her a drink, but she knew that wasn't what they wanted. They wanted sex, like all men. Back when she was in high school and even middle school, she probably would have been willing to give Chet a run for his money by slipping him some Ecstasy and then taking advantage of him. But that was back when she considered sex a sport, when it gave her a sense of power, and when it drove her parents crazy. Now she didn't need it anymore. In fact, it was a big pain in the ass with all the nonsense that had to go along with it. It was a waste of time, especially since it was far easier and quicker to take care of herself when she was in the mood.

Finishing her sit-ups, Jazz got to her feet and looked at herself in the mirror. She straightened to the full extent of her lean, muscled, five-foot-ten stature. She liked what she saw, particularly the definition of her arms and legs. She was in better shape than she was after naval boot camp, when the idea of exercise had first been introduced to her.

With her towel in one hand, she stooped down to pick up her water bottle. There was only a little left, and she polished it off. Then she started for the locker room. As she walked, she could see most of the men's eyes slyly following her. She was careful to avoid any eye contact and kept an expression of disdain on her face, which was easy, considering that was how she felt. She also caught a glimpse of Mr. Ivy League talking to the birdbrain who'd processed her paperwork when she joined the club a month earlier. Blond Mr. Polo now had his hands on his hips and a sad, hangdog expression on his face. Jazz had to suppress a smile when she thought about him bragging to her that he was a doctor, as if it was going to impress her! Jazz knew too many doctors, and they were all jerks.

She tossed the empty water bottle in the container by the door before heading out of the weight room. When she passed the main reception desk, she saw that it was almost nine-forty, meaning she'd better fire her afterburners and get a move on, since she liked to have the option of getting to work early if she lucked out and got another assignment. There had been a bit of a lull before the previous night's mission, which she was hoping would be the start of a whole new series. But she couldn't complain about the lull because, overall, she was lucky indeed. Sometimes she wondered how they had found her, but she didn't dwell on it. It was about time that things were starting to work out, considering all her effort, especially her so-called formal schooling after she got out of the military. Having to go to that community college with all those retards in order to go from corpsman to RN had been the biggest trial of her life.

Just inside the locker-room door was a table with a large tub of iced soft drinks. Jazz helped herself to a Coke, popped the tab, and took a satisfying swig. Next to the tub was a clipboard with a little sign requesting that she write her name and indicate what she'd taken so that her account could be charged. As she took another pull from the can and headed off to the VIP section, where she had her own assigned locker, she wondered what kind of fool would actually write their name down, but then again, she knew that a fool was born every minute.

A shower was a quick affair for Jazz. After lathering up, including a shampoo, she liked to stand for a few minutes with her eyes closed and allow the water to drum on her head and run down the crevices of her well-tuned body. Closing her eyes had the added benefit of shielding her from having to look at the other women, some of whom had butts the size of small countries, with skin that resembled the surface of the moon. Jazz couldn't believe they had such little self-respect to allow themselves to get to such a pathetic state.

After the shower, her cropped coif needed only a short stint with the hairdryer. When she'd been young, she'd agonized over her hair, but being in the military had cured her. It had also cured her of a long-standing hang-up about cosmetics. Now all she used was a little lipstick, and that was more to keep her lips from drying out than anything else.

Next came the green scrubs, over which

she pulled on a medium-length white coat with a stethoscope crammed in the side pocket. The breast pocket boasted a collection of pens, pencils, and other nursing paraphernalia.

"Are you an ER nurse?" a voice asked.

Jazz looked around. One of the large-ass women was sitting on the bench in front of her locker, swaddled in her towel like a sausage. Jazz debated whether or not to ignore her. Generally, Jazz stayed above the usual locker-room drivel, preferring to be expeditious about showering. Yet the stereotyping, which the comment implied, begged for a retort.

"No, I'm a neurosurgeon," Jazz said. She took her oversized, olive-drab military coat from her locker and pulled it on. It had pockets as deep as gold mines. The contents of the pockets bumped up against her thighs, particularly on the right.

"A neurosurgeon!" the woman marveled with a look of disbelief. "No kidding!"

"No kidding," Jazz echoed with a tone that did not invite any more conversation. She stuck her sweaty bodysuit in her gym bag, then closed and locked her locker. Although she did not look at the woman who'd spoken to her, she sensed that the woman was watching her. Jazz didn't care if the woman believed her or not. It didn't matter.

Without the exchange of another word, Jazz struck off through the locker room and out into the main corridor. After she pushed the down button of the elevator, she stuck her hand into the overcoat's right pocket and fondled her favorite possession, a subcompact nine-millimeter Glock. Its molded composite handgrip gave her a reassuring feeling of power, while awakening recurrent fantasies of being accosted by lowlifes like Mr. Ivy League in the parking garage. It would all happen so fast that the guy's head would spin. One minute he'd be making some inane comment, the next he'd be looking down the barrel of the gun's suppressor. Jazz had made the effort to outfit the gun with a silencer because another ongoing fantasy was to take out one of her nursing supervisors.

Jazz sighed. For her whole life, she'd been saddled with the albatross of incompetent authority personnel. It had started in high school. She could remember as if it were yesterday the time she'd been called into the guidance counselor's office. The dork had said he was mystified because she'd tested off the charts for intelligence but was doing so poorly. What was the cause?

"Duhhh!" Jazz voiced out loud as she recalled the incident. The guy was so slow mentally that he couldn't comprehend that nine-tenths of all the teachers were from the same shallow end of the gene pool that he was from. It was a waste of time going to high school. He'd warned her that she wouldn't get to go to college if she kept doing what she was doing. Well, she didn't care. She knew that the only real way out of the cesspool of her life was the military.

The trouble was that the military wasn't a whole lot better. It was okay at first, because she had a lot of ground to make up, getting into shape and all. Aptitude tests had supposedly pointed her in the direction of becoming a hospital corpsman, which was a joke, since she always lied on those stupid tests. But she played along; becoming a corpsman sounded fine, especially the idea of being on her own. Eventually, she opted for being an independent duty corpsman with the marines. But when she eventually got assigned, things started to go downhill. Some of the officers she had to deal with were half-wits, especially over in Kuwait, when her squadron infiltrated the Kuwait salient in February 1991. She had gotten a kick out of shooting Iraqis until her commanding officer took her rifle away as if she was not supposed to have any fun. He told her to restrict her activities to the health needs of the real men. It had been embarrassing.

Things came to a head in San Diego almost a year later. The same cretin of an officer came into a bar where she and some of the regular grunts were tossing back a few beers. He got sloshed and grabbed a feel when Jazz wasn't looking. As if that wasn't bad enough, he called her "a freaking dyke" when she spurned an offer to drive out to the tip of Point Loma with him to get laid. That had been the last straw, and Jazz had shot him in the leg with her sidearm. She hadn't been aiming for the leg, but he still got the appropriate message. Of course, that had been the end of her military career, but by then she didn't care. She'd had enough.

Going from the military into the community college turned out to be like going from the frying pan into the fire. But Jazz had persevered. She'd thought that getting her RN would be her ticket, because nurses were so much in demand, and she could call the shots. Unfortunately, the eventual reality was no different from her experience in the military when it came to supervisors, forcing her to move from job to job with the vain hope that things would be better at different institutions. But they never were. Now, it didn't matter.

When the elevator stopped on the upper parking level, Jazz got off, pushed out of the glassed elevator lobby, and walked over to her second-favorite possession, a brand-spanking-new, shiny, black-as-onyx H2 Hummer. She ran her fingers appreciatively along the vehicle's side, catching a view of her reflection in the windows. Except for the windshield, all the glass was tinted to the extent that it appeared to be black mirrors. Before she opened the door, she stepped back and took in the vehicle's boxy outline and its squat, threatening stance, both of which made it look like a weapon system ready to do battle on the streets of New York City.

Jazz climbed in, tossed her gymbag onto the passenger seat, and took her Blackberry out of her coat but left it in her lap. She started the engine. The low growl issuing from the tailpipes added to the car's allure. She couldn't help but smile. Getting into the car gave her a thrill like a line of coke, only better. It also reminded her how rewarding the day had been when Mr. Bob had approached her. She still didn't know his full name, which was stupid. He'd told her it was a matter of security, which she questioned at the time, but now she felt it didn't matter. At that first meeting, she'd seen him come at her out of the corner of her eye and thought it was just going to be another typical male come-on, but it wasn't. He got her attention immediately by calling her "Doc JR," which was the nickname the jarheads in her first marine squadron had given her. She'd not heard the name for several years, so she was surprised and guessed that Mr. Bob had been a marine himself. He had been waiting for her to come out of the hospital in New Jersey, where she was working on the evening three-to-eleven shift. He said he had a business proposition for her and asked if she was interested in earning extra money—a lot of extra money.

Sensing that her ship had finally come in, Jazz accepted his invitation to join him in his H2 Hummer, which was a spitting image of her own. Before she got in the vehicle, she made sure that there wasn't anybody else inside. She also made sure that she had her hand around the Glock nestled in her pocket. Back then, the pistol didn't have the silencer, so it was easy to draw. If Mr. Bob did anything untoward, she would have shot him where she'd meant to shoot the marine officer. She didn't believe in threatening. If the gun came out, it would be used.

But she hadn't needed to be worried. Mr. Bob was all business. They ended up at a small, smoky bar in downtown Newark, where Mr. Bob commiserated with her about her experience in the military and even apologized about her treatment and unwarranted discharge. He said that it was precisely because of her exemplary service that she was being recruited for an important mission, for which she would be compensated accordingly. Mr. Bob went on to say that they—Jazz had yet to know who "they" were—recognized her unique qualifications to provide the service they required. He then had asked if she was interested.

Jazz laughed as she put her Hummer in reverse and backed out of the parking slot. When she thought back, it was crazy for him to be asking if she was interested before she knew exactly what she would be doing, and she told him so at the time. From then on, he stopped beating around the bush. He told her they needed people like Jazz to help eliminate doctor incompetence, which he said was rampant although hard to ferret out because of a conspiracy of silence on the part of the medical profession. That was when Jazz was convinced that she was well suited to help. She was an expert on recognizing incompetence, since there had been a wellspring of it in every institution she'd been associated with. Mr. Bob said that her job would be to communicate to him by e-mail all episodes of adverse outcomes, particularly related to anesthesia, obstetrics, and neurosurgery, but he emphasized that they weren't choosy. They wanted everything she found. For her efforts, she would be paid two hundred dollars per case, with an added bonus of a thousand dollars for each that resulted in a malpractice suit and an extra five hundred if the judgment was for the plaintiff.

So that had been the beginning. Following Mr. Bob's recommendation, she switched from evenings to nights, which was easy, because the graveyard shift was the least popular. The benefit was that during the wee hours of the morning, there was less oversight, which made roaming the floors, checking the charts, and generally catching the gossip much easier than during the day or even during the evening. Mr. Bob had had other helpful recommendations as well, which he explained came from the fund of experience they'd had over several decades. He said that Jazz was joining an extensive, elite underground.

Jazz had flourished from the start. The clandestine nature of the operation was an added benefit; it even made going to work fun. The money was wired into an offshore account that had been set up for her by whoever "they" were. It grew rapidly, and it grew tax-free. The only problem was that in order to use the money, she had to go down to the Caribbean, a necessity that she found was hardly an imposition.

But then, after four years and several moves to different hospitals, the last being to St. Francis in Queens, things got even better. Mr. Bob reappeared to say that as a consequence of her outstanding work, she'd been commissioned along with a very select group to be raised in rank within the underground task force. She was now going to participate in an even more important mission, for which her compensation would be greatly increased. At the same time, so would the level of secrecy. It was a highly classified operation code-named "Operation Winnow."

Jazz remembered that he laughed after telling her the name. He said he had nothing to do with its selection, since it reminded him of "minnow." But his laughter quickly died off, and he again emphasized the secrecy. He said, "There are to be no ripples on the surface." He had asked if Jazz understood. Of course she understood.

Mr. Bob had gone on to explain that the circumstance would be the opposite of the setup with the "adverse outcomes," which she was to continue as well. With Operation Winnow, she would receive a patient's name by e-mail. Then, following a carefully devised protocol, which she had to follow to the letter, she would sanction the patient.

There had been a pause at that point. At first, Jazz didn't get his drift. She was confused by the word "sanction" until it finally dawned on her. When it did, it gave her a shiver of anticipation.

"This protocol has been masterminded by professionals, and it is completely foolproof," Mr. Bob had said. "There is no way it can be discovered, but you must follow it exactly as specified. Do you read me?"

"Of course I read you," Jazz had replied. What did he think she was, stupid?

"Are you interested in becoming part of the team?"

"That's affirmative," Jazz had said. "But you haven't told me the compensation."

"Five thousand a case."

Jazz could remember the smile that had appeared on her face. To think she would be paid five thousand dollars to do something challenging and fun was almost too good to be true. And it turned out to be better than she imagined. After the first five missions, which went off without a hitch, thanks to the protocol provided, Mr. Bob had appeared along with the Hummer.

"It's a token of our appreciation," he had explained while handing Jazz the keys and the papers. "Think of it as the antithesis of the pink Cadillac given out by that cosmetic company. Enjoy it in good health!"

Jazz exited the health club's parking garage onto Columbus Avenue. Stopping at the first red light, she activated her Blackberry. From experience, she knew that reception was marginal inside the garage. She was rewarded with a message from Mr. Bob. With mounting excitement, she opened it. It was another name!

"Yes!" Jazz shouted with a grimace of determination like an athlete who had just executed a perfect move. Simultaneously, she punched the air with a fist. But then she quickly reigned in her response. Her military training immediately kicked in to bring her back to a proactive calmness. Getting another name after having gotten one the evening before suggested that she was about to begin another series. Although the names came in random intervals, they tended to be grouped together. She had no idea why.

Reaching over, Jazz put the Blackberry in the traylike indentation on the dash over the glove compartment. The motion caused her to hesitate when the light turned green. The taxicab to Jazz's right lurched forward with the intention of cutting into Jazz's lane to avoid a stopped taxi in his own lane. Jazz stomped on her accelerator to unleash the full power of the Hummer's V-8. The SUV shot forward and gobbled up the lead of the taxi in short order, forcing the driver to slam on his brakes. Jazz flipped him the finger as she shot by.

After several other close calls with taxis along Central Park South, Jazz worked her way over to the East Side and then north on Madison to the Manhattan General Hospital. It was ten-fifteen when she pulled into the complex's mammoth garage. One of the other benefits of working the graveyard shift was a plethora of parking spaces right near the garage's entrance into the hospital on the second floor. Collecting her Blackberry and slipping it into her left coat pocket, Jazz crossed the pedestrian bridge and went into the hospital.

As she had planned, she was a little early. She went directly to floor six, where she was assigned. It was a general surgical floor and always busy. After safely stashing her coat, she sat down at one of the computer terminals and casually typed in "Darlene Morgan." The evening ward secretary ignored her, busy wrapping things up so she could leave.

Jazz was pleased to learn that Darlene Morgan was in room 629 on Jazz's floor, which made the mission that much easier. She could always go to other floors on her breaks and lunch hour, which she had done on previous missions, but there was always the mild concern about arousing attention.

Leaving floor six, she took the elevator down to the first floor. There, she walked into the emergency room. As usual, it was pure pandemonium. Evening was its busiest time, and the waiting area was jammed with people and crying babies in all manner of illness and injury. It was the kind of chaos Jazz counted on. No one questioned when she walked into the storeroom where the parenteral or intravenous fluids were kept. Although she didn't expect any interference, even if she was seen, she still looked around to make sure she wasn't being observed. It was a reflex. When it was clear no one was watching her, she reached into the cardboard box containing the concentrated potassium chloride ampoules, took one out, and slipped it into her jacket pocket. As Mr. Bob had said, in the busy ER, it would never be missed.

With the first part of her mission accomplished, Jazz returned upstairs to wait for the nursing report and for her evening shift to begin. More out of curiosity than anything else, she pulled Darlene Morgan's chart to see if there was anything interesting or, for that matter, any explanation. Of course, she didn't care whether there was or wasn't.

Mommy, I want you to come home tonight," Stephen whined.

Darlene Morgan patted the top of her eight-year-old's head and exchanged a worried glance with her husband, Paul. Stephen was big for his age and at times could act reasonably mature, although that wasn't the case at present. He was genuinely nervous about his mother being in the hospital and wouldn't let go of her hand. Darlene had been surprised when

Paul had showed up with the little guy in tow, since hospital rules dictated that visitors had to be twelve or older, and Stephen might have been big, but he didn't look twelve. But Paul had explained that Stephen pleaded to come to the point that Paul was willing to gamble that enforcement of the twelve-and-over rule would be minimal and that the floor nurses would turn a blind eye.

At first, Darlene had been glad to see Stephen, but now she was worried that there might be a tantrum if Paul inappropriately handled the departure issue. Paul had been trying to leave for half an hour and was understandably frustrated. With some difficulty, Darlene got her hand free and reached an arm around her son's waist and pulled him over against the side of the bed.

"Stephen," she said softly. "You remember what we discussed yesterday. Mom had to have an operation."

"Why?"

Darlene looked up at Paul, who rolled his eyes. Both knew that Stephen found the situation threatening, and he wasn't going to make it easy. Darlene had explained everything to him over the weekend, but he obviously hadn't comprehended.

"I had to have my knee fixed," Darlene said.

"Why?"

"You remember last summer when I hurt myself playing tennis? Well, I broke something in my knee called a ligament. The doctor had to make me a new one. Now I have to stay here overnight. Tomorrow night, I'll be home, okay?"

Stephen twirled the edge of the bedsheet in his fingers, avoiding his mother's eyes.

"Stephen, it's way past your bedtime. You go home with Dad, and then when you wake up, it will be the day I come home."

"I want you home tonight!"

"I know you do," Darlene said. She leaned over and gave her son a hug. Then she winced and let out a little groan from having moved her operated leg more than she had planned. The leg was partially immobilized in a motorized apparatus that slowly but continuously flexed the joint.

Paul stepped forward, put his hands on his son's shoulders, and urged him to step away. Stephen allowed himself to be backed up. He'd heard his mother's moan.

"Are you all right?" Paul asked his wife.

"Yeah," Darlene managed. She readjusted herself in the bed. "I just have to leave my leg still." She closed her eyes and breathed deeply, and the pain lessened.

"This is quite a setup," Paul said, nodding toward the apparatus. "We should thank our lucky stars we got into AmeriCare this fall. Otherwise, all this would have broken the bank."

"You're not suggesting I shouldn't have had the surgery, are you?"

"Not in the slightest! I'm just thinking our old insurance wouldn't have covered everything. Remember all those complicated deductibles and all that nonsense every time we tried to put in a claim? Hey, I'm just pleased everything is covered."

The little episode with the pain seemed to have a big effect on Stephen. It scared him enough to convince him that his mother needed to be in the hospital. Just a few minutes later, when Paul repeated that they had to go, he went without complaint.

All of a sudden, Darlene found herself alone. During the afternoon, there had been constant activity in the hallway, but now stillness reigned. No one passed her open door. What she didn't know was that all the nurses and aides from the evening shift, as well as those from the night shift, were having their report. The only sound was the distant, barely audible beep coming from a cardiac monitor someplace down the corridor.

Darlene's eyes roamed around her room, taking in the simple hospital furniture, the cut flowers from Paul on the bureau, the celery-green paint, and the framed Monet print. She shuddered to think of the life-and-death struggles the walls had witnessed over the years, but then quickly tried to erase the thought from her mind. It wasn't easy. She didn't like hospitals, and except for childbirth, had never been in one as a patient. Childbirth had been different. There was sense of happiness and anticipation that permeated the ward. Here, it was different and far more intimidating.

Turning her head and looking up, she watched the drops fall soundlessly from the IV bottle into an expanded portion of the IV line. Watching it was hypnotizing, and after a few minutes, it took a bit of effort to pull her eyes away. The reassuring part was that piggybacked to the IV line was a small pump containing morphine, which meant that to a controlled degree, she could medicate herself. So far she had done it only twice.

A TV was suspended above the foot of her bed, and she turned it on, more for company than anything else. The local evening news was in progress. She turned down the sound, preferring only to watch, her mind addled from a combination of the morning's anesthesia and the narcotic pain medication. The machine continued flexing her leg, but she was strangely detached from it, as if it were someone else's leg.

An hour passed effortlessly in a state midway between sleep and full consciousness. It was more like sleep when she remembered to lie still, and more like wakefulness if she happened to move her leg. She was vaguely aware that the local news had given way to the Letterman show.

The next thing she knew, she was being shaken awake by a nurse's aide. Darlene gritted her teeth because she'd inadvertently contracted her thigh muscle upon being disturbed.

"Have you passed urine since your operation?" the aide asked. She was an overweight woman with stringy red hair.

Darlene tried to think. In truth, she couldn't remember and said so.

"I think you would have remembered if you had, so you've got to go now. I'll get the bedpan." The aide disappeared into the bathroom and returned with the stainless-steel container. She placed it on the edge of the bed, against Darlene's hip.

"I don't have to go," Darlene said. The last thing she wanted to do was move herself onto the bedpan. Even the thought made her wince. The surgeon had told her she might have some discomfort after the operation. What an understatement!

"You have to," the aide stated. She checked her watch, as if there was no time for discussion.

A combination of the aide's attitude and Darlene's drugged state made Darlene's dander rise. "Leave the bedpan; I'll do it later."

"Honey, you're doing it now. I got orders from above."

"Well you tell whoever is 'above' that I'm doing it later."

"I'm getting the nurse, and let me tell you, she doesn't brook contrariness."

The aide disappeared again. Darlene shook her head. "Contrariness" was a word she associated with preschoolers. She moved the ice-cold bedpan away from her thigh.

Five minutes later, the nurse burst into the room with the aide in tow, causing Darlene to start. In contrast to the aide, the nurse was tall and lean with exotic eyes. With her hands on her hips, she leaned over Darlene. "The aide tells me you refuse to urinate."

"I didn't refuse. I said I would do it later."

"You're doing it now or we'll cath you. I trust you know what that means."

Darlene had an idea, and it wasn't appealing in the slightest. The aide went around to the other side of the bed. Darlene felt surrounded.

"It's your call, sister," the nurse added when Darlene didn't respond. "My advice to you is to get that butt of yours in the air."

"You could be a little more empathetic," Darlene suggested as she prepared to raise her backside by putting her two palms against the bed.

"I got too many sick patients to be empathetic about passing a little urine," the nurse said. She checked the IV line while the aide got the bedpan into place.

Darlene breathed a sigh of relief. Getting on the bedpan hadn't been as bad as she had imagined, although the cold metal was shocking. Urinating was another matter. It took her a few minutes of concentration before she could start. Meanwhile, the nurse and the aide had left. She passed more urine than she thought she could, which made her recognize that the ordeal was necessary. At the same time, it made her remember why she didn't like hospitals.

Once she was finished, she had to wait. She could move her pelvis up and down without discomfort, but to get the bedpan out from under her, she'd have to lift one of her hands off the bed. That meant tensing muscles that hurt her knee, so she was stuck. After five minutes, her back started to complain, so she gritted her teeth and managed to move the bedpan to the side. Almost on cue, both the nurse and the aide reappeared.

While the aide dealt with the bedpan, the

nurse offered Darlene a sleeping pill and a small paper cup of water.

"I don't think I need it," Darlene said. With all the drugs she'd had during the day, she felt like she was floating.

"Take it," the nurse enjoined. "It's been ordered by your doctor."

Darlene looked up into the nurse's face. She couldn't tell if her expression was brazen or bored or disdainful. Whatever it was, it seemed inappropriate. It made Darlene wonder why the woman had gone into nursing. Darlene took the pill, swallowed it, and chased it with the water. She gave the cup back to the nurse. "You could be a little more personable," she suggested.

"People get what they deserve," the nurse said, taking the cup and crushing it in her hand. "I'll be back to see you later."

Don't bother, Darlene thought but didn't say. Instead, she merely nodded as the nurse and the aide left. Recognizing her neediness and vulnerability, she didn't want to cut off her nose to spite her face. With her leg bound up in the flexing machine and with as much pain as she got when she moved her knee, she was totally dependent on the nursing staff.

Darlene gave herself a dose of her pain medication to dull her toothache-like discomfort after the bedpan ordeal. She soon felt calm and detached. The emotions evoked by the run-in with the nurse and the aide faded into insignificance. The important thing was that the surgery was over. The anxiety she'd felt the night before was a thing of the past. She was now on the road to recovery, and, according to the doctor, she could look forward to playing tennis in six months or so.

Without being aware of the transition, Darlene fell into a deep, dreamless, drugged slumber. She was unaware of the passage of time until she was rudely yanked back to consciousness by a searing pain racing up her left arm. A moan escaped from her lips as her eyes shot open. The TV was off, and the room was dim with only a single low-wattage nightlight down near the floor. For an instant, Darlene was disoriented, but she quickly recovered. With the pain now spreading into her shoulder, she lunged for the call button. But she didn't get to it. Instead, she felt a hand grab her wrist. Raising her eyes, she saw a white figure standing at the bedside, the face lost in shadow.

Darlene opened her mouth to talk, but the words caught in her throat. The room dimmed and began to spin before Darlene felt herself falling from the light into darkness.

six

"Shelly, watch out!" Laurie yelled. "Stop!" To her utter horror, her brother was running full tilt toward a stagnant lake, the shore of which was ringed with deadly mud capable of swallowing an elephant. She couldn't believe it. She'd warned him of the danger, but he wouldn't listen. "Shelly, stop!" she repeated as loud as she could.

Filled with the agonizing frustration of powerlessness in the face of imminent disaster, Laurie began running. Although she knew she would be helpless when Shelly blundered into the mud, she couldn't stand there and let the tragedy unfold without trying to do something. As she ran, she frantically looked for a long stick or a log that she could extend to her brother once he was caught in the muck, but the surrounding landscape was barren, with nothing but bare rock.

Then, suddenly, Shelly stopped about ten feet from the quicksand-like muddy border of the lake. He turned and faced Laurie. He was smiling in the same taunting fashion as he had when they were children.

Relieved, Laurie came to a halt. Panting, she didn't know if she should be thankful or angry. Then, before she could say anything, Shelly turned around again and recommenced his mad dash toward calamity.

"No!" Laurie shouted. But this time, Shelly reached the lake and ran out as far as he could go before his legs became hopelessly mired. Again, he looked back, only now his smile was gone. In its place was a look of terror. He reached toward Laurie, who'd run to the very edge of the dry land. Again, she looked for something to use to reach out to him, but there was nothing. Rapidly and relentlessly, her brother sank into the muck, with his pleading eyes riveted to Laurie's until they disappeared into the filth. All that was left was a hand vainly grasping at the air, but it, too, soon disappeared from view, swallowed by the enveloping mud.

"No! No! No!" Laurie shouted, but her voice was drowned out by a jarring jangle that pulled her from the depths of sleep. Quickly, she stretched out and quieted her ancient windup alarm clock. She flopped back onto the bed and stared up at the ceiling. She was perspiring and breathing heavily. It was an old nightmare that, mercifully, she'd not had for several years.

Laurie sat up and put her feet over the side of her bed. She felt terrible. The night before, she'd stayed up too late, compulsively cleaning her dirty apartment despite her exhaustion. She knew it had been a stupid thing to do, but it had been symbolically therapeutic. The literal and figurative cobwebs had to be cleaned.

She couldn't believe how much her life had changed in forty-eight hours. Although she was confident that her friendship with Jack would remain strong, her intimate relationship with him was probably over. She had to be realistic about her needs and his reality. On top of that were the concerns about her mother, as well as the worry about her own health.

Getting to her feet, Laurie went into her tiny bathroom and started her morning routine of showering, washing and drying her hair, and putting on the small amount of makeup she'd become accustomed to using. It was restricted to a touch of coral blush, a bit of eyeliner, and a natural-color lipstick. When she was finished, she looked at herself in the mirror. She wasn't pleased. She appeared tired and stressed, despite her attempts to hide it, and even with additional blush and a few dabs of concealer, she didn't look any better.

Laurie had always been a healthy person, and had taken health for granted except during a brush with bulimia in high school. Suddenly, the threat of carrying the marker for a BRCA1 mutation changed that dramatically. It was a scary, disturbing idea that a genetic conspiracy might be covertly residing inside every one of her trillion cells. Although she had hoped the previous evening's research would have been reassuring, it hadn't been. She now knew a lot more about the BRCA1 problem from an academic point of view; namely, that the normal gene functioned as a tumor-suppressor gene but that in its mutated form, it acted the opposite.

Unfortunately, bookish information was not a lot of help when she thought about the issue personally, particularly when she coupled what she had learned with her desire to have children. Prophylactically losing her breasts was bad enough, but losing her ovaries was much worse: It was castration. To her horror, she'd learned that if she had the marker for BRCA1, she not only had an increased chance of developing breast cancer before age eighty but also an increased chance of ovarian cancer! In other words, her biological clock was ticking even louder and faster than she had thought.

It was all very depressing, especially combined with her exhaustion from lack of sleep. The question was: Should she be tested for the BRCA marker? She didn't know. She certainly would not consent to having her ovaries removed, at least not until she had had a child. And her breasts? She didn't think she'd consent to that, either, so what would be the rationale for having the test? In her mind, such a quandary was the current problem with modern genetic testing: Either there was no cure for the illness in question, or the cure was too horrific.

After a quick breakfast of fruit and cereal, she got out of her apartment only fifteen minutes later than she would have liked. Mrs. Engler didn't disappoint her. She cracked open her door on cue and looked out at Laurie with her bloodshot eyes as Laurie repeatedly hit the elevator button in the hope of speeding it up. Laurie smiled and waved at the woman but got no response other than Mrs. Engler clicking the door shut.

The walk up First Avenue was uneventful. It had turned colder than it had been the previous few days, but Laurie didn't try to hail a cab. With her down coat zipped up to her neck, she was warm enough. She also enjoyed the distraction that the pulsating city provided. For her, New York had a dynamism like no other place on the planet, and her problems mercifully retreated into the recesses of her mind. In their place surfaced thoughts about the McGillan case and the hope that she would get slides from Maureen and a report from Peter. She also found herself wondering what kind of cases she'd get that day. She hoped they would be as absorbing and distracting as McGillan's.

Laurie entered the OCME through the front door. In contrast with the previous morning, the reception area was empty. The administration area to the left was also empty. She waved to Marlene Wilson, the receptionist, who was enjoying the solitude and leafing through the morning paper. She waved back with one hand while buzzing Laurie into the ID room with the other. Laurie slipped out of her coat as she walked into the office.

Two of the more senior medical examiners, Kevin Southgate and Arnold Besserman, were sitting in the two brown vinyl club chairs, deep in conversation. Both waved to Laurie without interrupting their dialogue. Laurie waved back. She noticed that Vinnie Amendola was not in his usual spot, hiding behind his newspaper. She approached the desk where Riva was busy reviewing the cases that had come in overnight. Riva looked up, peering at Laurie over the tops of her glasses. Riva smiled. "Did you get more sleep last night?" she asked.

"Not a lot more," Laurie confessed. "I was apartment cleaning until almost two."

"I've been there," Riva said with an understanding chuckle. "What happened at the hospital?"

Laurie told her about the visit and that her mother was doing fine. She talked briefly about her father but didn't mention the BRCA1 problem.

"Jack is already down in the pit," Riva said.

"I guessed as much when I noticed Vinnie wasn't here reading the sports page."

Riva shook her head. "Jack was already in here, rooting around in the cases, when I arrived before six-thirty. That's too early for him to be in here. It's pathetic. I told him to get a life."

Laurie laughed. "That must have gone over well."

"I also told him about your mom. I hope that was okay. He had asked where you had gone yesterday afternoon. Apparently, he'd come by our office just after you'd left for the hospital and I had gone down to talk with Calvin."

"That's fine," Laurie said. "Now that I've been told, it's no secret."

"I hear you," Riva said. "I can't understand why your mother wouldn't want to confide in you. Anyway, Jack was taken aback; I could tell."

"Did he say anything in particular?"

"Not about your mom. He was quiet for a few minutes, which is not like Jack."

"What kind of case is he doing?" Laurie asked.

"An ugly one," Riva said. "He is amazing; I have to give him credit. The more difficult the case, whether emotionally or technically, the better he likes it. This one was particularly troubling from an emotional point of view. It was a four-month-old infant that had been abraded all over its little body, then brought into the ER, dead. The ER personnel were in an uproar of indignation, since the parents tried to say they had no idea what had happened. The police were called, and now the parents are in jail."

"Oh, God!" Laurie voiced with a shudder. Despite thirteen years as a medical examiner, she still had trouble doing children, especially infants and abuse cases.

"I was in a muddle when I read the investigative report," Riva admitted. "There was no question the child had to be posted, but there wasn't anyone I disliked enough to assign it to."

Laurie tried to laugh because she knew Riva was joking, but she only managed a smile. Riva liked everyone and vice versa. Laurie also knew that Riva would have taken the case herself, had Jack not volunteered.

"Before Jack went downstairs, he mentioned another case," Riva said as she searched through the files before holding one up. "He said he'd had his usual informal tête-à-tête with Janice on his way in, and that she had told him there'd been a case of another young adult at the Manhattan General strikingly similar to McGillan's. He said that you would probably want it, and that I should assign it to you. Are you interested?"

"Absolutely," Laurie said. Her brows knitted as she took the folder. She opened it and rifled through the pages to find the investigative report. The patient's name was Darlene Morgan, age thirty-six.

"She was the mother of an eight-year-old," Riva said. "What a tragedy for the child."

"My word," Laurie voiced as she skimmed the report. "It does sound similar—strikingly similar." She looked up. "Do you know if Janice is still here?"

"I haven't the faintest idea. She was when I passed the PA's office, but that was before six-thirty."

"I think I'll check," Laurie said. "Thanks for the case."

"My pleasure," Riva said, but she was talking to Laurie's back, because Laurie was already on her way.

Laurie moved quickly. Technically, Janice was off at seven, but she frequently stayed later. She was compulsive about her reports and often could be there as late as eight. It was seven-forty as Laurie passed through the clerical room. A minute later, she leaned into the investigator's doorway. Bart Arnold looked up from his desk. He was on the phone.

"Is Janice still here?" Laurie asked.

Bart hooked his thumb over his shoulder

to point into the depths of the room. Janice's head popped out from around a monitor. She was sitting at the desk in the far corner.

Laurie walked in and grabbed a chair. She pulled it over to Janice's desk and sat down. She waited until Janice finished a strenuous yawn.

"Sorry," Janice said when she had recovered. She used a knuckle to wipe under her eyes; they were watering.

"You're entitled," Laurie said. "Was it a busy night?"

"Volume-wise it was the usual. Nothing like the night before, although there were a couple of heartbreakers. I don't know what's getting into me. I didn't used to be so sensitive. I hope it's not affecting my objectivity."

"I heard about the infant."

"Can you imagine? How can people be like that? It's beyond me. Maybe I'm getting too soft for this job."

"It's when you stop being affected by such cases that you have to worry."

"I suppose," Janice with an exhausted sigh. She straightened herself up in her chair as if pulling herself together. "Anyway, what can I do for you?"

"I've just scanned your report on Darlene Morgan. The case strikes me as being disturbingly similar to that of Sean McGillan."

"That's exactly what I told Dr. Stapleton when I ran into him this morning."

"Is there anything you can tell me that's not in here?" Laurie said, waving the report in the air. "Like any impressions you might have gotten while talking to the people involved, like the nurses or the doctors or even the family members. You know, a step beyond the facts. Something that you sensed intuitively."

Janice kept her brown eyes glued to Laurie's while she thought. After a minute, she shook her head slightly. "Not really. I know what you mean, kind of a subliminal impression. But nothing came to mind. It was just another hospital tragedy. An apparently healthy, young-to-middle-aged woman whose time was up." Janice shrugged. "When someone like that suddenly dies, it certainly makes you realize we are all living on the edge."

Laurie bit her lip while she struggled to

think of what else she should ask. "You didn't talk to the surgeon, did you?"

"No, I didn't."

"Was it the same surgeon who operated on McGillan?"

"No, there were two different orthopedic guys involved, and my impression from the resident was that both are held in high regard."

"It seems that both patients died at about the same time in the morning. Did that seem strange to you?"

"Not really. In my experience, that two-to-four-A.M. time frame is quite popular for deaths to occur. It's my busiest time during my shift. A doctor one time suggested to me it had something to do with circadian hormone levels."

Laurie nodded. What Janice was saying was probably true.

"Dr. Stapleton told me that you did the post on Sean McGillan. Is the reason you are asking these questions because you didn't find much pathology?"

"I found none," Laurie admitted. "What about anesthesia? Any similarities there, like the same personnel or same agents?"

"I have to confess I didn't look into that. Should I have?"

Laurie shrugged. "Both were about eighteen hours postsurgery, so they would still have remnants of the anesthesia on board. I think we're going to have to look into everything, including all the medication they got and in what order and dosage. I asked Bart to get the McGillan chart. I'm going to need the Morgan chart also."

"I can put in the request before I go," Janice said.

Laurie stood up. "I appreciate it. I hope you don't think my coming in here is a negative reflection on your investigative report, because it is quite the contrary. Your reports are always first-rate."

Janice flushed. "Well, thank you. I try. I know how important it can be to have all the information, especially in mysterious cases like these four."

"Four?" Laurie questioned with surprise. "What do you mean 'four'?"

"As I recall, the week before last there were two others, both from the Manhattan General, that were similar from my end."

"How similar? Were they patients who

were in their first day postoperative, like McGillan and Morgan?"

"That's my recollection. What I do remember for certain is that they were young and generally in good health, so that it was a big-time unpleasant surprise to everyone that they had cardiac arrests. I also remember both were found by the nurse's aide while doing routine postoperative temperatures and heart rates, which is how Darlene Morgan was found, suggesting they had to have suffered some kind of major medical catastrophe. I mean, there was no warning. At least with Sean McGillan, he'd had a chance to ring his call button. Also, just like with McGillan and Morgan, the resuscitation team had zero luck. I mean, they got nothing but a flat line."

"This could be very important," Laurie said, pleased that she had come to seek out Janice.

"Anyway," Janice said, "I was planning on pulling copies of the investigative reports, but I haven't had time yet."

"Were they orthopedic cases?"

"I don't remember exactly what kind of surgery they had, but it will be easy to find out. If I had to guess, I'd say they were both general surgery cases, not orthopedic. Would you like me to pull the investigative reports?"

"Don't bother. I'm certainly going to want to have the whole folders. Do you remember which doctor posted them?"

"I don't think I ever knew. I don't have much contact with the doctors, besides you and Dr. Stapleton."

"Do you remember what was the final, official cause of death?" Laurie asked.

"Sorry," Janice admitted. "I don't even know if they have been signed out yet. Sometimes I follow up on cases that interest me, but not on the two we're talking about. I have to admit that at the time, they seemed like a couple of pretty routine, unexpected major cardiac problems. I guess saying something is routine and unexpected is an oxymoron, so maybe routine is not the right word. I mean, people die in the hospital, as tragic as that may be, and a lot of times it's not from the problem that brought them into the hospital in the first place. It wasn't until this morning when I was writing up the Morgan case and thinking about the nurse's aide angle that I even remembered them."

"What were the names?" Laurie asked. She felt a shiver of excitement. This curious, unexpected yet potentially important snippet of information was exactly the reason she had wanted to talk with Janice. It made her feel more strongly that her medical-examiner colleagues who ignored the experience and expertise of the forensic investigators and the mortuary techs did so at their professional peril.

"Solomon Moskowitz and Antonio Nogueira. I wrote them down with their accession numbers." Janice handed the paper to Laurie.

Laurie took the paper and looked at the names. Whether she was actively seeking a major diversion from her own personal problems she didn't know. What she did know was that she had found one.

"Thanks, Janice," Laurie said sincerely. "I've got to hand it to you. Associating these cases might be important." One of the problems of there being eight medical examiners at the OCME is that such associations could slip through the cracks. There was a Thursday-afternoon conference where cases were vetted in an open forum, but it usually involved only the more academically interesting or even macabre ones.

"Don't mention it," Janice said. "It makes me feel good when I think I'm really part of the team and contributing."

"You most certainly are," Laurie responded. "Oh, and by the way, when you put in the request for Morgan's chart, will you also ask for Moskowitz's and Nogueira's as well?"

"I'll be happy to," Janice said. She made a notation on a Post-it and put the reminder on the side of her monitor.

With her brain in a twitter, Laurie hustled out of the forensic investigator's office and took the elevator up to the fifth floor. Concerns about BRCA1 and even Jack were pushed to the back of her mind. She couldn't take her eyes off the two names on the paper that Janice had given her. Going from one curious case to four was a huge leap. The question was simply whether these four cases were indeed related. For her, this was what being a medical examiner was all about. If the cases were related by a common drug or procedure, and if she could figure it out, then she would have the rewarding opportunity to prevent more deaths. Of course, such information would also tell her if the deaths were accidental or homicidal, and that thought gave Laurie a shiver.

Entering her office, Laurie quickly hung up her coat behind the door, then sat down at the computer. She typed in the accession numbers of the two cases, learning that neither had been signed out as of yet. Mildly disappointed, she did get the names of the two doctors who had done the autopsies: George Fontworth had posted Antonio Nogueira, and Kevin Southgate had posted Solomon Moskowitz. Having seen Southgate down in the ID office earlier, she picked up her phone and dialed his extension. She let it ring five times before hanging up.

Returning to the elevator, Laurie descended to the first floor and wended her way back to the ID room. She'd hoped Kevin would still be there, talking with Arnold, and she wasn't disappointed. She waited patiently for a break in their animated conversation. The two incessantly argued about politics: Kevin, the inveterate liberal Democrat, and Arnold, the equivalent conservative Republican. Both had been at the OCME for almost twenty years and had come to resemble each other. Both were overweight with ashen complexions and were haphazard about their hygiene and dress. In Laurie's mind, they were the stereotypical coroners in old Hollywood movies.

"Do you remember posting a Solomon Moskowitz about two weeks ago?" Laurie asked Kevin after apologizing for interrupting. As usual, he and Arnold seemed to be just shy of exchanging blows. They frustrated each other, since neither had a snowball's chance in hell of changing the other's entrenched opinions.

After joking that he couldn't remember the cases he did yesterday, Kevin's doughy face screwed up in thought. "You know, I think I remember a Moskowitz," he said. "Do you happen to know if it was a Manhattan General case?"

"That's what I was told."

"Then I remember it. The patient had an apparent cardiac arrest. If it's the one I'm thinking about, there wasn't much on the post. I don't believe I've signed it out yet. I imagine I'm waiting for the microscopic to come back."

Yeah, sure, Laurie thought to herself. Even in the busiest of times, it didn't take two weeks to get slides. But she wasn't surprised. Kevin and Arnold were notorious for failing to get their cases out on a timely basis. "Do you remember if the patient had had recent surgery?"

"Now you're pushing your luck. I tell you what, why don't you stop up to my office, and I'll let you go over the folder."

"Sounds like a good idea," Laurie responded. She was momentarily distracted by seeing George come in through the door to the ID room, removing his coat. Allowing Kevin and Arnold to get back to their bickering, Laurie joined George at the coffee machine.

George had been at the OCME for almost as long as Kevin and Arnold, but he hadn't picked up any of their personal habits. He appeared significantly more stylish, with pressed pants, a clean shirt, and a colorful tie, all of which were reasonably contemporary, which was how he liked to present himself. He also looked dramatically younger by avoiding the common middle-age weight gain. Although Laurie knew Jack did not hold George in high esteem professionally, she had always found him easy to work with.

"I heard your gunshot case yesterday had a surprising denouement," Laurie said.

"What an ordeal," George complained. "If Bingham ever offers to do another case with me, remind me to graciously refuse."

Laurie laughed and chatted about the case for a few minutes before switching to her real interest. As she'd spoken with Kevin concerning Moskowitz, she asked if George remembered doing Antonio Nogueira some two weeks earlier.

"Give me a hint," George responded.

"I'm guessing at the details, since I don't know them for certain," Laurie said, "but I believe he would have been relatively young, he would have been within twenty-four hours of having surgery at the Manhattan General, and he would have been suspected of having suffered some sort of cardiac catastrophe."

"Okay, I remember the case: a real teaser. I found zilch on the post and nothing to hang my hat on with the microscopic. The folder is up on my desk, waiting for toxicology possibly to come up with something. Otherwise, I'm going to be forced to sign it out as a spontaneous ventricular fibrillation or a massive heart attack that was so sudden and so global that there wasn't any time for pathology to develop. Of course, that means whatever caused it had to magically disappear. One way or the other, the heart stopped. I mean, it couldn't have been that his breathing stopped, because there was no cyanosis." He shrugged and gestured helplessly with his hands.

"So the microscopic didn't show much in the coronary vessels?"

"Minimal."

"And the heart muscle itself looked normal? I mean, like something capable of causing a sudden lethal arrhythmia. Was there any sign of inflammation?"

"Nope! It was completely normal."

"Do you mind if I look at the folder later this afternoon?" Laurie asked.

"Be my guest! Why the interest? How did you hear about it?"

"I heard about it from Janice," Laurie said. "I'm interested because I had a case surprisingly similar yesterday." Laurie felt mildly guilty about not mentioning the two other cases, but not guilty enough to bring them up. For one thing, her suspicion that they were connected in any way was purely speculative, and second, at this early stage she couldn't help but feel proprietary about what she was beginning to think might be some kind of series.

Leaving the ID office, Laurie descended a floor and sought out Marvin. She found him in the mortuary office. As she had hoped, he was already in his scrubs.

"Are you ready to rock and roll?" Laurie asked. She was eager to start.

"You're on, sister!" Marvin said as if it today was a rerun of the previous day.

Laurie gave him Darlene Morgan's accession number before going into the locker room to change into scrubs. She was excited. It was the first time in her career as a medical examiner that she hoped to find nothing on the autopsy, meaning Morgan would be like McGillan, Nogueira, and Moskowitz. The longer the series idea played out, the better the diversion it would be and the less apt she'd be to agonize over personal unpleasantries.

Leaving the locker room, she crossed over to the storage room and rescued her battery pack from the charger. Fifteen minutes later, she was in the moon suit and pushing into the pit from the anteroom where she'd gloved. There was only one case under way. She had no trouble distinguishing between Jack and Vinnie, since Vinnie was shorter and considerably slighter. Jack was peering through the viewfinder of a camera set on a tripod. Laurie tried not to look at the tiny, naked infant splayed out on the table. Laurie blinked by reflex when the camera's flash went off.

"Is that you, Laurie?" Jack called out. He had straightened up and turned in her direction in response to the sound of the door closing.

"It is," Laurie said. Not finding Marvin in the autopsy room, she twisted around to look through the wire-embedded glass in the door leading out to the corridor. Marvin was approaching with a gurney in tow. At the back, pushing, was another mortuary tech, Miguel Sánchez. Laurie guessed there had been a problem. Marvin was customarily super-efficient and invariably waiting for her.

"Come on over here!" Jack said with some excitement. "I have something to show you. This case is a corker."

"I'm sure it is," Laurie said. "But I think I'll

let you tell me about it after the fact. You know that autopsies on children are not my cup of tea."

"I'm pretty certain this case is another one like those yesterday," Jack said. "I'm more than ninety percent sure the cause and manner of death are going to surprise everyone. I'm telling you, it's textbook!"

Despite her distaste for dealing with kids in the autopsy room, her professional curiosity urged her over to Jack's side. With some difficulty, she made herself look down at the hapless child. Just as Riva had described, the poor little girl appeared bruised, abraded, and burned over much of her tiny body, including her face. The awfulness of the image made Laurie sway slightly, as if dizzy. She spread her feet to stabilize herself. Behind her, she heard the door open, followed by the squeak of the wheels of an old gurney as it was pushed in.

"What if I told you the whole body X-ray of this infant was completely negative for fractures, old or new? Would that influence your thinking about this case?"

"Not particularly," Laurie said. She tried to look in at Jack's face, but it was difficult with the overhead lights reflecting off his plastic face mask. They hadn't seen each other or talked for almost twenty-four hours, and when they first met that morning, she had hoped for something other than a repeat of his playful professorial role.

"What if I told you that in addition to the X-ray being normal, the frenulum is intact?"

"It certainly wouldn't negate what I'm looking at," Laurie responded. Despite her repugnance, Laurie bent over and looked closely at the skin lesions, particularly where Jack had made a small incision through one of the abrasions. There had been no blood or edema. All at once, she knew now what Jack was implying when pointing out signs that suggested abuse was not at issue. "Vermin!" she said suddenly. She straightened up.

"Give this lady a prize!" Jack said like a carnival barker. "As expected, Dr. Montgomery has expertly corroborated my impression. Of course, Vinnie isn't convinced, so we have a five-dollar bet riding on finding nonspecific evidence of an asphyxial death when we do the internal part of the autopsy, and everybody knows what that would imply."

Laurie nodded. The chances were good that the child in front of her had died of sudden infant death syndrome, or SIDS, which shows signs of asphyxial death on autopsy. Although on first glance she had thought all the skin lesions had been inflicted prior to death, she now guessed they were most likely postmortem damage caused by a variety of vermin, such as ants, cockroaches, and possibly mice or rats. If this indeed proved to be the case, then the manner of death was not homicidal but accidental. Of course, that didn't lessen the tragedy of the young life lost, but it surely had very different implications.

"Well, I better get cracking here," Jack said as he detached the camera from the tripod. "This child was maimed by the circumstances of poverty, not abuse. I've got to get her parents out of jail. Keeping them there is like adding insult to injury."

Laurie made her way over to where Marvin was aligning the gurney next to one of the autopsy tables, trying not to dwell on her disappointment about Jack's blithe repartee and apparent mind-set. She also couldn't help but wonder if Jack's case was another preternatural hint to remind her that things were not always quite what they seemed at first glance.

"Did you have some trouble?" Laurie asked Marvin as the two techs moved the body onto the autopsy table. Marvin positioned the head on a wooden block.

"A slight hitch," Marvin admitted. "Mike Passano must have written down the wrong compartment number. But with Miguel's help, we found the body in short order. Any special requests for this case?"

"It should be straightforward," Laurie said as she checked the accession number and name. "In fact, I hope it turns out to be a mirror image to the first case we did yesterday." Marvin shot her a perplexed glance as she started the external exam.

Laurie's trained eye began recording her observations. The body was that of a Caucasian woman in her mid-thirties with brunette hair in a normal distribution who appeared to have been in good health, although slightly overweight, with extra adipose tissue across her abdomen and on the lateral aspect of her thighs. Her skin had the usual pallor of death and was lesion-free, save for a few innocuous nevi. There was no cyanosis. There was no evidence of recreational drug use. There were two freshly sutured incisions on the lateral surfaces of her left knee and no signs of inflammation or infection. A capped-off intravenous line ran into her left arm, with no extravasations of blood or fluid at the site. An endotracheal tube that was correctly positioned in her trachea protruded from her mouth.

So far, so good, Laurie said to herself, meaning the external exam was comparable with Sean McGillan Jr.'s. She took the scalpel offered by Marvin and began the internal portion. She worked quickly and intently. The activity in the rest of the room receded from her consciousness.

Forty-five minutes later, Laurie straightened up after tracing the veins in the legs up into the abdominal cavity. She had found no clots. Other than several insignificant uterine fibroids and a polyp in the large intestine, she had found no significant pathology and certainly nothing that would have explained the woman's demise. Exactly like McGillan, she would have to wait for the microscopic and the toxicological if she was going to find a cause of death.

"A clean case," Marvin commented. "Just like you wanted."

"Very curious," Laurie said. She felt vindicated. She looked around the room, which had practically filled during her intense concentration. The only table that wasn't in use was immediately adjacent to where Jack had been working. Apparently, he'd finished and left without so much as a word. Laurie wasn't surprised. It seemed consistent with his recent behavior.

At the table on the other side of hers, Laurie thought she recognized Riva's diminutive frame. When Marvin went out into the hall to get a gurney, Laurie stepped over to check. It was Riva.

"Interesting case?" Laurie asked.

Riva looked up. "Not particularly, from a professional point of view. It's just a hit-and-run on Park Avenue. She was a tourist from the Midwest, and she was holding on to her husband's hand when she was struck. He was only a step ahead of her. It always amazes me pedestrians aren't more careful in this city, considering how fast the traffic moves. How about your case?"

"Extremely interesting," Laurie said. "Almost no pathology whatsoever."

Riva looked at her officemate askance. "Interesting and no pathology? That doesn't sound like you."

"I'll explain later. Meanwhile, do I have another case?"

"Not today," Riva said. "I thought you could use a little down time."

"Hey, I'm okay. Really! I don't want any special treatment."

"Don't worry. It's a relatively light day. You've got a lot on your plate."

Laurie nodded. "Thanks, Riva," she said, although she would have preferred to keep busy.

"I'll see you upstairs."

Laurie returned to her table, and when Marvin came back with the gurney, she thanked him for his help and said that she was finished for the day. Ten minutes later, after the usual cleaning process, she hung up her moon suit and attached her battery to the charger. Planning on heading to histology and toxicology, she was surprised to see Jack blocking her exit from the storeroom.

"Can I buy you a cup of coffee?" he asked.

Laurie glanced up into his maple-syrup-colored eyes and tried to gauge his mood. She'd had quite enough of his lightheartedness; considering the circumstances, it was ultimately humiliating. Yet there was no impish smirk like he'd worn the previous afternoon when he'd appeared in her office doorway. His expression was serious, almost solemn, which she appreciated, since it was more apropos to what was going on between them.

"I'd like to talk," Jack added.

"I'd love a cup of coffee," Laurie responded. With some difficulty, she tried to reign in her expectations about what Jack had in mind. This seemed to be almost too-appropriate behavior for him.

"We could head up to the ID office or the lunchroom," Jack said. "It's your call."

The lunchroom was on the second floor. It was a loud room with an old-fashioned linoleum floor, bare concrete walls, and a bank of vending machines. At that time in the morning, it would be reasonably crowded with secretarial and custodial personnel on break.

"Let's try the ID office," Laurie suggested. "We should have the place to ourselves."

"I missed you last night," Jack said as they waited for the back elevator.

My word, Laurie thought. Despite her concerns, her hopes of having a significant conversation rose. It was not customary for Jack to admit to his feelings quite so directly. She looked up at his face to make sure he wasn't being sarcastic, but she couldn't tell for certain, since his face was averted. He was absorbed in watching the floor indicator above the elevator door. The numbers were decreasing with their typical agonizing slowness. The back elevator was used for freight and moved at a glacial pace.

The door opened, and they boarded the cab.

"I missed you, too," Laurie admitted. Concerned that she was allowing herself to be set up for a fall, she felt embarrassingly self-conscious and now avoided eye contact. From her perspective, they were both acting like a couple of preteens.

"I was a hopeless case on the basketball court," Jack said. "I couldn't do anything right."

"I'm sorry," Laurie said, but then immediately wanted to take it back. It sounded as though she was apologizing, when she was merely sympathizing.

"As I expected, the internal on my case was consistent with SIDS," Jack said to change the subject. It was obvious that he was equally uncomfortable.

"Really?" Laurie said.

"How was yours?" Jack asked as the elevator began its ascent. "When I bumped into Janice, she mentioned it seemed similar to your McGillan case, so I told Riva that you'd probably want it."

"I appreciate it," Laurie said. "I did want it. And you were right. It was exactly like McGillan to an uncomfortable degree."

"What do you mean 'uncomfortable'?" Jack asked.

"I'm beginning to think that your suggestion yesterday about forensics establishing a manner of death opposite to what was expected could be applicable. I'm thinking I might be dealing with homicide, sort of the Cromwell case in reverse. In other words, I might have stumbled onto the work of a serial killer. I can't help but think about some of those infamous health-institution serial murders, particularly the recent one over in New Jersey and Pennsylvania." Laurie did not have the same reservations about mentioning her suspicions to Jack as she had had with Fontworth.

"Whoa!" Jack said. "When I was talking about forensics providing some surprises, I was talking in general. I wasn't suggesting anything about your case."

"I thought you were," Laurie said.

Jack shook his head as the elevator door opened on the first floor. "Not at all. And I have to say that I think you're taking a quantum leap going from natural to homicide with the case you described to me. Why on Earth did it even occur to you?" He gestured for Laurie to exit ahead of him.

"Because I've now autopsied in successive days two relatively young, healthy people who have died suddenly, yet have no associated pathology. None!"

"Your case today didn't have any emboli or obvious cardiac abnormalities?"

"Absolutely none. It was clean! Well, there were a few uterine fibroids, but that was it. Like McGillan, she was within twenty-four hours postsurgery with general anesthesia. Like McGillan, she had been completely stable without complications, and then . . . bingo! She arrests and is totally unable to be resuscitated!" Laurie snapped her fingers for emphasis.

They passed through the communications room. The secretaries were bunched together and chatting. For the moment, the phone lines were quiet. After the mayhem of the morning commute, death generally took a breather in the city.

"Two cases don't make a series!" Jack asserted. He was dumbfounded by Laurie's suggestion of a serial killer.

"I think it is four cases, not two," Laurie said. "That's too many to be a coincidence." While they helped themselves to the communal coffee, Laurie described her conversations with Kevin and George. As she spoke, she and Jack sat down in the two brown vinyl club chairs that Kevin and Arnold had been in earlier.

"What about toxicology?" Jack questioned. "If there turns out to be no pathology on gross or histologically, then the answer is going to come from toxicology, whether there was hanky-panky going on or even if there wasn't."

"George said he's still waiting on toxicology for his case. Obviously, for mine I've got a wait. Be that as it may, we're dealing with a curious set of circumstances here."

Jack and Laurie sipped from their respective cups, eyeing each other over the brims. Both were aware of the other's current mind-set in regard to Laurie's serial-killer theory. Laurie's expression was challenging, while Jack's reflected his feeling that she was out in left field.

"If you want my opinion," Jack said finally, "I think you're letting your imagination run wild. Maybe you're upset because of our problems, and you're looking for a diversion."

Laurie felt a wave of irritation spread through her. It came from a combination of Jack's being patronizing on the one hand and his being correct on the other. She averted her gaze and took a breath. "What is it you wanted to talk about? I'm sure it wasn't our respective cases."

"Riva told me about your mother yesterday," Jack said. "I was tempted to call last night to ask you about her and extend my sympathies, but under the circumstances, I thought it better to talk in person."

"Thank you for your concern. She's doing fine."

"I'm glad," Jack said. "Is it appropriate if I send some flowers?"

"That's completely up to you."

"Then I will." Jack said. He paused, fidgeted, and then said hesitantly, "I don't know if I should bring this up about your mother . . ."

Then don't, Laurie said to herself. She was disappointed. She had allowed herself to be set up after all. She didn't want to talk about her mother.

". . . but I'm sure you are aware there is a hereditary aspect to breast cancer."

"I am," Laurie said. She looked at Jack with exasperation, wondering where he was going with this conversation.

"I don't know if your mother has been tested for the markers indicating BRCA gene mutations, but the results would have significance concerning treatment. More important for you, it would have significance concerning prevention. One way or the other, I think you should definitely be tested. I mean, I don't want to alarm you, but it would be prudent."

"My mother is positive for a BRCA mutation," Laurie admitted. Some of her anger, although not her disappointment, abated when she realized that Jack was being solicitous about her health and not just her mother's.

"That's an even greater reason for you to be tested," Jack said. "Have you thought about it?"

"I've thought about it," Laurie admitted. "But I'm not convinced it would have much significance and may just add to my anxiety. I'm not about to have my breasts and ovaries removed."

"Mastectomy and oophorectomy are not the only preventive measures available," Jack said. "Last night, I went on the Internet and read up on all this."

Laurie found herself almost smiling. She wondered if she and Jack had visited the same websites.

"More frequent mammograms is another option," Jack added. "Eventually, you might even consider tamoxifen treatment. But that's down the road. Anyway, the bottom line is that it just makes sense. I mean, if this predictive information is available, you should do it. In fact, I would like to ask you to do it. No, I take that back. I would like to plead with you to do it . . . for me."

To Laurie's surprise, Jack leaned forward

and gripped her forearm with unexpected strength to emphasize his commitment to the cause.

"You're really convinced?" Laurie questioned, marveling at the "for me" part.

"Absolutely! No question!" Jack responded. "Even if the only effect is to make you more prone to have regular checkups. That would be an enormously positive effect. Laurie, please!"

"Is it a blood test? I don't even know."

"Yes, it's a simple blood test. Do you have a primary-care physician over at the Manhattan General, where we are now obligated to go?"

"Not yet," Laurie admitted. "But I can call my old college chum, Sue Passero. She's on staff in internal medicine. I'm sure she could set me up."

"Perfect," Jack said. He rubbed his hands together. "Should I call to make sure you do it?"

Laurie laughed. "I'll do it."

"Today."

"All right, for goodness' sakes. I'll do it today."

"Thank you," Jack said. He released Laurie's arm that he'd been firmly clutching.

"Now that we've got that settled, I want to ask about whether we can compromise about your moving out of my apartment."

For a moment, Laurie was nonplussed. Just when she thought Jack wasn't going to bring up their relationship, he did.

"As I said," he continued, "I missed you last night. Worst of all, my basketball game was a disaster. The defenses I had carefully erected against your absence had been undermined by a pregame run-in with a pair of your pantyhose."

"What pantyhose?" Laurie asked, raising her guard again. She purposefully didn't laugh at Jack's reversion to witty sarcasm. For her, there was nothing funny about suggesting that Jack's prowess on the basketball court was a determining factor in her moving back to his apartment.

"A pair you left in the bathroom. But don't worry, they're safely ensconced in the bureau."

"What do you mean by 'compromise'?" Laurie asked dubiously.

Jack fidgeted in his chair. It was apparent that he was uncomfortable with the question. Laurie let him take all the time he wanted. Finally, he made a gesture of confusion by hunching his shoulders and extending his free hand, palm up. "We'll agree to make sure we discuss the issues on a regular basis."

Laurie's heart sank. "That's no compromise," she said with a voice that reflected her discouragement. "Jack, we both know what the issues are. At this point, more talk is not going to solve anything. I know that sounds contrary to what I've usually said about the importance of communication. The fact of the matter is that I've been compromising from the beginning, and particularly over the last year. I think I understand where you are coming from, and I'm sympathetic, which is what has kept me in a circumstance that has not been satisfying my needs. It's really as simple as that. I believe we love each other, but we're at a crossroads. I'm not twenty-five anymore. I need a family; I need commitment. To use one of your expressions, the ball is in your court. It's your decision. Talk is superfluous at this point. I'm not going to try to convince you, which, at this stage, talk would begin to sound like. And one final point: I didn't leave in a moment of pique. It's been a long time coming."

For a few minutes, they merely stared at each other without moving. Finally, Laurie was the one who moved. She leaned forward and gave Jack's thigh a squeeze just above the knee. "This doesn't mean I don't want to talk in general," she said. "It doesn't mean we're not friends. It just means that unless we can truly compromise, I'll be better off staying at my apartment. And meanwhile, I'll get back to my diversion."

Laurie stood up, smiled down at Jack without rancor, and then walked back through the communications room en route to the elevator.

seven

With a mighty yawn that brought tears to her eyes, Laurie put down her pencil, stretched, and then viewed her handiwork. She had created a matrix on a piece of graph paper that had the names of the four patients of her supposed series on the left-hand side of the page. Running along the top of the page and creating columns were all parameters of the cases that she thought might be important, including: the age of the patient, the sex of the patient, the type of surgery involved, the name of the surgeon, the anesthesiologist and anesthetic agent used, the sedative and pain medication employed, where in the hospital the patient was boarded, how the patient was discovered and by whom, the time the patient was discovered, who did the autopsy, any potentially relevant pathology, and the toxicology results.

Currently, Laurie had preliminary entries in all the boxes of her matrix, except for the names of the surgeons and anesthesiologists, the type of anesthetic and drugs used, the toxicology results on the two cases she had posted, and any possible relevant pathology on Darlene Morgan. To fill in the empty boxes, she needed the hospital charts and the continued cooperation of Peter and Maureen. In the toxicology boxes of the two cases posted by Kevin and George, Laurie had written: negative screen, further testing pending.

One piece of information that the matrix had already brought to her attention, which she thought important and mildly damning for her theory of a serial killer, was that the cases were not on the same ward. Two of the patients had been on the general surgical floor, while the other two had been on the orthopedic and neurosurgical floor. Since none of the patients had had neurosurgery and since one of the orthopedic cases had been on general surgery, Laurie had already called the Manhattan General admitting office for an explanation. The explanation turned out to be simple: Because the hospital operated at near capacity, beds frequently had to be allocated irrespective of the type of surgery.

From the moment Laurie had left Jack in the ID room, she had been a human dynamo in regard to investigating the four patients. Her motivation was twofold. There was the continued need for a diversion to keep from obsessing about her own problems, as Jack had surmised. That hadn't changed. What had changed was a strong desire to vindicate her intuitive belief that these cases did not represent a coincidence. Jack's blithe dismissal of the idea had been both belittling and galling.

First, she had gone up to histology to see Maureen, who'd been happy to present her with a tray of McGillan's HE-stained microscopic sections in less than twenty-four hours. With the burden of processing eight thousand autopsies a year, overnight histology-slide service was unheard-of. Laurie had thanked her profusely for her efforts and had immediately taken the slides back to her office to study them painstakingly. As she had suspected, she found no pathology in general, and specifically, she found the heart entirely normal. There were no signs of active or healed inflammation of the cardiac muscle or the coronary vessels, and she saw no abnormalities of the valves or conduction system.

Next, she had gone down to the fourth-floor toxicology lab, where she'd run into a minor setback by bumping into John DeVries. Thanks to the bad blood between them and John's territoriality, he'd demanded to know what she was doing wandering around in his laboratory. Not wishing to get Peter in trouble with his boss, Laurie had to be creative. She happened to have been standing next to the mass spectrometer, so she said she had never completely understood mass spectrometry and was hoping to learn something about it. Mollified to a degree, John had provided her with some printed literature before excusing himself to go down to the serology lab.

Laurie had found Peter in his windowless, Lilliputian office, and his eyes lit up when he saw her. Although Laurie didn't remember Peter from their life prior to the OCME, Peter remembered her when they both had attended Wesleyan University in the early eighties. He had been two years behind her.

"I ran a toxicology screen on McGillan," Peter had said. "I didn't find anything, but I have to warn you that sometimes compounds can hide out in the peaks and valleys on the readout, particularly when the concentration is very low. It would be a big help if you gave me more of a hint of what you are looking for."

"Fair enough," Laurie had said. "Since the autopsies on these patients suggested they suffered a very rapid demise, their hearts had to suddenly stop pumping blood. I mean, one minute everything was fine, and the next minute there was no circulation. That means we have to eliminate cardiac toxins like cocaine and digitalis, and any other drugs that can cause changes in the heart rate, either by affecting the center that initiates the beat or the conduction system that spreads the impulse around the heart. On top of that, we even have to rule out all the drugs that are used to treat abnormal cardiac rhythms."

"Wow! That's a rather big list," Peter had commented. "The cocaine and the digitalis I would have seen, because I know where to look on the readout, and they'd have to be big doses to do what you are talking about. The others, I don't know, but I'll look into it."

At that point, Laurie had asked about Solomon Moskowitz and Antonio Nogueira, whose autopsies had been done several weeks earlier. She told Peter that the cases mirrored McGillan's. Using his keypad in front of his monitor and his password, Peter accessed the laboratory database. Both toxicology screens had been normal, but he offered to run them again now that he had a ballpark idea of what she was looking for.

"One other thing," Laurie had said when she was about to leave. "I did another case this morning whose samples should be on the way up. Again, it was strikingly similar to the others, which tells me there's something weird going on over at the Manhattan General. Since I can't find any pathology,

I'm afraid the major burden is going to be on your shoulders to find out what it is."

Peter had said he'd do his best.

After her visit to toxicology, Laurie had gone up to George's office to get a look at Antonio Nogueira's folder. George had surprised her by having copies of the salient portions waiting for her. Kevin had not been so accommodating, but he didn't mind if Laurie made copies. Taking the material back to her office, Laurie had gone over it in detail, filling in her matrix as she went along.

Taking the sheet containing the matrix and twisting around in her chair, Laurie waited for Riva to hang up on a call she was on with a local doctor about her hit-and-run case that morning.

"Check this out!" Laurie said, extending the graph paper to her officemate as she hung up the receiver.

Riva took the sheet and studied it, then looked over at Laurie. "You're being very industrious. This is a great way to organize this information."

"I'm fascinated by this puzzle," Laurie admitted. "I'm also intent on figuring it out."

"I suppose this is why you were pleased

when you found no pathology on Morgan, meaning you had yet another case."

"Precisely!"

"So what is your thinking at this point?" Riva asked. "With all this effort, you must have a better idea."

"I think I do. It's become pretty clear to me that the mechanism of death was ventricular fibrillation for all four. The cause is another matter, as is the manner."

"I'm listening."

"Are you sure you want to hear? I mentioned my ideas to Jack, and he was irritatingly dismissive."

"Try me!"

"All right! In a nutshell, since I've decided that the mechanism of death was ventricular fibrillation or cardiac standstill, and since the hearts have been structurally normal, the cause of death has to be some arrhythmia-producing drug."

"That seems pretty reasonable," Riva said. "Now what about the manner of death?"

"This is the most interesting part," Laurie said. She leaned forward and lowered her voice as if she were afraid someone might hear. "I'm thinking the manner of death is homicide! In other words, I think I have stumbled onto the handiwork of a clever serial killer in the Manhattan General."

Riva started to say something, but Laurie held up her hand and moderated her voice. "As soon as I get the hospital charts, I'll be able to fill in the rest of my matrix that will include the preop drugs, the anesthetic agent, as well as the postoperative medication. We'll talk again and see what your response is. Personally, I don't think the extra information is going to make any difference. The occurrence of four cases of fatal ventricular fibrillation unresponsive to resuscitation in young, healthy people undergoing elective surgery in the same hospital using customary protocols within a couple of weeks is too much of a coincidence."

"It is a very busy hospital, Laurie!" Riva said, simply not wanting to argue.

Laurie breathed out forcibly. In her sensitized state, she interpreted Riva's tone as condescending and not all that different from Jack's. Laurie reached out and snatched her matrix from Riva's hand.

"It's just my opinion," Riva said, sensing Laurie's reaction.

"You're entitled to your opinion," Laurie

said, swinging back around to face her desk.

"I don't mean to irritate you," Riva said to Laurie's back.

"It's not your problem," Laurie said without looking back. "I'm a bit thin-skinned these days." She turned around again and faced Riva. "But let me tell you this: What made those previous incidences involving serial killers in healthcare facilities go on for so long was a low index of suspicion."

"I think you are right," Riva said. She smiled, but Laurie did not return the peace gesture. Instead, she spun back around and picked up the phone. She might have found it aggravating to share her ideas with Jack and Riva, but the process of vocalizing them had put everything more in focus and had served to make her even more confident that she was correct. Her friends' objections had done nothing to shake her beliefs. She was now even more committed to her serial-killer scenario. As such, she realized that even if it were premature in the sense of having no definitive proof, it was incumbent on her to see that someone over at the Manhattan General was informed. Unfortunately, from bitter experience she knew that such a decision was not hers to make. It had to come from administration and go through public relations. Consequently, she dialed Calvin's extension and asked Connie Egan, Calvin's secretary, for a moment of Calvin's time.

"The deputy chief is due to leave for an Advisory Board luncheon in a few minutes," Connie said. "If you want to try to catch him, I'd advise you to come down immediately. Otherwise, you'll be looking at sometime after four, and even that is dependent on his getting back here, and there's no guarantee of that."

"I'll be right down," Laurie said. She hung up and got to her feet.

"Good luck," Riva said, overhearing the conversation.

"Thanks," Laurie responded without a lot of sincerity. She picked up her matrix.

"Don't be disappointed if Calvin is even more dubious than I," Riva called after her. "And he might bite your head off with such a suggestion of criminality. Remember, he has a soft spot for the Manhattan General, since he trained over there as a medical student and resident in its former life as a major university-affiliated teaching hospital."

"I'll keep that in mind," Laurie yelled back. She felt a little guilty about her behavior toward Riva. Being in such a bad mood was out of character for Laurie, but she couldn't help herself.

For fear of missing Calvin, she wasted no time. She took the front elevators and in less than five minutes, she was walking into the administration area. A number of people were seated on a long couch, waiting to see the chief, whose office door was closed and guarded by his secretary, Gloria Sanford. Laurie could remember a few times sitting there herself, waiting to be bawled out for doing something she was now avoiding by going to see Calvin. Laurie had been a good deal more headstrong, as well as apolitical, when she had first started at the OCME.

"You can go right in," Connie said as Laurie approached her desk. Calvin's door was ajar. He was on the phone with his legs perched on the corner of his desk. As Laurie came in, he motioned with his free hand for her to take one of the two chairs facing him. Laurie's eyes glanced around the familiar room. It was less than half the size of Bingham's and didn't connect with the conference room. Still, it was mammoth when compared to the space Laurie had to share with Riva. The walls were covered with the usual array of diplomas and awards and pictures with major city politicians.

Calvin concluded his conversation, which Laurie could tell dealt with the agenda of the up-and-coming Advisory Board luncheon. The Advisory Board had been set up by the mayor almost twenty years ago, to make the OCME less beholden to both the executive branch and law enforcement.

Calvin let his heavy legs plop down on the floor. He peered at Laurie through his newly acquired, rimless progressive lenses. Laurie felt herself tense. Thanks to a lingering, mild problem with male authority figures from an early age, Calvin had always intimidated Laurie, even more than the chief. It was a combination of his imposing physical presence; his unwavering cold, black eyes; his legendary stormy temperament; and his occasional chauvinism. At the same time, she knew him to be capable of warmth and gentlemanly behavior. What worried her at any given encounter was which side would be dominant.

"What can I do for you?" Calvin began. "Unfortunately, we have to make this short."

"It won't take but a moment," Laurie assured him. She handed over the matrix she had prepared. Then she quickly summarized the history of the four cases as they had unfolded, followed by her ideas concerning the possible mechanism, cause, and manner of death. It took only a few minutes, and when she was done, she fell silent.

Calvin was still studying the matrix. Finally, he looked up. His eyebrows were arched. Settling back into his seat, which complained with a squeak, he arched his index fingers with his elbows on the desk, and shook his head slowly. His expression was of confusion. "I guess my first question has to be why you are telling all this to me at this early stage? None of these cases has been signed out yet."

"Purely because I thought you might want to warn someone over at the Manhattan General what our thinking was, to raise the index of suspicion."

"Correction!" Calvin boomed. He took a fleeting glance at his watch, which wasn't lost on Laurie. "I would be warning them what your thinking was, not mine. Laurie, I'm surprised at you. You're using grossly inadequate data here to make a premature and ridiculous leap." He slapped the matrix with the back of his free hand. "You're suggesting that I communicate pure speculation, which could be extraordinarily detrimental to the Manhattan General Hospital if it got out into the wrong hands, something that happens all too frequently. It could even cause a panic. We deal in facts here at the OCME, not fanciful supposition. Hell, we could lose all credibility!"

"I have a strong intuition about this," Laurie countered.

Calvin slammed his sizable palm down onto the surface of his desk. A few papers went wafting off. "I have zero patience with female intuition, if that's what this is boiling down to. What do you think this is, a sewing club? We're a scientific organization; we deal in facts, not hunches and guesswork."

"But we're talking about four essentially unexplained cases within a two-week period," Laurie said while inwardly groaning. It seemed that she had awakened Calvin's dormant chauvinism.

"Yeah, but they do thousands of cases over at the Manhattan General. Thousands! I happen to know they have a low death rate, well below the bellwether three percent. How do I know? I serve on the board. Come back with some facts from toxicology or infallible evidence of low-voltage electrocution and I'll listen to you, not some cockamamie story of serial killer on the loose with no facts to back it up."

"They were not electrocuted," Laurie said. At one point, she had briefly considered the idea, since standard 110 voltage was capable of causing ventricular fibrillation. But she'd dismissed the idea because patients weren't routinely subjected to power sources. Maybe one could have been exposed to an aberrant piece of equipment, but surely not four, particularly since none had been monitored.

"I'm just trying to make a point," Calvin yelled. He stood up abruptly, causing his desk chair to roll back on its casters and strike the wall. He handed Laurie her paper. "Go back and get some facts if you are so motivated! I don't have time for this foolery. I've got to go to a meeting where we deal with real problems."

Embarrassed at being chastised like a schoolgirl, Laurie fled the administration area. Calvin's office door had been open during the exchange, and the people waiting to see Bingham watched her departure with expressionless faces. She couldn't imagine what they thought about what they had heard. She was relieved to catch an empty elevator to pull herself together. As she had said to Riva, she knew she was thin-skinned at the moment, and under normal circumstances, she probably could have brushed off Calvin's crusty response to her concerns. Yet combining Calvin's reaction with Jack and Riva's, she felt like a modern-day Cassandra. She couldn't believe that people whom she respected could not see what was so clear to her.

Back in her office, she threw herself into her chair and for a moment buried her head in her hands. She was stymied. She needed further information but was paralyzed by having to wait for the charts to come over from the Manhattan General through the usual channels. There was no way she could speed up the system. Other than that, she had to wait for Peter to work his magic with the gas chromatography and mass spectrograph. Short of getting yet another similar case the following day, which she was not wishing for, there was nothing to be done.

"I have to assume your meeting with Calvin was not as auspicious as you hoped," Riva said.

Laurie didn't respond. She was feeling even more temperamental than earlier. From when she was a little girl, she'd always sought approval from authority figures, and when she didn't get it, she felt terrible. Calvin's reaction was a case in point, making her feel that all the disparate segments of her life were unraveling. First was the situation with Jack, next her mother and the BRCA1 problem, and now it seemed that even her job was in disarray. On top of it all, she felt physically exhausted from insufficient sleep two nights in a row.

Laurie sighed. She had to pull herself together. Thinking about the BRCA1 problem reminded her that she had agreed with Jack to have herself tested for the marker by calling her old college roommate, Sue

Passero. At the time, Laurie had not been completely forthright, since she actually hadn't entirely decided to do it, so her acquiescence was more to assuage his unexpected insistence than a real decision. Yet suddenly, she saw the idea in a new light, since getting away from the OCME, even for just a couple of hours, sounded like a good idea. The thought also occurred to her that she could kill two birds with one stone. Knowing Sue as well as she did, Laurie was confident that while getting tested, she could pass along her concerns about the possibility of a serial killer that would give the hospital a reason to be vigilant without the need to cite herself or the OCME as the source.

Laurie got out her address book for Sue's office number and made the call. They had been close in college and in medical school, and having ended up practicing in the same city, they got together every month or so for a dinner. They always vowed to see each other more often, but somehow it never happened.

Laurie got one of the clinic secretaries where Sue worked and asked for Sue. Laurie's intention was just to leave a message for Sue to call back at a convenient time, but when the secretary asked who was calling and Laurie said "Dr. Montgomery," the secretary went off the line before Laurie could explain. The next thing she knew, she was talking with her friend.

"This is a nice surprise," Sue said cheerfully. "What's up?"

"Do you have a minute to talk?"

"A minute, what's on your mind?"

Laurie said she needed to be tested for BRCA1 for reasons that she would explain later. She also mentioned that she had been switched to AmeriCare but had not yet made arrangements for a primary-care doctor.

"No problem. Come over anytime. I can set you up with a script and send you down to the lab."

"How about today?"

"Today is fine. Come on over! Have you had lunch?"

"I haven't." Laurie smiled. It was going to be three birds with one stone!

"Well, get your rear end over here, girl! The cafeteria food is not something to write home about, but the company will be good."

Laurie hung up and got her coat from behind the door.

"I think you are doing the right thing about being tested," Riva said.

"Thank you," Laurie responded. She looked at her desk to be sure she wasn't forgetting something.

"I hope you're not cross with me," Riva said.

"Of course not," Laurie responded. She gave Riva's shoulder a reassuring squeeze. "As I said earlier, I know I'm oversensitive these days, and everything is bothering me more than it should. Be that as it may, and I know you're not my secretary, but I'd appreciate it if you would once again take messages, especially from Maureen or Peter. I'll make it up to you."

"Don't be silly. I'll be happy to answer your phone. Are you going to be back this afternoon?"

"Absolutely. It's going to be a quick lunch and a simple blood test, although I might stop and say hello to my mother as well. Anyway, I'll have my cell if you need to call."

Riva waved and went back to her work.

Laurie walked out the OCME entrance on First Avenue. There was a bite to the air.

The temperature had dropped as the day progressed, so it was colder than when she'd walked to work that morning. As she descended the front steps toward the curb, she got her zipper started and pulled it up to her chin. Standing on the curb, she was shivering slightly as she raised her hand to hail a cab.

The ride to Manhattan General was a little longer than the ride she'd taken the previous day to University Hospital. Both institutions were on the Upper East Side and approximately equal distance to the north from OCME, but the General was farther west, sprawled along Central Park. It took up more than an entire city block, with several pedestrian walkways spanning the surrounding streets to connect with outlying buildings. The complex had been constructed of gray stone in fits and starts during the course of almost a century, so the various wings were of slightly different architectural design. The newest wing with the most modern silhouette and named for the benefactor, Samuel B. Goldblatt, stuck off the back of the main structure at right angles. It was the VIP wing, the equivalent of where Laurie's mother had been roomed over at the University Hospital.

Having been to the Manhattan General on a number of occasions, including visiting Sue, Laurie knew where she was going, which was helpful, since the hospital was always mobbed. She headed directly to the Kaufman outpatient building. Once inside, she walked down to the internal medicine section and inquired after her friend at the main check-in desk. When Laurie mentioned her own name, the secretary handed her an envelope. Inside was a completed script for a screen for the BRCA1 marker, as well as a note from Sue. The note told her where the genetics lab was located in the central building on the second floor. There were also instructions for Laurie to go first to admitting. As a new AmeriCare subscriber, she had to get a hospital card. The final line in the note said that Laurie should go directly to the cafeteria when she was finished, and that Sue would meet her there.

Obtaining the hospital card took more time than the blood test. She had to wait in line to see one of the customer-service representatives. Still, it took only fifteen minutes, and she was soon on her way up to the laboratory on the second floor. Sue's directions were clear, and Laurie found the genetics diagnostics lab without difficulty. Inside, it was surprisingly serene in comparison to the rest of the hospital. Canned classical music issued from wall speakers. Framed prints of Monet's "Water Lilies" from the Museum of Modern Art lined the walls. No patients were in the waiting room when Laurie handed over Sue's script to the receptionist. It was apparent that walk-in genetic testing was in its infancy, but Laurie knew it would soon be changing, and with it, medicine in general.

Sitting in the waiting area, Laurie was again forced to confront the reality of what might be lurking deep within the core of her being. It was a disturbing revelation to think she was possibly carrying an instrument of her own death in the form of a mutated gene. It was a kind of unconscious suicide or built-in self-destructive device, which was certainly the reason she'd been actively avoiding thinking about it. Would she be positive or negative? She didn't know, and being in the hospital made her feel like a gambler, something she was never comfortable with. Had Jack not insisted, she most likely would have put off doing the test indefinitely. But now that she was there, she would have the blood drawn, and then she would forget about it, a trait Laurie shared with her mother.

After the blood was drawn, a deceptively simple procedure, Laurie returned to the first floor and waited in line at the main information desk. She had no idea where the cafeteria was located in the extensive complex. When it was her turn, the pink-smocked volunteer asked Laurie if she wanted the main cafeteria or the staff cafeteria. Momentarily indecisive, Laurie said the staff cafeteria and was given directions.

The directions were complicated but made easier by the volunteer's last suggestion—namely, to follow a purple line on the floor. After a five-minute walk, Laurie found herself in the staff cafeteria. Since it was quarter past twelve, the place was bustling. Laurie had no idea the staff of the Manhattan General was as large as it was, especially considering that the crowd represented only a portion of one shift out of three.

Laurie looked around at the teeming

faces both sitting at tables and waiting in the steam-table line. The babble of reverberating conversation reminded her of the noise of a wetland sanctuary on a late summer night. With such a crowd, Laurie couldn't help but be immediately pessimistic about hooking up with Sue. The plan smacked of trying to meet a friend in Times Square on New Year's Eve.

Just when Laurie was about to head over to the cashiers to ask for a house phone to page her friend, a hand tapped her on the shoulder. To Laurie's delight, it was Sue, who enveloped her in a big hug. Sue was a big-boned, athletic woman of color who had excelled at college soccer and softball. Laurie felt tiny in her embrace. As usual, Sue looked fetching. In contrast to most of her colleagues, she was dressed in a stylish and flattering silk dress overlaid with a highly starched white coat. Similar to Laurie, she liked to indulge her feminine side with her attire.

"I hope you didn't bring your appetite," Sue teased while gesturing toward the steam-table line. "But joking aside, the food's not that bad."

As they descended the steam-table line

and chose their food, they maintained a superficial banter about their respective professional roles. While waiting in the cashiers' line, Laurie asked about Sue's two children. Sue had gotten married just after medical school and had a boy, fifteen, and a girl, twelve. Laurie couldn't help but be jealous.

"Except for the agony of adolescence, everything is hunky-dory," Sue said. "What about you and Jack? Any light at the end of the tunnel? Seems to me you've got to get a move on, girl! I happen to know you are sneaking up to the big forty-three in a few days, since I'm close behind."

Laurie felt her face flush, along with a twinge of irritation that she was incapable of hiding anything. She could tell that Sue had caught the reaction, and since she and Sue had been friends for almost twenty-six years, she had confided in her about her desire for children and the situation with Jack, particularly over the last two years. Laurie was not going to be able to get away with platitudes.

"Jack and I are history," Laurie said, deciding to be more forthright than she actually felt, "at least intimacy-wise."

"Oh, no! What's wrong with that boy?"

Laurie wrinkled her forehead and shrugged to say she had no idea. She didn't want to get into a long, drawn-out emotional conversation in her current state.

"Well, you know something . . . good riddance. You've been more than patient with that indecisive nincompoop. You should get a medal, because he ain't going to change."

Laurie nodded and had to restrain herself from defending Jack, even though what Sue was saying was true.

Sue wouldn't let Laurie pay for her lunch and insisted on putting the charges on her house account. With their trays in hand, they managed to get a table for two by the window. The view was of an inner courtyard with an empty fountain. In the summer, it was lush with flowers, water gushing from the fountain's multiple tiers.

They talked casually for a few more minutes about the situation with Jack, with Sue doing most of the talking. She then insisted that she would find someone more suitable for Laurie, and Laurie teased her by daring her to try. The conversation then switched to why Laurie had to have the BRCA1 screen. Laurie told the story about her mother and the fact that as usual, her mother had hidden the information from her. Sue's only comment was that she would arrange an appointment for Laurie with a top-notch oncologist if the test came back positive.

"What about a primary-care physician?" Sue asked after a short pause. "Now that you are officially a subscriber, you're going to need one."

"How about you?" Laurie suggested. "Are you taking new patients?"

"I'd be honored," Sue replied. "But are you sure you would be comfortable with me as your doc?"

"Absolutely," Laurie said. "I'll also have to switch my gyno."

"I can help you with that as well," Sue said. "We've got some terrific people on staff, including the woman I use my myself. She's quick, gentle, and knows her stuff."

"Sounds like a good recommendation. But there's no rush; I'm not due for a yearly checkup for another six months."

"That might be true, but I think we should get it in the works. The woman I'm thinking of is awfully popular. For all I know, she has a six-month wait for a first appointment. She's that good."

"Then by all means," Laurie said.

For a few minutes, they both concentrated on eating. It was Laurie who broke the silence. "There's something else important that I wanted to talk to you about."

"Oh?" Sue commented. She put down her teacup. "Fire away!"

"I wanted to talk to you about SADS."

Sue's face screwed up into an expression of complete confusion. "What the hell is SADS?"

Laurie laughed. "I just made it up this second. You've heard of SIDS, sudden infant death syndrome."

"Of course! Who hasn't?"

"Well, I've coined SADS for sudden adult death syndrome, which is a good name for a problem that's been occurring over here at the Manhattan General."

"Oh?" Sue questioned. "I think you'd better explain."

Laurie leaned forward. "Before I do, I have to say that it has to be in strictest confidence that the information I'm about to tell you came from me. I had suggested to our deputy chief that someone over here at the

Manhattan General should be warned, but he blew his top, contending that it was all mere speculation with no proof, and as such, might hurt the hospital's reputation. Yet I feel like the researcher caught in the bind of conducting a double-blind study on a life-saving procedure, which has quickly suggested its worth. Even though I'd be destroying the integrity of the study, which might keep the FDA from approving the treatment, I've got to leak the results so the people getting the placebo can be saved."

Laurie leaned back and laughed at herself. "Wow! Am I getting melodramatic or what? But it is true that I have no specific proof concerning what I'm about to tell you, mainly because I haven't finished investigating the cases. I don't even have copies of their hospital charts yet. I just feel it strongly, and someone has to know sooner rather than later. Anyway, this kind of medical politics drives me up the wall. It's the one bad thing about my ob."

"Now you've got my curiosity up. Way up! Come on! Spill the beans!"

Leaning forward again and lowering her voice, Laurie proceeded to tell the story in the chronology it had unfolded by starting with McGillan, then adding the two cases posted by Kevin and George, and ending with her case that morning. She talked about the ventricular fibrillation and the fact that the autopsies had been completely clean. She then told Sue that she felt that with no pathology on gross or microscopically, the chances of four cases happening by chance was about the same as the sun not coming up the following morning.

"What exactly are you saying?" Sue questioned dubiously.

"Well . . ." Laurie said with hesitation. Knowing Sue as well as she did, she was aware that what she was about to say was the figurative equivalent of slapping her friend in the face. "Although I suppose there is still a minuscule chance the cause of these deaths was accidental in the form of a late anesthetic complication or maybe an unexpected side effect of a drug, I sincerely doubt it. And when I say minuscule, I mean infinitesimally small, because our toxicology screens have so far been negative. Anyway, the bottom line is this: I'm concerned about the possibility that these deaths are homicides."

For a few minutes, neither Laurie nor Sue

said a word. Laurie was content to let the information sink into Sue's brain. She knew Sue was enormously quick-witted and patriotic about the Manhattan General. She'd done all her residency training within its walls.

Sue eventually cleared her throat. It was obvious that what Laurie had said had troubled her greatly. "Let me get this straight. You think we have some kind of a grim reaper wandering around our wards at night?"

"In a way, yes. At least, that's my worry. Before you dismiss the idea out of hand, just call to mind those cases in the news over the last couple of years, where deranged healthcare workers were dispatching patients under their care. You remember them, don't you?"

"Of course I remember them," Sue said, seemingly taking offense at the comparison. She sat up straighter in her chair. "But we're not out in the boonies here or operating a fly-by-night nursing home. This is a major medical center with layers of oversight. And these patients you've been describing weren't bed-ridden or at death's door."

Laurie shrugged. "It's hard to argue with the facts that we have namely, no explanation for four deaths. And as I remember it, at least some of the institutions involved in those serial-murder cases were highly regarded. The double tragedy is that they went on for so long."

Sue took a deep breath and let her eyes wander around the room blankly.

"Sue, I'm not expecting you to do anything about this personally," Laurie said. "Nor should you feel defensive about the Manhattan General. I know it is a fine institution, and I'm certainly not trying to sully its reputation. What I was hoping is that you would know whom you or I should inform to try to keep it from happening in the future. Seriously, I'll be happy to tell this individual exactly what I told you, provided my identity can stay out of the picture, at least until the OCME officially gets involved."

Sue visibly relaxed. She gave a quick, mirthless laugh. "Sorry! I guess I take any criticism of the place to heart. Silly me!"

"Do you know someone like I described: someone on a clinical administrative level? Or what about the head of anesthesia? Maybe I should talk to him."

"No, no, no!" Sue repeated for emphasis. "Ronald Havermeyer has an ego as big as a tectonic plate, with the usual associated volcanic eruptions. He should have been a surgeon. Don't talk to him! He'd definitely take it personally and want to take revenge on the messenger. I know because I've sat with him on several hospital committees."

"What about the hospital president? What's his name again?"

"Charles Kelly. But he'd be as bad as Havermeyer, and maybe worse. He's not even a doctor, and he clearly thinks of this whole operation as a business. There's no way in hell he'd be sensitive to your situation, and he'd be looking for a scapegoat immediately. No, it has to be someone with a bit of finesse. Maybe a member of the mortality/morbidity committee."

"Why do you say that?"

"Simply because dealing with something like this is their mandate, and they meet once a week to keep tabs on what is going on."

"Who serves on it?"

"I served on it for six months. Someone from the clinical side serves on a rotating basis. The permanent members are the risk management officer, the quality-control chief, the chief counsel for the hospital, the president of the hospital, the nursing supervisor, and the chief of the medical staff. Wait a second!"

Sue lunged across the table and grasped Laurie's forearm so quickly that Laurie jumped. Laurie's eyes darted around the room, as if she expected an imminent physical threat.

"The chief of the medical staff!" Sue repeated with enthusiasm. She let go of Laurie's arm and gestured widely with her hands. "Why didn't I think of him before? Oh my gosh, he's perfect!"

"How so?" Laurie questioned, having recovered from her momentary fright.

It was now Sue's turn to lean forward and lower her voice in a conspiratorial tone. "He's in his late forties, single, and he's a doll. He's only been here for three or four months. All the single nurses are gaga over him, and if I weren't happily and irrevocably married, I would be, too. He's tall and lean and has this smile that melts ice. He does have a rather big snout, but you don't even notice it. Best of all, he's got an IQ in the stratosphere and a personality to go with it."

Laurie couldn't help but wryly smile. "He sounds charming, but that's not what I'm looking for. I need someone in a position of power who can be discreet. It's that simple."

"I told you, he's the chief of the medical staff. What more power can you ask for? And as far as being discreet is concerned, he's the definition of the word. I tell you, you have to pry personal information out of him with a crowbar. It took me a quarter of an hour at the Christmas party just to find out that before coming here, he'd been with Médecins Sans Frontières, which took him all over the world. I had to bite my tongue when Gloria Perkins, the head nurse in the OR, butted in and asked him to dance."

"Sue, I think you are telling me more than you need to. I don't need to know the guy's history. All I want to know is if you're reasonably confident he'll listen to what I have to say, act on it, and leave my name out of it until there's official word from the OCME. Is that your take?"

"I told you he's the picture of discretion. And personally, I think you two will hit it off famously. And all I ask in return is that you name your firstborn after me. I'm joking, of course. Now, let's see if he's here." Sue pushed back her chair, stood up, and started scanning the crowd.

Aghast at suddenly comprehending Sue's romantic intentions, Laurie reached out and tugged insistently on her white coat. "Hold on! This is not the time or place to try to fix me up."

"Hush, girl!" Sue said, batting Laurie's hand away while continuing to search the room. "You dared me to find somebody suitable, and this dude fills the bill. Now, where in tarnation is he? He's always here with women around him like he's dressed in flypaper. Ah, there he is, and no wonder I couldn't see him. He's holding court at the far table."

Without a second's hesitation, and oblivious to Laurie's appeals to the contrary, Sue strode off. Laurie watched her wend her way among the crowded tables. Almost fifty feet away she tapped a medium-brown-haired man on the shoulder. He stood up, and being a head taller than Sue, Laurie guessed he was close to Jack's height. For a moment Sue talked with him, utilizing lavish hand gestures capped off with her finger pointing in Laurie's direction. Laurie felt herself blush, and she looked down at her tray. The last time she had experienced this kind of social humiliation was in middle school, and although that episode turned out reasonably well, she didn't feel confident now.

The next few minutes crawled by. Laurie redirected her eyes out the window at the empty fountain, wondering if she should flee. The next thing she knew, Sue was tapping her shoulder and calling her name. With a sense of resignation, Laurie turned and found herself looking up into the rugged, smiling face of an attractive and vigorous-appearing man standing next to her friend. He could have been a sailor or someone who had spent a good deal of time in the sun. He was carefully groomed, dressed in a dark blue suit with a white shirt and colorful tie. Over his clothes, he had on a clean, highly starched white coat similar to Sue's. All in all, he exuded an urbane, refined, even elegant aura that stood out markedly from the other mostly frumpy doctors. As far as the nose was considered, Laurie felt it fit in just fine.

"I want you to meet Dr. Roger Rousseau," Sue said. Her hand gripped his shoulder.

Laurie scrambled to her feet and shook the hand that was extended toward her. It was warm and forceful. Looking into his eyes she was surprised to find them a pale blue. After stumbling over saying she was glad to meet him, Laurie winced internally. She felt like she was acting as she had back in middle school, during that previous awkward introduction.

"Please call me Roger," the man said warmly.

"And me Laurie," Laurie added, regaining her composure. She noticed the man's smile that Sue had described and found it appealing.

"Sue mentioned that you had some confidential information that you were willing to share with me."

"I do," Laurie said simply. "I assume she also mentioned it has to stay anonymous. A leak could put my job in jeopardy. Unfortunately, I've had some bad experiences in the past."

"I have no problem with your need for secrecy. I give you my word." He glanced around the busy cafeteria. "This isn't the best place for a confidential conversation. May I invite you up to my modest but at least private office? We won't have to shout, and we surely won't be overheard."

"That would be fine," Laurie said. She glanced at Sue, who winked, smirked, and waved good-bye all at the same time. When Laurie started to pick up her tray Sue motioned for her to leave it, saying she'd take care of it.

Laurie followed Roger as he threaded his way out through the cafeteria entrance, which was now even more crowded than when Laurie first arrived. Just beyond the throng, Roger stopped and waited for Laurie to catch up. "It's only one flight up. I usually take the stairs. Do you mind?"

"Heavens, no," Laurie said. She was surprised he'd even thought to ask.

"Sue told me you were part of the Médecins Sans Frontières," Laurie said as they climbed.

"I was indeed," Roger said. "For about twenty years."

"I'm impressed," Laurie said, knowing something of the good works carried out by the organization, for which it had received a

Nobel Prize. Out of the corner of her eye, she noticed that Roger was taking the stairs by twos. "How did you happen to join that organization?"

"When I finished my residency in infectious diseases in the mid-eighties, I was looking for some adventure. I was also an idealistic, far-left liberal who wanted to change the world. It seemed like a good fit."

"Did you find adventure?"

"Most assuredly, as well as training in hospital administration. But I found some disillusionment as well. The need for even the most basic medical care in so much of the world is staggering. But don't get me started."

"Where were you located?"

"The South Pacific first, then Asia, and finally Africa. I made sure I made the rounds."

Laurie remembered her trip to West Africa with Jack and tried to imagine what it would be like to work there. Before she could mention her experience, Roger sprinted ahead and opened the door at the top of the stairs.

"What made you leave the organization?" Laurie asked as they descended the busy main corridor en route to the administration area. As Roger was a relatively new employee she was impressed by how many people greeted him by name as they passed.

"Partly the disillusionment of not being able to change the world, and partly because I felt the need to come home and settle down and have a family. I'd always seen myself as a family man, but it wasn't going to happen in Chad or Outer Mongolia."

"That's romantic," Laurie said. "So love brought you back from the wilds of Africa."

"Not quite," Roger said as he held open the door that lead into the carpeted, peaceful realm of the administrative offices. "There was no one here waiting for me. I'm like a migratory bird instinctively flying back to the nesting site where I began as a chick, hoping to find a mate." He laughed as he waved to the secretaries who were not at lunch.

"So you're from New York," Laurie commented.

"Queens, to be exact."

"Where did you go to medical school?"

"Columbia College of Physicians and Surgeons," Roger said.

"Really! What a coincidence! So did I. What year did you graduate?"

"Nineteen eighty-one."

"I was eighty-six. Did you happen to know a Jack Stapleton in your class?"

"I did. He was one of the best basketball players in Bard Hall. Do you know him?"

"I do," Laurie said without elaborating. She felt strangely uncomfortable, like she was cheating on her relationship with Jack just by bringing up his name. "He's a colleague of mine over at the OCME," she added lamely.

They entered Roger's office, which was, as he had said, modest. It was situated on the inside area of the administration wing and accordingly had no windows. Instead, the walls were covered with framed photos of numerous places around the world where he had worked. There was a number of himself with either local dignitaries or patients. Laurie couldn't help but notice that in all of them, Roger was smiling as if each photo had recorded a celebratory event. It was particularly noticeable, since the other people were expressionless or actually frowning.

"Please, sit down!" Roger suggested. He angled a small straight-back chair toward the desk. After closing the door to the hall, Roger sat at the desk, leaned back, and folded his arms. "Now then, tell me what's on your mind."

Laurie again emphasized the need to keep her name out of the situation, and Roger assured her that she had nothing to fear. Reasonably confident, Laurie told the story as she had told it to Sue. This time, she used the term "serial killer." When she was finished she reached over and put a three-by-five index card with the four names directly in front of him.

Roger had been silent throughout Laurie's monologue, staring at her with increasing intensity. "I can't believe you are telling me this," he said finally. "And I am enormously appreciative of your making this effort."

"My conscience dictated that someone should know," Laurie explained. "Perhaps after I get copies of the charts or if toxicology comes up with something surprising, I'll have to eat my words. That would be fine, and no one would be happier than I. But until then, I'm worried something weird is going on."

"The reason I'm so surprised and appreciative is because I have been the scorned gadfly here like you have been over at the OCME, and for the same reasons. I've brought up each of these cases at the morbidity/mortality meeting. In fact, the last time was this morning with Darlene Morgan. And every time, I've been met with denial, even anger, particularly from the president himself. Of course, I haven't had the added benefit of the autopsy results, since we haven't gotten them yet."

"None of the cases have been signed out," Laurie explained.

"Whatever," Roger said. "These cases had me worried right from the first one, Mr. Moskowitz. But the president has put a gag order on our even discussing them, lest something leak out to the media and put the efficacy of our CPR program in question. The on-call docs were unable to get even a rudimentary heartbeat going on any of these cases."

"Has there been any investigation of any sort?"

"Nothing, which flies in the face of my strenuous recommendations. I mean, I've personally looked into it to a degree, but my hands are tied. The problem is, our mortality is very low, below two-point-two percent. The President said we'd do something when it gets to three percent, the usual level of concern.The rest of the committee agrees, particularly the quality-control person, the risk-management person, and the damn lawyer. They are all convinced beyond a shadow of doubt these episodes are merely unfortunate and unavoidable complications in the inherently risky environment of a tertiary-care center. In other words, they are within statistical predictions. But I don't buy it. For me, they're sticking their heads in the sand."

"When you looked into it, did you find anything at all?"

"I didn't. The patients have been on different floors, with different staff, and different doctors. But I haven't given up."

"Good!" Laurie said. "I'm glad you are on top of it, and I'm glad to have had a chance to satisfy my conscience." She stood up, but the second she did, she wished she hadn't, yet she couldn't sit back down for fear of embarrassing herself. The problem was Jack. In fact, lately it seemed that the problem was always Jack. She had enjoyed talking with this man and the feeling made her uncomfortable. "Well, thanks for listening to me," she added, extending her hand toward Roger in an attempt to regain a modicum of control. "It has been nice meeting you. As I mentioned, I'll be getting copies of the charts, and I have our best toxicologist working on it. I'll let you know if anything comes up."

"I'd appreciate it," Roger said, shaking her hand but then holding on to it. "Now, may I ask a few questions?"

"Of course," Laurie said.

"Would you mind sitting back down?" Roger asked. He let go of Laurie's hand and gestured toward the chair Laurie had just vacated. "I prefer you sitting, so I don't have to worry you'll flee out the door."

Somewhat confused by Roger's last comment and why he might believe she'd want to flee, Laurie sat back down.

"I have to confess that I have an ulterior motive in being uncharacteristically glib about answering personal questions. If you would indulge me, I'd like to ask you a few personal questions, since Sue made it a point to tell me that you were single and unattached. Is any or all of that correct?"

Laurie immediately felt dampness in the palms of her hands. Was she unattached? Being put on the spot by an attractive, interesting man who was expecting an answer made her pulse race. She didn't know what to say.

Roger leaned forward and dipped his head to try to look Laurie in the eyes. Her eyes had lowered in response to her emotional confusion.

"I apologize if I am upsetting you," Roger said.

Laurie straightened up, took a deep breath, and smiled wanly. "You're not upsetting me," she lied. "I just didn't expect to be asked that kind of question, especially on this potentially kamikaze career-wise mission of mine over here to the Manhattan General."

"Then an answer would be nice," Roger persisted.

Laurie smiled again, mostly at herself. She was again acting like a teenager. "I am single and mostly unattached."

" 'Mostly' is an interesting choice for an

adverb, but I'll accept it on face value, since we all live in a social web of sorts. Do you live in the city?"

An embarrassing snapshot of her tiny apartment with its seedy entrance flashed through Laurie's mind. "Yes, I have a flat downtown." Then, to make it sound better than it was, she added, "Not too far from Gramercy Park."

"Sounds good."

"How about yourself?"

"I've only been back for a little over three months, so I wasn't sure where the best place was to live currently in the city. I took a year's lease on an apartment on the Upper West Side—Seventieth Street, to be exact. I like it. It's close to that new Sports L.A. club, the museum, and Lincoln Center, plus I have the park at my fingertips."

"Sounds good," Laurie said. She and Jack had frequented restaurants in that area over the last several years.

"My next question is whether you'd care to have dinner with me tonight."

Laurie smiled inwardly as the aphorism "Be careful what you wish for, since it may come true" occurred to her. Over the last number of years with Jack, she'd progressively come to realize how much she appreciated decisiveness in her significant other, something Jack lacked in his personal life. Roger, on the other hand, seemed to be the opposite. Even during this brief encounter, she sensed his personality embodied the term.

"It doesn't have to be a late night," Roger added when Laurie hesitated. "It can be a restaurant of your choosing right around where you live."

"How about on the weekend?" Laurie suggested. "I happen to be free."

"That could be held out as a bonus if you enjoy yourself tonight," Roger said zealously, taking Laurie's suggestion as an auspicious response. "I'm afraid I must insist on tonight, provided, of course, you are free. That gives you an easy out, since you can always say you are busy. But I hope you don't. I have to admit right up front I have not been bowled over by interesting, accomplished women in this town, and I have had my antennae fully extended."

Laurie was flattered with Roger's insistence, especially compared to Jack's indecisiveness, and having been introduced to him by Sue, Laurie felt there was no reason why she shouldn't accept. She had been looking for a diversion, and this was the healthiest. "Okay," she said. "We have a date!"

"Great! Where? Or would you prefer I pick?"

"How about a restaurant in SoHo called Fiamma," Laurie suggested. She wanted to steer clear of any of the places she and Jack had frequented, even if there was a low probability of running into him. "I'll call and make a reservation at seven."

"Sounds good. Should I pick you up at your apartment?"

"Let's meet at the restaurant," Laurie said, as a sudden brief image of Mrs. Engler's bloodshot eye peering out from behind her door popped into her head. She did not want to subject Roger to that. Not at this stage.

Fifteen minutes later, Laurie walked out of the Manhattan General Hospital with a definite spring to her step. She was both surprised and thrilled at what felt like an adolescent infatuation. It was a type of excitement she'd not experienced since being in the ninth grade at the Langley School for Girls. She knew from experience that the feelings were premature and that they probably wouldn't stand the test of time, but she didn't care. She was going to enjoy the euphoria while it lasted. She deserved it.

Standing at the curb, she looked at her watch. With time to spare and with the University Hospital in proximity, she decided to head over and pay a quick visit to her mother before returning to the OCME.

eight

5 WEEKS LATER

Jasmine Rakoczi was reasonably certain that there were at least two snipers positioned on the rooftop of the gutted building to her right. Directly ahead was an open space of no more than fifteen feet leading into a building taller than the sniper's position. Her plan was simple: dash across the divide, dive into the building, and then head for the roof. At that point, she could dispatch the snipers and then move deeper into the ravaged city to accomplish her mission.

Rubbing her hands together in anticipation of her bolt across the open space, she made herself as ready as possible. Her heart was racing and her breathing was rapid and shallow. Calling on her military basic training, she calmed herself, took a deep breath, and then made the move.

Unfortunately, things didn't go as she had planned. Halfway across the open space and just when she was fully exposed, she hesitated as something caught her attention out of the corner of her eye. The result was predictable. She was shot, and having been shot, she certainly was not going to be promoted.

Voicing a few choice swear words she had learned in the marines, Jazz sat back, took her hands from the keyboard, and vigorously rubbed her face. As a stand-in for a Russian conscript in the battle of Stalingrad, she had been concentrating intently for several hours while playing the computer game Call of Duty. She'd been doing fantastic until this current debacle, which meant she'd have to start over. The goal was to complete progressively more difficult missions and be promoted up through the ranks to reach the level of tank commander. Now it wasn't going to happen. At least not tonight.

Letting her hands drop down into her lap, she looked over to the side of her computer screen to see what had messed her up. It was a small, blinking, pop-up window she'd set to appear when she got an e-mail. Imagining that she was going to be even angrier when she found some stupid porn solicitation or a Viagra advertisement, Jazz clicked on it. To her delight, it was a message from Mr. Bob!

A shiver of excitement coursed down Jazz's spine like a bolt of electricity. She'd not heard from Mr. Bob for over a month and was beginning to think Operation Winnow had been terminated. Over the last week, she'd become depressed enough to be tempted to use the emergency number Mr. Bob had given her, even though he had made it crystal clear that the number was only for emergencies from her end. As that was not technically the case, she'd resisted, but as the days had worn on and her discouragement mounted, she'd begun to warm to the idea. After all, she was getting to the point where she might have to move on from the Manhattan General Hospital, which was the hospital where Mr. Bob had specifically asked her to become employed.

The reason Jazz was thinking of moving was because her relationship with the night-shift charge nurse, Susan Chapman, had deteriorated to the point of ridiculousness, as did her relationship with the rest of the shift's nurses, for that matter. Jazz had come to believe the night shift was the place where nursing incompetents hid from the world. She had no idea how Susan had ever gotten to be in charge of anything, much less the surgical floor at the General. Not only was Susan a fat blob, but she knew crap and was always bossing Jazz around to do this or do that, and finding fault with everything Jazz did, which was easy, since the other nurses kept ragging on her about everything, especially when she'd duck into the back room to put her feet up for a few minutes and read a magazine.

Worst of all, Susan always assigned the worst cases to Jazz, as though she was thumbing her nose at her every night, letting the other nurses have the easy ones. Susan even had the nerve to complain to

Jazz about Jazz nosing around in the charts of the cases not assigned to her and to question why Jazz frequently went to the obstetrics floor when she was supposed to be at lunch. Susan said the obstetrics charge nurse had called to complain.

Jazz had bit her tongue at the time and resisted the temptation to ream Susan out the way she deserved or, better yet, to follow her home and use the Glock to get rid of her once and for all. Instead, Jazz dreamed up an explanation involving her need for continuing education . . . blah, blah, blah. It was all bull, but it seemed to work, at least temporarily. The problem was that Jazz needed to go to obstetrics and neurosurgery most every night, since it was the only way she could keep up with what was happening in those specialties. Even though Jazz had not had any patients to sanction, she had kept up with reporting adverse outcomes, which were mostly in obstetrics, involving druggies giving birth to screwed-up babies. Unfortunately, such reporting was not that challenging or fun, and the money was piddling compared to the pay for sanctioning patients.

Holding her breath, Jazz opened Mr.

Bob's e-mail. "Yes!" she shouted while she punched the air over her head with both hands like a professional cyclist winning a leg on a grand tour event. The e-mail was simply the name, Stephen Lewis, meaning Jazz had another mission! Suddenly, going to work was not going to be the grim experience it had become. Putting up with Susan Chapman and the rest of the schmucks wasn't going to be any easier, but at least there was a reason.

Beside herself with excitement, Jazz quickly accessed her off-shore bank account. For a pleasurable moment, she just stared at the balance. It was thirty-eight thousand nine hundred and sixty-four dollars and some odd cents. The best part was that by tomorrow, it would be five thousand higher.

For Jazz, the idea of having money in the bank meant power. Even if she didn't do anything particular with it, she knew she could. Money gave her options. She had never had money in the bank, any money that came into her hands went right out for whatever she wanted at the moment, in a vain attempt to obscure the reality of her life. In middle school and high school, that meant drugs.

As a child, Jazz had grown up in near-poverty conditions in a tiny, one-bedroom apartment in the Bronx. Her father, Geza Rakoczi, the only son of a Hungarian freedom fighter who'd immigrated to the USA in 1957, had sired her at age fifteen. Her mother, Mariana, was the same age and from a large Puerto Rican family. For religious reasons, the youths were forced by their respective families to drop out of school and marry. Jasmine was born in 1972.

Life for Jasmine was a struggle from the very beginning. Both parents shunned the Church, which they blamed for their plight. Both became alcoholics as well as drug abusers, and fought almost continually when they were sober enough. Her father worked intermittently at various manual occupations, disappeared on occasion for weeks at a time, and spent time in jail for various felonies and misdemeanors, including domestic violence. Her mother worked at a series of odd jobs but was constantly fired for absenteeism or poor performance secondary to drunkenness. Ultimately, she became remarkably obese, which limited what she could do.

Jasmine's life outside the home was no better than within. The neighborhood and the schools were caught in a web of gang-related violence and drugs that reached down into the grammar school. Even kindergarten teachers spent more time dealing with behavior problems than teaching.

Forced into a precarious and dangerous world where the only consistency was constant change, Jasmine learned to cope by trial and error. Every time she came home from school she had no idea what to expect. A sibling boy born when she was eight and whom she thought would be her soul mate died of SIDS at age four months. It was the last time she cried.

As Jazz gazed at her nearly forty-thousand-dollar offshore account balance, she remembered the only other time she had thought she had a lot of money. It was the year after baby Janos died, and it had snowed enough to actually accumulate. With an old coal shovel Jazz had found in the basement of their tenement, she'd walked around the neighborhood and shoveled walks. By five o'clock, she had amassed a fortune: thirteen dollars.

Feeling proud, she'd returned home with the roll of singles clutched in her hand. In retrospect, she should have known better, but at the time, she couldn't help but flaunt her newly acquired wealth as evidence of her worth. The result was predictable, as Jazz now knew. Geza had snatched the money away, saying it was about time she contributed to the family larder. Actually, he used the money to buy cigarettes.

A slight smile played across Jazz's face as she remembered her revenge. The only thing her father loved at the time was a yappy mutt the size of a rat, with long hair, which someone had given him where he was temporarily employed at the time. While Geza was drinking beer and watching the fights on TV, she'd taken the dog into the bathroom where the window was always open to help with the smell from the broken toilet. She could remember as if it were yesterday the expression on the dog's face as she held it out the window by the scruff of its neck while it tried furiously to regain the sill. When she let go, it let out a little yelp before plunging four stories down to the concrete below.

Later, Geza had rudely awakened her to demand if she knew anything about the dog's demise. Jazz had denied it vehemently, but she still got knocked around, as did Mariana, who more truthfully denied knowing how the dog fell from the bathroom window. But Jazz had felt the beating was worth it, even though at the time she was terrified. Of course, she was always terrified when her father hit her, which was entirely too often until Jazz got big enough to hit back.

Jazz closed her offshore account window and checked the time. It was too early to go to work, but there was not enough time to go to the gym. As far as starting another session with Call of Duty, she was too antsy to sit still. Instead, she decided to head down to the local Korean twenty-four-hour sundry store to get a few basics. She was out of milk, and she knew she'd want some the following morning when she got back from the hospital.

Pulling on her coat, her hand instinctively went into her right pocket to fondle the Glock. She pulled it out with ease, despite its lengthy suppressor, and aimed at herself in the small mirror she had on the wall next to the door. The hole in the end of the barrel looked like a pupil of a one-eyed maniac. Jazz chuckled as she lowered the gun and compulsively checked the clip. It was full, as it always was. She rammed it home with a reassuring click. Then she got her canvas bag that she used for shopping and slung it over her shoulder.

Outside, it was fairly mild. March was like that in New York. One day, it could feel like spring, but the next could be like the depths of winter. Jazz walked with her hands thrust into her pockets, clutching the Glock on one side and her Blackberry on the other. Holding on to her possessions gave her a sense of comfort.

Since it was just after eight-thirty in the evening, there was a fair number of pedestrians on the sidewalk as well as vehicular traffic on the side street as Jazz headed down toward Columbus Avenue. Passing her beloved Hummer, she stopped for a moment to admire its shimmering surface. She'd used the balmy weather that afternoon as an excuse to wash it. Continuing on, she marveled, as she often did, how lucky she had been to run into Mr. Bob.

Columbus Avenue was even busier, with tons of people and lots of buses, taxis, and cars vying for space. The sounds of the diesel engines, the beeping horns, and the screeching tires could have been overwhelming if Jazz had stopped to listen, but she was accustomed to the general din. The canopy of sky seen between the buildings was a dull gray from the reflected city lights. Only a few of the brightest stars were visible.

The store was open to the street with shelving filled with fruits, vegetables, cut flowers, and a wide assortment of other products. Like the avenue itself, the interior was crowded with a line of customers waiting at the only cash register. Jazz walked around and made her selections, which included bread, eggs, a few PowerBars, and bottled water in addition to the milk. Once she had what she wanted, and with a touch of exhilarating tenseness, she wandered out onto the sidewalk and pretended to examine the fruit. When she thought it was the most opportune time, with the owner engrossed at the register and his wife in the back getting something, Jazz merely turned and started for home. When she was far enough away to know that she wasn't going to be accosted and forced to come up with some lame excuse for walking away, she laughed to herself what fools the proprietors were. With multiple entrances into the store, it was so easy to leave without paying. She wondered why anyone bothered. As for herself, she couldn't remember the last time she had.

Back in her apartment, Jazz put away her groceries in the refrigerator and checked the time. It was still too early to go to work. It was at that moment that she caught sight of her computer screen. There, against her screen's wallpaper, was that same pesky blinking window announcing that she had e-mail.

Fearing that the Stephen Lewiss mission may have been canceled, even though such a situation had never happened in the past, Jazz quickly sat down and clicked on the window. Her concern ratcheted up a notch when she saw that it was a second message from Mr. Bob. With some trepidation, she opened the e-mail. To her astonishment and delight, it was a second name: Rowena Sobczyk.

"Yes!" Jazz blurted while shutting her eyes tightly, grimacing, and balling her hands into tight fists with excitement. After getting no names for more than a month, receiving two in the same night was unbelievable. It had never happened before. She was almost faint from holding her breath when she reopened her eyes and looked again at the screen. She wanted to make sure she wasn't fantasizing, and she wasn't. The name was still there, boldly standing out against the white background. Vaguely, she wondered what kind of name Sobczyk was, since the juxtaposition of consonants vaguely reminded her of her own.

Jazz stood up and began peeling off her street clothes as she headed over to her closet. It was still too early to go to the hospital, but she didn't care. She was going anyway. She was too keyed up to sit around and do nothing. She thought she could at least reconnoiter at the hospital and come up with a general plan of attack. She got out her scrubs and pulled them on. Next came the white coat. While she dressed, she thought about her offshore account. By that time the following evening, the balance would be close to fifty thousand dollars!

Once in the Hummer, Jazz actively calmed herself. It had been okay to celebrate for a time, but now it was time to get serious. She understood that dispatching two patients would be more than twice as difficult as dispatching one. She briefly thought that perhaps she should do them on successive nights but abandoned the idea. If that was the way Mr. Bob wanted it, he would have e-mailed on successive days. It was obvious to Jazz that she was supposed to sanction them together.

En route to the hospital, Jazz didn't even challenge the taxicabs. She was intent on keeping herself composed and focused. She parked the Hummer in its usual location on the second floor and walked into the hospital. After stashing her coat in its customary place, she descended to the first floor and sauntered into the emergency room. She was glad to see that the usual chaos reigned. As had been the case on all her previous missions, she obtained the two potassium chloride ampoules with no problem whatsoever. With one in each side of her white coat, she went back to the elevators and rode up to the sixth floor.

In comparison to the ER, the surgical floor seemed peaceful, but Jazz could tell it was busy. A glance at the chart rack let her know that every room on the floor was occupied, and a glance in the empty utility room meant that all the nurses and nurse's aides were out in patients' rooms. On quiet nights, by that time, the evening-shift nurses were already gathered in the back room, kibitzing and getting ready for report to pass the baton into the hands of the night people. The only person in sight was the ward clerk, Jane Attridge, who was busy getting a stack of laboratory reports into the right charts. Jazz looked into the drug room to make sure Susan Chapman wasn't around yet. She always came in early.

Jazz sat down at a monitor and typed in "Stephen Lewis." She was pleased to learn that his room was 424 in the Goldblatt Wing. Although she'd never been there, she felt it was auspicious. Being the fancy VIP part of the hospital she knew that there would be less nursing activity than on regular floors, which undoubtedly would make things easier for her. The only thing she had to check was whether the guy had a private-duty nurse, which she doubted, because the patient was only thirty-three and all he was in for was a rotator cuff repair.

With Stephen taken care of, Jazz typed in Rowena Sobczyk's name. As soon as she did so, a smile spread across her face. Rowena was right there in room 617, just down the corridor. She thought it would be ironic if she were assigned the case, which was a distinct possibility, and if she were, it would make the sanction that much easier. One way or the other, she felt confident that doing both people was going to be like a turkey shoot.

"You're in awfully early," a voice quipped.

Jazz's eyes popped up, and a shot of adrenalin coursed through her veins. She found herself looking into Susan Chapman's chubby face, with its rounded features demarcated by a slight seborrheic rash in the creases. Susan's expression was more challenging than friendly as she looked over Jazz's shoulder at the monitor screen. Jazz hated the way she wore her hair pulled back in an old-fashioned, tight bun. Jazz couldn't help but think she looked like some kind of nursing anachronism, especially with her old-fashioned lace-up leather-soled shoes with inch-thick heels.

"What, may I ask, are you doing?" Susan demanded.

"Just trying to familiarize myself with our cases," Jazz managed. Swallowing her anger at this woman, she forced herself to smile. "It seems like we have a full house."

Susan stared at Jazz for what seemed like minutes before speaking. "We almost always have a full house. What's with this Rowena Sobczyk; do you know her?"

"Never saw her in my life," Jazz responded. Her smile lingered but now looked more real since she had recovered from her initial alarm at being discovered accessing Rowena's record. "I was trying to take a peek at all the new patients to get a jump on the night."

"I think looking at the new patients is my job," Susan said.

"Fine and dandy," Jazz said. She blanked out the screen and stood up.

"We've been over this before," Susan snapped. "We have a rule in this hospital that protects patient confidentiality. I'm going to have to report you if I find you doing this in the future. Do I make myself clear? Looking at records is on a need-to-know basis."

"I'm going to need to know if I'm assigned."

Susan breathed out audibly as if exasperated. She stared at Jazz with her hands on her hips like an irate grammar-school teacher.

"It's funny," Jazz said, breaking the silence. "I would have thought you and the rest of the brass would encourage individual initiative. But seeing that you don't, I'll just take myself down to the coffee shop instead." She arched her eyebrows questioningly and waited for a beat for Susan to respond. When she didn't, Jazz flashed one more fake smile and headed down toward the elevators. As she walked, she could feel Susan's eyes boring into her back. She shook her head imperceptively. She was learning to detest the woman.

Descending to the first floor in case Susan was watching the floor indicator, Jazz followed the twisting corridors past the closed day clinics and walked into the Goldblatt lobby. She could have gotten off on the fourth or pediatric floor and headed into the Goldblatt Wing from there, but she was worried that Susan was getting too suspicious about her meanderings.

Even on the first floor, the Goldblatt Wing was different in all regards from the rest of the hospital. The walls were paneled in mahogany, and the corridors were carpeted. Oil paintings hung beneath their picture lamps. The visitors who were disembarking from the elevators and leaving were dressed nattily, and the women sparkled with diamonds. Outside were limousines and valet attendants.

Despite an elaborate security setup at the front entrance, no one questioned Jazz's arrival from the hospital proper. She stood at the elevators, waiting for a car, with a few other nurses coming on duty. She noticed they were dressed like Susan Chapman, in old-fashioned nurses' outfits. Several even wore hats.

Jazz was the only person to get off on the fourth floor. Like the lobby downstairs, it was carpeted and paneled and decorated with fine art. A number of departing visitors waited for a down elevator. Several smiled at Jazz, and she smiled back.

It hardly seemed like a hospital. Her

cross-trainers hardly made a sound on the carpet. Glancing into the patient rooms, she could see that they were decorated in an equally refined manner, with upholstered furniture and draperies. Visiting hours were ending and people were saying their good-byes. As she came abreast of room 424, she slowed. About fifty feet ahead was the central nurses' station, a beacon of bright light compared to the subdued illumination of the hall.

The door to room 424 was ajar. Jazz glanced up and down the corridor to make sure she went unnoticed. Stepping into the room's doorway, she had a full view of the interior. As she expected, there was no private-duty nurse. There were also no visitors. The patient was a muscular African-American man stripped to the waist. A large bandage swathed his right shoulder, and an IV ran into his left arm. He was sitting in the hospital bed with the back cranked up, watching a TV suspended from the ceiling over the bed's foot. Jazz could not see the screen, but from the sound, she could tell it was a sporting event.

Stephen's eyes pulled away from the TV

and looked over at Jazz. "Can I help you?" he called.

"Just checking to make sure everything is okay," Jazz said, which was true. She was pleased. It was going to be a walk in the park.

"Things would be better if the Knicks would get their game together," Stephen said.

Jazz nodded, waved to the patient, then retreated back to the elevator.

With her reconnoitering accomplished, Jazz returned to the first floor and went into the coffee shop. She was pleased.

The first half of the night shift went as expected. Jazz had been assigned as nurse manager for eleven patients, which was one more than the other nurses, but she didn't complain. She was teamed up with the best nurse's aide, so things evened out. Unfortunately, she had not been assigned to Rowena Sobczyk, and as busy as Jazz was, there was no chance to do anything for Mr. Bob until her lunch break, which had just started.

Jazz descended in the elevator with the

two other nurses and two nurse's aides who were sharing the lunch slot, but she made sure she lost all of them in the cafeteria. She didn't want to get caught up with their chitchat and have trouble getting away. Instead, she wolfed down a sandwich and polished off a pint of skim milk without sitting down. She had only thirty minutes, and she had a lot to do.

During the course of the shift, Jazz had added a couple of syringes to the potassium ampoules in her jacket pockets. Leaving the cafeteria, she ducked into the ladies' room. A quick check beneath the stalls convinced her that she was alone. For added privacy, she went into one of the stalls and closed the door. Taking out the ampoules one at a time, she snapped off their tops and carefully filled both syringes. With their needle caps back on, the syringes were returned to the depths of her jacket pockets.

Back out in the main part of the lavatory, Jazz quickly rolled the empty ampoules up in a number of paper towels. Still, no one had come in. Placing the roll on the tile floor, she crushed it with the heel of her shoe. The glass made a faint popping sound. She then tossed the flattened wad of paper and glass into the waste container.

Jazz looked at herself in the mirror. She ran her fingers through her fringed hair, straightened her jacket, and adjusted the stethoscope that was draped around her neck. Satisfied, she started for the door, now armed and ready for action. It had been as simple as that. She was beginning to appreciate the efficiency of doing two cases in the same night. It was like an assembly line.

She took the main elevators up to the fourth floor, avoiding the Goldblatt lobby, lest she arouse the curiosity of the security people. The fourth floor was all pediatrics, and as she descended the long hallway en route to the Goldblatt Wing, the thought of sick infants in the various rooms brought back an unpleasant memory of little Janos. Jazz had been the one who'd found him that fateful morning. The poor kid was as stiff as a board and slightly blue, lying facedown in his rumpled blanket. Being a child herself, Jazz had panicked, and desperate for help, she'd dashed in to where her parents were sleeping to try to wake them. But no matter what she did, she couldn't raise them from their drunken slumber. Jazz ended up calling 911 herself and later letting the EMTs in through the front door.

A heavy fire door separated the Goldblatt Wing from the hospital proper. It was as if it was rarely opened, and after an unsuccessful tug, Jazz had to put one foot up against the jamb and use her leg muscles to get it to budge. Stepping over the threshold, she was again reminded of how different the Goldblatt décor was. What particularly caught Jazz's attention was the lighting. Instead of the usual institutional fluorescents, there were incandescent sconces and picture lights, which had been dimmed since Jazz's earlier visit.

She put her shoulder against the fire door just to be a hundred percent sure it would reopen for her retreat. It moved with significantly less effort than it had the first time. Jazz set off down the corridor at a deliberate pace. She'd learned from experience not to be hesitant, since such behavior invited attention. She knew where she was going, and she acted like it. Despite a long vista down the hallway, she saw no one, not even at the distant nurses' station. As she passed patient rooms, she heard the occasional beep of a monitor and even caught a glimpse of a nurse bending over a patient.

As Jazz neared her objective, she began to feel the same excitement she'd experienced in combat in Kuwait in 1991. It was a sensation that only soldiers who'd been in war could understand. Sometimes there was a flicker of it when she was playing Call of Duty, but not with the intensity of the real thing. For her, it was a little like speed, but better and without the hangover. Jazz smiled inwardly. Getting paid for what she was doing made it even more of a pleasure. She came to room 424 and didn't hesitate. She walked right in.

Stephen was still propped up in bed but fast asleep. The TV was off. The room was relatively dark, with the only illumination coming from a combination of a dim night-light and a vanity light in the bathroom. The bathroom door was open just a crack, causing a stripe of light to fall across the foot of the bed and along the floor like a narrow line of fluorescent paint. The IV was still in place.

Jazz checked her watch. It was three-fourteen. Quickly but silently, she moved over to the bedside and opened up the IV. Within the Millipore chamber, the drops became a steady stream. She bent over and looked at the IV site where the needle went into Stephen's arm. There was no swelling. The IV was running just fine.

Back at the door to the hall, Jazz leaned out and looked up and down the corridor for one last check. Still, no one was in sight. All was calm. Returning to the bedside, she pushed the sleeves of her jacket up above her elbows to get them out of the way. She then pulled out one of her full syringes and took the needle cap off with her teeth while holding the IV port in her left hand. Despite her excitement, she steadied herself before inserting the needle. Straightening up, she listened. She heard nothing.

With a strong, steady push, Jazz emptied the syringe into the IV port. As she did so, she saw the level of fluid in the Millipore chamber rise, which she expected. The potassium chloride solution was backing up the IV fluid. What she didn't expect was a rather loud groan from Stephen, followed by his eyes popping open to their fullest extent. Even more unexpected was Stephen's right hand lunging across his chest and grabbing Jazz's forearm with shocking strength. A muffled cry of pain escaped from Jazz's mouth as sharp nails dug into her skin.

Dropping the syringe onto the side of the bed, Jazz desperately tried to break the hold Stephen had on her arm, but she couldn't. At the same time, Stephen's groan melded into a shriek. Abandoning her attempt to release his grip on her arm, Jazz slapped her free hand over Stephen's mouth and leaned her torso into him in a desperate attempt to quiet him. It worked, although he bucked to try to worm himself free.

There was a continued brief struggle, but Stephen's strength quickly ebbed. As his grip on Jazz's arm weakened, his fingernails were drawn down her forearm, scratching her and causing her to cry out again.

As quickly as the scuffle started, it ended. Stephen's eyes rolled up inside his head, and his body went limp, his head flopping onto his chest.

Jazz detached herself. She was furious. "You bastard!" she murmured through clenched teeth. She checked her arm. Several of the scratches were bleeding. She felt like punching the guy, but she held herself in check since she knew the guy was already dead. She snatched up the syringe and then got down on her hands and knees to find the damn needle cap that she'd been holding in her teeth and had dropped when she'd cried out. She quickly gave up. Instead, she merely bent the needle around 180° before putting the empty syringe back in her jacket pocket. She couldn't believe what had happened. Since she had started dispatching patients, this was the first one to pull off such a stunt.

After slowing the IV back to where it was when she'd first come in and replacing her stethoscope around her neck, Jazz quickly went to the door. She glanced up and down the corridor. Thankfully, apparently no one had heard Stephen's cry, since the corridor remained as quiet as a morgue. She gingerly straightened the sleeve of her jacket over the scratches on her forearm, glanced back once more at Stephen to make sure she wasn't forgetting anything, then stepped out into the hallway.

Wasting no time, she retraced her steps back to the fire door. Once on the other side she leaned her back up against the door. She was a bit unnerved by the unexpected complication, but she quickly collected herself. She reasoned that she had to expect problems once in a while, despite her planning. She then examined her forearm in the better light. She had three gouges on the volar surface of her forearm from Stephen's nails, with trailing linear scratches about three inches long extending down toward her wrist. Two of them were oozing blood. She shook her head, thinking that Stephen certainly had it coming to him.

Jazz warily replaced her sleeve and checked her watch. It was three-twenty, and she had one more sanction to accomplish. She knew it was an opportune time, because the nurse assigned to Rowena was on break with her and wouldn't be back for another ten minutes. But she couldn't dillydally. Walking rapidly, Jazz returned to the main elevators and went back up to her floor.

There was only one person at the nurses' station. It was Charlotte Baker, a pixieish nurse's aide. She was busy writing nurse's notes. Jazz glanced in the utility room and the drug room, the Dutch door of which was open on the top. Both were empty.

"Where's our fearless leader?" Jazz questioned. She looked down the corridor in both directions. She didn't see anyone.

"I believe Ms. Chapman is down in room 602, helping with a catheterization," Charlotte said without looking up. "But I'm not entirely sure. I've been holding down the fort here for fifteen minutes or so."

Jazz nodded and looked down toward 602. That room was situated in the opposite direction from Rowena's room. Sensing that the time would not get any better, she pushed away from the counter that overlooked the nurses' station, made sure Charlotte was not paying her any attention, and headed toward 617. Once again, her pulse quickened as she anticipated action, only this time the thrill was tinged with anxiety after her experience with Stephen Lewis. A mild ache from the scratches on her forearm was a reminder that she couldn't control all the variables.

A patient caught a glimpse of Jazz as she hurried past his door, and he called out to her, but she ignored it. Checking her watch, she figured she had six minutes before anyone was scheduled to return from their lunch break, including the nurse assigned to Rowena, but since no one was ever early, she had a bit of a buffer. Six minutes was plenty of time.

The stage was similar to what she'd found in Stephen's room, but without the carpet, fancy drapes, upholstered furniture, and fine art, and the only light was a night-light. The bathroom door was ajar, but the lights were off. Rowena Sobczyk was asleep in the bed with both feet bandaged from a bilateral hallux valgus repair. She was on her back and snoring slightly. Jazz looked down at the woman. Although she was twenty-six, she appeared much younger, with tiny features and a mop of dark, unruly hair splayed out against the white pillow.

Jazz opened the IV to run freely, then bent over to check for any swelling. There was none, so all was set. She pulled out the full syringe and, holding it in her right hand, lifted the IV port with her left. Just as she'd done in Stephen's room, she used her teeth to remove the needle cap. Immediately, she inserted the needle into the port and then repositioned her hand with her thumb over the syringe's plunger. After taking a breath and holding it, she smoothly depressed the plunger.

Rowena stirred, writhing her upper body. Jazz removed the syringe, and as she did so, she heard footsteps out in the hall on the composite flooring. Her intuition immediately flashed a warning as the sound of the footfalls made her think of Susan's clodhopper nursing shoes. She glanced briefly at the half-open door to the hall, then back at Rowena, who was now clutching at her arm with the IV and making gurgling noises.

In a panic, Jazz dropped both the syringe and the needle cap into her pocket and backed up from the patient. For a second, she thought about hiding in the bathroom in case Susan heard the noises, but then discarded the idea as it might make a bad situation worse. Instead, she started for the door, thinking the best defense was offense.

Confirming her worst fears, Jazz literally ran into Susan coming into the room just after Susan had stepped over the threshold.

Susan took a step back, acting indignant and looking up at Jazz with the same challenging expression she had had earlier.

"Charlotte said you'd come down here. What the hell are you doing? This is June's patient."

"I was passing in the hall, and she called out."

Susan bent around Jazz, who was trying to fill the doorway, and squinted into the half-light of the room. "What was the matter?"

"I guess she was dreaming?"

"She looks like she is moving around. And the IV is running full tilt!"

"Really?" Jazz questioned. Susan pushed by, forcing Jazz to step aside.

Susan slowed down the IV as she bent over Rowena. "My God," she said. Then, turning to Jazz, she shouted: "Hit the lights! We've got a code here!"

Jazz did as she was told while Susan sounded the alarm. Susan then directed Jazz to help get the opposite-side bed rails down. Seconds later, the code was announced over the hospital PA system.

"She's got a thready pulse, or she did!" Susan barked. She had her fingers pressed into Rowena's neck to feel her carotid artery. She let go and climbed up to kneel on the bed. "We've got to start CPR. You breathe, and I'll do the compressions."

With great reluctance, Jazz pinched Rowena's nostrils shut and placed her mouth over Rowena's. She blew in and inflated the lungs. There was little resistance, suggesting to her that the patient was essentially flaccid. She was the only one who knew that at this stage, trying to resuscitate Rowena was a joke.

Charlotte and another nurse named Harriet arrived and managed to get an EKG hooked up and going. Susan was continuing the compressions, and Jazz, for appearances' sake, continued with the breathing.

"We have some electrical activity," Harriet said. "But it looks like strange complexes to me."

At that point, the resident cardiopulmonary resuscitation team arrived and quickly took over. Jazz was pushed to the side as Rowena was expertly intubated and started on pure oxygen. Drug orders were barked out, and the drugs were given. Arterial blood was drawn and sent off to the lab for a stat report on blood gases. The strange complexes as noted by Harriet at the outset had quickly disappeared. The EKG traced a straight line, and the residents began to lose their enthusiasm. Rowena wasn't responding to anything.

While the resuscitation was still technically going on, Jazz walked out of the room. She went back to the nurses' station and stepped into the utility room. She sat down and cradled her head in her hands. She needed a few minutes to pull herself together. She had been unnerved by what happened with Stephen Lewis, and then having something untoward happen with Rowena seemed like too much. Jazz couldn't believe it. She'd never had any problem whatsoever on all her previous cases. She couldn't help but wonder if she would be spooked on her next mission.

Out of the corner of her eye, she saw Susan appear out at the nurses' station. Jazz couldn't hear but assumed Susan had asked the aide manning the desk where Jazz was, because the aide was soon pointing in Jazz's direction. When Susan started toward the utility room, Jazz knew that she was about to weather another confrontation.

Susan came in and closed the door. She

didn't talk, even after she sat down. She just stared at Jazz.

"Are they still trying to resuscitate the patient?" Jazz asked, discomforted by the silence. Jazz wanted to get it over with if they were going to have an argument.

"Yes," Susan said simply before another pause. Jazz felt it was like some kind of weird staring contest, so she decided to wait it out. Finally, Susan said, "I want to ask you again why you were in Sobczyk's room. You say the patient called out. What exactly did the patient say?"

"I don't remember if it was any words. I just heard her, okay? So I went in to check."

"Did you talk with her?"

"No. She was asleep, so I just turned around and came out."

"So you didn't see that the IV was wide open."

"That's correct. I didn't look at the IV."

"Did she seem all right to you?"

"Of course! That's why I was coming out when we bumped into each other."

"What are those scratches on your arm?"

The way Jazz was sitting with her elbows on the built-in desk, her sleeve had fallen just enough to reveal the three scratches and a bit of dried blood.

"Oh, these?" Jazz questioned. She took her arms off the desk and shook her sleeve back down to cover the wounds. "It happened in my car. It's nothing."

"They've been bleeding."

"Maybe a little, but it's no problem, really."

Jazz again found herself having the same weird staring contest, as if they were in the third grade. For almost a minute, Susan didn't say anything and hardly blinked. Jazz had had enough. She pushed back and stood up. "Well, time to get to work." She skirted Susan and opened the door.

"It strikes me as a strange coincidence you being in that room," Susan said as she swung around and faced Jazz.

"Obviously, when the patient called out, it was the beginning of whatever caused her code. It just wasn't apparent when I went in there. Maybe I should have checked her better than I did. But tell me! Are you trying to make me feel worse than I already do or what?"

"No, not really," Susan admitted. She looked away.

"Well, you're doing a pretty good job, whether you're trying or not," Jazz said before walking out to find the nurse's aide she'd been assigned to work with that night.

At first, Jazz felt like she had talked herself out of a potentially problematic situation with Susan, but as the rest of the shift wore on, she got progressively paranoid. It seemed like every time she turned around, Susan was staring at her. By the time report rolled around and the morning-shift nurses were hearing about the evening, including the code on Rowena Sobczyk, the problem had advanced to a point of ridiculousness. With Susan's behavior, there was no question in Jazz's mind that she was suspicious. All Jazz could think about was Mr. Bob telling her that there could be no ripples. As far as Jazz was concerned, this situation with Susan wasn't threatening ripples—it was portending a tidal wave.

Jazz's biggest fear was that Susan would take off after report and go directly to blab her suspicions to the nursing supervisor, Clarice Hamilton, an enormous African-American woman who Jazz thought was as big a dud as Susan. If that happened, all hell would probably break loose, and Jazz would surely have to use the emergency number to call Mr. Bob. Yet what Mr. Bob could do at that point was fairly limited.

The moment report was over, Jazz remained where she was and pretended to be doing a bit more chart work. Susan spent another five minutes debriefing the day charge nurse about specific problems. As close as Jazz was, she could hear most of the conversation. Luckily, Susan didn't say anything about Jazz. When that was over, Susan got her coat, and laughing and carrying on with June, she went down to the elevators. That was when Jazz got her own coat. She also grabbed a pair of latex gloves from a box on the utility-room desk next to the door.

At that time in the morning with the shift changing, the elevator area was crowded. Jazz made sure she stayed in the periphery, as far from Susan and June as possible. When the car came, she wormed her way to the very back. She could tell where Susan was by her ridiculous bun.

When the elevator stopped on the second floor, Jazz pushed her way to the front and disembarked, along with a half dozen other people, including Susan. Jazz knew that Susan, like herself, drove to work. Like a clutch of cackling hens, the group walked down to the door that opened onto the connecting bridge that crossed over to the parking garage. Jazz hung back to bring up the rear. As she walked, she pulled on the latex gloves.

Once in the garage, the group splintered off to their respective vehicles. At that point, Jazz upped her pace. She had her hands in her pockets with her right hand gripping the Glock. She closed the distance between herself and Susan so that when Susan slipped in along the driver's side of her Ford Explorer, Jazz was doing the same on the passenger side. The second Jazz heard the unlocking mechanism activate, she opened the passenger-side door and slipped into the front seat.

Jazz had timed it perfectly. It was almost as if she'd been sitting there when Susan climbed in. Under different circumstances, Susan's shocked expression would have been hilarious. The trouble was, Jazz wasn't finding any of this funny.

"What the hell?" Susan questioned.

"I thought maybe we could talk in private

and mend fences," Jazz said. She had both hands in her pockets with her shoulders scrunched up and her arms straight.

"I don't have anything to talk to you about," Susan snapped. She put her key in the ignition and started the engine. "Now get out of my car. I'm going home."

"I think we have plenty to talk about. You've been giving me the evil eye all night. I want to know why."

"Well, you are an odd duck."

Jazz laughed with derision. "That's funny, coming from you."

"That's the kind of comment that underlines my impressions," Susan spat. "To be honest, I've never felt confident in you. I don't know why you are a nurse. You don't get along with anyone. You have no compassion. Every night, I have to give you the easiest cases."

"Oh, bull!" Jazz sputtered. "You give me all the junk cases."

For a second, Susan stared at Jazz just the way she had been doing all evening. "I'm not going to argue with you. In fact, if you don't get out of my car, I'm going to go get security and let them deal with you."

"You still haven't told me why you have

been gawking at me. I want to know if it has anything to do with Rowena Sobczyk."

"Of course it has something to do with Rowena Sobczyk. It's too much of a coincidence with you coming out of her room when she wasn't your patient. And I happen to remember you were seen coming out of Sean McGillin's room, and he wasn't your patient, either. But talking to you about all this is not my job. It's the nursing supervisor's job, so you'll be talking with her I'm sure."

"Oh, yeah?" Jazz sneered. "I don't think you should be so sure, you freaking loser." With a little effort, Jazz got the Glock out of her pocket.

Susan saw the gun coming and was only able to raise her right hand when Jazz shot her twice in the side of the chest. Susan slumped laterally against the door, with her cheek pressed up against the glass.

Despite the suppressor, the noise within the car was more than Jazz expected. So was the smell of the cordite. With her free hand, she fanned the fumes. Twisting around, she looked out the back of the SUV. Multiple cars were coming into the garage, but all were going by and up the ramp, since all the second-tier slots were taken. A few cars were going out. With all the noise and commotion, Jazz was confident that no one would have heard the double thump of the Glock. Jazz worked the gun back into her pocket.

Reaching over, she grabbed Susan by her bun and righted her, letting her head fall against her chest but keeping her upright. *What a loser,* she thought as she positioned the woman's lifeless arms to rest on the steering wheel. *And losers deserve to lose.* She switched off the car's ignition.

Next, Jazz opened Susan's purse and rifled through it to find her wallet. Opening the wallet, she took out the cash and the credit cards. Then she tossed the wallet and the cards on the floor, hoping for the appearance of a fatal mugging. Twisting around again, Jazz looked through the back window at the door to the connecting bridge. As she did so, a group of nurses emerged and waved to each other as they split up to go to their respective vehicles. Jazz hunkered down until they were out of sight.

Sitting back up, she eyed her Hummer. It was only two cars away. After a quick check to make sure the coast was clear, Jazz got out of Susan's vehicle and away from it by going around the front of the immediately adjacent car.

Inside her own SUV, she stripped off the latex gloves and pocketed them. She started the engine, backed out, and headed for the exit. As she passed behind Susan's car, she glanced inside. It looked as though Susan was taking a catnap after a hard night. It was perfect.

Out in the morning traffic, Jazz allowed herself to take a deep breath. She hadn't realized how tense she'd been. It had been a hard night, but she was confident she'd handled it well. She was ten thousand dollars richer, and she'd managed to eliminate a potential problem. Operation Winnow was alive and kicking. Life was good.

nine

Laurie's ancient windup alarm jangled in the morning's half-light, and she reached out to turn it off without even opening her eyes. As she settled back into the warmth of her bed, she shivered, not from cold but from nausea. Her eyes blinked open. She'd experienced a touch of nausea the previous morning as well, but she had ascribed it to the scallops she'd had the night before with Roger. She loved scallops, but there had been a few times in the past when they had made her feel queasy the following day. Luckily, yesterday's nausea had not lasted. By the time she had walked around a bit, it had all but disappeared.

Laurie sat up. She shivered again. After taking a sip of the water she had at her bedside, she felt a bit better. The problem was that this time, she hadn't had scallops for dinner. In fact, she'd had some reasonably bland chicken, the memory of the nausea in the back of her mind.

As she clutched her sheets around her, she noticed a new symptom along with the nausea: mild right lower quadrant discomfort. It wasn't strong enough to call pain. Using her fingers, she gingerly pushed in her abdomen in the general area over the crest of her hip. She couldn't tell if it made the discomfort any worse, since pushing in her stomach mostly reminded her of her full bladder.

Throwing back the bedcovers, she pulled on her robe and slipped her toes into her slippers. As she walked into the bathroom she could feel the discomfort more distinctly. Now it was more like pain, but still quite mild.

As a doctor considering these two symptoms, Laurie's first concern was early appendicitis. She knew there were a lot of things that could go wrong in the right lower quadrant, and that the diagnosis could be challenging at times. But she knew she was jumping the gun. It was the kind of hypochondriasis she had indulged when she was a medical student. She smiled as she remembered a simple headache in her first year that made her worry that she was coming down with malignant hypertension simply because she'd studied the syndrome the night before. Of course, she didn't have malignant hypertension, and in a similar fashion, her discomfort and nausea were almost completely gone when she got out of the shower.

Laurie wasn't hungry, but she forced herself to eat a piece of toast. When that went down okay, she had some fruit. She was convinced that having something in her stomach would help, and it did. By the time she was ready to leave for the OCME, she felt pretty much like her old self.

She waved to Mrs. Engler when the woman's door cracked open. This time, the bleary-eyed harpy actually spoke, advising

Laurie to get her umbrella, since it was supposed to rain.

It was a mild morning, and although overcast, it wasn't yet raining. Laurie walked north along First Avenue, oblivious to the crush of traffic, wondering if her nausea could be psychosomatic due to stress. *What else is new?* she thought dejectedly, since she'd never seemed to be able to get her social life to run as smoothly as her professional life.

Laurie's whirlwind five-week relationship with Roger had recently hit an unexpected bump. They had been seeing each other two or three times a week, as well as every weekend. Laurie didn't consider the current bump an insurmountable obstacle, but it had been jarring to a degree and made her remember that back in the beginning of their acquaintance, she'd warned herself that adolescent infatuations often did not withstand the test of time. The case in point was Laurie learning only two nights earlier that Roger was married. There had been plenty of opportunities for him to have told her this important fact, but he had chosen not to, for reasons Laurie couldn't fathom. It was only after Laurie had forced herself to ask him directly that he'd owned up to the truth. He had married a Thai woman some ten years ago when he was stationed in Thailand, and had never gotten a divorce, although he was supposedly now seeking one. Even more upsetting for Laurie was that he'd had several children.

The story became somewhat less damning as it unfolded. The woman was from a wealthy, privileged family, to which she had selfishly returned, according to Roger, essentially abducting the children when Roger was transferred to Africa. Yet his withholding such information set a bad precedent and made Laurie wonder if Roger was not quite the person she had envisioned. It also underscored a growing uneasiness that Laurie felt about the speed of the relationship, coupled with Roger's pressure for physical intimacy. On top of everything were her unresolved feelings for Jack.

The night before, as she sat in her apartment feeling sorry for herself about the previous night's revelations, she had had a mini-epiphany. For the first time, she had acknowledged to herself that she actively and deliberately suppressed issues she didn't want to talk about or even think about. She'd recognized this trait in her parents, particularly her mother, from as far back as Laurie could remember, and her mother's way of dealing with her recent bout with breast cancer was a case in point. Laurie had always despised the trait. Yet she had never looked at herself in the mirror as her parents' child. What made her come to the realization was that Roger's marital status hadn't been the surprise she liked to pretend. There had been hints, but Laurie had assiduously kept herself from acknowledging any of them. She simply did not want to believe that he was married.

At the corner of 30th Street, Laurie waited for the light to cross First Avenue. As she did so, she thought about how her newly acknowledged personality trait applied to her ailing relationship with Jack. With sudden clairvoyance, it seemed rather clear. She had wanted to put all the blame on him for being noncommittal about their future and for not bringing up the issue of marriage and children. Now she realized she had to share some of the blame as she had failed to bring it up herself. She also realized that his offer to broach the subject on a regular basis had actually been a concession on his part, maybe not a monumental one, but a concession nonetheless. How she was going to communicate all this to Jack, she had no idea. The last time they had spoken on any kind of personal level had been five weeks earlier.

As the light changed and she hurried across First Avenue and up the front steps of the OCME, she thought that having met Roger complicated things. Rather than having problems with one man, she now had problems with two. Although she cared for both of them, she knew she loved Jack, and she found herself longing for his uncompromising candor. Part of the reason she'd gone out with Roger in the first place was to make Jack jealous, an adolescent machination worsened by two complications: First, she hadn't expected to be as attracted to Roger as she had become; and second, she hadn't expected the jealousy ploy to work so well.

Although Laurie felt that Jack loved her, his enduring reluctance to make any commitment convinced her his love was not the same as hers. Specifically, he had never made her feel that he valued their relationship as much as she did. She was convinced that he wasn't going to change and that he was incapable of jealousy.

But now, thanks to his current behavior, she felt differently. The tone of their interactions and conversations had deteriorated over time. When she had first moved back to her apartment, there'd been flippant sarcasm. After she started seeing Roger, it had become nastier, and it made Laurie feel terrible. A month ago, when Jack had asked her to have dinner with him and she told him she had plans to go to the symphony with Roger on the evening in question, Jack had responded by telling her to have a good life. He didn't suggest an alternative date. The implication was that he didn't even want to remain her friend.

Waving to Marlene, the receptionist, as she buzzed her into the ID room, Laurie had to smile. The whole situation smacked of a soap opera, and she told herself to put thoughts of the two men out of her mind. Clearly, changing her behavior or anyone else's was not going to be the easiest thing in the world.

Laurie draped her coat over one of the club chairs in the ID room, placed her umbrella on top, and went directly to the coffee machine. It was Chet's turn to decide which cases needed to be posted, and he was hard at work, bent over a stack of folders.

Laurie stirred her coffee and checked the time. It was still before eight, but certainly not as early as she used to get in with Jack. She noticed that Vinnie wasn't there reading his newspaper, suggesting that he was already down with Jack, doing an autopsy. The only sounds Laurie could hear were the chatter of the operators in the communications room, preparing for the day. Laurie enjoyed the relative solitude, knowing that in an hour, the place would be humming with activity.

"Is Jack already downstairs?" Laurie asked, taking a sip of her coffee.

"Yup," Chet said without lifting his head. Then, suddenly, he looked up when he recognized the voice. "Laurie! Great! I was supposed to give you a message if you came in before eight. Janice is very eager to talk with you. She's been in here twice."

"Was it about a recent postoperative patient from the General?" Laurie questioned, her eyes lighting up. She had asked Janice to be sure to let her know if another such case surfaced. If it had, it would mean that not thinking about the two men in her life would be considerably easier, as her four suspicious homicide cases would grow by a hefty twenty-five percent. The two cases she had posted, McGillin and Morgan, she had yet to sign out. The other two had been signed out by Kevin and George, citing the manner of death as natural, a conclusion that Laurie had opposed.

"No, it wasn't a patient from the General," Chet said with a teasing smile that Laurie failed to detect. Laurie's shoulders slumped in disappointment. "It wasn't one, but rather two!" He reached out and tapped the top of two folders he'd put aside. He then gave them a gentle push in Laurie's direction. "And both obviously need to be posted."

Laurie snatched them up and looked at their names: Rowena Sobczyk and Stephen Lewis. She quickly checked their ages: twenty-six and thirty-two, respectively. "Are they both from the Manhattan General?" she asked. She wanted to be sure.

Chet nodded.

For Laurie, it seemed almost too good to be true from the standpoint of a diversion. Her series would grow to six cases, not five. That was a fifty percent increase. "I'd like to do these two cases," she said hastily.

"You got them," Chet responded.

Without another word, Laurie grabbed her coat and umbrella. With the folders under her arms, and balancing her coffee as best she could, she quickly headed through communications and the clerical room on her way to the forensic investigators' office. She was beside herself with curiosity. She'd had to eat a bit of crow over the course of the previous five weeks, as her supposed serial-killer scenario had failed to materialize as a viable possibility and had been dismissed by everyone except Roger. Jack had used the issue to tease her rather sarcastically on several occasions. Even Sue Passero had been dismissive after making what she described as multiple, discreet inquiries around the hospital. Luckily, Calvin had not brought up the issue at all. Nor had Riva.

The hospital charts on the original four cases had eventually arrived in Laurie's office, and she had completely filled in her matrix but found no smoking gun. In fact, there was no way the cases were related. There were different surgeons, mostly different anesthetists, a variety of anesthetic agents, a significant variation of preoperative and postoperative drugs, and differing locations in the hospital. Worst of all, the toxicology results were completely negative, despite Peter pulling every trick that he could think of with the gas chromatograph and the mass spectroscopy. For Laurie's benefit, he had truly gone out of his way to find even the most minute traces of an offending agent. And with no agent, no one was willing to give the serial-killer idea any credence, especially since there had been no more cases after Darlene Morgan. Everyone relegated the four cases to the wastebasket of statistical oddities occurring in the inherently dangerous environment of the hospital.

As Laurie popped into the forensic investigators' office, Bart looked up from his desk. "You're just in time," he said, and pointed to the rear of the room to make his point. Janice was in the process of pulling on her coat.

"Dr. Montgomery," she said. "I was afraid I was going to miss you. I've run out of steam, and my bed is calling." She peeled off her coat and after draping it over her desk chair, sat down heavily.

"Sorry to hold you up," Laurie said.

"No problem," Janice said gamely. "This won't take but a minute. Are those the Lewis and Sobczyk folders you've got?"

"They are," Laurie said, pulling up a chair. Janice took the folders, opened them, and took out her reports, handing them back to Laurie.

"Both these General cases remind me of the other four you were interested in," Janice said as Laurie scanned the write-ups. Janice cupped her tired face in her hands and leaned her elbows on the desk. She took a deep breath before continuing. "In short, both were young and healthy, both seemed to die of an unexpected cardiac problem, both had had minor surgery less than twenty-four hours earlier, and both obviously could not be resuscitated."

"They sound remarkably similar," Laurie agreed. She looked up. "Thanks for giving me a heads-up. Was there something in particular you wanted to tell me that's not in your summaries?"

"It's all there," Janice said. "But there is something I want to emphasize. Although most parameters with the Sobczyk woman are the same, there is one thing that is different. When she was found by the nurses, she was in extremis but still alive. Unfortunately, that quickly changed, despite strenuous intervention. Lewis, on the other hand, had no cardiac or respiratory activity when he was found by nurse's aides."

"Why do you think that's important?"

"Just because it's different," Janice said with a shrug. "I don't know, but last time you spoke with me, you asked me if I had sensed something intuitively about the Darlene Morgan case. I hadn't, but with Sobczyk, the fact that she was still alive jumped out."

"Then I'm glad you told me," Laurie said. "Anything else?"

"That's it. The rest is in the reports."

"Needless to say, I'll like copies of the hospital charts."

"They have already been requested."

"Great!" Laurie said. "I'm glad you told

me this. If you think of anything else, you know where to find me."

Laurie gathered up her belongings and went out to the back elevator, eager to get to work. She couldn't remember being this excited in weeks. As the elevator rose, she thought about what Janice had told her. She wondered if it would be important.

Dashing into her office, Laurie hung up her coat and put her umbrella on top of the file cabinet. Sitting at her desk, she opened both folders and again took out Janice's reports. After rereading them more carefully, she leaned over, opened one of her desk drawers, then took out the matrix she had drawn from the original four cases. It was attached with a rubber band to the Morgan and McGillin folders, along with copies of the pertinent portions of the other two cases. Undoing the parcel, she held the McGillin folder for a second. She hadn't been able to give the definitive word to Dr. McGillin about his son's death as she had so confidently promised, and it made her feel guilty. She hadn't even spoken with the man in weeks, even though she'd promised to get back to him. As she put the folder down with the other, she made a mental note to call him. She wondered what the man would say if she told him she was entertaining the idea of a serial killer.

Feeling confident in Janice's assessment, Laurie went ahead and added Lewis and Sobczyk to the matrix, even though she had yet to do the posts. Since Janice anticipated Laurie's interest, she had done a very complete job on both cases. Even without the hospital charts, Laurie could fill in the boxes for the patients' ages, the times they had been pronounced dead, their MDs, the surgical procedures they'd undergone, and where in the hospital they'd had their rooms. While Laurie was busy doing this, Riva arrived.

"Adding to that matrix of yours?" Riva questioned, glancing over Laurie's shoulder.

"There are two more presumed cases. That's going to make six. Obviously, I haven't done the posts yet, but they sound exactly the same. Want to change your idea about the manner of death? I mean, this is going to be a fifty percent increase."

Riva laughed. "I don't think so, especially since the toxicology has been negative, and I for one happen to know how hard

Peter has tried. By the way, how's your mother? I keep forgetting to ask."

"She's doing surprisingly well," Laurie said. "Of course, I don't hear much, since she's acting like the whole thing never happened."

"I'm glad she's doing well," Riva said. "Give her my best! Hey, how is that new beau of yours? You've been uncharacteristically silent about him."

"It's going well," Laurie said vaguely. Riva was right; Laurie had not shared much about Roger. Picking up her phone before Riva could ask any more questions, she called down to the mortuary office. She was pleased when Marvin answered. She told the tech about the two cases and said she wanted to do Sobczyk first. With his usual alacrity, he told Laurie he'd be waiting for her.

"See you in the pit," Laurie said to Riva as she scooped up Sobczyk and Lewis's folders. As she descended in the elevator she prepared herself mentally for the cases, which was easy, since she half assumed and half hoped she wasn't going to find much. By the time she had changed into scrubs, donned her moon suit, and pushed into the autopsy room, Marvin was almost ready. On the way to her table, she had to pass Jack's.

Recognizing Laurie, Jack glanced at the wall clock before straightening up from the opened body of a sizable elderly lady. A portion of her gray, stringy hair had been shaved to reveal a punched-out, depressed fracture of the skull on the top of her head. "Dr. Montgomery, it appears as if you are adopting banker's hours these days. Let me guess! I bet the explanation is that you were out painting the town red with your French boyfriend."

"Very funny," Laurie said. She fought against her irritation and the urge to walk on. "Actually, you are wrong on both counts. I was home last night, and Roger is as American as you or I."

"That's strange," Jack said. "Rousseau sounds so French to me. Wouldn't you agree, Vinnie?"

"Yeah, but my name's Italian, and it doesn't mean I'm not American."

"My gosh, you're right!" Jack said with false contrition. "I guess I'm jumping to conclusions here. Sorry!"

Laurie was embarrassed at Jack's behavior and the jealous anger he was doing a bad job of repressing. But under the circumstance of being in the autopsy room with Vinnie, she chose to change the subject. She pointed to the elderly woman's depressed skull fracture. "I see you have a rather obvious cause of death here."

"The cause maybe, but not the manner," Jack said. "Such cases are becoming my specialty."

"Would you care to explain?" Laurie questioned.

"Are you really interested?"

"I wouldn't be asking if I weren't."

"Well, the victim was hastily off-loaded from a cruise ship in the middle of the night. The cruise company claimed an inebriated elderly lady had a fatal fall in the bathroom of her stateroom. They reported there was no suspicious behavior and no violence involved. But I don't buy it, although she might have been drunk."

"Tell me why you don't buy it."

"First, the punched-out, depressed fracture is on the top of the head," Jack said, warming to the conversation. "That's hard to do if you're falling in a bathroom, unless you're a contortionist. Second of all, look at these patterns of bruises on the inside of her upper arms!" Jack pointed to linear groupings of petechiae, which Laurie could see when she looked closer.

"Next, notice the tan lines on her wrist and ring finger. She'd spent some serious time in the sun on the cruise, with what looks like quite a rock on her finger and a wristwatch. And guess what? No ring and no watch in the stateroom. I have to hand it to the tour doctor. Despite the hour, he was thinking in high gear. They had cleaned up the stateroom and the bathroom, but he still asked the right questions."

"So you think it was homicide."

"No question, despite the cruise company's comments to the contrary. Of course, I'll just be reporting the findings, but if anybody asked my opinion, I'd tell them that this woman was viciously knocked on the head with some kind of hammer, rudely dragged by her arms into her stateroom while still alive, robbed, and left to die."

"Sounds like a good case to emphasize that deaths among the elderly are in some respects similar to deaths involving child abuse."

"That's exactly right," Jack said. "Since the elderly are expected to die, there is less suspicion of foul play than with a younger person."

"It's a good teaching case," Laurie said, trying to put on a good face before moving on to her table. Although she was leaving the exchange on a reasonable note, its overall character was more evidence of how difficult it was going to be to have any kind of serious discussion with Jack about their relationship even if he was so inclined. But she put the thought out of her mind as she looked down on the body of Rowena Sobczyk.

"Do you suspect anything out of the ordinary on this case?" Marvin asked.

"Nope. I believe it is going to be straightforward," Laurie said as her trained eye began the external exam. Her first impression was that the woman looked considerably younger than the reputed twenty-six years. She was tiny with delicate, almost preadolescent features as well as thick, youthful-appearing curly black hair. Her skin was almost blemish-free and ivory-white, except for areas of dependent lividity. Both feet were bandaged, consistent with her surgery. The bandages were clean and dry.

Like with McGillin and Morgan, the remnants of the resuscitation attempt were still in place, including the endotracheal tube and the IV line. Laurie checked them carefully before removing them. She looked for signs of drug abuse and found none. She took off the bandages. The surgical incisions showed no signs of inflammation, and only minimal drainage.

The internal portion of the autopsy was the same as the external: negative for any obvious pathology. In particular, the heart and the lungs were entirely normal. The only finding was several cracked ribs from the resuscitation attempt. As with the other cases, Laurie made certain that she got more than adequate samples from all the usual places for toxicology screening. She was not about to give up hope that Peter would succeed with his magic on one of the cases.

"Do you want to do the second case right away?" Marvin asked when they had finished sewing the body back together.

"Absolutely," Laurie said. To expedite the transition, Laurie helped. As they passed

Jack's table on the way out and again on the way in, Laurie made sure she didn't hesitate. She didn't want to be embarrassed again by any of his comments. If he saw her, he did not let on. By that time, the room was in full operation with lots of people coming and going, and in their moon suits, everyone looked rather similar. Thanks to the glare of the overhead lights, it was difficult to see through the plastic face masks.

As soon as they moved Stephen Lewis onto the table and into position, Laurie began her external exam. Meanwhile, Marvin went to get the specimen bottles and other materials for the case. Laurie forced herself to follow her usual protocol to avoid missing anything. Although her expectations were high that Stephen Lewis would be like the others in the sense of having no significant pathology, she wanted to be thorough, and her methodical approach paid off almost immediately. Barely discernable but definitely present was a small amount of crusted blood under the nails of his right index and ring finger. If she hadn't specifically looked, she would have missed it. It was something she'd not seen with Sobczyk,

Morgan, or McGillin, and George and Kevin had not described it in the autopsy notes on the other two cases.

Putting Lewis's hand back down on the table, Laurie began a careful search for any scratches on the man's body that might account for the dried blood. There were none. Nor was there any bleeding at the IV site. Next, she removed the bandages covering the right shoulder. The surgical incision was closed and showed no signs of inflammation, although there was some evidence of postoperative bleeding, with a bit of crusted blood along the suture line. Laurie thought there was a chance this blood could have been the source of the blood under the nails although it seemed strange, since it was his right hand.

When Marvin came back, Laurie asked for a sterile swab and two specimen containers. She wanted to do a DNA fingerprint on both samples just to make sure they matched the victim. When she took the samples, she sensed that there was a small amount of tissue as well. In the back of her mind was the titillating thought that if her serial-killer idea had any merit and if Lewis had had a hint of the killer's intentions and if he could have gotten hold of him, maybe he could have scratched him. That was a lot of ifs, but Laurie prided herself on being meticulous.

The rest of the case went quickly. Laurie and Marvin had become accustomed to each other such that they functioned as a well-orchestrated team that required minimum conversation. Each anticipated the other's motions like tango dancers. Once again, there was almost no pathology. The only findings were minimal atheroma formation in the abdominal aorta and a benign-appearing polyp in the large intestine. There was no explanation for the man's sudden death.

"Is this your last case?" Marvin asked after taking the needle holder from Laurie when she had finished sewing up the body.

"It seems that way," Laurie said. She looked around the room to see if she could make out Chet, but she couldn't. "I guess we're done. Someone would have said something to me by now."

"Both these cases this morning remind me of those two we did a month or so ago," Marvin said as he began cleaning up the instruments and collecting the specimen bottles. "Remember those two when we found nothing significant? I can't remember their names."

"McGillin and Morgan," Laurie said. "Certainly I remember, and I'm impressed you do as well, considering the number of cases you're involved with."

"I remembered them because of how much they bugged you not finding anything. Hey, do you want to take these specimen samples with you, or do you want them to go up with all the rest?"

"I'll take the toxicology and DNA samples," Laurie said. "The microscopic can go with the others. And thanks for reminding me. I must say, I'm appreciating you more and more."

"That's cool," Marvin responded. "Likewise from my end. I wish all the docs were like you."

"Now that would be boring," Laurie said with a laugh as she gathered up the samples. She walked past Jack's table once again without stopping. She could hear him and Vinnie laughing over what had probably been some black humor. Laurie disinfected herself and the sample bottles before emerging into the hallway.

Not wasting any time, she got out of her protective gear and plugged her battery into the charger. Without even changing out of her scrubs, she headed for the back elevator. She carried the clutch of sample bottles against her chest to keep from dropping them. The two folders were under her arm. As she rode up to the fourth floor, she could feel her pulse in her temples. She was excited. The posts had confirmed Janice's assessment. Laurie was now confident that her series now stood at six.

Getting off on the fourth floor, Laurie cautiously peered into the toxicology lab. In her attempt to avoid the temperamental lab director, Laurie was reduced to sneaking around. Luckily, he stayed mostly in the general lab on the floor below. Feeling like a cat with its ears down, Laurie scurried diagonally across the lab and into Peter's tiny office. She was glad when she didn't hear someone call out her name. She was even more glad that Peter was at his desk, meaning she didn't have to seek him out.

"Oh, no!" Peter moaned teasingly when he looked up from his work and spotted the samples in Laurie's arms.

"I know you're not happy to see me,"

Laurie said. "But you are the man! I need you more than ever. I've just posted two more patients that are the mirror image of the others. There are now six."

"I don't know how you can say I'm the man, because so far, I've come up with a big blank."

"I haven't given up hope, so you can't, either." Laurie dumped the samples onto Peter's desk. Some of them threatened to roll off. Peter grabbed several and righted them. "Now that there are six cases, the idea of skulduggery goes up. Peter, you've got to find something. It has to be there."

"Laurie, I did everything I could think of with the other four cases. I looked for every known agent that affects cardiac rhythm."

"There has to be something you haven't thought of," Laurie insisted.

"Well, there are a couple of other things."

"Okay, like what?"

Peter made a face and scratched his head. "I mean, this is way out in left field."

"That's okay. We need some creativity here. What are you thinking about?"

"In the back of my mind, I remember reading something when I was in graduate school about a poison frog from Colombia called *Phyllobates terribilis.*"

Laurie rolled her eyes. "I'll say you're getting a bit far afield. But it's okay. What about these frogs?"

"Well, they contain a toxin that's one of the most toxic substances known to man. If I remember correctly, it's capable of causing cardiac arrest."

"Sounds interesting! Have you tested for it?"

"Not really. I mean, so little of the toxin is needed, like millionths of a gram. I don't know whether it would show up with the sensitivity of our machine. I'll have to find out where to look."

"That's the spirit. I'm sure you are going to find something, especially with these two additional cases."

"I'll go online and see what I can learn."

"I appreciate it," Laurie said. "And keep me posted!" She picked up the DNA samples and started to leave, but then she stopped. "Oh, by the way, there was something slightly different with one of these cases. Let me check which one it was." She opened Sobczyk's folder and checked the accession number against the sample bottles. Finding the correct one, she held it up, then put it directly in front of Peter. "It's this one. This was the only patient out of the six who apparently had some cardiac and respiratory activity when she was found. I don't quite know what to make of that, but I thought you should know. If it were an unstable toxin, maybe it would have the highest concentration of all the cases."

Peter shrugged. "I'll keep it in mind."

Laurie looked out into the lab proper. Seeing that the coast was clear, she waved to Peter and quickly dashed out into the hallway. She used the stairs on her way up to the sixth floor. Halfway up, she stopped. All of a sudden, the right lower quadrant abdominal discomfort she'd had that morning reappeared. Once again, she used her fingers to press over the area. At first, it made the discomfort worse, reaching the threshold of what she would call pain, but then, as quickly as it had appeared, it vanished. Laurie felt her forehead to make sure she didn't have a fever. Convinced she didn't, she shrugged and continued on her way.

The sixth floor housed the DNA laboratory. In contrast to the rest of the building, the DNA lab was state-of-the-art. It was less than a half dozen years old and sparkled with white tiled walls, white cabinetry, white composite flooring, and the newest instrumentation. Its director, Ted Lynch, was a former Ivy League football jock. He wasn't in Calvin's league in terms of size, but not far behind, though he had a personality the opposite of Calvin's. Ted was an even-tempered, friendly individual. Laurie found him hovering over his beloved sequencer machine.

Laurie gave Ted a bit of background on the case and then asked him if he'd do a rush screen. Along with the samples from under Lewis's nails, she gave him a sample of Lewis's tissue.

"Yeah, yeah, yeah!" Ted voiced with a laugh. "You and Jack are quite a pair. Every time you bring me something, it's got to be stat, like the sky is going to fall if you don't get it. Why can't you two be more like the rest of the lazy gang? Hell, they hope they don't hear from me, because when they do, it creates work for them."

Laurie couldn't help but smile. She and Jack had created a reputation for themselves. Laurie told Ted just to do the best he could. She then descended a floor and walked quickly down toward her office. She couldn't wait to get to the phone. The person to whom she was most excited about giving the news of the two new members of her series was Roger.

Sitting at her desk, Laurie dialed Roger's extension at the Manhattan General. She drummed her fingers as she waited for the call to go through. Her heart was beating even faster than it had been earlier. She knew Roger would want to know about the two new cases if he didn't already. Unfortunately, when the line was picked up, it was Roger's voicemail. Laurie silently cursed. Of late it seemed that all she ever got was people's voicemail, never a real person.

After listening to Roger's outgoing message, Laurie merely said it was she who was calling and to call her back. She couldn't help but feel a twinge of disappointment at not getting hold of him right away. As she hung up the phone, she left her hand on the receiver as she thought about Roger being the only person who seemed to share her concern about the possibility of a grim reaper stalking the halls of the Manhattan General, which was the derogatory way Sue Passero had referred to her suspicions. Yet with her new self-honesty, she wondered how sincere his support really was. After the marriage revelation, she didn't know how much to trust him. As Laurie thought back over the last five weeks, she had to admit that he'd been almost too solicitous at times. She hated to be cynical, but that was the consequence of his dishonesty.

Laurie jumped as the phone rang under her hand, and snatched up the receiver in a mini-panic.

"I'm looking for Laurie Montgomery," a pleasant female voice said.

"Speaking," Laurie responded.

"My name is Anne Dickson. I'm a social worker here at the General, and I'd like to make an appointment with you."

"An appointment?" Laurie questioned. "Can you tell me what case this is about?"

"Your case, of course," Anne said, confused.

"My case? I'm not sure I understand."

"I work here in the genetics lab, and I believe you came in a little more than a month ago for a genetic screen. I'm calling to arrange for you to come back in so we can schedule a meeting."

A complex array of thoughts flashed through Laurie's mind. The BRCA1 test was yet another example of her putting unpleasant things out of her mind. She'd completely forgotten about having given the blood. This woman calling her up out of the blue brought back the whole disturbing issue like an avalanche.

"Hello? Are you still there?" Anne questioned.

"I'm still here," Laurie said as she tried to organize her thinking. "I suppose this means the test was positive."

"It means that I'd like to see you in person," Anne said evasively. "It's our normal procedure for all our clients. I'd also like to apologize. Your folder has been on my desk for a week or so, but it mistakenly got put in the wrong basket. It's my fault entirely, so I'd like to see you sooner rather than later."

Laurie felt a wave of impatient irritation. She took a deep breath and reminded herself that the social worker was only trying to do her job. Still, Laurie would have preferred just to be told the results than suffer some drawn-out protocol.

"I've had a cancellation for one o'clock today," Anne continued. "I was hoping that might work. If it's not convenient, the next opening is a week from today."

Laurie closed her eyes and took another deep breath. She wasn't going to allow herself to be in limbo for a week. Although she expected that the phone call meant the test was positive, she wanted to know for certain. She looked at her watch. It was eleven forty-five. There was no reason she couldn't run over to the General. Maybe she could have lunch with Roger or Sue. "One is fine," she said with resignation.

"Wonderful," Anne said. "My office is in the same suite where you came for the blood to be drawn."

Laurie hung up the phone. With her eyes again closed, she bent over her desk and ran her fingers roughly through her hair, scratching her scalp. All the nasty consequences of the BRCA1 gene flooded into her consciousness, along with a wave of sadness. What particularly bothered her was the acknowledgment of the upcoming need to make what she called "an end decision," a decision that eliminated options, such as having children.

"Knock, knock!" a voice called out.

Laurie glanced up to find herself looking at the smiling face of Detective Lieutenant Lou Soldano. He appeared particularly dapper with a clean, pressed shirt and a new tie. "Hey, Laur," he said cheerfully. Laur was a nickname that Lou's son, Joey, had given Laurie back when Laurie and Lou had briefly dated. At that time, Joey was five. Now he was seventeen.

Laurie and Lou had not had a falling out but rather a mutual understanding that a romantic relationship wasn't appropriate. Although they continued to have great respect, understanding, and admiration for each other, the passion part didn't work. Instead of romance, a close friendship developed and blossomed over the years.

"What's the matter?" Lou asked. Laurie had started to talk, but instead of saying anything, her eyes filled up with tears. She'd slapped a hand over her forehead, pressing in on her temples with her thumb and index finger.

Lou closed the door. He pulled Riva's chair over and sat down, then put his hand on Laurie's shoulder.

"Hey, come on! Tell me what's going on here!"

Laurie took her hand away. Her eyes were still brimming, but no tears had spilled out. She puffed up her cheeks then smiled weakly. "Sorry," she managed.

"Sorry? What are you talking about? There's nothing to be sorry for. Come on! Tell me what's cookin'? But wait! I think I know."

"You do?" Laurie questioned. She opened one of her desk drawers and took out a tissue to blot her eyes. Once she had the watery eyes under control, she looked back at Lou. "What makes you think you know what's bothering me?"

"I've gotten to know you over the years: both you and Jack. I also know you and him are on the outs. I mean it's not like it's a secret."

Laurie started to protest, but Lou took his hand off her shoulder and held it up to shush her. "I know it's none of my business, but it is my business, since I'm crazy for both you guys. I know you've been seeing some other doctor, but I think you and Jack should patch things up. You guys were meant for each other."

Laurie had to smile in spite of herself. She gazed at Lou with loving eyes. The man was a dear. Back when she and Jack started to be romantically involved, she'd been concerned that he'd be jealous, since the three had become fast friends. Instead, he'd been generously supportive right from the beginning. Now it was Laurie's turn to put her hand on Lou's shoulder. "I appreciate your thoughts," she said sincerely. If he wanted to think her little bout of emotionalism was due to her relationship with Jack, that was fine with her. The last thing she wanted to do was get into a discussion of the BRCA1 problem with Lou.

"I know for a fact that your seeing this other guy is driving Jack crazy."

"Really," Laurie said. "Well, you know something, Lou: I'm actually surprised about that. I didn't think Jack would care one way or the other."

"How could you think that?" Lou questioned with an expression of total disbelief. "Did you forget about the way he acted when you almost got engaged to that arms dealer, Sutherland? Jack was a basket case."

"I thought that was because both you

guys didn't think Paul was the right man, which he wasn't. I didn't think it was jealousy on Jack's part."

"Mark my words: It was jealousy, loud and clear."

"Well, we'll see what we can do. I would like to talk to Jack if he'll let me."

"Let you?" Lou questioned with equal disbelief. "Hey, I'll box him around the ears if he doesn't."

"I hardly think that would help," Laurie said with another smile. She blew her nose with the tissue she had in her hand. "But be that as it may, to what do I owe this midmorning visit, especially as decked out as you are? I know you didn't come here solely as Jack's advocate."

"That's for damn sure," Lou said. He straightened up in his seat. "I got a problem, and I need some help."

"I'm all ears."

"The reason I'm spiffed up is because I had to head out to Jersey with Michael O'Rourke, my captain. Unfortunately, his wife's sister was murdered this morning here in the city, and we went out to tell the husband. Needless to say, I'm under a ton of pressure to come up with a suspect. The body's already downstairs in the cooler. What I'm hoping is that either you or Jack could do the case. I need a break, and between the two of you, you always seem to come up with the unexpected."

"Gosh, I'm sorry, Lou. I can't do it now. If it can wait until later this afternoon, I'm sure I can help."

"What time?"

"I don't know for sure. I have an appointment over at the Manhattan General."

"Really," Lou commented with a wry smile. "That's where Michael's sister-in-law got mugged: right in the parking garage."

"That's terrible. Was she on the hospital staff?"

"Yeah, for years. She was a head nurse who worked nights. She got whacked getting into her car on her way home. It's a crying shame. Two young kids, too, ten and eleven."

"Was she robbed or raped or both?"

"Just robbed, or so it seems. Her credit cards were strewn about the car. Her husband guesses she had less than fifty bucks, and for that she loses her life."

"I'm sorry."

"Not as sorry as I'm going to be unless I

make some headway. What about Jack? He wasn't in his office when I went by."

"He's down in the pit, or he was when I left about a half hour ago."

Lou stood up and rolled Riva's chair over to her desk.

"Wait, Lou," Laurie said. "As long as you're here, there's something I want to mention to you."

"Oh, yeah? What?"

Laurie briefly told Lou about her series of six cases. She touched on only the highlights, but it was enough for Lou to pull Riva's chair back so he could sit down again.

"So you really think these cases are homicides?" Lou questioned when Laurie fell silent.

Laurie chuckled mostly at herself. "You know, I'm not sure," she admitted.

"But you just said you thought someone was doing this to these patients. That's homicide."

"I know," Laurie said. "The problem is, I don't know how much I believe it myself. Let me explain. Starting this morning, I've been on a self-honesty gig that's making me rethink a lot of things. I've been stressed emotionally over the last month and a half with Jack, with my mother, and other things, and I know I've been looking for a diversion. This series of mine certainly falls into that category."

Lou nodded in understanding. "So you think you might be making a mountain out of a molehill."

Laurie shrugged.

"Have you run this serial-killer idea by anybody else here at the OCME?"

"Just about everybody who will listen, including Calvin."

"And?"

"Everybody thinks I'm jumping to conclusions, because toxicology can't find anything remotely suspicious, like insulin or digitalis, which was used in documented healthcare institution serial murders in the past. Well, it's not completely accurate to say that everybody has disagreed. The doctor I've been seeing socially, whose name, by the way, is Roger and who works at the General, has supported me, but this morning I've found myself questioning his motives. But that's another issue entirely. Anyway, that's the whole story about the serial-killer idea."

"You've run it by Jack?"

"Certainly. He thinks I'm off the wall."

Lou stood back up and returned Riva's chair. "Well, keep me informed. After that corneal-cocaine conspiracy you ferreted out ten years ago, I probably would give your intuition more credit than you."

"That was twelve years ago," Laurie said.

Lou laughed. "That just shows to go you that time flies when you're having fun."

ten

"How's that?" Jack asked. He backed up a step to survey his handiwork.

"Okay, I suppose," Lou answered.

Jack had helped Lou into a moon suit and connected his battery pack. Jack could hear the hum of the ventilation fan pulling air through the HEPA filter. "Can you feel the breeze?"

"Some breeze," Lou commented derisively. "I don't understand how you can work in this contraption every day. For me once a month is too much."

"It's not my idea of a good time," Jack admitted as he began climbing into his own suit. "When I'm on call on weekends, I sometimes surreptitiously revert to the old mask and gown, but every time Calvin finds out, I get read the riot act."

They gloved in the anteroom, then pushed into the autopsy room proper. Five of the eight tables were in operation. On the fifth lay the naked remains of Susan Chapman. Vinnie was busy arranging the specimen bottles.

"You remember Detective Soldano, don't you, Vinnie?"

"Yeah, sure. Welcome again, Lieutenant."

"Thanks, Vinnie," Lou said as he stopped some six feet from the table.

"Are you okay?" Jack asked. Lou was a relatively frequent autopsy observer, so Jack was not worried that he'd pass out and fall over backward, as some visitors did. Jack had no idea why he'd stopped, although he did notice the detective's facemask had fogged, suggesting he was overbreathing.

"I'm okay," Lou murmured. "It's a little hard seeing someone you know rudely stretched out like this, waiting to be gutted like a fish."

"You didn't say you knew her," Jack responded.

"I suppose I'm exaggerating. I didn't actually know her. I'd met her a few times at Captain O'Rourke's house."

"Well, move on in here! You're not going to see anything from left field."

Lou took a couple of tentative steps forward.

"Looks like she had a thing for Krispy Kremes," Jack said, surveying the body. "What did she weigh out as, Vinnie, old boy?"

"A hundred and eighty-three."

Jack whistled, which sounded muffled behind his plastic mask. "That's a bit much for what I'd say is about a five-foot-three-frame."

"Five-four," Vinnie said. He went back to the cabinet for syringes.

"I stand corrected," Jack said. "Okay, Lou, fill me in! You railroaded me in here so fast, I haven't read the investigator's report. Where was she found?"

"She was sitting upright in the driver's seat of her SUV like she was taking a nap. Her head was resting down on her chest. That was why she wasn't discovered right away. A few people had seen her but thought she was sleeping."

"What else can you tell me?"

"Not much. She was apparently shot in the right chest."

"And your impression was that of a robbery?"

"Certainly looked like it. Her cash was gone, her wallet and credit cards were thrown on the floor, and her clothes were intact."

"Where were her arms?"

"Poked through the steering wheel."

"Really? That's odd."

"How so?"

"Sounds to me like she was positioned."

Lou shrugged. "Could be. If so, what do you read into it?"

"It's just not common with a garden-variety mugging." Jack picked up the woman's right hand. A section of the thenar eminence below the thumb was gone, causing a grooved defect. The rest of the ball of the thumb and most of the palm was heavily stippled with tiny penetrations. Part of the first metacarpal bone was visible in the defect. "My guess, this is a defensive wound."

Lou nodded. He was still a full step away from the table.

Jack lifted the right arm away from the body. Within the armpit were two small dark red circles with some adherent fabric fibers. The surface within the circles looked like dried chopped meat with a bit of yellow adipose tissue peeking out.

Vinnie came back with the syringes and after dumping them alongside the corpse, pointed to the view box on the wall. "I forgot to tell you I put up the X-rays. There are two slugs in the chest to match the two entrance wounds."

"How right you are!" Jack said. He stepped over to the view box and peered at the films. Lou came up behind him and looked over his shoulder. The two bullets stood out dramatically as two pure white defects in the mottled, varying gray field. "My guess is that one is in the left lung and the other's in the heart."

"That confirms the two nine-millimeter

shell casings found in the vehicle," Lou said.

"Let's see what else we can find," Jack said as he returned to the table and recommenced his external exam. He was meticulous, literally going from the top of the head to the bottom of the feet. In the process, he pointed out the fine stippling around the entrance wounds.

"What's that mean?" Lou asked. He'd finally moved close enough to see.

"Since this area was clothed, it tells me the muzzle of the gun was close, maybe only a foot away, but not as close as it was to the hand."

"Is that significant?"

"You tell me. It raises the question whether the attacker was sitting in the car when the gun was fired rather than just reaching in."

"Yeah, so?"

Jack shrugged. "If the attacker was sitting in the car, you may want to question if the victim knew the attacker."

Lou nodded. "Good point."

For the internal portion of the autopsy, Jack stood on the victim's right, with Vinnie on the left. Lou stood at the head and bent over when Jack pointed out a particular finding.

The autopsy was routine, except when Jack traced the bullets' trajectories. Both had penetrated ribs, which Jack thought probably accounted for the lack of exit wounds. One bullet had gone through the aortic arch to lodge in the left lung. The other had passed through the right side of the heart to embed itself in the wall of the left ventricle. Jack retrieved both slugs, handling them with extreme care so as not to alter their external markings. He dropped them into evidence pouches with custody tags that Vinnie had prepared.

"I'm afraid this is all I'm going to be able to give you," Jack said, handing the sealed pouches to Lou. "Maybe your ballistics people can help out."

"I hope so," Lou said. "We got no prints from the scene, even from the passenger-side door handle. There weren't even any latents on the wallet other than the victim's, so we got zilch from the scene. On top of that, the nighttime attendants didn't see anybody suspicious coming in or hanging around."

"It sounds like it's going to be a tough case."

"You got that right."

Leaving Vinnie to clean up, Jack and Lou went into the storeroom to get out of the protective suits. From there, they walked into the locker room to change from scrubs to street clothes.

"Once a doctor, always a doctor, so I hope you don't mind my saying that it looks like you're getting a paunch there, Lieutenant."

Lou's eyes dropped to take in his expanded girth. "Sad, isn't it?"

"Sad and unhealthy," Jack said. "You're not doing yourself any favors with that extra weight, especially since you haven't stopped smoking."

"What do you mean?" Lou questioned as if offended. "I've stopped smoking a hundred times. Why, the last time was just two days ago."

"How long did that last?"

"Till I could bum one off my partner: about an hour." He laughed. "I know, I'm pathetic. But the reason I'm carrying around all this extra baggage is that I can't find the time to work out with all the homicides in this fair city." He pulled on his shirt and buttoned it over his protruding waist.

"You're going to have to be indicted for your own death if you don't change your ways."

Standing alongside Jack in front of the mirror Lou slipped the loop of his tie over his head. He hadn't untied the knot earlier. He cinched it up to his neck, thrusting out his chin in the process. "I had a conversation with Laurie before I came down here to find you."

"Oh?" Jack questioned. He paused, tying his knit tie, and stared at Lou in the mirror.

"She was upset about you guys and got all teary-eyed."

"That's curious, considering she's having a mad, passionate affair with some creep over at the Manhattan General."

"His name is Roger."

"Whatever. Actually, he's not a creep, and that's part of the problem. In fact, he sounds kind of perfect."

"Well, you can relax about that. I definitely didn't get the impression she's so wild about the guy. She even said she wants to talk to you about patching things up."

"Ha!" Jack grunted in disbelief. He went back to tying his tie.

Knowing that he was putting words into Laurie's mouth and feeling a little guilty about it, Lou avoided eye contact with Jack while he got his jacket out of the locker and slipped it on. He justified his machinations as a friend helping friends. He used his fingers to comb back his closely cropped hair.

Jack's eyes followed Lou until Lou finally looked at him. Jack then said, "I find it hard to believe she wants to talk about patching things up when a couple of weeks ago, she wouldn't give me the time of day outside of talking about cases here at the morgue. I tried to get together with her a number of nights in a row. She blew me off each time, saying she was busy going to the symphony or to the museum or the ballet or some other disgustingly cultural event. I mean, she was booked up solid and never suggested an alternate date." Like Lou, Jack used his fingers to sweep his Caesar-style hair off his forehead with rapid, irritated strokes.

"Maybe you should try again," Lou suggested. He sensed that he should tread rather softly. "As I told her, you guys are meant for each other."

"I'll think about it," Jack said evasively. "I'm not big on self-humiliation these days."

"She also mentioned her confusion about a series of suspicious deaths over at the Manhattan General. It almost sounded like she was trying to talk herself into them being homicides. She said she'd talked to you about it. What's your take? She said you thought, in her words, she was 'off the wall.' "

"That's a bit strong. I just think she's gotten a little ahead of herself with those four cases."

"Six! She got two more today."

"No kidding?"

"That's what she said. She also admitted she might be using the serial-killer idea as a diversion."

"She said that specifically? I mean, she actually used the word 'diversion'?"

"Scout's honor!"

Jack shook his head with surprise. "I'd say that was a reasonable assessment, considering toxicology has drawn a complete blank. I'd also have to say it was impressively self-aware."

With the March sun still making its diurnal transit in the southern sky, a shaft of midday sunlight that had suddenly knifed through the rapidly moving cloudcover penetrated into the Manhattan General's southerly oriented cafeteria window. It was like a laser beam, and Laurie had to lift her hand to shield her eyes from its sudden intensity. Dr. Susan Passero, who was sitting across from her with her back to the window, became a featureless silhouette against the glare.

Keeping her hand over her forehead, Laurie dropped her eyes to her tray in front of her. She had hardly touched her food. Although her selections sounded appetizing when she got them, once she sat down, she realized she wasn't hungry at all. Having no appetite was not usual for Laurie. She attributed it to the stress she felt about her upcoming meeting with the social worker and the inevitable news she was about to get. In some ways, she felt humiliated about being forced to see a mental-health professional.

When Laurie had arrived at the hospital forty minutes earlier, she'd first gone to Roger's office, but he still wasn't available. One of the secretaries had told her he was closeted with the hospital president. Laurie had then gone to seek out Sue, who was graciously willing to join her for lunch on short notice.

"Getting a call from one of the genetics lab social workers doesn't necessarily mean your test was positive," Sue said.

"Oh, come on," Laurie complained. "I just wish the woman would have told me."

"Actually, by law, they are not supposed to tell you over the phone," Sue said. "With the new Health Information Privacy Act, phone reporting is frowned upon. Laboratory personnel can never be sure exactly with whom they are speaking. They could inadvertently give the information to the wrong person, which is what the new HIPA is supposed to prevent."

"Why haven't they sent you my results?" Laurie asked. "You're my official primary-care physician."

"I wasn't, technically, when the test was

ordered. But you're right. I should have heard. At the same time, I'm not surprised. The walk-in genetics lab is just getting their act together. To tell you the truth, I'm surprised they didn't require you to have a session with one of their specially trained social workers before they took your blood. That was my understanding of the proactive way they were going to handle things. You don't have to be a rocket scientist to know that genetic testing is going to be upsetting, no matter the outcome."

Tell me about it, Laurie thought to herself.

"What's wrong with your food?" Sue asked, leaning over to look at it. "You haven't touched a bite. Do I have to take this personally?"

Laurie laughed and gave Sue a dismissive wave of her hand. Laurie confessed to being not hungry with everything going on in her life.

"Listen," Sue said, assuming a more serious tone. "If the BRCA1 test turns out to be positive, which obviously you expect, I want you to come right over to the clinic so I can get you in to see one of our top oncologists. Do we have a deal?"

"We have a deal."

"Good! Meanwhile, what's the scoop with Laura Riley? Did you get set up with a gyno appointment for your routine check?"

"I did. I'm set."

Laurie glanced at her watch. "Oops! I've got to get a move on. I don't want to be late. The social worker might decide I'm being passive-aggressive."

The women parted ways in the hall. As Laurie climbed the stairs up to the second floor, the right lower quadrant discomfort came back, causing her to hesitate. She wondered why stairs tended to aggravate whatever the nuisance was that was bothering her. It was like what she used to call a "stitch" when she ran too much as a child. True to form, it faded after only a minute. Making a fist with her right hand, she tapped against her back. The idea had occurred to her that it might be kidney or ureteral pain, but the tapping did not re-evoke the discomfort. She pushed in on her abdomen but felt nothing abnormal. She shrugged and continued on her way.

The reception room of the genetics diagnostics lab was as serene as it had been on Laurie's previous visit. The same classical music floated out of wall speakers and certainly the same impressionist prints hung from the walls. What was different was Laurie's mind-set. On the first visit, there was more curiosity than trepidation. Now it was the reverse.

"Can I help you?" a pink-smocked receptionist asked.

"My name is Laurie Montgomery, and I have an appointment with Anne Dickson at one o'clock."

"I will let her know you are here."

Laurie sat down and picked up a magazine, flipping through the pages aggressively. She looked at her watch. It was exactly one. She wondered if Ms. Dickson was going to humiliate her further by making her wait.

Time crept forward. Laurie continued flipping through the magazine without concentration. She found herself getting progressively more anxious and more irritated at the same time. She closed the magazine and put it back on the table with the others. Instead of trying to read, she sat back and closed her eyes. By force of will, she calmed herself. She thought about lying on a beach in the hot sun. If she tried, she could almost hear the waves lapping against the shore.

"Ms. Montgomery?" a voice asked.

Laurie looked up into the smiling face of a woman half her age. She was dressed in a simple white sweater with a single strand of pearls around her neck. Over her sweater was a clean white coat. In her left hand was a clipboard tucked against her side. She had her right hand extended. "I'm Anne Dickson."

Laurie got to her feet and shook the woman's hand. She then followed the woman through a side door and down a short hall. She was directed into a small, windowless room with a couch, two club chairs, a coffee table, and a file cabinet. Centered on the coffee table was a box of tissues.

Anne motioned for Laurie to sit on the sofa. She closed the door and then sat down in one of the chairs, the box of tissues conveniently between them. Anne consulted her clipboard for a moment and then looked up. From Laurie's perspective, she was a pleasant-appearing woman who could have been a mere college student in a work-study program rather than a person with at least a master's degree and probably extra training in genetics. She wore her straight, medium-length, brown hair parted in the middle, requiring her to frequently sweep it off her face and tuck it behind her ears. Her lipstick and nail polish were a dusky red-brown color.

"I appreciate you coming in on such short notice," Anne said. Her voice was soft with a slight nasal twang. "And I apologize again for having misplaced your folder."

Laurie smiled, but she could feel herself getting progressively impatient.

"I wanted to give you some background concerning what we do here in the genetic diagnostics lab," Anne continued. She crossed her legs and settled the clipboard between them. Laurie could see a small tattoo of a snake on the inside of her leg just above the ankle. "I also wanted to explain why you are talking with me rather than with one of our staff doctors. It's purely a matter of time: I have a lot, and they have a little. What that means is that I can be with you here for as long as you would like and answer all your questions. And if I can't answer them, I have immediate access to people who surely can."

Laurie didn't comment or change her expression while she silently ordered Anne to cut the fluff and just give her the damn results of the test. She leaned back abruptly, crossed her arms, and tried to remind herself that she shouldn't blame the messenger. Unfortunately, Anne and the situation was irking her to no end. She particularly found the convenient box of tissues patronizing, as if Anne expected her to break down emotionally, even though, knowing herself, Laurie knew it was a possibility.

"Now," Anne said after consulting her clipboard again and making Laurie feel as though she was getting a canned presentation. "It is important for you to know something about the science of genetics and how the field has all changed with the decoding of the human genome, meaning the sequence of all three-point-two billion nucleotide base pairs. But first let me say that you can interrupt at any moment if you don't understand something."

Laurie nodded impatiently. She couldn't help but wonder how much Anne knew about nucleotide base pairs, despite how flippantly she mentioned them. Nucleotide base pairs are the portions of the DNA molecule that form the ladder part of the molecule, and their linear order is responsible for conveying genetic information.

Anne went on to discuss Gregor Mendel's laws of genetics concerning dominant and recessive traits discovered by the monk's work with garden peas in the nineteenth century. Laurie couldn't believe what she was being subjected to, yet she didn't interrupt nor remind Anne that she was dealing with a physician who obviously would have come across Gregor Mendel's work in the course of her biological study. Laurie let the woman drone on about genes and how certain traits could be linked with other traits to form specific haplotypes that were inherited over generations.

At one point, Laurie even tuned the social worker out and concentrated on the woman's tics, which included, in addition to the almost constant sweeping of her hair behind her ear, a sustained blepharospasm when she was making a point. But Laurie's attention was drawn back to the woman when she started talking about single nucleotide polymorphisms, which she quickly began to refer to by using the acronym SNP. This was an arena of genetics that

Laurie was not quite as knowledgeable about and had been learning about only recently.

"SNPs have become extremely important," Anne said. "They are specific sites in the human genome where a single nucleotide base pair has changed by mutation or deletion or even more rarely by insertion. Between any two people, there is an average of one SNP for every thousand or so nucleotide bases."

"Why have they become so important?" Laurie found herself asking.

"Because there are now millions of them mapped across the whole human genome. They now stand as convenient markers that are linked hereditarily to specific abnormal genes. It is much easier to test for the marker than to isolate and sequence the affected gene, although we generally do both just to be one hundred percent sure. We want to be confident we are giving our patients the correct information."

"Right," Laurie said irritably. Anne's comment about abnormal genes had rudely yanked Laurie back to the reality of why she was having this conversation. It was not an intellectual exercise.

Seemingly oblivious to Laurie's mind-set and after consulting her clipboard, Anne continued her monologue in her nasal twang. All at once, Laurie had had enough. Her patience came to an abrupt end. She uncrossed her arms and raised her right hand for Anne to stop speaking. Anne caught the cue, stopped in mid-sentence, and looked at Laurie questioningly.

"With all due respect," Laurie said, trying to modulate her voice to sound calm, "there is one significant piece of information, which you either don't have or have forgotten. I happen to be a physician myself. I appreciate this background material, but I assume that the real reason I am here is because you have the results of my test. I want to know what they are. So, if you could be so kind, I would like you to tell me."

Flustered to a degree, Anne again consulted her clipboard. When she looked up, her blepharospasm was significantly more pronounced. "I didn't know you were a physician. I saw the doctor title, but I assumed it was some other kind of doctor. It wasn't down as an MD."

"It's quite all right. Am I positive for the marker for the BRCA1 gene?"

"But we haven't talked about implications."

"I am aware of the implications, and any other questions that I might have, I will direct to my oncologist."

"I see," Anne said. She looked down at her clipboard as if it might provide some help in what she was obviously finding as an uncomfortable situation.

"I don't mean to sound unappreciative of your efforts," Laurie added, "but I need to know."

"Of course," Anne said. She straightened up in her chair and looked Laurie in the eye. There was no blepharospasm. "You are indeed positive for the marker for BRCA1, which has been confirmed by sequencing the gene. I'm sorry."

Laurie looked away with unseeing eyes while she bit her lower lip. Although she fully expected the news, she could feel tears amassing on the emotional horizon. She fought against it as a matter of principle. She was determined not to use the tissues on the table in front of her. "Okay," Laurie heard herself say. She also heard Anne start to speak, but Laurie did not listen. Although Laurie was generally acutely aware of others' feelings, under the circumstances, she didn't care. She knew she was blaming the messenger to some degree.

Laurie stood up, gave Anne what amounted to a crooked smile, and headed for the door. With her palms as wet as they were, she had no intention of shaking the woman's hand. She could hear Anne following her and calling her name, but she didn't even look back. She crossed the reception area of the clinic with a determined step and walked out into the hospital corridor.

On the first floor, Laurie appreciated being surrounded by the surging crowds coming and going in the busy hospital. The anonymity provided an unexpected solace from her mental turmoil. There was a bench opposite the information booth, and Laurie took a moment to sit down. She took a deep breath. She was calming down. What she needed to do was decide what to do next. She'd promised Sue she'd come over to the clinic ASAP to set up an appointment with the oncologist, but as Laurie sat there, she felt the need for a more personal interaction. She thought of Roger and wondered if he'd be available.

The administrative area was close, and as the connecting door closed behind her, Laurie realized that she now preferred the calmness to the hospital lobby's chaos. Her shoes didn't make a sound on the carpet. Trying not to think about the reality of a genetic time bomb ticking away in every one of her cells, she walked down to the area of Roger's office. One of the secretaries recognized her from earlier.

"Dr. Rousseau is in his office now," the secretary said, looking at Laurie from behind her monitor.

Laurie nodded an acknowledgment and walked to Roger's doorway. His door was ajar. He was sitting at his desk, going over paperwork. Laurie knocked on the jamb, and Roger looked up. He was dressed as he usually was at the hospital, in a freshly laundered, crisp white shirt. He had on a golden silk tie, the texture and color of which contrasted nicely with his craggy, permanently tanned face.

"My word!" he said, catching sight of Laurie and leaping to his feet. "I just left a message on your voicemail two seconds ago. What a coincidence." He came around from behind his desk, and closed his door.

Turning back to her, he gave her a quick hug and a kiss on the forehead. He didn't notice that her arms stayed limp at her sides. "I'm so glad you are here. I have so much to talk with you about." He turned his two straight-backed chairs around to face each other. He motioned for Laurie to sit, and he did the same.

"You can't believe the morning I've had," Roger gushed. "There were two more post-operative deaths last night, just like the previous four: both of them young and healthy."

"I know," Laurie said in a subdued voice. "I've already autopsied both of them. It was what I was called you about earlier."

"And what did you find?"

"There was nothing: no pathology," Laurie said in the same quiet manner. "They were like the previous four."

"I knew it! I knew it!" Roger said, punching the air with a fist. He stood up and paced back and forth in his tiny office. "I called an emergency meeting of the morbidity/mortality committee this morning, despite our having just met two days ago. I presented the two cases as evidence that these past five weeks have been no more than a pause. I argued vainly that we have to do something. But, oh, no, we're not to rock the boat, since the media might get wind of it. I have half the mind to make an anonymous call to the media so it wouldn't be an issue, but of course I won't. I even went into the president's office after the meeting to try to convince him to change his stance, but it was like talking to the wall. I even managed to get him angry at me by what he called my 'damned dogged determination.' "

Laurie watched Roger pace but couldn't make eye contact. At the moment, the series of suspicious deaths at the Manhattan General was not what was on her mind, but she didn't have the emotional strength to counter Roger's current vehemence about them.

"And then, to make matters worse," Roger added, "we had a homicidal mugging in our parking garage this morning. I mean, I'm starting to get a complex about all this. None of this happened before I came on board."

Roger finally stopped moving and made eye contact with Laurie. His expression suggested that he was looking for sympathy, but it changed when he noticed hers. "Why the long face?" he asked. He bent over to look more closely, then quickly sat down. "I'm sorry. Here I've been ranting and raging and ignoring you, and you're upset. What's wrong?"

Laurie shut her eyes tightly and looked away. Roger's sudden solicitousness reawakened the emotions she'd felt the moment Anne Dickson had given her the definitive news. She felt Roger's hand on her shoulder.

"What is it, Laurie? What's wrong?"

At first, Laurie could only shake her head, for fear that talking would release a flood of tears. She hated her emotionalism. It was such a damn handicap. She straightened up and took a deep breath, letting it out in a sustained huff. "I'm sorry," she managed.

"You don't have anything to be sorry about. I was the one carrying on like a selfish, insensitive brute. What's happened?"

Laurie cleared her throat and began her BRCA1 saga, and once she started talking, she ironically got progressively less emotional, as if her professional persona was able to take over. She talked about her mother and her recent surgery and the fact that she was also positive for the mutated gene. She also mentioned her father's advice to get the test. Leaving out Jack's role, she described how she'd come over to the Manhattan General and had the blood drawn the day she and Roger had met. She then explained how she had successfully forgotten all about it until the call she had gotten that morning from Anne Dickson. She concluded by saying that she'd just come from an interview where she'd been told that she was positive for the BRCA1 marker and for the mutated gene itself, so there was no chance for laboratory error. She admitted she'd blamed the messenger, despite trying to avoid not doing so, and joked that she'd denied the poor woman the opportunity to ask her the quintessential therapist's question: how Laurie felt about the news. Laurie ended by chuckling.

"I'm amazed you can find humor in this," Roger said.

"I feel better after talking to you."

"I'm so sorry about all this," Roger said with a voice that suggested utter sincerity. "What are you going to do? What's the next step?"

"As soon as I leave here, I'm supposed to head over to the clinic to see Sue Passero. She's offered to help arrange an appointment in the near future with an oncologist."

She gave Roger a pat on the thigh and started to stand up.

"Hold on," Roger said, reaching out and pressing down on her shoulder to keep her in her seat. "Not so fast! Since the social worker didn't have a chance, let me ask you how you feel. I imagine it's something like finding out your best friend is your mortal enemy."

Laurie peered into the depths of Roger's dark brown eyes. She found herself wondering if he was asking the question as a close friend or as a doctor. If it was the former, was his interest truly sincere? He seemed to have a knack for saying the right thing, but what was his motivation? Then she chided herself for questioning, but after the marriage and children flap, she wasn't sure of anything.

"I guess I haven't had time to feel much of anything," Laurie said after a pause. She was tempted to say something about her newly recognized ability to compartmentalize her thoughts to the point of just not thinking about anything she didn't want to. But then she decided it was too long a story, since she wanted to get over to the Kaufman Clinic building to see Sue. In the long run, it was the oncologist who was going to be key, and the sooner the appointment was scheduled, the better she would feel.

"There must be something you can share with me," Roger persisted. He still had his hand resting on her shoulder. "You can't learn something as disturbing as this without having some specific fears."

"I suppose you are right," Laurie admitted reluctantly. "For me, some of the suggested prophylactic measures and their side effects are the scariest. For instance, the idea of electively losing my fertility by having my ovaries removed is . . ."

Laurie stopped in mid-sentence. For her, the thought that suddenly raced through her mind like a tornado was the equivalent of being rudely slapped in the face. It brought an instantaneous adrenaline rush that caused her pulse to race and the ends of her fingers to tingle. For a moment, she even felt dizzy, such that she had to grasp the edge of her chair to keep from toppling over.

Luckily, the dizziness passed as quickly as it had appeared. She could tell Roger was talking, but for the moment, she couldn't hear him, as the idea that had occurred to her kept reverberating in her mind with an effect akin to claps of thunder. The old adage "Be careful what you wish for because it might come to pass" again flashed into her consciousness.

Laurie stood up abruptly, effectively pulling Roger to his feet as well, since he still had his hand on her shoulder. All at once, she wanted to be by herself.

"Laurie!" Roger demanded. Using his two hands, he gave her shoulders a shake. "What's wrong? You didn't finish your sentence."

"I'm sorry," Laurie said in a voice that was calmer than she felt. She peeled Roger's reluctant hands from her shoulders. "I have to go."

"I can't let you go like this. What are you thinking about? Are you depressed?"

"No, I'm not depressed. Not yet, anyway. I have to go, Roger. I'll call you later."

Laurie turned to leave, but Roger grabbed

her arm. "I have to be sure you won't hurt yourself in any way."

Catching Roger's drift, Laurie shook her head. "Rest assured, I'm not going to hurt myself. I just need to be alone for a while." She extracted her arm from Roger's grasp.

"You'll call me."

"Yes, I'll call you," Laurie said as she opened the door.

"Am I going to see you tonight?"

Laurie hesitated in the doorway and then turned around. "Tonight's not going to work. But I'll be in touch."

Laurie left Roger's office, rounded the nearest secretary's desk, and walked deliberately down the hallway, resisting the inclination to run. She could feel Roger's eyes on her back, but she didn't turn around. Passing through the doorway that separated the administrative area from the rest of the hospital, she slipped into the crowd. Once again, the anonymity was comforting. Instead of dashing out of the building, which was her initial intention, she regained her seat opposite the information booth and spent the next quarter of an hour thinking of the consequences of her disturbing notion.

eleven

The Thursday-afternoon conference at the Office of the Chief Medical Examiner was a command performance, according to the dictates of the chief, Harold Bingham. Although he frequently did not attend himself, citing pressing administrative duties, everyone else under his command in the five boroughs of New York had to attend. The rule was strictly enforced by the deputy chief, Calvin Washington, unless prior dispensation had been granted, which required deathbed illness or the equivalent. Consequently, the forensic pathologists from the branch offices in Brooklyn, Queens, and Staten Island all had to make the weekly hajj to Mecca for the questionable enlightenment that the conferences offered. For those medical examiners assigned to the home office serving Manhattan and the Bronx, the onus was far less of an imposition, since all they had to do was take the elevator from the fifth floor down to the first.

Laurie generally found the conferences entertaining to a degree, particularly the informal social period prior to the meeting. It was during this time that the examiners traded war stories of the week's more intellectually challenging or plainly bizarre cases. Laurie rarely contributed to these "sidewalk" discussions but enjoyed listening. Unfortunately, enjoyment was not the situation on this particular Thursday. After learning that she was positive for the BRCA1 marker and then having the disturbing worry emerge in Roger's office, she felt shell-shocked, almost numb, and certainly didn't feel social in the slightest. Coming into the room, she didn't join the group around the coffee and donuts, but rather had taken a seat near the door to the hall in hopes of possibly slipping away at some convenient and unobtrusive time.

The conference room was of moderate size, and its décor had a particularly tired look that suggested it was much older than its purported forty-four years. To the left, where a door communicated directly into Bingham's office, stood a scarred and scratched lectern with its own little picture lamp that no longer worked and a goose-necked microphone that did. Arrayed in front of the podium were four rows of equally battered seats fixed to the floor and outfitted with hinged writing surfaces. The seats gave the room the appearance of a small lecture hall and allowed it to fulfill its major function: Bingham's news conferences. In the back of the room stood a library table that presently supported the refreshments, and around which were grouped the city's medical examiners: everyone except the two higher-ups and Jack. A babble of voices interspersed with laughter floated around the room.

Unlike Laurie, Jack did not like anything about the Thursday conferences. Jack had had a run-in with one of the medical examiners from the Brooklyn office over the sister of one of Jack's basketball buddies and refused to even socialize with the man. The same feelings were extended to the branch chief when he supported his underling in the dispute. Even though Jack denied that it was deliberate, he always arrived late, to Calvin's irritation.

The door to Bingham's office opened, and Calvin's massive body appeared. He was clutching a folder, which he opened on the lectern. His dark eyes scanned the room, briefly connecting with Laurie's before moving on. He was obviously taking attendance.

"All right!" Calvin bellowed when no one paid him any heed. Thanks to the microphone, his voice reverberated around the room like a kettledrum. "Let's get under way here."

Calvin kept his head bent down while he organized his papers on the lectern's slanted surface. The medical examiners quickly broke off from their conversations and filed into the rows of chairs to take their seats. Calvin began the meeting the way Bingham used to, back when the chief regularly attended. First, he launched into a summary of the previous week's statistics.

As Calvin's voice droned on, Laurie's mind wandered. Although she was usually good at slipping into her professional persona on command and leaving her personal problems for another time, she couldn't do it presently. Her new worry kept popping back unpleasantly into her consciousness, such that it even trumped the BRCA1 concern. The problem was that she had no idea what she would do if her fears were realized.

The hall door immediately to Laurie's left opened, and Jack walked in. Calvin stopped his presentation, glared at Jack, and said sarcastically, "I'm so glad you were able to grace us with your presence, Dr. Stapleton."

"I wouldn't miss it for the world," Jack answered, causing Laurie to wince. With her fear of authority figures, she couldn't understand how Jack could be so transparently brazen with Calvin. She thought it was a kind of masochism on Jack's part.

Jack looked down at Laurie with an exaggerated questioning expression. She was sitting in the seat he always preferred, and for the same reason Laurie had taken it. He gave her shoulder a squeeze before taking the aisle seat directly in front of her. With Jack's head in the line of her vision, she found it even harder to concentrate on what Calvin was saying. It was a visual reminder that, one way or the other, she was going to have to have a serious conversation with him.

After giving the statistics, Calvin launched into his usual discussion of cogent administrative issues that usually involved some decrease in city funding, and this week's conference was no different. Instead of listening, Laurie watched Jack. Although he had just sat down, his head started the telltale bobbing that suggested that he had already begun falling asleep, causing her to worry that Calvin was going to notice and fly into a rage. When authority figures got angry, even if it wasn't directed at her, it still made her feel uncomfortable.

Either Calvin didn't notice or he just elected to ignore the disrespect, because he concluded his remarks without making a scene and introduced the chief of the Brooklyn office, Dr. Jim Bennett.

Each one of the chiefs from the respective borough offices stood up to give their presentations. When Dick Katzenburg from Queens got behind the microphone and started speaking, Laurie had a flashback to her cocaine conspiracy twelve years earlier. It was at a Thursday-afternoon conference that she had the idea of discussing her overdoses with the group, and the ensuing discussion had been helpful, thanks to Dick. She wondered why the idea of doing the same with the Manhattan General cases hadn't occurred to her, and she thought about bringing it up. But then she changed her mind. She was too stressed-out to deal with the anxiety of talking in front of the group. But then she waffled again when she reminded herself that Calvin seemed to be in a reasonably tolerant mood.

At the end of Margaret Hauptman's presentation of the Staten Island statistics, Calvin reclaimed the podium and asked if anyone else wanted the microphone for any other business. It was a pro forma offer that was rarely accepted, since people were eager to leave. After a moment of painful indecision, Laurie tentatively raised her hand. Any chance of changing her mind was dashed when Calvin quickly but reluctantly recognized her. Jack twisted around in his seat in front of her and gave her an exasperated questioning expression that implied: *Why are you extending this agony?*

Laurie walked unsteadily up to the podium. She felt a jolt of adrenaline, since speaking in front of groups always intimidated her. As she adjusted the microphone, she berated herself for getting into such a situation. She certainly didn't need any more stress.

"First, let me apologize," Laurie began. "I hadn't prepared for this, but it just occurred to me that I would like to get some general response from everyone about a current series of mine."

Laurie looked down at Calvin and could tell that his eyes had narrowed. She sensed that he knew what was coming and didn't approve. She glanced back at Jack, and as soon as her eyes connected with his, he positioned his fingers like a gun and pretended to shoot himself in the head.

With such negative vibes, Laurie felt even more insecure. To collect her thoughts, she looked down at the lectern's defaced wooden surface with its myriad initials and doodles encased with ballpoint-pen marks. Vowing to avoid making eye contact with either Calvin or Jack, she raised her eyes and launched into a short description of her Sudden Adult Death Syndrome, or SADS, a term she admitted she'd coined when talking with a professional colleague five weeks ago, about four totally unexpected, hospital-based cardiac arrests that had resisted resuscitation. She said she now had six cases spanning a six-week period, all of which had similar demographics: young, healthy, and within twenty-four hours of elective surgery. She went on to say that there was no pathology on gross or microscopic, although on the last two cases, she had yet to do the microscopic, since they had been posted that very morning. She concluded by saying that despite toxicology failing to come up with any possible arrhythmic agent, she suspected that the manner of death in these cases was not natural or accidental.

Laurie let her voice trail off. Her mouth was bone-dry. She would have loved a drink of water, but she stayed where she was. The implication of her monologue was immediately clear to the group, and for a few seconds, silence reigned in the conference room. Then a hand shot up, and Laurie called on the individual.

"What about electrolytes: sodium, potassium, and particularly calcium?"

"The lab reported all electrolytes from all the usual sample sources to be entirely normal," Laurie responded. She then called on another person who raised his hand.

"Are the patients related in any way other than all being young, healthy, and having just had surgery?"

"Not that is apparent. I've made it a point to search for commonalities, but I haven't found any other than what I have mentioned. The cases involve mostly different doctors, different procedures, different anesthetic agents, and, for the most part, different medications, even for postoperative pain."

"Where have they occurred?"

"All six have been at the same hospital: the Manhattan General."

"Which has an extremely low death rate," Calvin snapped. He'd had enough. He stood up, approached the podium, and used his bulk to nudge Laurie aside. He bent the microphone up, and a harsh squeal emanated from the speakers as if in protest. "Calling these disparate cases at this stage 'a series' is misleading and prejudicial because, as Dr. Montgomery has admitted, they are not related. I've told Dr. Montgomery this before, and I'm telling her again. I'm also telling this august assemblage that this is an in-house discussion that doesn't leave this room. OCME is not going to tarnish the reputation of one of the city's premier tertiary-care centers with unsubstantiated innuendo."

"Six is rather a lot for a coincidence," Jack said. He had revived when Laurie got up to speak. Although he was not asleep, he was slouched back in his seat with his legs draped over the seat in front of him.

"Would you kindly show some respect, Dr. Stapleton," Calvin growled.

Jack put his feet down on the floor and sat up. "Four was borderline, but six is too many when they are all at the same hospital. Still, I'm going to vote for accidental. Something in the hospital is affecting these patients' conduction systems."

Dick Katzenburg raised his hand. Calvin motioned with his head for him to speak.

"My colleague at the Queens office just

reminded me that we saw some similar cases," Dick said. "It's our recollection that the demographics were quite similar: all relatively young and supposedly healthy. The last case was at least a few months ago, and we haven't had one since."

"How many overall?" Laurie asked.

Dick leaned toward Bob Novak, his deputy, and listened for a moment, then straightened up. "We think it was also six. But it was spread over a period of several months with a number of examiners. Just when we began to be a bit curious about them, they stopped, and as a consequence, they have sort of dropped off our radar. It's my recollection that all were eventually signed out as natural, even though no significant pathology was found. I know for certain that toxicology was negative on all of them, because that would have certainly been brought to my attention."

"Were they postoperative?" Laurie asked. She was taken aback, excited, and pleased. It would be déjà vu if her series were to double from having brought up the issue at a Thursday conference. And if it did double, the profile of these cases would surely be even more of a mental diversion than it had been to date.

"I believe so," Dick said. "Sorry that I can't be more definitive."

"I understand," Laurie said. "Where did these deaths occur?"

"At Saint Francis Hospital."

"Ah, the plot thickens," Jack commented. "Isn't St. Francis another AmeriCare hospital?"

"Dr. Stapleton!" Calvin snapped. "Kindly maintain a modicum of decorum! Allow yourself to be recognized if you wish to contribute to the conversation."

"It is an AmeriCare institution," Dick said, turning toward Jack and ignoring Calvin.

"How soon can I get their names and accession numbers?" Laurie asked.

"I'll e-mail them to you as soon as I get back to the Queens office," Dick said. "Or we can just call my secretary. I think she could find the list."

"I'd like them as soon as possible," Laurie said. "I'd like to get their hospital charts, and the sooner I get the accession numbers to one of our investigators, the better."

"Fine by me," Dick said agreeably.

"Any other business?" Calvin asked. He

scanned the group, then concluded the meeting. "See you all next Thursday."

As most of the medical examiners stood up, stretched, and recommenced their conversations that the meeting had cut short, Dick made his way over to Laurie. He had his cell phone pressed up against his ear and was describing the location of a folder in his desk. He motioned for Laurie to wait.

Glancing over at Jack, Laurie saw him immediately duck out of the conference room. She had hoped to talk with him, even if only briefly, and thank him for being ultimately supportive during her mini-presentation.

"Do you have something to write on?" Dick asked.

Laurie produced a pen and the back of an envelope. While Laurie kept her finger on the envelope to keep it steady on the writing surface of one of the chairs, Dick wrote down the names and the accession numbers. He thanked his secretary and rang off. "Well, there you have them," he said. "Let me know if I can be of assistance in any other way. I have to say, it does seem curious."

"I imagine I'll be able to access what I

need from the data bank, but if I can't, I'll be in touch. Thanks, Dick! This is the second time you have helped me out. Do you remember those cocaine cases twelve years ago?"

"Now that you mention it, of course I remember, although it seems like it was in a different lifetime. At any rate, I'm glad to be of service."

"Dr. Montgomery!" Calvin called. "Can I speak to you for a moment?" Although his comment was presented as a request, it was more of a command.

Laurie gave Dick a parting wave and then stepped warily over to Calvin. "If these cases of Dick's turn out to resemble yours demographically, I want you to let me know. In the meantime, the proscription of talking about your supposed series with anyone outside of the OCME still holds. Am I clear on that? You and I have had disagreements about information leaks to the media in the past, and I don't want it to happen again."

"I understand," Laurie said nervously. "Don't worry! I learned my lesson, and I certainly would not go to the media. At the same time, I must admit I have been speaking with the chief of the medical staff over at the Manhattan General right from the beginning about the cases. He happens to be a friend."

"What's his name?"

"Dr. Roger Rousseau."

"Since he's on the staff, I suppose it's safe to assume he is aware of the sensitive nature of the issue."

"Most definitely."

"I suppose it's equally safe to assume he's not apt to go to the media."

"Hardly," Laurie said. She was feeling more confident. Calvin was definitely in a mild-mannered mood. "Yet Dr. Rousseau is rightfully concerned, and I believe he would want to hear if Dick's cases are indeed similar. It would give him the opportunity to talk with his counterpart at Saint Francis and make him feel he's not the only one with such a problem."

"Well, I don't see any harm in talking with him, provided you are clear the OCME officially does not currently agree with your assessment of the manner of death, and at the moment will back the Queens office's disposition."

"Certainly, and thank you," Laurie said. It was good to clear the air. She'd carried a twinge of guilt from having talked to Roger about the deaths when she'd first met him, despite Calvin's wishes.

Leaving the conference room, Laurie headed directly to the investigators' office. She was beginning to calm down from the anxiety of talking in front of the group and from having to confront Calvin. She felt even better when she found Cheryl Meyers at her desk, since her workday had officially ended an hour earlier. In Laurie's estimation, Cheryl was the most talented investigator at the OCME and just as hard a worker as Janice. Laurie had Cheryl copy the list of names and accession numbers Dick had provided, and Laurie asked her to put in a request for copies of the patients' charts from St. Francis Hospital.

"What about the autopsy folders and death certificates?" Cheryl asked.

As Laurie had told Dick, she said she'd first try to see what she could obtain from the computerized database. If she needed help for hard copies, Laurie said she'd get back to her.

Clutching her envelope and silently reading the names over and over, Laurie rode up in the elevator. Her intuition told her loudly and clearly that the demographics and details of this new list of victims was going to match her own. Her SADS series was now twelve people.

Once on the fifth floor, Laurie hesitated. It took her a moment to build up her confidence. She wanted to go down to Jack's office and talk to him, even if only briefly, about her disturbing, potential epiphany she had had in Rogers office. She thought it would assuage her anxieties to share them, but she didn't quite know what she wanted to say or even how to begin. Attempting to steel herself against all the uncertainties, she took a fortifying breath and started off.

The closer she got, the slower she walked. She hesitated again before stepping into view in the doorway, appalled at her indecision. She was becoming either a coward or hopelessly wishy-washy, or a mixture of both. Laurie looked back longingly over her shoulder at her own door some forty feet away and waffled.

Hearing a desk chair scrape back within the office in front of her, and sensing that Jack was coming out, Laurie almost fled in a panic. Fortunately, there wasn't enough time, and it wasn't even Jack. It was Chet who literally bumped into her in his haste.

"Oh, gosh, I'm sorry!" Chet offered as he grabbed Laurie by the shoulders to keep from bowling her over as the two stumbled back a step. He immediately let go of Laurie and bent down to pick up the jacket he'd dropped.

"It's quite all right," Laurie said. She recovered quickly, although her pulse was racing.

"I'm off to my body-sculpting class," Chet offered as an explanation. "Obviously, I'm late. And if you are looking for Jack, you missed him. He had some important basketball game at his neighborhood court and bolted out of here ten minutes ago."

"Oh, too bad," Laurie said. She was actually relieved. "No problem. I'll catch him in the morning."

Chet waved good-bye and ran down the corridor toward the elevator. Laurie walked toward her office. Suddenly, she was very tired. The day had taken its toll. She looked forward to getting back to her apartment and taking a hot bath.

As Laurie suspected, her office was empty. She sat down at her desk and typed in her password. For the next thirty minutes, she downloaded the records on the six cases from Queens. Although the forensic investigators' reports were not even close in quality to those done by Janice, there was enough information for Laurie to conclude that the cases were indeed similar to hers. The deaths were all in the early-morning hours between two and four, the ages ranged from twenty-six to forty-two, none of the patients had a history of cardiac problems, and all were within twenty-four hours of elective surgery.

When she was finished, Laurie reached for her phone and dialed Roger's number. She had promised to call, and this was as good a time as any, especially since she had something particular to say besides explaining her behavior in his office. As the call went through, she found herself hoping on this occasion to get his voicemail to avoid having to resist being drawn into a conversation about things that she didn't want to discuss, but unfortunately, Roger answered on the second ring with his usual cheerful voice. When he realized it was Laurie, he became immediately solicitous.

"Are you all right?" he asked anxiously.

"I'm holding my own," Laurie answered. She wasn't going to lie. "I'm looking forward to getting back to my apartment. It hasn't been my idea of a great day. In the meantime, I've learned something within the hour that I think you will find interesting. During our Thursday-afternoon interdepartmental conference, it was brought to my attention that there had been six deaths at Saint Francis Hospital in Queens that so far sound strikingly similar to those at the Manhattan General."

"Really?" Roger questioned. He was both surprised and interested.

"I've downloaded their death certificates and investigative reports, and I've ordered copies of their hospital charts. Getting the charts will take a while, but in the interim, I'll get what I can over to you tomorrow. I assume you'll want to discuss this with the chief of the medical staff at Saint Francis."

"Most definitely, if only to commiserate with him." Switching gears, Roger added, "Now, let's talk about you. I have to say I've been worried sick since you mysteriously stopped in mid-sentence here in my office and then essentially walked out. What's going on in your mind?"

Laurie twisted the phone cord in her fingers while she tried to think of something appropriate to say. It was not her intent by any stretch of the imagination to cause Roger anxiety, but there was no way she wanted to discuss what was dominating her thoughts, especially when she didn't even know for certain that her worries were justified.

"Are you still there?" Roger questioned.

"I'm still here," Laurie assured him. "Roger, I'm all right. Truly! And as soon as I feel comfortable talking about what is on my mind, I promise I will do so. Can you accept that for the time being?"

"I suppose," Roger said without enthusiasm. "Is it about your being positive for the BRCA1 marker?"

"Indirectly, to some extent. But please, Roger, no more questions."

"Are you sure you don't want to get together tonight?"

"Not tonight. I'll call you in the morning. I promise."

"Okay, I'll be waiting to hear from you. But if you have a change of heart, I'll be home all evening."

Laurie hung up the phone, leaving her

hand resting on the receiver. She felt guilty about causing Roger distress, but she was not about to talk to him about what was on her mind.

Pushing back from the desk and standing up, Laurie looked down at the stack of new material from the OCME database. She thought about taking the papers home with her and adding the names to her matrix, but then quickly dismissed the idea. She could deal with her burgeoning series the following day.

With her coat over her arm and her umbrella in one hand, Laurie turned off the light and locked her office door. Next stop was the drugstore, and after that, her apartment. As Laurie pushed the elevator's down button, she could almost feel the delicious sensation of slipping into an enveloping hot bath. For her, a bath was as much a therapeutic experience as it was an opportunity to get clean.

twelve

". . . One hundred ninety-nine, two hundred," Jazz counted to herself before stopping her sit-ups. She lay back on the inclined plane of the sit-up apparatus, keeping her hands behind her head while she stared up at the ceiling panels of the health club's weight room. She was breathing heavily from pushing herself during her entire workout by doing twice her normal number of repetitions with each exercise and at each weight station. Such exertion usually had a cathartic effect on her, cleansing her mind, and today was no different. She felt better. She closed her eyes and let her body relax, despite her head being lower than the rest of her, causing her blood to rush to her head.

The problem had been that Jazz hadn't been able to stop fretting about the snafus with Lewis and Sobczyk to the point that sleep had been difficult. Prior to those two messy episodes, she'd done ten missions without a speck of trouble. It irritated her that people could be so difficult, especially Lewis grabbing her arm the way he did. Sobczyk hadn't been much better, the way she gurgled and writhed around at just the wrong time. The only good part was that that sorry situation had pushed her over the edge as far as Susan Chapman was concerned. Jazz had fantasized about getting rid of her from day one, and now it was done.

Jazz slipped her feet from beneath the padded restraints and swung her legs over to the side. She stood up and glanced in the mirror at her very red and perspiring face. She grabbed her towel and wiped the sweat off her forehead before glancing up at the clock. Although she had essentially doubled her entire workout routine, it had taken her only thirty minutes longer.

Letting her eyes briefly sweep around the room, she caught the inevitable furtive looks from the mostly male occupants, including blond Mr. Ivy League, whom she hadn't seen for a while. In the mood she was in, she almost wished he'd try to talk to her again. This time, she wouldn't be so nice.

Knowing that she had to get a move on if she was to get to work reasonably early, Jazz headed for the locker room. Now that she had her irritation about the Lewis and Sobczyk episodes under control, she was able to think more clearly about them. Both were hardly her fault. Rotating her left arm, she looked at the still-raw scratch marks. She couldn't believe the guy had had the nerve to scratch her like that, and she hoped to hell he wasn't HIV-positive. He certainly deserved what he got. In the future, Jazz reminded herself, she should steer clear of the subject's free hand. As far as the Sobczyk debacle was concerned, that was Chapman's fault, and now that

Chapman was history, there was little to worry about.

With her towel and her Walkman in one hand, Jazz used the other to push into the woman's locker room. She tossed the towel into the convenient hamper, and with the Walkman under her arm, she took a Coke from the ice-filled tub. After a glance around to make sure no one was watching, she walked on. She flipped the tab and took a long, satisfying slug.

Ultimately, the real threat of the foul-ups with Lewis and Sobczyk was the possibility of discovery. Mr. Bob had warned about ripples, and both episodes had been like ten-foot waves. Participating in Operation Winnow had been the best thing that had ever happened to Jazz, and she shuddered to think of what might have occurred had she not wasted Chapman when she did. Or, worse yet, what might have happened if Chapman had gone directly to the nursing supervisor that morning instead of walking out to her car. Jazz didn't even like to think about it, because everything she had worked for could have gone down the drain. Back at the beginning of her relationship with Mr. Bob, she had decided that she was not going to let anything or anybody stand between her and her newfound success. Just before she came to the health club, she'd gone online and checked her account. As she had anticipated, her balance was now close to fifty thousand dollars. Just looking at the figures had made her feel like she had died and gone to heaven.

"Hey," someone taunted. "I heard you were a nurse, not a neurosurgeon!"

Jazz stopped and turned to look at the person who had spoken to her. She was a fleshy woman, trussed up in a towel like a cannoli. "Do I know you?"

"You told me you were a neurosurgeon," the woman said disdainfully. "And the trusting person I am, I believed you. Well, I know differently now."

A derisive half-laugh escaped from Jazz's mouth. Vaguely, she remembered making such a comment, but the fact that this tub of lard remembered it and had the nerve to bring it up was a bad joke. "Why don't you get a life, you porker?" Jazz scoffed and then walked on before the woman could respond. Jazz shook her head and wondered if she should begin checking out another health club. At her current one, it used to be just the men who irked her, but now that the women were starting, it might be time to move on.

Jazz didn't take long in the shower, nor did she dillydally, climbing into her scrubs and white jacket. When she pulled on her oversized olive-drab coat, she checked her pockets as she always did. She fondled the Glock and the Blackberry while she scanned the locker to make sure she'd taken everything she wanted.

As Jazz rode down in the elevator, she wondered when she'd get her next mission for Operation Winnow. She hoped it would be soon, and not just for the money. With the problems on the last two cases making the possibility of discovery a realistic concern, she worried about being spooked. She'd learned about dealing with such negative thoughts in the military. The idea was to jump right back into the water.

On the upper garage level, she headed over toward her waiting car. It gleamed in the garage's raw fluorescent light and looked awesome despite the fact that it was no longer virginal. On the back left quarter panel was a smudge of yellow paint and a slight dent from a recent run-in with a taxicab. Jazz wasn't happy about the defect in the vehicle's otherwise flawless surface, but the damage to the taxi and the irritation of the driver compensated for the minor blemish.

When Jazz was about ten feet away, she activated the door release, and she could hear the mechanical clicks as the doors unlocked. Coming alongside, she glanced at her reflection in the tinted windows and fluffed her fringed hair with her fingers. She opened the driver's-side door, tossed her gym bag into the passenger-side seat, and swung herself up behind the wheel. As she stuck the key in the ignition with anticipation of hearing the roar of the V-8, a hand gripped her shoulder.

Jazz almost went through the roof. Spinning around fast enough to jab herself in the hip with the steering wheel, she shot a glance into the backseat. In the half-light of the interior, made dim by the darkly tinted windows, all she could see were the outlines of two men. Their faces were hidden in shadow. While Jazz frantically struggled to get her hand into her coat pocket to get the

Glock, one of the men spoke: "Howdy, Doc JR!"

"Jesus, Mr. Bob!" Jazz blurted. She gave up on the Glock. Instead, she slapped her hand over her forehead. "You scared me half to death."

"That wasn't the intention," Mr. Bob said unapologetically. "We're just being discreet." He was sitting on the passenger side of the back seat, leaning slightly forward. The other man was sitting back with his arms crossed.

"How the hell did you get in here?" Jazz questioned. She squinted to try to get a look at the other guy while rubbing the top of her iliac crest. It was throbbing from its painful contact with the steering wheel.

"Easy. We kept a key when we delivered the vehicle. I'd like you to meet a colleague of mine: Mr. Dave."

"I can't see either one of you," Jazz complained. "Should I turn on the interior light?"

"It's not necessary, and I prefer you don't."

"What are you doing here?"

"We came for reassurance."

"Reassurance about what?"

"For one thing, we want to be certain the

two patients whose names you got yesterday were sanctioned."

"Absolutely. I did them both last night." Jazz felt her pulse quicken. Nervously, she worried that Bob had somehow learned about the screwups.

"Then there's the little matter of a nurse getting whacked in the Manhattan General's parking lot, supposedly for a measly fifty bucks. What can you tell us about that sorry incident?"

"Nothing. I haven't heard a thing. When did it happen?" Jazz ran her tongue around the inside of her mouth. It had gone bone-dry. But she purposefully didn't look away or squirm in her seat, thanks to her military interrogation training.

"This morning, between seven and eight. The name was Susan Chapman. Did you know her?"

"Susan Chapman! Of course I knew her. She was the incompetent charge nurse on my floor."

"That's what we thought, and frankly, that's why we are concerned. We wanted to be reassured you weren't involved, considering your reputation, Doc JR. I know that officer bastard in San Diego had it coming, but you did shoot him, even if not lethally. Are you sure this Susan Chapman didn't get in your face and push you over the edge, something like the marine officer? We feel it is kind of a coincidence she got shot, considering your history, and she being your immediate superior."

"Is that what this is about? You think I shot Susan Chapman? Hey, no way! I mean, Susan and I might have had our differences, but that was minor stuff like her always giving me the crap patients or giving me lip because I sat down for two seconds. There's no way I'd shoot her. Come on! What do you think I am, crazy?"

"The point here is that we have to be certain your behavior is beyond reproach. I made that very clear when I recruited you into the program. Remember! There can't be any ripples. Of course, all this is predicated on your wanting to remain an active participant in Operation Winnow."

"Absolutely," Jazz said with conviction.

"You're happy with your compensation, and I trust this SUV we're sitting in has been an enjoyment?"

"There's no question. I'm very happy."

"Good! Now, do I have your word that if

there's a problem in any aspect in relation to your position, or your fellow workers, or the work that you do for us, you'll give me a call with the special number I gave you? I trust you still have the number?"

"I thought that telephone number was just for emergencies."

"I'd consider what I'm talking about an emergency. I want you to call if you are ever tempted to do anything out of the ordinary, particularly anything violent that might stimulate an investigation like I'm certain this murder of the charge nurse will do. Remember! I told you from the beginning that for us, security is of the utmost importance, since any breach could put the entire operation in jeopardy. I'm sure you don't want to do that."

"Of course not."

"We consider any type of investigation worrisome, especially if you are drawn into it."

"I agree."

"Then we see eye to eye."

"Most definitely."

Mr. Bob turned to his companion. "Is there anything you'd like to say or ask Doc JR?"

"How many days a week do you come to this sports club?" Mr. Dave asked. He uncrossed his arms and leaned forward slightly.

Jazz shrugged. "I don't know, maybe five or six, sometimes even seven. Why?"

"So, other than your apartment or the hospital, this is the only other place you spend significant amounts of your time?"

"I suppose."

"Any current boyfriends or close girlfriends?"

"Not really," Jazz said. Although she could not see the man's face, from his voice, she felt that Mr. Dave was younger than Mr. Bob. "What the hell are these questions for?"

"We always like to know our agents," Mr. Bob said, "and the more facts we have, the better we know them."

"Seems rather personal to me."

"That's the kind of operation this is," Mr. Bob said with a smile. His teeth looked particularly white in the dim light. "Do you have any questions for us?"

"Yeah! What are your real names?" Jazz laughed nervously. She felt she was at a distinct disadvantage with them knowing about her and she knowing nothing about them.

"Sorry, that's confidential."

"Then I don't have any questions."

"Okay," Mr. Bob said. "We have something for you: another name. I trust that you are working tonight."

"Absolutely! I'm on the next four nights, so I'm available. What's the name?"

"Clark Mulhausen."

Jazz repeated the name. With a new mission, she was now fully recovered from the shock of the men surprising her in the Hummer and from Chapman's murder being mentioned. In fact, she was now elated. She was, in her words, jumping right back into the water.

"So you'll be able to do Clark tonight?"

"Consider it done," Jazz said with a confident, wry smile.

Mr. Bob opened his door and got out. Mr. Dave did the same on his side. "Remember! No ripples!" Mr. Bob reminded her before closing his door.

"No ripples," Jazz repeated over her shoulder, but she wasn't sure the men had heard, because both rear doors closed simultaneously as she spoke. She watched the two men walk down the row of cars toward an H2 Hummer that was a spitting image of hers. Jazz hadn't noticed it when she'd come into the garage. As soon as the men climbed into their vehicle, Jazz started her engine and backed out of her slot.

"Creeps," she muttered as she drove toward the ramp leading up to the street. Although she was excited about getting another name and glad everything was copacetic about Operation Winnow, she was aggravated by the way she was being treated. She didn't like being subservient and talked down to, which is what the conversation with Mr. Bob and Mr. Dave had been like. Even the names of the two men were stupid and a slap in the face. She also vaguely wondered how much they were being paid for each sanction if she was getting five grand. *Hell,* she thought, she was doing all the work.

So, what do you think?" David Rosenkrantz asked Robert Hawthorne.

Bob was in the driver's seat, slowly drumming his fingers on the steering wheel and staring out the windshield at the bare concrete wall while he mulled over their conversation with Jazz. He had yet to start the car. Dave was in the passenger seat, eyeing his boss.

"I don't know," Bob said finally, throwing both hands into the air. He shook his head and turned to his underling. Bob was a big, athletic-appearing man with coarse features that contrasted with his Italian suit. The natty dress was a relatively new affectation. Most of his life had been spent in military fatigues, roaming the world on special ops as a member of the Army's Special Forces. "Running this operation is a classic catch-22. We spend so much effort finding and cultivating these antisocial fruitcakes who are willing to carry out the missions without compunction, but then we have to deal with their craziness. This Rakoczi is a case in point. Can you imagine she actually tried to shoot that marine officer in the nuts just because he made a pass at her?"

"Yet she's effective," said Dave. Dave was in his mid-twenties, almost half Bob's age. He was of a slighter build but equally athletic. He'd been recruited by Bob in prison, where both had done time: Bob for nearly killing a gay man who had made the mistake of approaching him in a bar, and Dave for simple grand larceny.

"She's the best we have," Bob answered. "That's why I'm torn. There's no pussyfooting around with Radoczi. We give her a name and bam, the person's gone the same night. Not once has there been any hesitation and excuses like we've had to put up with with all the others. But like I implied to her, I'm afraid she might be a loose cannon."

"Do you think she was involved with the murder of the nurse?"

"To tell you the truth, I have no idea, although I wouldn't put it past her. At the same time, I know she wouldn't do it for fifty bucks, so maybe it was a mugging. I just don't know. I'd hoped that by surprising her, we'd have a better idea."

"She didn't react much when you first mentioned the nurse's name, but then she seemed to get a little mad."

"I got the same impression, but I don't know how to interpret it. Like most of our emissaries, she has a history of not getting along with her superiors, so the news that Chapman was dead might have just made her feel good about not having her around anymore." Bob started the vehicle's engine and twisted around to back out of the parking slot.

"I think we'll just have to hold tight and see what happens," Bob said. Once he got the car in the clear, he put it in drive and started for the ramp. "If there are any more coincidental shootings, we'll have to suspect the worst, and she'll have to go. If that happens, you'll be the man."

"Yeah, I know," Dave said. "That's why I asked her about her habits."

"I guessed as much," Bob said, pulling up to the booth. "But take what she said with a grain of salt. People like Rakoczi have as much qualms about lying as they do about polishing their shoes."

Dave nodded, but he wasn't concerned. Rakoczi's loner inclinations would make dealing with her a breeze.

thirteen

Laurie put the small plastic cap on the device after she thought it was adequately saturated, and placed it on the edge of the sink. She certainly wasn't going to sit and watch it for the required time. Instead, she climbed into the shower and lathered herself with a body wash and shampooed her hair. She then stood under the stream of water for a few minutes, allowing it to cascade over her head. For Laurie, a shower wasn't quite the therapeutic experience that a bath was, but it was as calming just the same.

It had been a restless night for Laurie, with her mind refusing to turn off. When she was able to sleep, it was in snatches, haunted by disturbing dreams, including the recurrent nightmare about her brother sinking into the mud. When the alarm had sounded, there was a certain relief that the long night was finally over. She hardly felt rested but was relieved to get out of bed. The covers and sheets were in such disarray from her tossing and turning that it appeared as if there had been a wrestling match.

Similar to the previous two mornings, when she had initially stood up, she had a touch of nausea. As she turned off the shower, there was still a remnant, but assuming the situation would be the same, she expected she'd feel almost normal after a bit of breakfast.

Laurie stepped out onto the bath mat, dried herself off, then turned and bent her head back into the shower stall to shake her thick mane of hair like a dog emerging from a dip in a pond. She then vigorously hand-dried her hair and wrapped it up in the towel. Only then did she hazard a look down at the innocent piece of plastic resting on the edge of the sink.

Laurie caught her breath. With slightly trembling fingers, she picked up the device as if by holding it closer there might be a different result. But there wasn't. In the small window in the plastic sheath were two pink lines. Laurie closed her eyes and held them shut for an extended moment. When she reopened them the pink lines were still there. She wasn't conjuring them up in her mind. Having studied the directions on the side of the box, Laurie knew that the test was positive. She was pregnant!

With trembling knees, Laurie put down the top of the toilet seat and sat down. For a moment, she felt completely overwhelmed. Too many disconcerting things had happened in too short a time. It had all started with her semi-split with Jack, followed quickly by her mother's cancer, the situation with the BRCA1 mutation, and then her whirlwind relationship with Roger. And now she was being drawn into yet another potential tumult. Most of her life, she had dreamed about what it was going to be like to be pregnant, but now that she was, she didn't know how to feel. It was like her life was spinning out of control.

Laurie put the testing device back on the edge of the sink and looked at the box it had come in, which she had placed on top of the hamper. Once again, she was tempted to blame the messenger, as if being pregnant was the fault of the pregnancy test. Laurie could have done it the night before, but she read that it was the most reliable and sensitive in the morning. So she had waited. It was obvious to her that she had been procrastinating and putting off the inevitable. When the thought of possibly being pregnant had suddenly occurred to her in Roger's office, she was almost certain she was. After all, it would explain the morning nausea, which she had been foolishly trying to attribute to scallops.

Laurie shook her head in dismay. The fact that being pregnant had come as such a surprise was yet another example of her ability to put things that she didn't want to think about out of her mind. She distinctly remembered acknowledging to herself that she had missed a period three weeks before. But with everything else going on, she had decided not to worry about it, and she didn't. After all, she had missed periods before, particularly when under stress, and currently, there was certainly no dearth of stress in her life.

Lowering her head to look at her abdomen, Laurie tried to understand that there was the beginning of a child inside of her. Although she had always considered the idea to be natural, now that it was actually happening, it seemed so phenomenal as to defy belief. She immediately knew when the conception had occurred. It had to have been that morning when she and Jack had found themselves both strangely wide awake in the middle of the night. At first, they had been careful not to bother the other, but when they had discovered that they were both not sleeping, they started talking. The talking led to a caress, and the caress progressed to an embrace. The resulting lovemaking had been natural and initially fulfilling, but later, when Laurie found herself still awake, the intensity of the lovemaking had ironically made her realize what she was missing: a family with children. Now the ultimate irony was that the lovemaking had actually created a child she'd longed for, although without the marriage.

Laurie got to her feet and stood sideways in front of the mirror. She tried to see if there was any bulge to her abdomen, but then openly laughed at herself. She knew that at five weeks, an embryo was no bigger than about eight millimeters, or a third of an inch, hardly enough to cause any visible external changes.

All at once, Laurie stopped laughing and stared at herself in the mirror. Being pregnant under the current circumstances was hardly a laughing matter. It was a mistake with serious consequences for her life, and for others as well. Thinking in that vein made her wonder how it had happened. She had always been careful to avoid lovemaking when she thought she might be fertile, so how did she mess up? She thought back to the night they had made love, and as soon as she did so, she realized what had happened. At two o'clock in the morning, it was technically the next day. The previous day had been her tenth day, and it probably would have been okay, but certainly not the eleventh day.

"Oh, my word!" Laurie said out loud in a

despairing voice as the reality of the situation began to sink in. She truly felt overwhelmed, and even a little depressed. The need to talk with Jack had suddenly changed from a desire to a necessity, yet at the moment, she wondered how she was going to find the emotional strength. There were too many problems swirling in her mind, not least of which was the knowledge that she was positive for the BRCA1 marker. How was that going to play into her being pregnant? She had no idea, but the thought invariably brought up the word "abortion." Despite being a medical doctor, Laurie had always associated the word more with its political connotations concerning women's rights than with a procedure that she would consider herself. Suddenly, all that changed.

"I've got to get a grip!" Laurie said to her image in the mirror with more determination than she felt. She got out her hair dryer and began drying her hair. Her one refuge was her professional persona. Despite her problems, she had to get to work.

As she'd expected, Laurie's queasiness all but disappeared after she'd had some breakfast. Bran Flakes without milk turned out to be the most palatable. While she ate, the right lower abdominal discomfort she'd felt on occasion over the last few days returned. With her fingers, she pushed in over the area. It accentuated the feeling, especially when she moved her fingers closer to the midline, but it still wasn't anything she would have called pain. Vaguely, she wondered if it was a normal sensation of early pregnancy. Since she had never been pregnant before, she didn't know if implantation caused such a feeling. Intellectually, she knew that the process involved a kind of invasion of the uterine wall, so it wasn't out of the realm of possibility. There was also the chance the discomfort could be from the right ovary. One way or another, it wasn't her biggest concern.

When Laurie arrived at the OCME, it was only about seven-fifteen, but she was still pessimistic about catching Jack in the ID office. Lately, he seemed to be coming in earlier and earlier. Her assumption was corroborated when she saw Vinnie's preferred location vacant and his newspaper, open to the sports page, abandoned on the desk, which undoubtedly meant he was already down helping Jack. Chet was hard at work, sitting at the main desk and going through the folders of the bodies that had come in during the night. It was to be his last day for the job that week. Laurie was the medical examiner on call for the upcoming weekend, which also meant that the following week's duty of deciding which cases needed to be posted and distributing them would fall to her.

"Is Jack already downstairs?" Laurie asked as she took her first sip of coffee. Believing the caffeine would help check her melancholy mood, she hoped her stomach would tolerate the strong brew.

Chet's head popped up. "You know Jack. When I got here, he'd already been cherry-picking through all the folders and was eager to get a jump on the day."

"What kind of case is he doing?" The warmth of the coffee gave her a contradictory shiver.

"It's interesting you should ask. He took a case just like the two you got yesterday."

Laurie took the cup away from her lips. Her mouth opened in an expression of surprise. "You mean a case from the Manhattan General?"

"Yup! Fairly young guy who'd had a routine hernia repair and then promptly checked out for good."

"Why did Jack take it? He knows I'm interested in those cases."

"He did it as a favor."

"Oh, come on, Chet. What do you mean as a favor?"

"Apparently, Calvin had left word with Janice that if another such case came in, she was to give him a call. Obviously, she did, because he came in just about the same time as Jack and checked it out. When I arrived, he told me specifically he didn't want you doing it. In fact, he said that you were to have an official paper day today, so you're free and clear. Anyway, Jack then offered to do the case because he said you'd probably want the results sooner rather than later."

"Why did Calvin say that he didn't want me doing it?" Laurie questioned. It seemed like a deliberately low blow, since the diversion of her series was the only thing she had going for herself in the face of all her problems.

"He didn't say. And you know Calvin; it wasn't as if he was about to offer. He just made it crystal clear you weren't to do it.

He also said that when I saw you, I was supposed to tell you he wanted to see you in his office ASAP. So the message has been delivered. Good luck!"

"That's weird. Did he sound angry?"

"No worse than normal." Chet shrugged. "I'm sorry. That's all I can tell you."

Laurie nodded as if she understood, but she didn't. Leaving her coat on one of the ID office's club chairs, she retraced her route back out through the ID room and into the main reception area. She was nervous. With everything else in her life, in her words, "going to hell in a handbasket," she wouldn't have been surprised if her career was somehow in jeopardy as well, although she had no idea what she could have done to irritate Calvin, other than perhaps giving her impromptu talk at yesterday's conference. But after the fact, when she'd spoken with him, everything seemed to be all right.

Laurie had Marlene buzz her directly into the administration area, which was tomb-like in its stillness. None of the secretaries had yet arrived. Calvin, however, was in his office, scanning documents from his in basket and hastily signing them. He continued the last couple even after Laurie had announced herself. He motioned for her to sit while he gathered up the stack of signed papers and slipped them into his out basket. Then he sat back and eyed Laurie over the top of his rimless glasses, with his chin practically on his chest. "If you don't already know, the name of the potential new case is Clark Mulhausen, and I suppose you want to know why I insisted you don't do it."

"That would be nice," Laurie said. She was relieved. Calvin's tone was hardly strident, suggesting that he wasn't mad and she wasn't about to be harangued or, worse yet, put on administrative leave.

"The long and short of it is that you have yet to sign out those original cases in your so-called series from over a month ago. At this point, you can't be waiting for any other lab work or whatever, so you've got to get them done. To be honest, the chief has been feeling some heat about them from the mayor's office for God knows what reason. Whatever it is, he let me know he wants them signed out, which means I'm getting heat. Maybe it has something to do with insurance and the families. Who knows? One way or the other, get them done! I gave you a paper day to make sure it happens. Fair enough?"

"I haven't signed them out because I can't in good conscience say they were either accidental or natural, and I know you don't want me to say they were homicides, because that would suggest a serial killer, and I don't have any proof—at least not yet."

"Laurie, don't give me a hard time," Calvin said. He leaned forward intimidatingly, extending his huge head toward her and impaling her with his dark, menacing eyes. "I'm trying to be nice about this. I'm also not trying to stop you from looking into the possibility they are causally related, but for now you've got to choose between accidental or natural. I favor natural, like Dick Katzenburg, because there's no more proof they were accidental than homicidal. The death certificates can always be amended if and when new information becomes available. We can't leave the cases in limbo forever, and you can't create a PR firestorm by calling them homicidal or even accidental without some specific justification. Be reasonable!"

"All right, I'll do it," Laurie said with a defeated sigh.

"Thank you! But damn! You make it sound like I'm asking for the moon. And while we're on the subject, what have you found out about the Queens cases? Do they fit the same demographics?"

"So far," Laurie said in a tired voice. She slouched forward, looking down at the floor with her elbows resting on her knees. "At least from what I could get out of the investigator's reports. I'm waiting on the charts."

"Keep me apprised! Now, get up there to that office of yours and sign out those Manhattan General cases!"

Laurie nodded and got to her feet. She gave Calvin a crooked smile and turned to leave.

"Laurie," Calvin called after her. "You're acting browbeaten, which is not like you. What's up? Are you all right? You've got me worried here. It distresses me to see you, of all people, moping around."

Laurie turned back to face Calvin. She was taken aback. It was not like him to ask personal questions, much less suggest concern. She hardly expected that from any authority figure, especially not the often-curmudgeonly Calvin. The surprise caused unwelcome stirrings of emotion within her, which immediately threatened to surface. Since the very last thing she wanted to do was break down in front of her often-chauvinistic superior, she fought the impulse by taking a deep breath and holding it for a minute. Calvin's eyebrows slowly arched, and he leaned forward more, as if to encourage her to speak.

"I guess I've got a lot on my mind," Laurie said finally. She was afraid to make eye contact.

"Do you care to elaborate?" Calvin asked in a voice that was significantly more mellow than usual.

"Not at the moment," Laurie said while flashing Calvin the same crooked smile.

Calvin nodded. "Fair enough, but remember, my door is always open."

"Thank you," Laurie managed before fleeing. As she walked down the main first-floor corridor, she felt a mixture of feelings to add to her chaotic thoughts. On the one hand, she felt lucky to have gotten away without an emotional scene, while at the same time, she was irritated with herself about yet another episode of her embarrassing demonstrativeness. It was ridiculous that she had to fight against shedding a tear because her boss evidenced a bit of solicitude. On the other hand, she was impressed at having witnessed a side of the deputy chief that she had never seen. And after the nervous pessimism that the call to Calvin's office had evoked, she felt relief that she was still employed. If she'd been put on leave for some real or imagined transgression, she wasn't sure she could have handled it. With the new concern about being pregnant combined with her other anxieties, the diversion that her job provided was needed more than ever.

Sticking her head into the investigator's office, she asked the chief investigator, Bart Arnold, if Janice was still around. Laurie wanted to learn the details of the Clark Mulhausen case, to be certain it was another to be added to her series.

"You missed her by about ten minutes," Bart said. "Anything I can help you with?"

"Not really," Laurie said. "How about Cheryl? Is she available?"

"You're striking out. She's already out on a case. Should I have her call you when she returns?"

"You can relay a message," Laurie said. "Yesterday, I asked her to put in a request for hospital charts from Saint Francis Hospital out in Queens. I'd like her to amend the request and make it urgent. I need them as soon as possible."

"No problem," Bart said, as he made a note on a Post-it. "I'll put this on Cheryl's desk. Consider it done."

Laurie headed back toward the ID office to retrieve her coat, but she thought of Jack down in the pit doing the autopsy on Clark Mulhausen. He would have the folder with Janice's investigative report, which would have all the particulars. Reversing her course, she headed for the back elevator. Not only could she make sure Mulhausen fit the demographics of her series, she'd have an excuse to talk with Jack. Remembering her waffling the previous afternoon outside of Jack's office, it would be good to have a professional reason to break the ice with him and give her the opportunity to suggest that they get together away from the OCME for a personal discussion. The thought of the kind of conversation she needed to have with him made her tense. In his current state of mind, she had no idea whether or not he'd be receptive either to meet with her or to what she had to tell him. Lou had suggested he would be, but Laurie didn't know.

In days past, a gown, a hat, and a mask were all that was needed to drop into the autopsy room for a visit to check out a finding or have a short conversation. Times had changed. Now Laurie had to go into the locker room and change into scrubs before heading over to the supply room to get into her full protective gear, as if she was doing a case herself. Calvin had established the new rules, and they were supposedly cut in stone.

"Ahhh!" Laurie whimpered as she extended her arm while hanging up her blouse in the locker. She had gotten a sudden stitch in that same abdominal location that had been intermittently troubling her over the previous few days. This time, it was definitely a sharp pain that made her wince as well as withdraw her hand. Gingerly, she placed it over the bothersome area. Thankfully, the pain quickly eased and then disappeared as suddenly as it had appeared. Carefully, she pressed in over the area, but there was no residual tenderness.

She extended her arm as she had done when hanging the blouse, but still there was no discomfort. Shaking her head with confusion over whether it had anything to do with being pregnant, she thought maybe she should ask Sue whether she had experienced anything similar during her two pregnancies.

With the memory of the pain fading into the background, Laurie continued changing into scrubs, and then headed across the hall to climb into her moon suit. A few minutes later, she pushed into the autopsy room. As the heavy door thumped against the jamb behind her, the two people in the room straightened up from bending over the body splayed open in front of them. They both looked over at her.

"Well, glory be!" Jack quipped. "Is this really Dr. Montgomery already in full regalia, and it is not even eight o'clock? To what do we owe this great honor?"

"I just want to find out if this case truly fits into my series." Laurie said as lightly as she could while bracing herself for Jack's probable continued sarcasm. She advanced to the foot of the table. Jack was on her left and Vinnie on her right. "Please! Go back to work! I don't mean to interrupt."

"I don't want you to think I took this case away from you. Do you know why I'm doing it?"

"I do. Chet told me."

"Have you seen Calvin yet? I couldn't read him this morning. He was acting weird. Is everything hunky-dory between you two?"

"Everything is fine. I was worried myself when Chet told me I was to have an official paper day and that Calvin wanted to see me ASAP. It turned out that all he wants is for me to sign out the earlier cases in my series. I'm supposed to say they were natural."

"Are you going to do it? I'm thinking there's no way they were natural."

"I don't have a lot of choice," Laurie admitted. "He laid it on the line. I hate the political pressures of this job, of which this situation is becoming a prime example. But, be that as it may, what's your take on Mulhausen. Does this case belong in my series?"

Jack looked down into the corpse's open thorax. He'd already removed the lungs and was in the process of opening the great vessels. The heart was in full view. "So far, I'd have to say yes. The demographics are the same, and I don't see any suggestion of pathology of any note. I'll know for sure in a half hour or so when I finish with the heart, but I'll be very surprised if we find anything."

"Do you mind if I look at the investigator's report in the folder?"

"Mind? Why would I mind? But I can save you the trouble by giving you the facts. The patient was a healthy thirty-six-year-old stockbroker who'd had an uncomplicated hernia repair yesterday morning and was doing fine. Four-thirty this morning, he was discovered dead in his bed. The nurses' notes said he was practically room temperature when he was found, but they tried to resuscitate him anyway. Obviously, they got nothing. So, do I think he fits your series? I do. What's more, I think you are genuinely onto something with this series idea. Obviously, I didn't at first, but I do now, especially now that you've got seven cases."

Laurie tried to see the nuances of Jack's expression, but she couldn't through his plastic screen. Still, she was encouraged. Somewhat like Calvin, he was acting more affable than expected, and it made her feel optimistic on a number of fronts.

"What about those cases Dick Katzenburg mentioned yesterday?" Jack asked. "Have they panned out so far?"

"Yes. At least from the investigators' reports. I'm waiting for the hospital charts to be certain."

"It was a good pickup," Jack said. "Yesterday, when you got up to go to the microphone to give your little presentation, I was pissed, since it meant that the Thursday-afternoon torture session was going to be extended, but now I have to give you credit. If Dick's cases do turn out to match yours, your series doubles, which kind of casts a pall over AmeriCare, wouldn't you say?"

"I don't know what it says about AmeriCare," Laurie said. She was surprised at Jack's talkativeness. Even that seemed encouraging.

"Well, as the saying goes, something's rotten in Denmark: At thirteen cases, it's gone way beyond coincidence. But it's interesting there's no smoking-gun commonality, which is why I hesitate to support your homicide idea, although I'm warming to it. Tell me, have any of the cases occurred in the intensive care unit or the postanesthesia care unit?"

"None of mine. I don't know about Dick's. Mine have all been in regular hospital rooms. Why do you ask? Was Mulhausen in either?"

"No! He was in a normal room. I'm not sure why I'm asking. Maybe because drugs are handled differently in either the ICU or the PACU than they are on a regular hospital floor. Actually, I'm trying to think of some sort of systems error, like they are all getting a drug that they are not supposed to get. It's just something else to consider."

"Thanks for the suggestion," Laurie said without a lot of conviction. "I'll keep it in mind."

"I also think you should continue to press toxicology. I still think that ultimately, it's going to be toxicology that solves this conundrum."

"That's easy to say, but I don't know what else I can do. Peter Letterman has really gone out of his way, trying to the point of thinking about minutiae. Yesterday, he was talking about checking into some kind of unbelievablely potent toxin from a South-American frog."

"Whoa! That's a bit far afield. That calls to mind the adage, 'When you hear hoof beats, think of horses, not zebras.' Something is interrupting these people's cardiac conduction system. I can't help but believe it's got to be a garden-variety arrhythmia drug. How they are getting it is another story."

"But that certainly would have shown up in toxicology."

"That's true," Jack agreed. "What about a contaminant in their IV fluid? Have they all had IVs running?"

Laurie thought for a minute. "Now that you mention it, they have. But it's not unusual, since most people who've had surgery keep an IV for at least twenty-four hours. As far as a contaminant in the IV fluid is concerned, it passed through my mind, but it is extremely unlikely. If a contaminant were involved, we'd have more cases than we have, and it certainly wouldn't favor the relatively young and healthy, nor just patients having had elective surgery."

"I don't think you should eliminate anything out of hand," Jack said. "Which reminds me of the question about electrolytes the fellow from Staten Island asked you yesterday after you made your presentation. You told him the levels all tested normal. Is that true?"

"Absolutely. I made it a point to ask Peter to check into that specifically, and he reported back that they were all normal."

"Well, it certainly sounds as if you are covering all the bases," Jack said. "I'll finish up with Mulhausen just to be sure there's no emboli or cardiac pathology." He repositioned the scalpel in his hand and bent over the corpse.

"I'm trying to think of all the possibilities," Laurie said. Then, after a moment's hesitation, she added, "Jack, could I speak to you for a moment on a personal note?"

"Oh, for Christ's sake!" Vinnie said suddenly. He'd been impatiently shifting his weight from one foot to the other during Laurie and Jack's extended conversation. "Can't we get this freaking autopsy done?"

Jack straightened back up and looked at Laurie. "What is it you want to talk about?"

Laurie glanced at Vinnie. She felt awkward in his presence, especially considering his impatience.

Jack noticed Laurie's reaction. "Don't mind Vinnie. With as much help as he is as an assistant, you can just pretend he's not here. I do it all the time."

"Very funny," Vinnie responded. "How come I'm not laughing?"

"Actually," Laurie said, "I don't want to talk with you now. What I'd like to do is arrange for us to get together. There are some important things I need to share with you."

Jack didn't answer right away but rather stared at Laurie through the plastic face masks. "Let me guess," he said finally. "You're getting married, and you want me to be a bridesmaid."

Vinnie laughed so hard it sounded as if he was choking.

"Hey, it wasn't that funny," Jack protested, although he was now laughing along with Vinnie.

"Jack," Laurie said, maintaining a calm voice with some difficulty. "I'm trying to be serious."

"I am, too," Jack managed. "And since you haven't denied the nuptials, I'll consider myself informed, but I'm afraid I'm going to have to decline the bridesmaid offer. Was there anything else?"

"Jack!" Laurie repeated. "I'm not getting married. I need to talk with you about something that involves you and me."

"Okay, fine! I'm all ears."

"I'm not about to talk to you here in the autopsy room."

Jack made a gesture around the room with all its gothic details. "What's wrong with this? I feel quite at home in here."

"Jack! Could you be serious for a moment? I said it was important."

"Okay, fine! What other venue do we have at our disposal that would better suit your needs? If you give me a half hour or so, I could meet you upstairs in the ID office, and we could chat over a nice cup of Vinnie's coffee. The only problem with that is that the other hoi polloi will just be arriving for their workday. Perhaps you'd prefer we rendezvous in our scenic second-floor lunchroom and have something delectable out of the vending machines. There, we could hobnob with the janitorial staff. What's your preference?"

Laurie eyed Jack as best she could through the plastic face shields. His reversion to angry sarcasm seriously eroded her earlier optimism about his receptivity, but she pressed on: "What I was hoping is that we could have dinner tonight, possibly at Elios, if we could somehow manage a reservation." Elios was a restaurant that had played a role in Laurie and Jack's long relationship.

For another extended moment, Jack stared back at Laurie. Although the day before he'd not given Lou's comments about Laurie much credence, he suddenly wondered if there had been a germ of truth to what he'd said. At the same time, Jack reminded himself that he was in no mood for further humiliation. "What's the matter with Romeo? Is he sick tonight?"

Vinnie chuckled again and then tried to suppress it when Laurie glared at him.

"I don't know," Jack continued. "It's kind of short notice, considering I was supposed to go bowling tonight with seventeen nuns from out of town."

Vinnie lost control and left the table. He wandered over to the sink and busied himself.

"Could you please be serious for a moment?" Laurie repeated. "You're not making this easy."

"I'm not making it easy?" Jack questioned superciliously. "That's a switch. I tried for months to arrange spending an evening with you, but you were always heading off to some major cultural event."

"It's only been a month, and you asked me twice, and both nights I had plans. I need to talk with you, Jack. Will you see me tonight or not?"

"It sounds like you are really motivated about this rendezvous."

"I'm very motivated," Laurie agreed.

"Okay, tonight it is. What time?"

"Is Elios all right?"

Jack shrugged. "It's fine."

"Then I'll call to see if I can make a reservation, and I'll let you know. It might have to be on the early side, since it's Friday night."

"Okay," Jack said. "I'll wait to hear from you."

With a final nod, Laurie left the table, opened the door to the hallway, and walked back to the storeroom to get out of her protective suit. She was pleased that Jack had finally agreed to get together, but, as Calvin had suggested earlier, she felt browbeaten about getting Jack to commit to their meeting, and, sensing his anger, she was no longer particularly optimistic about how he was going to react to her news.

After getting into her street clothes and rescuing her coat from the ID room, Laurie took the elevator up to the fourth floor. Her idea was to pay Peter a quick visit to give him a morale boost for his efforts and to make sure he hadn't struck gold with either Sobczyk or Lewis. As preoccupied as she was with personal thoughts, she didn't even consider the possibility of having to confront her nemesis, the laboratory director, John DeVries. Unfortunately, he was in Peter's office, apparently in the process of dressing down Peter. He had his hands angrily thrust onto his hips, and Peter had a sheepish expression on his face. Laurie had unknowingly run headlong into the fray.

"Such timing!" John exclaimed. "If it isn't the seductress herself!"

"Excuse me?" Laurie questioned. With such a sexist comment, she could feel her own ire rising.

"Apparently, you have been able to seduce Peter into becoming your own laboratory slave," John snarled. "You and I have had this discussion before, Dr. Montgomery. With the pittance I'm allocated to run this lab, no one gets special service, which invariably makes everyone else wait that much longer. Do I make myself clear, or do you want me to write it out for you? Furthermore, you can be sure that Dr. Bingham and Dr. Washington will be notified of this situation. Meanwhile, I want you out of here." To emphasize his point, John gestured toward the door.

For a moment, Laurie looked back and forth between John's gaunt face and Peter's. The last thing she wanted to do was make things any worse for Peter, so she refrained from telling John what she thought of him. Instead, she turned around and walked out of the lab.

As Laurie climbed the stairs, she felt more depressed than she had earlier. She hated run-ins with people, particularly people she had to work with. They often lead to inappropriate emotional responses like the one she'd had earlier with Calvin, although on this occasion with John, anger was ascendant. Thinking of Calvin, she vaguely wondered what the fallout would be, since John invariably made good on his threats.

She thought the chances were good that she'd hear from the deputy chief, and what that would mean, she had no idea. She truly hoped she hadn't caused any long-term problem for Peter, since he had to deal with John on a daily basis.

Entering her office, Laurie closed the door behind her. She hung up her coat and noticed Riva's hanging on its hook, which meant Riva was down in either the ID office or the autopsy room. Laurie sat down and thought about the telephone call she had to make. She'd been dreading it since the pregnancy test had been positive. In her mind, it was as if the process of making the call would finally and ultimately confirm the reality of her being pregnant. She had been trying to deny it to some degree, because of how big a mistake it was. As much as she wanted to have children, this was not the time, and she questioned what had gone through her mind to allow her to take the risk. Even though it was only a few weeks ago, she truly couldn't remember.

Reaching for the phone, Laurie reluctantly placed the call to the Manhattan General Hospital. As the connection went through, she looked down at the material from the Queens cases, which she needed to add to her matrix, along with the case Jack was currently doing.

When the operator came on the line, Laurie asked to be connected with Dr. Laura Riley's office. As the extension began to ring, Laurie was thankful that Sue happened to fix her up with a GYN doctor who also did OB. In the current medical malpractice milieu, that certainly was not always the case.

When Dr. Riley's scheduling secretary answered, Laurie explained her situation. She found herself stumbling over her words when she revealed she was pregnant according to an OTC test kit.

"Well, in that case, we certainly cannot wait until September," the secretary said brightly. "Dr. Riley likes to see her obstetrics patients at eight to ten weeks after the last period. Where are you?"

"It's been about seven weeks," Laurie said.

"Then we should see you next week or the week after." There was a pause. Laurie realized that her hand holding the phone was trembling.

"How about next Friday?" the secretary

said, coming back on the line. "That's a week from today, at one-thirty."

"That will be fine," Laurie said. "Thank you for squeezing me in."

"My pleasure. Now, can I have your name?"

"I'm sorry, I didn't realize I didn't give it to you. I'm Dr. Laurie Montgomery."

"Dr. Montgomery! I remember you. I spoke with you yesterday."

Laurie winced. Her secret was now quasi-public. Even though she had never met the secretary, the woman now knew a terribly private, intimate detail about her life that Laurie had not yet decided how she was going to handle. Difficult choices would have to be made.

"Congratulations!" the secretary continued. "Hold the line! I'm sure that Dr. Riley would want to say hello."

Without a chance to respond, Laurie found herself on hold, listening to music. For a brief moment, she thought about hanging up, but she decided she couldn't do it. To keep her mind in check, she looked down at the stack of death certificates and investigative reports from Queens. Anxious for a diversion, she picked up the first and began reading. The patient's name was Kristin Svensen, age twenty-three, who had been admitted to St. Francis Hospital for a hemorrhoidectomy. Laurie shook her head at the dimensions of the tragedy. It made her problems seem small compared to the death of a healthy young woman in a hospital after having her hemorrhoids removed.

"Dr. Montgomery! I just heard the good news. Congratulations."

"You can call me Laurie."

"Fair enough, and you can call me Laura."

"I'm not sure congratulations are in order. To be perfectly frank, this is an unexpected and rather an inconvenient surprise for me, so I'm not sure how I feel about it."

"I see," said Laura, reigning in her exuberance. Then, with sensitivity born of experience, she added, "We still have to make sure you and the conceptus are as healthy as possible. Have there been any problems?"

"A bit of morning sickness, but it's been very transient." Laurie found herself uncomfortable talking about the pregnancy and wanted to get off the line.

"Let us know if it gets any worse. There are lots of suggestions for dealing with it in the thousands of pregnancy books available. As for books, my advice is to stay away from the most conservative ones, because they'll drive you crazy, thinking you can't do anything, like take a hot bath. With that said, we'll see you next Friday."

Laurie thanked her and hung up the phone. It was a relief to get the call behind her. Picking up the computer printouts of the cases from Queens, she tapped them against the surface of her desk to align them. The motion caused an almost subliminal unpleasant sensation in the same location where she'd had the pain while down in the locker room. She wondered if she should have at least mentioned the feeling and pain to Laura Riley. She thought she should have, but wasn't about to call her back. Instead, she'd bring it up during her appointment, unless it became frequent or intense enough to warrant a call. She also wondered if she should have mentioned about being positive for the BRCA1 marker, but as with the discomfort, she decided it would be perfectly appropriate to discuss it on her first visit.

With the papers in one hand, Laurie reached for the phone again, but then hesitated with her hand on the receiver. She had it in her mind to call Roger for several reasons, not the least of which was feeling guilty about leaving him in the dark about what must have seemed strange behavior in his office. But she didn't know what she was going to say. She wasn't yet willing to tell him the whole truth for a number of reasons, but she knew she would have to say something. Ultimately, she decided she'd use the BRCA1 issue, as she'd already done.

Laurie picked up the phone and dialed Roger's direct line. What was really motivating her was her desire to take copies of the Queens materials over to him so she could talk with him directly about them. Despite the turmoil in her mind from her personal problems, she'd come up with an idea about the cases from Queens that might possibly solve the mystery of SADS.

fourteen

When Laurie got over to the Manhattan General Hospital, she was ushered directly into Roger's office, where he was waiting for her. The first thing he did was close the door. Then he gave her a sustained, silent hug. Laurie hugged him back, but not with equivalent ardor. On top of the residuals from the marriage flap, she knew she wasn't going to be entirely forthright with him about her own situation, and it made her feel self-conscious. If he noticed her restraint, he didn't mention it. After the embrace, he turned his two straight-backed chairs around to face each other just as he had done the day before. He had Laurie sit in one, and he took the other.

"I'm glad to see you," he said. "I missed you last night." He was leaning forward into her space with his hands clasped and his elbows on his knees. Laurie was close enough to smell his aftershave lotion. His day was just beginning. His fresh shirt still had the telltale creases from the laundry box.

"I'm glad to see you, too," Laurie said. She reached out and handed him the investigative reports and the death certificates on the six cases from Queens. She hadn't had time to make copies, but it didn't matter. She could just as easily download them again. By giving him the material, she hoped to deflect the conversation away from her mental state, at least for the moment. Besides, she was eager to tell him her idea.

Roger scanned the pages quickly. "My word! They do seem similar to ours, even to the extent of occurring at around the same time in the morning."

"That's my take. I'll know more details when I get the hospital charts. But for the sake of the discussion, let's assume they are mirror images. Does that suggest anything to you?"

Roger looked down at the papers, thought for a moment, and then shrugged. "It means the number of cases has doubled. We now have twelve cases, not six. No, we have thirteen, including the death last night. I assume you've heard about Clark Mulhausen. Are you going to be doing the autopsy?"

"No, Jack is doing it," Laurie said. She had told Roger a little about Jack during their five-week courtship, including the fact that she and Jack had been lovers. When Laurie had first met Roger, she had described herself as "mostly unattached." Later, when she and Roger had gotten to know each other better, she had admitted that she had used that particular description of herself because of unresolved issues with Jack. She had even gone to the extent of confiding that the problem involved Jack's reluctance to make a commitment. Roger had accepted the news with great equanimity, which had enhanced Laurie's estimation of his maturity and self-confidence, and the issue had never resurfaced.

"Look at the dates on the Queens cases," Laurie suggested.

Roger again glanced through the papers then looked up. "They were all in the late fall of last year. The last one was in the latter part of November."

"Exactly," Laurie said. "They were clumped pretty close together, at a frequency of slightly more than one a week. Then they stopped. Does that suggest anything to you?"

"I suppose, but it sounds like you have something specific in mind. Why don't you tell me?"

"Fair enough, but first listen! You and I are the only ones who suspect we might be dealing with a serial killer, but we've been effectively gagged. I can't get the OCME to take a stand on the manner of death, and you can't get the hospital authorities even to admit there's a problem. What we're fighting here is institutional inertia. Both bureaucracies would rather sweep the issue under the rug until something forces their hand."

"I can't argue with that."

"What's held us so effectively in check from your side is that your hospital has such a good mortality rate that these deaths aren't appearing on the radar. From my side, it is the failure of toxicology."

"They still haven't found anything remotely suspicious?"

Laurie shook her head. "And the chances they might in the near future just took a nosedive. I'm afraid our crotchety laboratory director discovered my undercover effort this morning. If I know him, from now on he'll make sure that any further work on our cases will go to the very back of the queue. And even when he does get around to them, he's surely not going to do anything special."

"So, where are you going with all this?"

"It means it's up to us alone to try to root out this possible serial killer, and we'd better do something if we're going to prevent any more senseless deaths."

"We've known that practically from day one."

"Yes, but up until now we have tried to work within the constraints of our institutions and our job descriptions. I think we have to try something else, and it seems to me these cases from Queens present an opportunity. If these deaths are homicides, my guess is that there is one serial killer, not two or more."

"I suppose I had assumed as much."

"Since Saint Francis is another AmeriCare institution you should have reasonable access to their personnel database. You're in the perfect position to get personnel information. What we need is a list of people, from janitors to anesthesiologists, who worked the eleven-to-seven shift at Saint Francis in the fall and Manhattan General in the winter. Once we have the list, then we could check the people out. This is where my idea gets a little fuzzy, but if we could come up with a couple of credible suspects, then maybe we'll be able to get the hospital or the OCME to take a stand."

A slight smile played across Roger's craggy face as he nodded. "An elegant idea! I'm glad I thought of it." He laughed and gave Laurie's thigh a playful pat. "You make it sound so simple. But that's okay. I think I should be able to cajole that kind of information out of someone, and wouldn't it be interesting if it really came to something? I mean, I wonder if there really will be such a list. I know another list that exists for sure, a list of the professional staff with admitting privileges at both institutions. I have direct access to it as chief of the medical staff."

"That might even be a better idea than mine," Laurie admitted. "If I were asked who I would consider the most likely suspect in the hospital community, I'd have to say a deranged doctor. It's passed through my mind that if these deaths are homicides, then whoever is responsible must have a significant knowledge of physiology, pharmacology, and maybe even forensics. Otherwise, we'd already know how he or she is pulling it off."

"And we both know which group of doctors is the most knowledgeable in those regards."

"Who?"

"Anesthesiologists."

Laurie nodded. It was true that anesthesiologists would be the most skillful at dispatching patients, yet despite her comments, she had trouble believing as a doctor herself that a doctor could be behind the killings. It seemed so contrary to a doctor's role, but then again, it was contrary to the role of all healthcare professionals. And, of course, there was the staggering case in England of a doctor suspected of murdering upwards of two hundred people.

"How about jumping on this idea," Laurie suggested. "I know it's Friday, and people are not excited about having a new task plopped in their laps just before the weekend. But we have to do something, and we have to do it fast, and not only because it might prevent more deaths. It might be that our supposed serial killer is also smart enough to know that it would be safer for him to move to another hospital after a certain number of episodes. The assumption here is that he has moved once after six episodes, so there's reason to believe he could move again after seven. If he does, then our equivalent colleagues at some other hospital, maybe even in another city, will be starting from square one. That was one of the reasons that the other recent, infamous healthcare serial killer here in the metropolitan area wasn't caught for so long."

"Hey, Queens might not have been his first hospital."

"You're right," Laurie said with a shiver. "I never thought of that."

"I'll get right on it," Roger promised.

"I'm on call all weekend," Laurie said, "which means I'll probably be at the OCME, so call me there. Whatever I can do to help, I'd be happy to do. I know the whole process will be more difficult than I have suggested."

"We'll see. Maybe I'll be able to find a computer nerd in personnel who could help us." Roger aligned the pages Laurie had given him. "Now, I have something rather interesting to tell you about our cases. By chance, I've uncovered a curious commonality."

"Oh?" Laurie questioned. She was fascinated. "What is it?"

"Now, I don't mean to suggest that this is significant, but it holds for all seven cases, including Mulhausen last night. All of them were relatively recent AmeriCare subscribers, having joined the plan within the year. I actually discovered it by accident, looking at their subscriber numbers."

For a moment, Laurie stared at Roger, and Roger stared back. Laurie mulled over this new fact and tried to think how it could be connected. Nothing came to mind although it reminded her of Jack's comment the day before during the afternoon conference when he learned St. Francis, another AmeriCare institution, had seemingly had a similar series of deaths like hers. He'd said, "The plot thickens." She'd not had a chance to ask him what he had meant, nor did she follow up this morning when he'd said the new cases "cast a pall over AmeriCare," but now that Roger had told her this new fact, she was even more eager to ask him to explain. Laurie knew that Jack had a visceral hatred for AmeriCare, which colored his thinking, but still, he was smart and also intuitive.

"I really don't know if this is significant," Roger repeated. "But it is curious."

"Then it has to be significant in some form or fashion," Laurie said. "But I don't know how. These victims have all been young and healthy. AmeriCare actively recruits such customers. It's to their detriment to lose them."

"I know. It doesn't make sense, but I thought I should inform you anyway."

"I'm glad you did," Laurie said. She stood up. "Well, I've got to get back. The reason I'm not doing Mulhausen's autopsy is that I was supposed to go right up to my office and sign out McGillin and Morgan's deaths as being natural this very morning."

"Not so fast!" Roger said. He caught Laurie's arm and, with a little pressure, eased her back down into her seat. "You're not getting away that easy. But first, who's forcing you to sign out the cases as natural?"

"The deputy chief, Calvin Washington. He claims that the Chief, Harold Bingham, is getting pressure from the mayor's office."

Roger shook his head. He had a disgusted expression on his face. "I'm not surprised, considering what the hospital president said to me yesterday. He said that I should know for my own good that AmeriCare wants this problem to fade into the woodwork."

"That's hardly surprising. It would be a PR nightmare. But how does it come through the mayor's office?"

"I'm new to the organization, but I've gotten the sense that AmeriCare puts a lot of stock on being politically connected, as evidenced by them landing the city contract. I don't have to remind you that healthcare is big business, and there's always a lot of lobbying going on about a myriad of issues."

Laurie nodded as if she understood, but she didn't. "I'm going to sign them out as natural deaths, but I'm hoping with your help I'll be changing the certificates in the near future."

"Enough of this business talk," Roger said. "More important, how are you? I've been really concerned, and frankly, I've had to hold myself back from calling you every fifteen minutes."

"I'm sorry I've made you concerned," Laurie said as her mind frantically searched for a way to placate Roger without lying and without telling him the crux of the problem. "But as I said yesterday, I'm holding my own. It's just a difficult time for me."

"I understand. I tried to imagine how I would feel if I had been told I had a marker for a gene that was associated with developing cancer and then allowed to walk out the door. The burgeoning field of medical genetics has to come up with a better way to present this kind of information to patients than they do now, along with some reasonable cures."

"As someone who's in the process of going through it, I'd have to agree, although the social worker did make an attempt. But American medicine has always been like that. Technology has been the driving force, pulling the sociology of patient care behind."

"I wish I knew how to be more supportive for you."

"I'm afraid at the moment you really can't be. I'm caught up in my own personal odyssey. But that doesn't mean I'm not appreciative of your thoughts, and you have been supportive."

"What about tonight? Can we get together?"

Laurie peered into Roger's pale eyes. It bothered her that she wasn't being forthright, but she could not get herself to tell him she was pregnant and was having dinner with Jack because she and Jack had conceived a child. It wasn't that she thought he couldn't handle it, because she thought he could. It was more because of her sense of privacy, and until she told Jack, she didn't want to share it with anyone, even someone she cared for, such as Roger.

"We could have an early dinner," Roger urged. "We don't even have to talk about the BRCA issue if you don't want to. Maybe I'll already have some personnel data from here or Saint Francis. I mean, it's possible I could get some, even though, as you say, it's Friday."

"Roger, with everything that has happened to me recently, I need some space, at least for a few days. That's the kind of support I need. Can you try to live with that?"

"Yes, but I don't like it."

"I appreciate your understanding. Thank you." Laurie stood up again, and Roger did the same.

"Can I at least call you?"

"I suppose, but I don't know how much I'll want to talk. Maybe it would be better for me to call you. I'm taking it a day at a time."

Roger nodded and Laurie did the same. There was a brief, awkward moment of silence before Roger reached out and gave Laurie another hug. Her response was as restrained as it had been earlier. Laurie flashed a weak smile and started to leave.

"One other question," Roger said. He stepped between Laurie and the door.

"Does any part of this 'difficult time' you've described have anything to do with my still being married?"

"To be honest, I suppose a small amount," Laurie admitted.

"I certainly regret not telling you, and I'm sorry. I know I should have earlier on, but at first it seemed presumptuous you'd care. I mean, I'd gotten to the point I didn't care myself, like it was a nonissue. Then, when we got to know each other, and I'd fallen in love, and I knew you would care, I was embarrassed for not having told you sooner."

"Thank you for apologizing and explaining. I'm sure it will help put the issue behind us."

"That's my hope," Roger said. He gave Laurie's shoulder a tender squeeze, then opened his office door. "We'll talk."

Laurie nodded. "For sure," she agreed, and then walked out.

Roger watched Laurie wend her way among the desks and start down the long corridor. He watched her until she was out of sight, then closed his door. As he moved around his desk and sat down, her scent wafted in the air like a wraith. He was concerned about her, and he was worried that he'd botched their relationship by not being forthright with her, and, more damning, he hadn't come clean. He was still holding back things that she had the right to know if their relationship was to grow, and, worse yet, he wasn't telling her the truth about things that he'd already told her. Contrary to what he had suggested, there were unresolved aspects of his relationship with his wife, including unrequited love on his part, which he had not had the courage to tell Laurie, even though she had had the courage to tell him something similar regarding her former boyfriend, Jack.

Roger's biggest secret from everyone, including his current employers, was that he was a former addict. While in Thailand, he had fallen into the trap of heroin addiction. It had started innocently enough, as a kind of experiment ostensibly so he could better understand and treat patients with the problem. Unfortunately, he had underestimated the drug's seductiveness and his own weaknesses, especially since the heroin was so freely available. It was at this time that his wife and children left him for the protection of her powerful family. It was also the reason he was transferred to Africa and eventually dismissed from the organization. And even though he had gone through an extensive program of rehabilitation and had been reasonably drug-free for years, the specter of the addiction problem still haunted him every day. One problem was that he knew he drank too much. He loved wine and was surreptitiously drinking at least a bottle a night, which made him worry that he was allowing alcohol to become a substitute for heroin. As a physician, particularly one who'd gone through rehab, he knew the risks.

Roger would have agonized longer, but luckily he had the series of suspicious deaths to occupy his thoughts. Although he had been curious about them on his own, it was Laurie's commitment to them that had fanned his interest. He'd used the series to foster a relationship with her, and it had worked superbly. As the weeks had gone by, he'd become enthralled with her and began to think that his idea of coming back to the States to salvage some kind of normal life with a new wife, new kids, and the proverbial white picket fence were within his grasp. Then, with a slip of the tongue, disaster had struck. Now he needed the series more than ever as a kind of glue to hold things together. The sooner he got the employee lists she suggested, the better. If he was really lucky and came up with something, he could call her that evening and take it over to her apartment.

Roger used the intercom on the phone to get in touch with Caroline, the most efficient secretary. He asked her to come into his office. Next, he got out the hospital phone directory and looked up the director of the human resources department. His name was Bruce Martin. Roger copied down his extension number, and while he was doing so, Caroline appeared and hovered expectantly in the doorway.

"I need some names and phone numbers over at Saint Francis hospital," Roger called out. His voice reflected his sudden zeal. "I want to talk to the chief of the medical staff and the director of human resources as soon as possible."

"Should I get them on the line," Caroline asked, "or do you want to make the call yourself?"

"Get them on the line!" Roger ordered.

"Meanwhile, I'll have a quick chat with our own Mr. Bruce Martin."

As Laurie came through the front door of the OCME office, she glanced at her watch. She was appalled. It was almost noon. The taxi ride from the Manhattan General Hospital had taken an incredible hour and a half. She shook her head. New York could be like that, with all of midtown snarled in traffic like an enormous blood clot. The driver had explained that some major dignitary was in town, although he didn't know whom. Unfortunately, the visit required certain streets to be closed off for the motorcade. As soon as that happened, the entire central portion of the city came to a screeching halt.

Marlene buzzed Laurie in through the main door such that Laurie had to pass the administration area. She was afraid to look through open door, lest Calvin catch sight of her. If she had known she was going to be gone for so long, she would have filled out the two pesky death certificates before she left.

Luckily, the elevator was waiting, so Laurie didn't have to stand fully exposed in the main hall to anyone coming out of administration. As she rode up, she wondered if Roger would follow up on her suggestion and do the detective work she proposed. The more she thought about the idea, the more optimistic she became that it would lead to something. But even if it didn't, it would at least give her the feeling that something was being done about the problem. She didn't even want to think about the individual tragedies that the deaths of young, healthy people in the prime of their lives were causing for their families and loved ones.

Getting off on the fifth floor, Laurie walked quickly down to her office. The door was ajar. Riva was there but on the phone. Laurie hung up her coat and sat down. Centered on her blotter were a series of Post-it notes in Riva's crisp handwriting. Three said merely "Jack came in." Two said "Calvin came in," followed by several exclamation points. The final one said to call Cheryl Meyers.

Hastily, Laurie opened the drawer where she kept the material from her potential serial-killer series and pulled out the McGillin and Morgan folders. From each she took the partially completed death certificates, then reached for a pen. The first certificate was McGillin's, and she positioned the pen over the place on the form where she had to indicate the manner of death. But she hesitated as a mental battle raged between her responsibility of duty as ordered by a superior and her sense of ethics. For her, it was akin to a soldier being ordered to do something that wasn't right, for which he could be held responsible. The only saving grace was that in Laurie's situation, it was not an irrevocable act, and it could be changed. With a sigh, she completed both forms.

At that point, Riva hung up her phone and spun around. "Where have you been? I've tried your cell phone a dozen times."

"I was over at the Manhattan General," Laurie said. She opened her bag, felt around for her phone, took it out, and checked the LCD screen. "Well, that's the explanation why I didn't get your call. I can't seem to remember to turn the blasted thing on. I'm sorry."

"Calvin's been in here twice. I wrote two notes so you'd get the message if you came in when I wasn't here. To say the least, he's not very happy you disappeared."

"I know what it's about," Laurie said as she held up the two death certificates. "This is what he was looking for, so all should be okay."

"I hope so. He was fit to be tied."

"I see Jack stopped by as well."

"That's the understatement of the year. He was here twenty times. Well, that's a bit of an exaggeration. But even he got a little sarcastic with his comments toward the end."

Laurie inwardly groaned. After the effort she'd expended getting Jack to agree to have dinner that night, she hoped her absence hadn't frustrated him enough that he'd call off their date. "Did Jack say what he wanted?"

"No! Just that he was looking for you. As for the last message from Cheryl, she said it wasn't important, but for you to give her a call."

Laurie got up, clutching the two death certificates. "Thanks for being a messenger service. I owe you."

"It wasn't a problem," Riva said. "But out

of curiosity, what were you doing over at the Manhattan General for so long?"

"Actually, I spent more time in the taxis than I did at the hospital. But I went over there because I had an idea that might help with my supposed serial-killer series."

"What is it?"

"I'll tell you later. Right now, I'm going to take these death certificates down to Calvin in person to smooth the waters."

"What should I say to Jack if he happens to come by yet again?"

"Tell him I'll be stopping by his office after I see Calvin."

Laurie retraced her steps to the elevator, feeling a twinge of guilt about not sharing her most current problem with Riva. Yet short of the OB office, she knew she didn't want to tell anyone that she was pregnant until she'd told Jack. Of course, she knew that if sharing it with Jack turned out to be as bad as it could possibly be, she might not be sharing it with anyone else.

As the elevator descended, Laurie glanced at the now-completed death certificates. Even though they could be changed, and in her estimation probably would, it still bothered her that she'd been forced to compromise her professionalism by filling them out as she had. It seemed to her that kowtowing to the needs of bureaucracy was not only ethically repugnant but also a disservice to the memory of the victims.

Once in administration, Laurie had to sit on the couch to wait. Calvin's door was closed, and his secretary, Connie Egan, told her the deputy chief was closeted with a police captain. Laurie wondered if it was Michael O'Rourke, Lou's immediate boss, who was an in-law to the Manhattan General mugging victim. While she waited, she thought about what she was going to say to Jack. If he'd been looking for her as hard as Riva had suggested, it was inevitable he'd ask where she'd been. If he were as jealous as Lou suggested, it was not going to help if he learned that Laurie had gone over to see Roger immediately after getting Jack to commit to having dinner. Yet Laurie promised herself that she wasn't going to fall into the trap of lying.

Thinking about Jack reminded her that she'd not made a dinner reservation. Since it was now afternoon, she knew it was an appropriate time. She eyed the phone on the side table next to where she was sitting. With no one paying her any heed, Laurie called Riva to get the number from her address book on her desk, and then put in the call. As she expected, the restaurant was heavily booked, and Laurie had to settle for a five-forty-five reservation.

Calvin's door opened and a bulky, quintessentially Irish-appearing police officer in his dress blues emerged. He shook hands with Calvin, nodded to Connie and even Laurie, put on his hat, and left. As Laurie's eyes turned back to Calvin, she found herself transfixed by his stare.

"Get in here!" Calvin barked.

Laurie got to her feet and sheepishly passed him to stand inside his office. Calvin shut his door, came over to Laurie, and snatched the papers from her hands. He leaned his backside against his desk while he checked the certificates. Satisfied, he tossed them onto his desk.

"It's about time," Calvin said. "Where the hell have you been? I gave you a paper day to do paperwork, not to go gallivanting around."

"I made what I thought was going to be a quick visit to the Manhattan General Hospital. Unfortunately, the traffic didn't cooperate, and it turned into a much longer errand than I'd expected."

Calvin eyed Laurie suspiciously. "And what were you doing over there, if I may ask?"

"I was talking with the gentleman I mentioned yesterday, the chief of the medical staff."

"You're not going to do anything that will turn out to be an embarrassment to the department, I trust."

"Not that I can imagine. I gave him the information about the Queens cases. It's in his hands to do whatever he thinks is appropriate."

"I don't want to hear you're overstepping your bounds like you've done in the past."

"As I said yesterday, I've learned my lesson." Laurie knew she was again being less than forthright.

"I should hope so. Now get your butt upstairs and sign out the rest of your cases or you'll be out pounding the pavement for alternative employment."

Laurie nodded respectfully and left Calvin's office. She was relieved. She had expected the worst, but the visit turned out to be surprisingly tame. She wondered if Calvin was mellowing.

While she was on the first floor, Laurie poked her head into the forensic investigators' office to see if she could save herself a call. She found Cheryl busy at her desk and asked her what was on her mind.

"I just wanted to let you know that I called Saint Francis and changed the chart request to urgent."

"Shucks! When I saw your message, I was hoping maybe you'd gotten them already."

Cheryl laughed. "Overnight hospital-chart service? That'll be the day! We'll be lucky to see them in a couple of weeks, even with the urgent classification."

Laurie went back to the front elevator, and as she waited, she wondered if it would be helpful if Roger intervened as far as the charts were concerned. In the back of her mind, she had the sense that somewhere in the charts from either St. Francis or the Manhattan General, there would be some hidden piece of information that would be the keystone of the mystery.

Gaining the fifth floor, Laurie hesitated for a moment, building up her courage. She wanted to drop in to Jack's office to talk with him but was concerned about what she'd be confronting, after what Riva had said. Although Laurie accepted that the current estrangement with Jack was largely her fault due to the affair with Roger, it didn't make it any easier. At the same time, she was not about to apologize.

Taking a fortifying breath, Laurie started down the hall. In contrast to the day before, she didn't hesitate. She let her momentum carry her all the way into the room, where she found both Jack and Chet bent over their respective desks, peering into their microscopes. Although she hadn't been trying, she'd come in silently, such that neither man knew she was there.

"I'd be willing to bet five bucks I'm right," Jack was saying.

"You're on," Chet responded.

"Excuse me!" Laurie called.

With obvious surprise, both men's heads bobbed up and turned to face their visitor.

"Forsooth!" Jack exclaimed. "Speak of the devil! The ghost of the missing Dr. Montgomery has just materialized in our midst."

"Miraculous!" Chet added. He drew back, pretending to be terrified.

"Come on, you guys!" Laurie said. "I'm in no mood to be made fun of."

"Thank God she's real!" Jack said as if relieved. He pressed the back of his hand against his forehead in the stereotypical fainting gesture.

In a similar fashion, Chet put his hand to his chest as if he were experiencing palpitations.

"Come on! Knock it off!" Laurie said while looking from one to the other. It seemed to her that they were carrying the charade a bit too far.

"We thought you were gone for good," Chet explained with a snicker. "The rumor was that it had been a sudden dematerialization. As the day's scheduler, I was supposed to know where you were, but I had no idea. Even Marlene in reception didn't see you leave."

"Marlene had stepped away from her desk when I went out," Laurie said. It was apparent to her that her absence had been the subject of speculation, which, under the circumstances, was not a good sign.

"We're all a little curious about where you

did go, since, according to Calvin, you were supposed to be in your office."

"What is this, the Spanish Inquisition?" Laurie asked, hoping a bit of humor would deflect the question. She looked directly at Jack. "Riva said you stopped by, so I'm returning the favor. Was there something specific on your mind?"

"I was going to give you the final lowdown on Mulhausen's autopsy," Jack said. "But first, we are all truly curious about where you so mysteriously went. Can't you fill us in? We've got a lot of money riding on it."

Laurie's eyes flicked back and forth between the two men. They were watching her expectantly. This was the question she feared, and she frantically tried to think up an appropriate response without lying. Nothing came to mind.

"I went over to the Manhattan General Hospital—" Laurie began, but Jack cut her off.

"Bingo!" Jack said. He pointed at Chet with his fingers positioned to make his hand appear like a gun. "You owe me five bucks, hotshot."

Chet rolled his eyes in apparent disappointment, shifted his weight to get his wallet out of his back pocket, and plopped a five-dollar bill in Jack's waiting hand.

Jack clutched the money triumphantly and looked back at Laurie. "Looks like I get to profit from your assignation after all."

Laurie felt her ire rising, but she held it in check. She didn't like this public gamesmanship at her expense. "I went over to the Manhattan General because I had an idea that might solve the mystery of my serial-killer series."

"Oh, sure!" Jack said. "And just by coincidence, you had to share this idea with your current flame."

"I think I'll head down and get some coffee," Chet said, hastily getting to his feet.

"You don't have to go on my accord," Laurie said.

"I think I will just the same," Chet responded. "It's time for lunch." He stepped out of the office and pulled the door shut behind him.

For a moment, Laurie and Jack eyed each other.

"Let's put it this way," Jack said, breaking the silence. "I find it demeaning that you would spend considerable effort convincing me to have dinner with you and then immediately disappear for four hours to see the man with whom you are currently having an affair."

"I can understand, and I'm sorry. It didn't dawn on me that it would affect you like this."

"Oh, please! Put yourself in my position!"

"Well, after the fact, I must admit I was afraid you would ask where I had gone. But, Jack, I went only for the reason I said. The Queens cases gave me an idea of how I might be able to come up with a list of potential suspects. It was not a tryst. Don't belittle me with that kind of talk!"

Jack tossed Chet's five-dollar bill onto his desk, lowered his eyes, and rubbed his forehead.

"Jack, believe me! Part of the reason I had the idea I did was your comments about the plot thickening and a pall being over AmeriCare. In fact, I wanted to ask you what you meant specifically."

"I'm not sure I had anything specific in mind," Jack said without taking his hand from his forehead. "It's just that if your series jumps to thirteen cases at two hospitals, both of which are AmeriCare institutions, it makes you wonder."

Laurie nodded. "I thought you had something about managed care in mind. If these are murders, I'm getting the impression they are not random. The demographics are too similar. For instance, I learned today that all of them, at least those at the Manhattan General, have been relatively recent AmeriCare subscribers. How that fits into the picture, I haven't a clue."

Jack took his hand away and looked up at Laurie. "So you're now thinking this might be some kind of conspiracy thing?"

Laurie nodded. "I thought that was what you were implying from your comments."

"Not really, and from a capitation standpoint, it doesn't make sense, so it can't have anything to do with managed care per se. On the other hand, medicine has become big business, and AmeriCare is one enormous organization. That means there are actuarial types and their bosses who are so far removed from patient care that they forget what the product of the company ultimately is. They see everything in terms of numbers."

"That may be true," Laurie said, "but getting rid of new, healthy subscribers is diametrically counterproductive to any actuarial goal."

"It might seem that way to us, but my point is that there are people involved, at high levels, whom we cannot hope to understand. Some kind of conspiracy still could be involved whose rationale might not be immediately apparent."

"Maybe so," Laurie said vaguely. She was disappointed. She thought Jack might have something specific to offer.

Laurie and Jack gazed at each other for a few beats. It was Jack who broke the silence. "Let me ask you something straightout that I alluded to down in the pit. Is this dinner date tonight some kind of elaborate setup to tell me you're getting married, because if it is, I'm going to go ballistic. I just want to warn you about that."

Laurie didn't answer right away, because the comment reminded her of how complicated everything in her life had become. It was hard for her to keep everything and everybody in perspective.

"This silence is not giving me a good feeling," Jack warned.

"I am not getting married!" Laurie said

with sudden vehemence, jabbing her finger at Jack. "I told you that in no uncertain terms down in the autopsy room. I told you that I needed to talk to you about something that involves you and me and no one else."

"I don't think you included that 'no one else' part down in the pit."

"Well, I am now!" Laurie barked.

"All right, all right. Calm down! I'm the one that's supposed to be upset, not you."

"You'd be upset if you were me."

"Now, that's a statement I can't interpret without a bit more information. But, you know, Laurie, I hate to see us going at each other like this. We're like two blind people flailing away in the dark."

"I couldn't agree more."

"Well, then, why don't you tell me whatever it is you need to tell me and put it behind us."

"I don't want to talk about it here in this setting. I want to be away from the OCME. It has nothing to do with work, and I don't want to be here. I made a reservation at Elios at five-forty-five."

"Whoa! Is that going to be dinner or a late lunch?"

"Very funny," Laurie said impatiently. "I warned you it might have to be early. It's Friday night, and they are booked. I was lucky to get what I did. Are you going to be there or not?"

"I'll be there, but it's going to be a big sacrifice. Warren is going to be disappointed I won't be showing up on the basketball court for the big Friday-night run. Well, actually, that's a lie. I've been playing so poorly since you left that he won't have me on his team. I've become a relative persona non grata on my own court."

"I'll see you at Elios," Laurie said, "provided you deign to show up." She turned and walked out of the office.

Jack leaped from his chair, and, holding onto the doorjamb, he leaned out into the hall. Laurie was already a good distance down the corridor in the direction of her office. There was no hesitancy in her step, and she was moving at a good clip. "Hey," he called out. "Saying it was a sacrifice meeting you for dinner was supposed to be a joke!"

Laurie didn't slow or turn around and soon disappeared from view into her office.

Jack righted himself and regained his

desk chair. He wondered if he had overdone his sarcasm. He shrugged because, knowing himself, it would have been hard for him not to do otherwise. Such repartee had become his defense against the uncertainties of life. In the current situation, he feared he was going to be blindsided by Laurie in some form or fashion. He had no idea what was on Laurie's mind. Yet Lou's comment that she wanted to patch things up still resonated and gave him a sliver of hope.

The combination of street basketball and work was usually Jack's solace, and with basketball not as satisfying, as he'd explained to Laurie, work had taken over. During the previous five weeks, Jack had been a virtual workhorse. Within the time frame of slightly more than a month, he'd gone from Calvin's nightmare in respect to getting cases signed out to Calvin's darling. Not only was Jack doing significantly more cases than anyone else, he was getting them out faster. Jack returned to his microscope and the trays of slides he'd just brought down from histology that morning.

Time flew by. Chet returned, and Jack insisted that Chet take back his fiver with the explanation that the bet hadn't been fair because Jack had been a hundred percent certain. After a time, Chet had gone out again, but Jack labored on. The progress he made calmed him and gave him a sense of satisfaction, but best of all, it made it possible not to think about Laurie.

"Hey, come up for air," a voice said, breaking Jack's concentration. He'd been staring at a strange hepatic parasite he'd stumbled onto in the liver of a gunshot-wound case. He looked up to see Lou Soldano standing in his doorway. "I've been watching you for five minutes, and you haven't moved a damn muscle."

Jack waved the detective into the office with one hand while he turned Chet's chair around with the other.

Lou sat down heavily and tossed his hat onto Chet's desk. He was wearing his usual sleep-deprived face such that he had wrinkled his forehead to keep his eyes open.

"I just heard the good news," Lou said. "I think it's great."

"What are you talking about?"

"I just stuck my head in Laurie's office. She told me you and she have a date tonight at Elios and that she asked you out.

What did I tell you? She wants to get back together."

"Did she tell you that specifically?"

"No, not specifically, but come on! I mean, she asked you out to dinner."

"She said she wanted to tell me something, but maybe it's something I don't want to hear."

"God, what a pessimist! You sound as bad as me. The woman loves you."

"Yeah, well, it's news to me! How did she happen to tell you we have a date, anyway?"

"I asked her. I don't hide the fact that I want you two back together, and she knows it."

"We'll see," Jack said. "Meanwhile, what's on your mind?"

"The freaking Chapman case, of course. We've been working flat out and have interviewed just about everybody over at the hospital. Unfortunately, nobody saw anybody suspicious, not that that's so strange. But we've got nothing. I was hoping that you might have come up with something. I know my captain came over to talk with Calvin Washington."

"That's weird. Calvin doesn't know anything about the case, and he didn't talk with me."

Lou shrugged. "I thought maybe you had. Anyway, do you have anything at all?"

"I haven't gotten the slides back, but they're not going to tell us anything. You got the slugs, which I think is about all you're going to get from the autopsy. What about the positioning of the victim and the fact that whoever shot her was probably sitting in the car? Are you working on the angle that the victim might have known the perpetrator?"

"We're working every angle. I tell you, we are interviewing everybody that had access to that garage. The problem is, we have no prints. Except for the shell casings, we've got nothing!"

"Sorry not to have been more help," Jack said. "On another subject, did Laurie say anything about her series of suspicious deaths that I mentioned to you yesterday?"

"No, she didn't."

"I'm surprised," Jack said. "Things are hopping in that regard. She's up to seven cases now at the Manhattan General, including one I posted today, plus she's come across six others at a hospital out in Queens."

"Interesting."

"I think it's more than interesting. In fact, I'm starting to believe she's was right about this from the start. I think she might be on to a serial killer."

"No kidding?"

"No kidding! So maybe you'd better start thinking about getting involved."

"What's the official take? Are Calvin and Bingham on board, too?"

"Hardly. In fact, I found out Laurie was pressured to sign out her first cases as natural deaths by Calvin, who was pressured by Bingham, who was pressured by somebody over in the mayor's office."

"Sounds political, which means our hands are tied."

"Well, at least I warned you."

fifteen

Jack put some serious muscle into his pedaling, and his bike responded. He was presently streaking past the United Nations building, heading north on First Avenue. Although the five-thirty traffic was at its peak, Jack had no altercations with any of the drivers. He had scaled back his aggressiveness to a degree following the recent arrival at the morgue of one of the city's many bicycle messengers. That poor fellow had had a dispute with a sanitation truck, for which he paid dearly. When Jack saw him in the morgue, his head had the diameter of large beach ball but the thickness of a quarter.

Ahead loomed the massively pillared viaduct of the Queensboro Bridge. Jack clicked into a higher gear as the roadway began to drop away in a gradual decline. With the help of gravity, Jack was neck and neck with the traffic, and the wind was whistling through his helmet. As usual, the exhilaration gave him a sense of detachment, and for a few minutes all his cares, worries, and bad memories evaporated in a wash of endorphins.

Earlier that afternoon, Jack had turned off his microscope light, put his desk in order, and walked down to Laurie's office with the idea of discussing with her how they should get to the restaurant. But he'd found her desk empty just like he had on his many visits that morning. On this occasion, Riva had explained that she had gone back to her apartment to change clothes. Jack gathered that his expression had been one of surprise, because Riva had gone on to explain that it was a woman thing, although that explanation only confused him more.

Laurie's attire had been perfectly appropriate for their early dinner. More than anyone else at the OCME, Laurie always dressed in a smart, feminine fashion.

Just beyond the Queensboro Bridge, the traffic snarled with backed-up cars vying to get onto the ramp leading to the FDR Drive north. Jack was reduced to slaloming between stopped cars, buses, and trucks until he was able to worm his way across the gridlocked 63rd Street intersection. Breaking away from the pack, he stood up on his pedals to regain his speed.

From that point north, Jack had no trouble. At the corner of 82nd Street and Second Avenue, Jack went up onto the sidewalk and dismounted. He secured his bike and helmet to a No Parking sign. When he walked into Elios, he was only three minutes late.

Jack stood by the mahogany bar just inside the door and took in the scene. Waiters in freshly laundered white aprons scurried about, making sure the linen-topped tables were in order. There were few customers sprinkled around the narrow but deep interior. To Jack's immediate right was a round table occupied by a loud group, several of whom Jack vaguely recognized as TV people, even though he didn't own a TV. At first, he didn't see Laurie and thought he was the first to arrive.

The owner, an elegantly tall woman, approached him; when Jack said he was there for a reservation under the name of Montgomery, she took his leather bomber jacket, which she immediately handed to an unoccupied waiter, and motioned for Jack to follow her. Halfway into the dining room, he saw Laurie at a table to the right, engrossed in conversation with a mustached waiter. In front of her was a bottle of sparkling Italian water, but no wine. He knew how much Laurie liked wine, and in the past, if he was ever late for a dinner together, she always went ahead and ordered a bottle. Why she didn't on this occasion, he had no idea.

Jack leaned over and gave Laurie a fleeting kiss on the cheek before he even thought about whether he should do it or not. He then shook hands with the waiter who was a remarkably friendly chap. As Jack sat down, the waiter asked him if he wanted any wine.

"Yeah, I guess," Jack said. He looked at Laurie.

"You go ahead," Laurie said pointing to her water glass. "I'm going to stick with this."

"Oh?" Jack questioned. He was already slightly off guard at a dinner date where he had no idea what to expect. He waffled for a moment, then told the waiter to bring him a beer. If Laurie wasn't going to drink wine, he wouldn't, either. He thought it was a matter of principle, even if he had no idea what the principle was.

"I'm glad you got here safely," Laurie said. "I was hoping after that courier case you'd rethink the advisability of courting death on a daily basis."

Jack nodded but didn't respond. To him, Laurie looked radiant. She was wearing one of his favorite outfits, and he wondered if she had chosen it on purpose. Not only had she changed clothes, she had washed her hair. At the OCME, Laurie wore her hair either piled on top of her head or in a French braid, but tonight it was down and cascaded over her shoulders to form a soft frame around her face.

"You look great," Jack said.

"Thank you. You look good, too."

"Oh, yeah, sure," Jack said with obvious disbelief. He looked down at his wrinkled chambray shirt, mildly spotted, dark blue knitted tie, and slightly grease-stained jeans. Next to Laurie's splendor, he felt like the poor relation.

While the waiter was off getting Jack's beer, they made small talk about the numerous times they had been at the restaurant. Laurie mentioned the time she had brought Paul Sutherland into Elios for a surprise meeting with Jack and Lou when she was thinking of marrying the man.

"Well, that wasn't my favorite night here," Jack admitted.

"It wasn't mine, either," Laurie agreed. "The reason it comes to mind is that just yesterday, Lou brought it up out of the blue and said that you and he were jealous."

"Really? Well, what does Lou know?"

"I have to tell you, just so you know, I never thought you were jealous."

The waiter returned with Jack's beer and a basket of bread. "Would you like to hear the specials now, or do you want to wait?"

"I think we'll wait for a few minutes," Laurie responded.

"Just give a yell," the waiter said agreeably. Jack and Laurie watched him head back into the kitchen.

"I'm sorry about suggesting this afternoon that having dinner with you was a sacrifice," Jack said when they looked back at each other. "I didn't mean to hurt your feelings. It was supposed to be funny."

"Thank you for your apology. Under normal circumstances, I wouldn't have reacted as I did. I'm afraid I'm not seeing much humor in things lately."

"Well, I didn't get a chance to tell you that Mulhausen was clean, just as you suspected. There was no pathology whatsoever on gross. And talking about Lou, you should know that I told him that I was coming around to your serial-killer idea and that his department might want to look into it."

"Really? And what did he say?"

"He wanted to know what the official OCME position was, and I told him."

"And?"

"He said under the circumstances, with neither the OCME or the hospital taking a stand and the mayor's office tangentially involved, his hands were, in a sense, tied."

"I'm going to try to change all that by coming up with a list of suspects."

"Actual suspects! Whoa! That would certainly alter the landscape. And strange that you should say that. I had a new thought along those lines."

"This should be interesting."

"Although the deaths in your series seem counterproductive to the actuarial interests of managed care, there are a couple of ways they could be related to the managed-care phenomenon."

"I'm listening."

"Managed care has had to be aggressive, taking over practices and hospitals in an often hostile way. Your serial killer could be someone as angry at AmeriCare as I am. I have to admit I'd harbored some murderous thoughts after AmeriCare gobbled up my practice. If it weren't for AmeriCare, I'd still be a conservative ophthalmologist back in the Midwest, walking around in a glen plaid suit and struggling to put a couple of girls through college."

"No matter how many times you tell me the story of your former life, I find it hard to picture. I'm sure I wouldn't recognize you."

"I wouldn't recognize myself!"

"But your point is well taken. A physician who has admitting privileges at Manhattan General and Saint Francis Hospital is one of the profiles that is being considered. What's your other idea?"

"Managed-care competition! It's a dog-eat-dog business world out there in the medical arena. As the two local giants in the industry, National Health and AmeriCare have bumped heads in the past with some strikingly underhanded machinations coming to light. I know National Health has generally conceded New York to AmeriCare, but they could have had a change of mind. Causing AmeriCare a major PR disaster, which your series will be sooner or later, would undoubtedly be a boon to National Health. And as long as I'm thinking in this vein, any individual or group who wanted AmeriCare stock to tumble could be involved, because once your series hits the media, investors are going to turn away in droves."

"Good points!" Laurie conceded. "I really hadn't thought of either one of those ideas. Thank you."

"Don't mention it."

Jack took a long pull on his beer, drinking it directly from the bottle. Laurie sipped her sparkling water. The restaurant was awakening from its daytime slumber. A few more patrons were seated. A bar crowd had materialized, raising the noise level with excited chatter and bursts of laughter.

Noticing the break in Jack and Laurie's conversation, the waiter came over to ask if they'd like to order appetizers. After Laurie and Jack exchanged glances to see if either objected, they both nodded, which keyed off an impressive performance on the waiter's part. He rattled off a long list of appetizer specials, explaining each in painstaking detail. Despite the enticing recital, Laurie ordered an arugula salad, and Jack settled on calamari. Both were from the regular menu.

After the waiter had gone and left them alone again, Jack eyed Laurie. She had her head down while busily repositioning her flatware that was already perfectly well positioned. Jack sensed that she was tense. After several more minutes went by, what had started out as a mere pause in the conversation seemed to Jack to become an awkward lull. He adjusted himself on the hard seat, and after a glance around the room to make sure they were being appropriately ignored, he broke the silence: "When would you like to talk about your important 'whatever' that involves you and me and no one else? Is it an appetizer subject, an entrée subject, or a dessert subject?"

Laurie looked up. Jack tried to read her blue-green eyes, but he couldn't tell if she was angry or anguished. His speculation about what she was going to say ran the full gamut from her wanting to patch things up, as Lou had suggested, to telling him she was tying the knot with her French-sounding boyfriend. The fact that she was dragging the mystery out was starting to wear thin.

"If it's not too much to ask, I would like you to kindly avoid any attempts at sarcastic humor. I'm sure it is obvious I'm having a hard time with this, and you could at least show some respect."

Jack took a deep breath. It was a tall order for him to abandon his most potent psychological defense in a situation when he feared he needed it the most. "I'll try," he offered, "but I'm all over the map trying to figure what this is all about."

"First, let me say that I learned yesterday that I have the marker for BRCA1."

Jack stared at his former lover while myriad thoughts reverberated inside his head. Along with a rush of sympathy and concern was what he considered a less noble sense of relief. Selfishly, he knew he could personally deal with the BRCA1 problem a lot better than he could with the idea that she was getting married.

"Aren't you going to say anything?" Laurie asked after a pause.

"I'm sorry! The news has just caught me unawares. I'm truly sorry to hear that you have the marker. On the positive side, I still think it is better that you know than if you didn't know."

"At the moment, I'm not convinced."

"I am. There's not a shred of doubt in my mind. For now, it will merely mean you'll have to be that much more vigilant, perhaps with mammograms or MRIs on a yearly basis. Remember that although the marker means you have an increased risk of developing cancer before the age of eighty, your mother, whose mutation you undoubtedly share, didn't develop the problem until she was in her eighties."

"That's true," Laurie said, recognizing that Jack had a point. Her face visibly brightened. "And my maternal grandmother who'd had breast cancer didn't develop it until her eighties, either. And my aunts who are all in their latter seventies haven't gotten it—at least not yet."

"Well, there you go," Jack said. "It seems reasonably clear to me that your particular family mutation determines an octogenarian illness."

"Maybe," Laurie said, retracting some of her optimism. "But there's no test for such an assertion, and it doesn't take into account the increased risk of ovarian cancer."

"Has anyone in your family on either side ever had ovarian cancer?"

"Not that I know of."

"It seems to me that is all very positive information."

"I suppose," Laurie said, going back to tinkering with her flatware.

Jack took another gulp of his cold beer. He felt hot and wondered vaguely if his face reflected it. He stuck a finger into his collar and pulled it away from his perspiring neck. He was dying to take off his tie, but he didn't dare, with the chic way Laurie was dressed. What was bothering him was the way Laurie had introduced the BRCA1 issue. She'd said "first," which made Jack worry there was a "second."

At that moment, the salad and calamari arrived. The waiter served the food and then busily rearranged the table and scooped up the breadcrumbs before disappearing. He'd not pestered them about their entrée order, which reminded Jack of one of the reasons he liked to eat at Elios. He'd never felt victimized by the inevitable bum's rush in an effort to turn the table, as he had at so many other "in" restaurants.

After taking a few bites of his calamari and another sip of beer, Jack cleared his throat. Superstitiously, he didn't want to ask the question, but the suspense was killing him: "Was there anything else you wanted to tell me tonight, or was it just this BRCA1 issue?"

Laurie put down her fork and locked eyes with Jack. "There is something else. I wanted to tell you that I am pregnant."

Jack swallowed, tipped his head slightly to the side as if something had just caromed off his scalp, and put his beer back on the table. He kept his eyes glued on

Laurie's. Laurie being pregnant was perhaps the last thing he expected to hear, and his mind was a jumble of complicated thoughts. He cleared his throat again.

"Who's the father?" Jack questioned.

Laurie's face clouded over like a sudden summer storm, and she leaped up so fast that her chair tipped over backward. The crash brought general conversation in the restaurant to a sudden standstill. She threw her cloth napkin down onto the top of her salad and started for the front of the room. Jack, who had initially recoiled from the unexpected flurry, regained his senses enough to reach out and catch Laurie by the forearm. She tugged back, but Jack held on tightly and wouldn't let her go. She glared down at him with nostrils flared.

"I'm sorry!" Jack blurted and then hastily added, "Don't run off! Obviously, we need to talk, and perhaps that wasn't the most diplomatic first question."

Laurie gave another tug to free her arm, but it was with less force than the first.

"Please sit down!" Jack said in as calm and reassuring a voice as he could muster.

As if suddenly becoming aware of her surroundings, Laurie's eyes swept around the room, and she saw that the restaurant had been seemingly caught in a freeze-frame, with all eyes directed at her. She looked down at Jack, nodded, and took a step back around the table. As if on cue, the waiter materialized, righted her chair, and took away both the napkin and plate of salad. Laurie sat down, and as soon as she did so, the conversation in the restaurant recommenced as if nothing had happened. New Yorkers were accustomed to the unexpected and took it in stride.

"How long have you known?" Jack asked.

"I suspected it yesterday but didn't get confirmation until this morning."

"Are you upset about it?"

"Of course I'm upset. Aren't you?"

Jack nodded and paused for a moment while he thought. "What are you going to do?"

"Do you mean whether or not I'm going to have the baby? Is that what you're asking with your damn question?"

"Laurie, we are having a discussion. You don't have to act angry."

"Your first question, as you called it, struck the wrong chord."

"That was apparent, but considering that you have been having what seems from the outside as an intense affair, my question isn't so inappropriate."

"It struck me as inordinately insensitive, since I have not had sex with Roger Rousseau."

"How am I supposed to know? Over the last few weeks, I've tried on a number of occasions to call you in the evening. One night I continued the effort until rather late, which lead me to believe you were not there."

"I have stayed at Roger's on a few occasions," Laurie admitted. "But there was no sex involved."

"That sounds like a rather suspect distinction, but let's move on."

The waiter reappeared with a fresh napkin and salad for Laurie. Sensitively, he quickly withdrew.

"How pregnant are you?" Jack asked.

"Six weeks, although the OB office would call it seven weeks. There is no doubt in my mind that it occurred that last night we spent together. It's rather ironic, wouldn't you say?"

" 'Surprising' is the adjective that springs

mostly to my mind. How could this have happened?"

"I hope you are not blaming me. If you remember the day before, you had asked me where I was in my cycle. I told you that it was probably safe, but that it was close. When we made love, it was technically the next day, and obviously not safe."

"Why didn't you put a limit on our love-making?"

Laurie glared at Jack. "You are starting to anger me again. It sounds like blame to me, and you know something, it was the two of us involved in the decision to make love, not just me, and we both had the same facts."

"Calm down," Jack said appeasingly. "I'm really not placing blame. Honest! I'm just trying to understand. Your being pregnant has taken me totally and completely by surprise. We had done well to avoid it in the past. Why did we mess up on this occasion?"

Laurie glare softened. She took a deep breath and let it out with a whoosh. "Well, at this point, it's probably best to be completely honest. That morning, when I began to suspect that we might make love, I did think that we were taking a chance, and I was certain you did, too. It wasn't a huge chance in my mind, considering I thought it was the tenth day, but a chance nonetheless. With as much as I wanted a family with you for both our sakes, I was comfortable with the risk. From your point of view, I thought that somewhere in the depths of your soul, you were of the same mind, with the idea that conceiving a child would help push you beyond your past to start a whole new personal life. Maybe I was projecting too much of my own desires onto you, I don't know, but that was the long and short of how I felt."

Jack mulled over what Laurie had said. Absently, he chewed the inside of his cheek in the process. Life had thrown him some curveballs, and this one seemed right up there with the best of them. The shock of being presented with the news that he had possibly fathered another child caught him completely off guard. It also terrified him, mainly because he feared he would love it too much and it would make him as vulnerable as he'd been in the past. Losing a family had been the biggest trial of his life, and he doubted he could survive it again. Yet on top of these disturbing thoughts was another, more positive one. If he had learned nothing else in the past miserable six weeks, he'd at least learned that he loved Laurie more than he had admitted. How that was going to play out in the current situation he had no idea. He had no idea how she felt about her current boyfriend.

"I have trouble with these silences of yours," Laurie said. "Not only is it not like you, but I need feedback. Anything, even if it is bad. I need to know how you feel. We have some decisions to make, or if you don't want to be involved, tell me. Then I'll make the decisions myself."

Jack nodded. "Of course I want to be involved, but this is a little unfair. It's difficult for me to have all this dumped in my lap and then be expected to respond in the spur of the moment. In fact, it seems to me to be unreasonable for you to expect that. I would have preferred that you told me the moment when you learned so that we could both have had a chance to think in tandem. Then, at this dinner we could have shared our thoughts."

"You have a point," Laurie admitted. "I don't mean to put you on the spot, even though I wish you would respond the way I want you to respond."

"And how is that?"

Laurie reached across the table and gripped Jack's forearm. "I'm not going to put words into your mouth other than to hope this event can be positive and draw you out of your grieving role. Having a child will not demean your late family. But go home and think about it. I'm on call this weekend, so if I'm not at home, I'll be at the OCME. I'll wait for your call."

"Fair enough," Jack said in a tired voice.

"Hey, don't get depressed on me," Laurie chided.

"I won't get depressed, but I can tell you one thing. I'm no longer hungry."

"Neither am I," Laurie said. "Let's call it a night. We're both strung out." Laurie raised her hand and the waiter came over on the run.

sixteen

Roger leaned back and stretched his arms up toward the ceiling. They felt cramped after the hours he'd spent leaning over the library table in the conference room of the human resources department of St. Francis Hospital. Stacked around the table in little individual piles were numerous pages of computer printouts, plus a recently burned CD. Sitting across from him was the department head, Rosalyn Leonard. She was a serious-appearing, tall, striking woman with inky black hair and porcelain skin who had initially intimidated Roger since she seemed immune to his charm, which Roger took personally. It was inordinately important for him to think of himself as attractive to women he thought were attractive. But persistence had paid off, and as the hours had passed, he had finally prevailed. Ever so slowly at first, she had begun to warm. During the last hour, he felt she was flirting in return. The fact that she was not wearing a wedding band was not lost on Roger, and as the day melded into evening, he had tactfully inquired about her social status. When he learned that she was single and currently between relationships, he even considered taking the risk of asking her for a dinner date, especially if things didn't work out with Laurie.

When Roger had come out to Queens from Manhattan earlier that afternoon it had been a little like going home, since the hospital was located in the East Side of Rego Park, which was a stone's throw away from the section of Forest Hills where he had grown up. Although both of his parents had passed away, he had several aunts and an uncle who still lived close to his boyhood home. As he'd peered out of the taxi window while cruising along Queens Boulevard, he'd even entertained the idea to pass by the old homestead when he was finished with his errand.

Roger had made significant progress. His meeting with Bruce Martin, who headed up the Manhattan General Hospital's department of human resources, had been quite fruitful, although not at the outset. When Roger had initially asked straight-out for employee records, Bruce had told him that there were all sorts of federal rules that restricted access to such information. That forced Roger to be creative in his request, by contending that in his role as the chief of the medical staff, he was starting a study about the interaction between the doctors and all the support and custodial staff, particularly in regard to new employees and particularly during the night shift, when the hospital was on, in his words, "cruise control." Roger assiduously avoided mentioning even a hint of his true goal.

By the time Roger had left Bruce's office, he'd been promised a list of all employees at the Manhattan General Hospital and a list of new employees since mid-November, with a particular emphasis on people who worked the eleven-to-seven night shift. There had been a slight worry in Roger's mind when he had proposed such a seemingly arbitrary commencement date for the new employees that Bruce would have become suspicious in some form or fashion, but Bruce had merely written it down without any reaction. He promised Roger he'd have the list before he left work that very afternoon, and would have it placed on Roger's desk.

The second thing Bruce had done was call Rosalyn Leonard, his counterpart at St. Francis Hospital, to tell her that Roger would be coming over and to give her an idea of what Roger needed. At the time, Roger didn't appreciate how helpful that had been. Had Roger walked in off the street with his requests, which was his initial plan, he wouldn't have gotten anywhere with Rosalyn. There was no doubt in Roger's mind that she would have been dismissive and unhelpful. Thanks to Bruce's call, she had already done some of the preliminary work before Roger arrived. It turned out that getting the kind of lists Roger wanted required accessing a number of different sources. Roger had been surprised that the various departments in AmeriCare hospitals more or less functioned as individual fiefdoms within the constraints of their centrally dictated budgets.

The other thing Roger had accomplished before leaving the Manhattan General was to get Caroline started on amassing the professional staff list, with particular interest in those physicians who had admitting privileges for both the Manhattan General and St. Francis. Roger had taken the time to see if that information was generally available by calling up a few individual doctor's records. Unfortunately, it was spotty. Caroline had promised him she would do what she could, as it wasn't specifically coded. She had said that she was hopeful, since she was personally friendly with one of the computer whizzes employed by the hospital, who could often figure out how to do the impossible.

"Well, there you have it," Rosalyn said, pushing a final, thin stack of papers in Roger's direction across the library table's varnished surface. She patted the top with the palm of her hand. "Here's a complete list of all Saint Francis employees as of mid-November, with a notation of those working the night shift; a list of St. Francis employees who either quit or were terminated between mid-November and mid-January; a list of our full-time professional staff, also as of mid-November; and finally, a list of our professional staff with admitting privileges. Is that all you want for your study? What about new employees since mid-November?"

"No need," Roger said. "I think this should do it for what I have in mind." He glanced through the pages containing all the hospital employees as of mid-November and shook his head in amazement. "I had no idea so many people were required to run an American hospital." He wanted to divert the conversation away from his putative study. As sharp as Rosalyn was, he guessed she'd see through his ruse rather quickly if he was forced to say too much.

"Like all AmeriCare hospitals, we're actually on the lower slope of the bell curve," Rosalyn said. "As with all managed-care organizations, one of the first things AmeriCare does when it takes over a hospital is reduce the personnel in most every department. I should know, since the unenviable task fell to me. I was responsible for a sizable number of pink slips."

"That must have been difficult," Roger offered in an unconsciously preoccupied tone. He put the full list aside and glanced at the list of the employees that had left St. Francis. Even that was much longer than he had anticipated. It also wasn't as detailed as he had hoped, particularly in respect to which particular shift individual employees worked, whether they were terminated or left on their own accord, and where they went. "I'm surprised there is as much turnover as this. Is this representative?"

"Generally speaking, yes, but it might be slightly on the high side, because the period you are interested in encompasses the holidays. If people are thinking of moving to a new job, and want to take a little time off in between, the holidays are a popular and predictable time."

"And it seems like it's mostly nurses."

"Unfortunately, that's the reality. There's a serious nursing shortage, which puts them in the driver's seat. We're constantly recruiting nurses, and other hospitals are recruiting ours like a tug-of-war. We're even being reduced to seeking prospective candidates abroad."

"Really?" Roger questioned. He knew the United States drained doctors from developing countries who came to America, presumably to train, but then stayed, but he wasn't aware that nurses were being recruited as well. Considering the health needs of the developing world, it seemed ethically questionable at best. "The list doesn't say where the individuals went."

Rosalyn shook her head. "That information isn't put into the main employee data bank. It might be in the individual record if the individual requested a recommendation be sent to another institution or if an inquiry came in from another institution. But we have to be very chary with those records, as you well know. There's always the threat of litigation unless the individual authorizes access."

Roger nodded. "What if I end up with questions about individual people for my study? I mean, questions about their records in regard to their general performance while at Saint Francis, like whether they got along with their coworkers or whether there was any disciplinary action taken for any reason."

"That will be difficult," Rosalyn said, nodding as if agreeing with herself. "Is this study of yours an in-house study, or is it something you're thinking of publishing?"

"Oh, it's definitely in-house with limited access, except at the highest administrative level. It's definitely not meant for publication."

"If that's the case, I can probably help you, but I'd need to run it by our president and general counsel. Do you want me to do that Monday? That would be the first chance I'd have."

"No, not really," Roger said quickly. The last thing he wanted was for the two presidents to have a chat about his so-called study. "Hold off until I see if I need any more personal information on any of these people. I probably won't."

"Just give me twenty-four hours' notice if you do."

Roger nodded and was eager to change the subject. He cleared his throat and finally got around to ask the key question on his mind. "Which, if any, of these employees who left Saint Francis came to the Manhattan General, meaning they stayed within the AmeriCare family? Is that information readily available?"

"Not that I'm aware of. As you know, AmeriCare operates its hospitals as individual entities. The only economies of scale relate to price and origin of basic supplies. If a Saint Francis employee leaves and goes to Manhattan General, for us it's no different than if they went to a non-AmeriCare hospital."

Roger nodded again. What he was realizing was that he was facing some serious collating time when he got back to his office. The chance that he'd have something to take over to Laurie's apartment that evening as an excuse to get together with her was looking slim. He lifted his wrist and glanced at his watch. It was a quarter to seven. The window behind Rosalyn was completely dark. Night had long since fallen.

"I'm afraid I've kept you here an unreasonably long time," Roger said. He smiled warmly. "I'm very appreciative of your help, but I'm afraid I'm feeling particularly guilty since it is Friday night, and I'm sure I have kept you from something much more entertaining and enjoyable."

"It has been my pleasure to help, Dr. Rousseau. Bruce was very flattering about you when he called. I understand you were with Médecins San Frontières."

"I'm afraid so," Roger said modestly. "But please call me Roger."

"Thank you, doctor," Rosalyn said and then laughed at herself. "I mean, thank you, Roger."

"There's no reason to thank me. It is I who should be thanking you."

"I've read about the work that Médecins Sans Frontières does around the globe. I'm very impressed."

"There is a great need in the world for even the most basic healthcare in the trouble spots of the world." Roger was pleased that the conversation had taken such a personal turn.

"I'm sure. Where did you go during your service?"

"South Pacific, the Far East, and finally Africa. A mixture of impenetrable jungle and arid desert." Roger smiled. He had this story down pat, and just like it had with

Laurie, it usually had an auspicious social outcome.

"It sounds like a movie. What made you leave Médecins Sans Frontières, and what brought you to New York?"

Roger's smile broadened. He took a deep breath before closing in on the pièce de résistance of his come-on. "The eventual realization I wasn't going to change the world. I'd tried, but it wasn't going to happen. Then, like a migratory bird, I felt the instinctive need to come back here to nest and start a family. You see, I was born in Brooklyn and grew up in neighboring Forest Hills."

"How romantic. Have you found the lucky lady?"

"Hardly. I've been too busy getting myself situated and adjusted to living in the civilized world."

"Well, I'm certain you will not have any trouble," Rosalyn said as she began amassing the papers from which she'd culled the lists she'd given to Roger. "I bet you have some fascinating stories to tell about your travels."

"Indeed!" Roger responded happily. He was relieved. He knew he'd piqued her interest. "I'll be happy to share a few of the less harrowing, if you'd allow me to buy you dinner. It's the least I can do after having kept you here for so long. That is, of course, if you are free. Would you allow me the honor?"

Somewhat flustered, Rosalyn shrugged. "I suppose."

"Then it's a deal," Roger said. He stood up and stretched his legs. "There's an Italian restaurant here in Rego Park that's been a fixture since the fifties as a hangout for the local mafioso. The food was great the last time I was there eons ago, and not a bad wine list, either. Are you game to see if it still exists?"

Rosalyn shrugged again. "It sounds intriguing, but I can't be out late."

"Me neither. Heck, I'm going back to the office tonight."

Jasmine Rakoczi!" a voice called.

Jazz stopped her repetitions on one of her favorite exercises. She was lying prone working her hamstrings and buttocks. Turning her head to the side, she could see that someone was standing next to the machine she was using. Surprisingly enough, the feet and legs were female, not male. Jazz took her earphones out, then twisted around to look up into the face of the individual. She couldn't see much, because the face was backlit from the fluorescent ceiling lights.

"I'm sorry to bother you," said the almost featureless face.

Jazz could not believe someone was harassing her in the middle of her routine, and it was more irritation than anything else that got her to extract her legs from the machine and sit up. She found herself confronted by one of the women who manned the front desk. She'd seen her earlier when she'd signed in.

"What's the damn problem?" Jazz demanded. She wiped her forehead with her towel.

"There are a couple of gentlemen out in the lobby," the woman said. "They said they needed to see you right away, but Mr. Horner wouldn't let them come back here."

A slight but distinctly uncomfortable shiver descended Jazz's spine. Mr. Bob and Mr. Dave's unexpected visit the evening before flashed into her mind. Something must be up. It wasn't like Mr. Bob to approach her in such a public place.

"I'll be out," Jazz said. She took a drink from her water bottle as she watched the health-club employee head out of the weight room. Jazz's first thought was that her Glock was back in the pocket of her coat, hanging in the locker. If there was going to be trouble, she wanted the Glock. But why would there be trouble? Mulhausen had gone smoothly, without a ripple. The only thing that came to her mind was the possibility of something happening in regard to the Chapman investigation. Like everyone else on the eleven-to-seven shift, Jazz had been approached by a couple of exhausted-looking detectives for routine questioning. But that had gone down just fine, as evidenced by the conversation they'd all had at nursing report. The buzz was that it had been a mugging, pure and simple. Hospital security had made a big point of promising they'd be beefing up patrols, particularly at the times when shifts changed.

Jazz walked quickly to the door. As preoccupied as she was she didn't even notice the men staring at her. Wasting no time, she went back to the locker room and grabbed a Coke at the entrance. Opening her locker, she pulled on her coat over her workout clothes, thrusting her hand into her right pocket to clutch her Glock.

With one hand in her pocket and the other holding the Coke, Jazz had to use her shoulder to open the door to the lobby. Beyond the sign-in desk, there was a rather spacious sitting room, and beyond that, a restaurant and bar. There was even a small sports-apparel shop.

Jazz quickly scanned the people sprinkled around the space, and not seeing Mr. Bob or Mr. Dave, she went over to the sign-in desk and asked the receptionist for the men who wanted to see her. She pointed to two men hidden behind newspapers. Clearly, they were not Mr. Bob and Mr. Dave. From the look of their lower halves, they could have been homeless bums.

"Are you sure they asked for me?" Jazz questioned. Her next worry was that they were a couple of deep-undercover detectives trying to scare up dirt about Chapman. With a sense of resignation, Jazz walked over to where the two men were sitting. Her hand still clutched the Glock in her pocket.

"Hello!" Jazz called irritably. "I was told you two were looking for me."

The men lowered their papers, and when they did so, Jazz could feel her face flush and her pulse pound in her temples. It was all she could do to keep from pulling out her gun.. One of the men was her father, Geza Rakoczi. He had a two-day growth of stubble on his face, as did his companion.

"Jasmine, dear, how are you?" Gesa questioned.

Jazz could smell the alcohol on his breath from where she was standing behind a shallow coffee table littered with magazines. Without answering, Jasmine looked at the other man. She'd never seen him before.

"This is Carlos," Geza said, noticing the direction of Jazz's attention.

Jazz looked back at her father. She'd not seen him for years and had hoped he'd drunk himself into the grave. "How did you find me?"

"Carlos has a friend who's good with a computer. He says you can find anything on the Internet. So I told him to find you, and he did. He said you played a lot of online games and used what he called 'chat rooms.' I don't know anything about all that malarkey, but he sure did find you. He even found out you were a member of this club." Geza's eyes roamed around. "Pretty fancy place. I'm impressed. You're doing all right, girl."

"What are you doing here?" Jazz demanded.

"Well, to tell you the truth, I need a little money, and knowing you're a fancy nurse and all, I thought I'd ask. You see, your mother died, God rest her soul. I got to come up with some money, or they'll be burying her out on some island in a plain wooden box."

For a moment, all Jazz could see in her mind's eye was the thirteen dollars she'd made shoveling snow. Remembering what happened to it only deepened her fury. As hard as she was holding the Glock, she was smart enough to take her finger out of the trigger guard.

"Get the hell out of here!" Jazz spat. She spun on her heels and headed back toward the locker room. She could hear Geza call out her name, and the next thing she knew, he had grabbed her shoulder, pulling her around.

Jazz yanked her hand out of her pocket—luckily, without the Glock. Later, she'd wondered how it had happened, since her instinct was to draw the weapon. She jabbed her finger into his face. "Don't you ever touch me again!" she snarled. "And don't come pestering me! You know what I'm saying? If you do, I'll kill you. It's that simple."

Jazz turned again and headed for the locker room. She could hear Geza try to complain, saying that he was her father, but she didn't stop, and he didn't try to follow. She returned to her locker, spun the combination, and put her coat away. Back in the weight room, she decided to start her routine from the top, even though when she'd been disturbed, she was close to finishing.

Jazz had needed the exertion to control her fury, and it worked to a large degree. By the time she returned to the locker room for her shower, she had regained control. She could almost see some humor in the pathetic creature that her father had become. She wondered when her mother had died.

Jazz was amazed she'd lasted this long, as obese as she was.

Since she was behind schedule after doubling her workout routine, Jazz showered and dressed hurriedly. Emerging from the locker room, she looked back into the lobby area where her father had been sitting, and was relieved that he'd taken the hint and left.

As she approached her car, she couldn't help but remember the previous night, and after opening the door, the first thing she did was check the backseat. She wasn't happy about Mr. Bob and Mr. Dave surprising her the way they did. She liked to think of herself as being wary and observant.

Climbing into the Hummer and buckling herself in, Jazz was looking forward to some fun on the way to the hospital. Dueling with taxicabs was a good way to deal with the remnant of anxiety that her father's surprise visit had aroused. Waiting in the short line to get out of the garage, she got out her Blackberry. After three names in the last two nights, she wasn't optimistic, but she wanted to check just the same.

At the first red light, she logged on for messages. To her delight, there was one from Mr. Bob. Hastily, she opened it. "Yes!" she cried out. There was another name on her LCD screen. It was Patricia Pruit.

A smile spread across Jazz's face. All was well. By that time the following night, her account balance would be more than sixty thousand dollars.

When the light changed, Jazz bolted ahead of the pack of cars and taxis. No one seemed to want to challenge her. Settling back into the seat, she thought about how her father had found her. She was a little surprised. Although she spent a lot of time in chat rooms on the Internet, she thought she had been careful about her identity and whereabouts, except for the few times she "hooked up." She decided she'd better be more careful, because she liked chat rooms and wasn't about to give up the pleasure. It was only online that she found people of like mind to whom she could truly relate, respect, and even love. It was such a far cry from the assholes she had to deal with in real life.

Roger's dinner with Rosalyn turned out to be an unqualified success. The fact that she had been aloof when they first met was more than adequately made up by her behavior during dinner, particularly after she'd had a few glasses of wine. Following the meal, Roger tried to put her in a taxi to take her home, but she insisted that they share one. Outside her Kew Gardens apartment, she mounted a hard-to-resist argument for Roger to come in for a nightcap. a term Roger hadn't heard since college.

Ultimately, Roger did resist, even after a sustained and passionate kiss on the sidewalk. Roger had kept one hand on the open taxi door. Despite being severely tempted to take advantage of her hospitality and whatever else her newly expressed physicality implied, Roger kept reminding himself about the work he planned to do in his office. He felt he was on a roll, and even if he couldn't have anything that evening to present to Laurie, the weekend was just beginning.

After a promise to keep in touch, Roger climbed back into the cab and waved out the back window. Rosalyn stood nailed to the spot, waving until she disappeared from view. Roger was pleased. The venture to Queens had been rewarding. Not only did he get most of the information he wanted, he'd met a woman who was a strong candidate for some interesting future encounters.

By the time he had gotten back to the Manhattan General, it was nearly eleven o'clock. The first thing he did was visit the coffee shop and have a cup of real coffee. By the time he got up to his office, he was wired, and he dove into his work with alacrity. By two A.M., he'd developed quite a bit of data. Laurie's idea, coupled with his decisions of how to expand it, had proved to be strikingly fertile. In fact, it appeared to be too fertile. When he had started, he'd wondered if he'd come up with any suspects. Now he had too many.

Roger rocked back in his chair and picked up the first sheet he'd printed, a list of five doctors with admitting privileges at both Manhattan General and St. Francis, and who had actually exercised those privileges at both institutions over the previous four months. The original list of the doctors with dual privileges was far too long to be workable. That was when he decided to restrict it.

As chief of the medical staff, Roger had

unfettered access to the credentialing information and records of all physicians associated with the Manhattan General. Three of the five doctors on his list had disciplinary problems. Two of the doctors were euphemistically called "impaired" because of addiction problems to which Roger could surely relate. They were on probation, with some minor limitations in respect to their privileges, after having gone through drug rehab six months ago. The other individual, Dr. Pakt Tam, was involved in multiple malpractice suits that were still pending, all of which involved untimely deaths, although not the ones in Laurie's series. The hospital had tried to revoke his privileges, but he had sued, and his privileges were reinstated by court order pending the trial.

Dr. Tam's case had stimulated Roger to look up all the doctors whose privileges had been either eliminated or curtailed over the previous six months, with the idea that they could be angry, vengeful, and deranged, or any combination. That inquiry had led to eight doctors. The problem was that he had no way of knowing if any of them had had an association with St. Francis. Quickly, he scribbled a note to himself to call and ask Rosalyn on Monday. He attached the note to the page with the eight doctors and put it off to the side.

The thought about an angry doctor had made Roger think about any disgruntled current or former employee of the hospital, particularly a nurse or someone else who had direct access to patients. If he was going to think about doctors, he had to think about everyone else in the hospital as well, so he'd made a note to talk to Bruce to get a list of employees terminated prior to the mid-November cutoff date, maybe even going back a year. He'd taped the note to the edge of his desk lamp so he'd be sure to see it. At that point, he had begun to get discouraged, but he had pressed on.

The next group Roger had considered was the anesthesiologists. As he had voiced to Laurie, and for the reasons Laurie had concisely specified, he felt their expertise made them prime suspects, and his intuition had paid off with a couple of interesting possibilities. Two had immediately jumped out at him. Both worked the night shift exclusively, and presumably by choice. One was Dr. José Cabreo, who had a history of impairment with OxyContin, as well as several malpractice suits. The other was Dr. Motilal Najah, a recent addition to the professional staff from St. Francis. Roger had printed out copies of both doctors' records and had drawn stars next to their names. Those papers were directly in front of him just off the central blotter. As far as he was concerned, they were his chief suspects, with Najah ahead of Cabreo. Although Najah's credentialing record was clean, the timing of his transfer was just too perfect.

The last group Roger had looked into was the rest of the hospital employees. Comparing the list of people leaving St. Francis after mid-November with the list of new employees at the Manhattan General during the same period, Roger had come up with a group of more than twenty people. At first, the number shocked him, but then, when he thought about it, it made a certain amount of sense. The Manhattan General was the flagship of the AmeriCare fleet, and if there was active recruiting going on, as Rosalyn suggested, it would be natural for most professionals and support personnel to prefer to be at the name institution.

Recognizing his limitations as an amateur sleuth, Roger had known immediately that twenty-three suspects were too many for him to consider. To narrow the group, he had used Laurie's suggestion of considering only those people who worked the night shift at St. Francis and moved to the night shift at Manhattan General. With such narrow parameters, he had no idea if he'd get any hits, but to his surprise, he did. He had gotten seven. The names were Herman Epstein from pharmacy, David Jefferson from security, Jasmine Rakoczi from nursing, Kathleen Chaudhry and Joe Linton from the laboratory, Brenda Ho from housekeeping, and Warren Williams from maintenance.

Roger picked up the sheet containing these seven names. Although it was more people than he had expected, he thought he could deal with seven. As he read over them again, he couldn't help but notice how much the surnames reflected the ethnic heterogeneity of American culture. He felt he could guess the general ancestral origins of all except Rakoczi, although if pressed, he'd say Eastern European. He looked at the various departments involved and realized that all of them would have access to patients in some form or fashion, particularly during the night shift, when oversight was at a minimum. Vaguely, he wondered if he should try to talk Rosalyn into getting him their St. Francis records. Now that he had the beginning of a personal relationship with her, perhaps he would be able to get the information without her sending up a red flag, but there were no guarantees. Yet how else was he to proceed?

Putting the paper down next to the list of anesthesiologists, Roger looked at his watch. It was now a quarter after two in the morning. He shook his head. He couldn't remember the last time he had stayed up so late working. He guessed it had been back in his medical residency. It was a bit depressing, thinking of most of the rest of the city sleeping, but at least he wasn't tired. The bolus of caffeine he'd gotten down in the coffee shop was still coursing around in his bloodstream, making him feel antsy. He even noticed that he'd been unconsciously tapping his right foot. He wished it were about ten P.M. instead of two A.M., because now that he had all these potential suspects, he would love to call Laurie and maybe even suggest that he pop over to her apartment. Unfortunately, that was out of the question. As upset as she was about her BRCA1 situation, he was surely not going to wake her up.

Thinking about the hour made Roger realize that for the first time since he'd been employed at Manhattan General, he was actually in the hospital during the night shift when all the questionable deaths that he and Laurie were interested in had occurred. With the caffeine on board, sleep was out of the question, and as long as he was in the sleuthing mood, he might as well check out the surgical floor where more than half of the questionable deaths had occurred and, while he was at it, at least some of his so-called suspects. With that idea in mind, he picked up the records of the two anesthesiologists and the sheet with the seven individuals who'd transferred from the night shift at St. Francis to the night shift at the General. He looked over them again, committing the names to memory.

Roger was about to get up when another thought occurred to him. Given how wired he was, he knew he'd be up most of the night. Since he'd need some sleep, he'd likely not be back to the office until late morning. With that in mind, Roger dialed Laurie's extension at work.

"It's me, Roger," he said to Laurie's voicemail. "It's after two in the morning, but your suggestion about Saint Francis was on target. It's produced a lot of potential suspects, certainly more than I expected, so I have to give you credit. I'm looking forward to sharing it all with you, and maybe we could get together tomorrow night for dinner. At the moment, I'm heading upstairs to do a bit more detective work, like check out the surgical floor and meet some of the people on my lists while they are on duty. As a teaser, let me tell you about one of the night-shift anesthesiologists, Motilal Najah. I interviewed him when he applied for a staff position. Anyway, I had forgotten that he had come from Saint Francis right after the holidays. Is that a coincidence or what? And he's just the tip of the iceberg. Anyway, I'm going to be here another few hours, so I might not be back here in my office until possibly noon or early afternoon. I'll call you as soon as I get in. Ciao!"

Roger hung up the phone and looked at the list of the seven nonphysicians who'd also transferred to the General during the period in question, and he wondered if he should have run down the list for Laurie. More than anything else, he wanted to fan her interest as much as possible, in the hope that she'd accept the idea of getting together. He thought about calling again to add to his message, but then decided the message he'd given was enough of a teaser.

After donning the long, white coat he wore whenever he ventured out into the hospital, Roger walked the length of the administration area. He'd been there a few times in the evenings, but never after midnight. At this hour, it was like a mausoleum.

The main hospital corridor was empty, save for a person using a floor polisher in the distance. As he rode up in the elevator, he was amazed at how wide-awake and energized he felt. He also recognized a touch of euphoria, which unfortunately reminded him of heroin. He shook his head. He didn't want to fall into that trap. For doctors, such temptation is harder to fight, with drugs so easily available.

Roger got out at the third floor and pushed through a pair of swinging doors into the OR complex. He found himself in a deserted corridor. To his right, the sound of a TV issued forth from the arched opening leading into the surgical lounge. Hoping to run into some of the surgical staff, he walked in.

The room was about thirty feet square, with windows that looked out onto the same courtyard as the staff cafeteria did. Two opposing doors led into the locker rooms. The furniture consisted of a couple of gray vinyl couches, a smattering of chairs, and several dictating desks. A central coffee table was littered with newspapers, outdated magazines, and an open box of pizza. A corner TV was tuned to CNN, but no one was watching. In another corner was a small refrigerator with a communal coffee pot on top.

Ten people were sitting in the room, all dressed in the same unisex scrubs. Some had hats or hoods, and some didn't. Although the OR appeared egalitarian, Roger knew otherwise. It was the most hierarchical domain of the hospital. Most of the people in the room were reading and munching on various snacks while sipping coffee, while others chatted.

Roger went over to the coffee machine. He debated having more, not to keep awake, but more as a social ploy, as well as an ostensible reason to be there. He hadn't recognized anyone in the room. Believing he was adequately wired, he opened the refrigerator and opted for a small orange juice.

With his drink in hand, Roger swept his eyes around to look more closely at the various people. No one had paid him any heed when he'd come in, but now a woman made eye contact and smiled. Roger walked over to her and introduced himself.

"I know you," the woman said. "We met at the Christmas party. My name is Cindy Delgada. I'm one of the nurses. We don't get admin visitors very often. What brings you up here in the middle of the night?"

Roger shrugged. "I was working late, and I thought I'd wander around a bit for some human contact and see the hospital in action."

A wry smile appeared on Cindy's face. "Not much excitement with this somnolent group. If you're looking for entertainment, I suggest the ER."

Roger laughed to be polite. "No cases tonight?"

"Oh, yeah," Cindy said. "We've done two, there's one going on right now in room six, and we have another coming up from the ER within the hour."

"Do you know Dr. José Cabreo?"

"Of course," Cindy said while pointing to a pale, heavyset man in a chair by the window. "Dr. Cabreo is right over there."

Hearing his name, José lowered his paper and looked over at Roger. He had a bushy mustache that hid most of his mouth. His eyebrows rose expectantly under the edge of his surgical cap.

Roger felt obligated to walk over. He hadn't necessarily planned to talk with the two anesthesiologists directly; his informal game plan had been to engage the OR staff in casual conversation about the men to see if he could get a feel for their personalities. Roger wasn't fooling himself. He was no psychiatrist and had no delusions that he'd be able to recognize a serial killer unless the person out-and-out told him, yet he had a vague idea that he would be able to sense if either man could be a potential suspect.

"Hi," Roger said self-consciously, since he didn't know what to say. He berated himself for not anticipating the possibility of such a confrontation.

"What can I do for you?" José questioned.

"Well," Roger said, trying not to sound as confused as he was. "I'm chief of the medical staff."

"I know who you are," José said. His voice had an edge, as if he was wary of what Roger wanted.

"You do? How is that?" José was one of many on staff he'd not met, which included just about everybody on the night shift.

José pointed to Roger's nametag.

"Oh, of course," Roger responded, bouncing the heel of his hand off his forehead. "I forget it's there."

There was an awkward pause. The rest of the room was quiet except for the TV whose volume was turned way down. Roger had the sense the other people in the room were listening.

"What is it you want?" José asked.

"I just wanted to make sure that you are content, and there are no problems."

"What do you mean, 'problems'?" José demanded. "I don't like your implication."

"There's no reason to get upset," Roger said soothingly. "My intention is merely to be proactive and meet the staff. We've not had the pleasure." Roger stuck out his hand toward José, whose face had flushed.

José eyed Roger's hand but made no attempt to shake it. Nor did he get to his feet. Slowly, his eyes rose and reengaged Roger's. "You've got a lot of nerve coming up here out of the blue and talking to me about problems," he said heatedly. He poked his finger threateningly toward Roger. "This better not have anything to do with ancient history, like dredging up the painkillers I needed for my back or my closed malpractice cases, because if it does, you and the rest of the administration will be hearing from my lawyer."

"Calm down," Roger urged softly. "I had absolutely no intention of talking about any such thing." He was taken aback at José's belligerence and defensiveness, yet he forced himself to remain cool and collected. If the man could get this wound up with such little provocation, maybe he was a loose cannon capable of the unthinkable.

To defuse the situation, Roger quickly added, "My real goal in stopping by was to ask how things were working out with Dr. Motilal Najah. You've been here a long time, and Dr. Najah is a relative newcomer. As the senior man, I was interested in your opinion."

Some of the hostility and tenseness drained out of José's face, and he motioned for Roger to take a seat next to him. As soon as Roger was seated, José leaned forward and lowered his voice. "Why didn't you say that straight off? Motilal is the one you should be talking with, if you're concerned about problems."

"How so?" Roger asked. José's eyes now had a conspiratorial glint. Roger found himself thinking that even if José wasn't a serial killer, he might be the last person Roger would want giving him anesthesia.

"The man is a loner. I mean, like, we're kind of a tight team on the night shift. Let me tell you, he doesn't interact with anyone except in a professional capacity. He eats by himself and never comes in here to socialize. And when I say never, I mean never!"

"He seemed personable enough when I

interviewed him," Roger said. Roger could distinctly remember being impressed by Motilal's easy candor and gentle manner. He seemed friendly enough, yet what he was hearing from José suggested that Motilal had some antisocial traits, and if that was true, he'd have to be considered a suspect.

"He fooled you then," José said. He sat back and then gestured around the room. "Ask anybody if you don't believe me."

Roger's eyes scanned the room. The people had gone back to their reading or conversation. Roger looked back at José. Roger was beginning to feel pessimistic about winnowing down his potential suspect list with what he was hearing about Motilal and the way José was acting.

"What about his professional skills?" Roger asked. "Is he a good anesthesiologist?"

"I suppose," José said. "But one of the nurse anesthetists would be better at evaluating that, since they have to work directly with the lazy bum. The problem that I have with him is that he is never here. He's always out wandering around the hospital."

"What's he doing when he's wandering around?"

"How should I know? All I know is I end up doing all the work. Like ten minutes ago, I had to page him to get his ass up here, since it was his turn to do a case. Hell, I had already done two tonight."

"Where was he when you paged him?"

"Down on the OB-GYN floor. At least, that's what he said when I asked him. But he could have been in one of the local bars, for all I know."

"So he's doing a case at the moment?"

"He better be, or our chief, Ronald Havermeyer, is going to hear about it. I'm tired of covering for that guy."

"Tell me something," Roger said, settling back into his seat. "Have you been aware that in the last couple of months there have been seven unexpected and unexplained deaths of healthy, relatively young people in our hospital within twenty-four hours of surgery?"

"No," José said—a bit too quickly, in Roger's estimation. José held his hand out toward Roger as if to quiet him. A wall speaker had crackled to life.

"Code red in 703," a disembodied voice announced. "Code red in 703."

José heaved himself to his feet, tossing his newspaper aside. "Wouldn't you know it? The second I get a chance to sit down, there's a cardiac code. Sorry to break this off so abruptly, but when we're not on a case, we're supposed to show up for a code. I urge you to talk with Motilal. If you're trying to head off problems, he's your man."

José rushed from the room with his stethoscope clasped in his hand. From out in the hall, Roger could hear the double doors leading to the elevator lobby bang open and noisily swing shut. Roger exhaled uneasily and glanced around the room. No one had reacted to their strange conversation, to the code announcement, or José's sudden departure, until his eyes reconnected with Cindy Delgada's. She smiled again and made a questioning gesture with her shoulders. Roger got up and walked back to her.

"Don't mind Dr. Cabreo," she said with a laugh. "He's a hopeless pessimist and our resident prophet of doom."

"He seemed a bit defensive."

"Ha! That's the understatement of the year. He's out-and-out paranoid, with a touch of misanthropy, but you know something? We give him some slack because he's a damn good anesthesiologist, and I should know, since I work with him almost every night."

"That's reassuring," Roger said, although he was hardly convinced. "Did you happen to hear what he said about Dr. Najah?"

"I got the gist."

"Is that the general feeling up here in the OR?"

"I suppose," Cindy said with a shrug. "It's true Dr. Najah doesn't socialize and hang around with us, but no one minds except José. I mean, this is the graveyard shift, after all."

"What does that mean?"

"We all have our quirks, which is why we work this shift. Maybe we're all a little misanthropic in our own ways. I know I like the fact that there's less supervision and a lot less bureaucratic crap. Why Motilal prefers this shift, I don't know. Maybe it's as simple as just being shy. He's hard to read since he's so quiet, but I'll tell you, he's definitely a good anesthesiologist, and don't get me wrong because I said it about José, because I don't say that about everybody."

"So you wouldn't say Dr. Najah is antisocial."

"Certainly not in the psychiatric sense. At least, I don't think so, but to be honest, I really don't know. I've probably only spoken ten words to him."

"José complained about him wandering around in the hospital. Do you have any idea where he goes?"

"I believe so. I think he visits all the in-house preops scheduled for morning. Why I think so is because he's always carrying around the next day's surgery schedule."

Roger nodded while silently reaffirming his opinion about his deficiencies as a detective. After chatting with José, hearing a little about the loner Motilal, and learning about the night shift in general, he wasn't eliminating anyone as a suspect, but he pressed on. "Did you hear what José said when I asked him if he was aware of the seven deaths we've seen over the last couple of months?"

"Yeah, I heard," Cindy said with a derisive chuckle and a dismissive wave of her hand. "I don't know what was going on in his mind, because he knows about them. We all know about them, particularly the anesthesiologists. I mean, we haven't exactly been dwelling on the issue, but it's been the topic of conversation on occasion, especially as the cases mount."

"Why would he tell me he was unaware of them?"

"Beats me. Maybe you should ask him when he comes back. The anesthesiologists never stay long on codes. They just pop in if they happen to be available to intubate the patient or, if the patient was already intubated, to make sure the patient was intubated properly."

"Thanks for chatting with me," Roger said. He then glanced around the room a final time. "I have to say, no one else seems particularly friendly."

"As I said, we have our quirks, but if you came up here on a regular basis, you'd find people friendly enough."

With a final wave and appreciative smile, Roger walked out to the elevator. His finger went toward the call button, but stalled in midair. His visit to the OR hadn't been particularly helpful. He had two anesthesiologists who were potential suspects before he arrived, and he still had two after he left.

The choices were simple. He could stay on the third floor and visit the pharmacy and try to find out something about Herman Epstein, who'd transferred from the night shift at St. Francis to the night shift at the General. He could go down to the second floor and visit the lab to find out what he could about the two lab technicians who were on the same list. He could go back down to the first floor and visit security or even to the basement to visit housekeeping and maintenance, where there were two more similar transferees. Yet something told him he wasn't going to learn anything, thanks to his total lack of investigative experience. His little chat with José had made it clear that he didn't even know what questions to ask, short of "Are you a serial killer who's been knocking off patients during the night shift?" Laurie's idea was good in theory, but in reality, there were just too many potential suspects. All the transferees had access to the hospital in general by virtue of their respective job descriptions.

The thought of directly asking people if they were a serial killer brought a smile to

Roger's face. It wasn't hard to guess what would happen to his reputation and job if he started asking such a question. Roger sighed and looked at his watch. It was now after three A.M. Although some of the caffeine euphoria was wearing off, the feeling of being wired hadn't. There was no way he would fall asleep if he went back to his apartment.

Impulsively, Roger pressed the up button on the elevator. He decided he'd pay a visit to the surgical floor, whose charge nurse had been mugged and killed and where four of the seven unexpected deaths had taken place. He also decided to take a quick tour through the fifth floor, which housed orthopedics and neurosurgery, where there had been two deaths. He reasoned that he'd never been in the hospital during the night shift, particularly on the patient floors, and having a sense of the ambience and locale might be helpful in his thinking.

Although he had assumed as much, the atmosphere of the surgical floor was completely different than it was during the day. Instead of controlled chaos, an unexpected and deceptive serenity reigned. Even the lighting was different, dimmed from its daytime starkness. As Roger walked from the elevator lobby toward the nurses' station, he saw no one. It was as if there had been a fire drill and everybody had run out of the building.

Reaching the nurses' station Roger looked at the bank of monitors displaying the EKGs and pulses of all the patients. With modern wireless technology, such telemetry was now easily available on regular hospital floors. The problem, of course, was that no one was there watching it.

Roger looked down the lengthy corridor in both directions. The composite floor gleamed in the half-light. At that moment, Roger heard the telltale squeak of a desk chair. Wondering where the sound had come from, he rounded the end of the nurses' station and walked over to an open doorway. It led into a utility room with a long built-in desk/countertop, under and over cabinets, and a refrigerator. Sitting at the desk with her feet propped up and reading a magazine was an arresting-appearing nurse. Her features reflected a hint of Asian exotic, which Roger had come to appreciate in his years in the Far East. Her eyes were appropriately dark, as was her cropped hair. Beneath her scrubs was the hint of a shapely, hard body.

"Evening," Roger said before introducing himself. He noticed that the nurse was reading a firearms magazine, which seemed mildly inappropriate.

"What's up?" the nurse inquired without removing her feet from the edge of the countertop.

Roger smiled inwardly. He remembered a time in the not-so-distant past when nurses were deferential to doctors to the point of acting intimidated, even in the United States. This one clearly wasn't.

"I'm just checking to see how things are going," Roger said. "I know you tragically lost your charge nurse yesterday morning. I'm sorry."

"Not a problem. Actually, she wasn't all that good as a charge nurse."

"Really?" Roger questioned. It seemed a curiously unsympathetic response. Such candor with a stranger was hardly the norm, whether what she said was true or not. He read her nametag: Jasmine Rakoczi. He remembered that she was on the transferee list.

"I'm not pulling your leg. She was a weird one, and nobody liked her much."

"I'm sorry to hear that, Ms. Rakoczi," Roger said. He leaned back against the countertop and crossed his arms. "Has Clarice Hamilton assigned a new charge nurse for the shift?"

"Not yet. We got a temp to tide us over, but just as another grunt. I kind of took charge and assigned the patients. Somebody had to do it, and the others were just sitting around, wringing their hands. Anyway, things are going just fine."

"I'm glad to hear it," Roger said. "Ms. Rakoczi, I'd like to ask you a question."

"Call me Jazz. I don't respond to Ms. Rakoczi."

"I assume you have been aware of the four deaths of relatively young, ostensibly healthy, postop patients that have occurred on this floor over the last six or seven weeks or so, with the last one just last night."

"Of course. It would be hard not to be aware."

"True," Roger agreed. "Have they bothered you?"

"How do you mean?"

Roger shrugged. The question seemed so self-evident. "Have they disturbed you psychologically?"

"No, not really. This is a big, busy hospital. People die. You can't get attached, because if you do, you'll go crazy and your other patients will suffer. You brass sitting in your fancy offices don't remember what it's like out here in the trenches, you know what I'm saying?"

"I suppose," Roger said. He detected a not-too-subtle change in the nurse's demeanor. She had started out breezy but now seemed wary and taut, almost to the point of anger.

"Are you asking me this because they occurred on my floor?"

"Obviously."

"There have been similar deaths on other floors."

"I'm aware of that."

"In fact, there was one tonight, just a half hour ago, up on the OB-GYN floor. Why don't you go up and hound them?"

A distinctly unpleasant tenseness gripped Roger's entire body, which he blamed on the caffeine. After the euphoria passed, he invariably felt as if all his nerves were exposed. Learning of yet another death right while he was there in the hospital supposedly looking for suspects, made him feel uncomfortably complicit, as if he should have been able to prevent it. "Were the specifics about the same?" he asked, hoping vainly for a negative reply.

"I suppose," Jazz responded. "The word is, it was a woman in her thirties, in for a hysterectomy. Seriously, why don't you go on up and ask the nurses if it bothered them."

For a beat, Roger stared at this exotic-looking nurse whom he had originally thought of being attractive and rather sexy, while she brazenly stared back. Now he thought she was almost eerie, reminding him to a degree of his reaction to Dr. Cabreo and to the story about Dr. Najah. He couldn't help but remember Cindy's comment about people working the night shift being quirky, though maybe "quirky" wasn't nearly strong enough. Maybe "neurotic" was closer to the mark. He couldn't help but wonder if he'd find the whole lot of people on his supposed suspect list equally bizarre. One way or the other, it was becoming clear he would have to work on

Rosalyn to get the transferees' personal records, no matter the risk.

"What is this?" Jazz sneered. "The silent treatment, or are we having some kind of juvenile staring contest?"

"Sorry," Roger said, breaking off eye contact. "I was just shocked to learn about yet another death. It's upsetting and alarming. I'm surprised you seem to be able to take it so lightly."

"It's called professional distance," Jazz said. "Those of us who actually treat people have to maintain it." She brought her feet down with a thud, tossed her magazine to the side, and stood up. "I got patients to see. Enjoy yourself upstairs on OB-GYN."

"Just a second," Roger said. He grabbed Jazz's arm as she tried to brush past him. He was surprised at its muscularity. "I have a few more questions."

Jazz looked down at Roger's hand gripping her upper arm. There was a tense moment, but she controlled herself. She raised her eyes to Roger's. "Let go of my arm or you will be very sorry. You hear what I'm saying?"

Roger let go and recrossed his arms to be completely nonthreatening. He didn't want to give this woman any excuse for physical violence, of which he intuited she was capable. In truth, she was scaring him. "I understand you transferred from Saint Francis recently. Would you mind telling me why?"

It was Jazz's turn to stare before responding. "What is this, an interrogation?"

"As I told you, I'm chief of the medical staff. There was a mild complaint about your attitude by one of the doctors, and I'm looking into it. Frankly, this doctor has a history of unfounded complaints, but I still am obligated to check into the allegation." Roger was lying, but he felt he had to come up with some explanation for his questioning her on the spur of the moment. The nursing staff was not under his jurisdiction.

"What's this freaking doctor's name?"

"I'm not at liberty to disclose the individual's identity."

Jazz broke off eye contact with Roger. Her eyes darted around the room. Roger could see that her nostrils were flared, and she was breathing deeply. She was no longer wary. She was now definitely angry.

"Let me explain," Roger said. "I'm inquiring if you left Saint Francis for a similar reason. Did you have trouble with any doctor on the Saint Francis staff? We have to ask."

"Hell, no!" Jazz snapped. "I might have had a few words with my charge nurse on occasion, but never a doctor. I mean, I could count on one hand the number of times I even saw a doctor over there on the night shift. They were all home, screwing their wives."

"I see," Roger said. He wasn't about to comment on Jazz's last inappropriate point but picked up on the first. "So you also felt your charge nurse over at Saint Francis was not as competent as you would have liked?"

A wry smile appeared on Jazz's face. "You guessed it, but it's not surprising. The night shift attracts some weirdoes."

Roger nodded. As a result of his first night-shift visit, he couldn't have agreed more. "Out of curiosity, did you ever think you might share some of the blame if you didn't get along too well with either charge nurse?"

Any vestige of a smile disappeared from Jazz's face. "Oh, yeah! It's my fault that these two fat ladies were so stupid. Give me a break!"

"So why did you transfer?"

"I wanted a change, and I wanted to move into the city."

"Why do you personally work the night shift?"

"Because there's a lot less bullshit. There's still some, I admit that, but it's a lot less than during the day or even during the evening. When I was a corpsman in the military, I was assigned to the Marines for independent duty. I like working on my own the best."

"So you were in the military."

"Damn straight! I was with the Marines during the first Gulf War."

"Interesting," Roger said. "Tell me, what is the background of the name Rakoczi?"

"Hungarian. My grandfather was a freedom fighter."

"One other question if you don't mind," Roger said, trying to be nonchalant. "Did you know that when you were at Saint Francis, there was a series of similar deaths, back in November?"

"It was the same: It would have been hard not to be aware."

"Thanks for your time," Roger said, pushing away from the countertop. "I think

I will follow your suggestion and go up to OB-GYN, but I might have a few more questions. Would you mind if I came back if that were the case?"

"Suit yourself."

Roger tried to smile reassuringly at Jazz before walking out of the utility room and heading toward the bank of elevators. As he walked, he shook his head imperceptively. He couldn't believe it. He'd talked to two people on his list and heard about a third, and he felt he could make a case for any of them possibly being deranged enough to be doing the unconscionable.

Jazz leaned out of the utility room just enough to watch Roger head down toward the elevators. She couldn't believe it. Trouble was coming out of the woodwork. The sanctioning had been going so well until Lewis, then all hell had broken loose. And just when she had eliminated one potential disaster, another one had popped up. "What a bastard!" she murmured. She knew from the way he dressed and spoke that he was another one of those damn Ivy League types.

When Roger reached the elevators and pushed the call button, he turned and looked back toward the nurses' station. Jazz pulled her head back. She didn't want him to see her staring after him like she was concerned. She shook her head, then slammed an open palm onto the countertop. A few loose papers wafted to the floor.

"What the hell should I do?" she murmured. She shook her head again. The thought went through her mind to call Mr. Bob, but she quickly dismissed it. She had the sense that if she complained about anything, she wouldn't get any more names. She'd be dismissed from Operation Winnow. It was as simple as that.

Jazz shrugged. She couldn't think of anything. Although the worry gnawed at her, she didn't know what to do. At the same time, she knew she had to be careful, because this freaking admin type could end up being a whole lot more than a ripple, the way he was talking.

The elevator door slid open and Roger stepped out onto the seventh floor. To the left, beyond double doors, was the medical ward, and to the right through similar doors was OB-GYN. He pushed into OB-GYN. In contrast to the surgical floor below, there were a lot of people in evidence both at the nurses' station and in the hallway. He even saw an orderly pushing a gurney with a patient shrouded in a sheet toward the patient elevators. Roger guessed it was the patient he'd come up to inquire about.

Advancing to the nurses' station, Roger stood for a moment and just watched. He guessed it was the resuscitation team along with some of the floor's nurses. The resuscitation cart with its defibrillator was parked against the corridor wall. The people were talking in small groups, most likely debriefing themselves about the failed resuscitation attempt.

"Excuse me," Roger said to a woman directly in front of him. She was busy writing in a chart but looked up. Like Jazz downstairs, she was dressed in scrubs, but unlike Jazz, she emanated both civility and respect. Also unlike Jazz, she was slightly obese, with a smattering of freckles across the bridge of her nose. "Could you tell me who is the charge nurse?"

"I am. I'm Meryl Lanigan. What can I do for you?"

Roger introduced himself and said that he was inquiring about the recent death.

"The name was Patricia Pruit," Meryl said. "This is the chart. Would you like to see it?"

"I would indeed. Thank you." Roger took the chart and rapidly scanned it. The demographics were as he had feared. Patricia Pruit was a healthy thirty-seven-year-old mother of three. The previous morning, she'd had an uncomplicated hysterectomy for fibroids. Her postoperative course had been entirely uneventful, and she had already been started on clear fluids by mouth. Then came disaster.

Roger looked back down at Meryl. She was waiting for the chart, which she took back.

"It certainly is a tragedy," Roger said. "And so unexpected, given her age and past health."

"It's heartbreaking," Meryl agreed. She opened the chart to the nurses' notes.

"There have been others quite similar on other floors over the last month or so," Roger said.

“So I’ve heard. Luckily, this is our first. We might take it harder than others, since we’re accustomed to much happier outcomes.”

“I have a couple of questions, if you don’t mind. Did you happen to see a Dr. Najah on your floor tonight?”

“We did, just like we usually do.”

“How about Dr. Cabreo?”

“We saw him as well, but only after the code was called.”

“How about a nurse named Jasmine Rakoczi, who goes by the name Jazz?”

“Funny you should ask.”

“How so?”

“We see a little too much of Ms. Rakoczi most every night. I’ve even complained to Susan Chapman, who used to be her charge nurse, saying that I didn’t want her up here. I’m going to have to go a little higher now that we don’t have Susan with us any longer.”

“What does Ms. Rakoczi do when she comes up here?”

“She tries to be friendly with the aides. Other than that, she’s always looking in the charts, which she has no business doing.”

"Do you recall specifically that she was up here tonight?"

"I remember, all right, because whenever I see her, I challenge her. I challenged her tonight, just like I always do."

"What did she say?"

"She said she was the acting charge nurse downstairs and needed some supplies. I can't remember what it was. I sent her into our supply room to get whatever she needed, but I told her then to please leave. I also told her she'd have to replace whatever she borrowed, which she promised she would."

"And she went into your supply room?"

"She did."

"And then what happened?"

"I guess she got what she needed and went back downstairs. I really don't know, because I was off taking care of a problem with one of the patients. And then, of course, we had the code."

"What room was Patricia Pruit in?"

"703. Why do you ask?"

"I'd like to take a look."

"Be my guest," Meryl said while pointing down the appropriate corridor.

Myriad thoughts were swirling around inside Roger's head as he walked toward the patient's room. In his estimation, Jasmine Rakoczi was becoming more and more of an enigma. He kept asking himself why she would constantly be coming up a floor to the OB-GYN section to hobnob with the aides when she seemed so asocial, and why would she be going through OB-GYN charts. It didn't make any sense. What did make sense was that both she and Dr. Najah had come to OB-GYN prior to the code. Of course, he wondered how many others on his transfer list had come as well. For all he knew, it could have been all of them.

Patricia's room was a mess. The debris from the cardiac resuscitation attempt littered the floor. In the frenzy of the event, some of the wrappers, syringes, medication containers, and the like had been merely tossed aside. The bed had been cranked down flat, raised to help with the CPR, and the resuscitation board was still in place. A few telltale droplets of blood were sprinkled across the wrinkled, white sheet.

Unfortunately, what Roger was looking for was not in evidence. The IV pole was in its usual position at the head of the bed, but without the bottle or plastic container of fluid that had to have hung there. As a consequence of being on the scene, Roger had gotten the idea of having the IV contents checked. Since Laurie had told him that toxicology had come up short, maybe testing the IV fluid would yield something.

Roger turned around and went back to the nursing station. He got Meryl's attention and asked her about the missing bottle.

Meryl shrugged her shoulders. "I don't have any idea where it is." She then turned around and yelled to the medical resident who'd been in charge of the resuscitation, asking the same question. He shook his head, indicating that he didn't know, either, before getting back to his sidewalk mini-conference. He and the other residents were still loudly debating why they had been unsuccessful.

"I guess it went down with the patient," Meryl said. "We always at least leave the IVs in place, along with any other tubes."

"This might be a silly question, but I haven't been on staff that long. Where exactly did the patient go?"

"To the morgue, or what we use as the

morgue. It's the old autopsy theater in the basement."

"Thanks," Roger said.

"Not at all," Meryl said.

Roger went back to the elevators. He pressed the down button but then eyed the sign for the stairs. He suddenly had it in his mind to ask Ms. Rakoczi why she went to the OB-GYN floor so often, and what it was that she needed that night. Since the elevator was taking its time arriving, Roger used the stairs. As he descended, he acknowledged that the caffeine was finally starting to wear off. His legs felt heavy. He decided that he'd have one more chat with Ms. Rakoczi, hunt briefly for the IV bottle, and then head for home.

The surgical floor was as quiet as it had been earlier. Roger surmised that the nurses were all attending to their patients. He saw some of them as he passed open doors into the patients' rooms. Rather than bother anyone, he thought he'd wait at the nurses' station for Ms. Rakoczi to return. To his surprise, he found her where he'd found her earlier, in the same position, reading the same magazine.

"I thought you said you had patients to

see," Roger said. He knew he was being abrasively provocative with someone with a volatile temperament, but he couldn't help himself. This woman was obviously gold-bricking.

"I saw them. Now I'm manning the nurses' station. Do you have a problem with that?"

"Luckily for both of us it's not my bailiwick," Roger said. "But I do have another question for you. I followed your suggestion and went upstairs to OB-GYN and spoke with Meryl Lanigan. She said you were a frequent visitor to her floor. In fact, she said you were up there earlier. I'd like to know why."

"For my continuing education," Jazz said. "OB-GYN interests me, but I didn't get much exposure to it with the Marines, for obvious reasons. So I frequently go up there on my breaks. Now that I've learned a bit about the field, I'm thinking of putting in for an opening in OB-GYN."

"So it was for continuing education that took you up there tonight?"

"Is that so hard to believe? Instead of going down to the cafeteria on my lunch hour with my half of the surgical-floor team and talking about drivel, I went up to OB-GYN to learn something. I don't know what it is about this place. Whenever you make an extra effort to improve yourself, you get nothing but grief."

"I don't want to add to your burden," Roger said, struggling to keep the sarcasm from his voice. "But there seems to be a discrepancy. Ms. Lanigan told me that when she confronted you earlier, you said you wanted to borrow something."

"Is that what she said?" Jazz questioned with a scornful laugh. "Well, she's right in one sense. I did need to borrow some infusion lines, thanks to central supply not restocking us, but that was an afterthought. What I was really doing up there was sucking up information from reading nursing notes. She probably doesn't want to admit that, because she's probably worried I'm gunning for her job."

"That wouldn't be my take," Roger said. "But what do I know? Thanks for your time, Ms. Rakoczi. I'll be back in touch if I have any more questions."

Roger walked out of the utility room and rounded the nurses' station countertop. He was now feeling genuinely fatigued. The caffeine had completely worn off. A few moments earlier, he'd entertained the idea after talking again with Ms. Rakoczi of returning to the OR to see if he could find Dr. Najah. As with Rakoczi, he wanted to ask him what he had been doing on the OB-GYN floor, but now he had second thoughts. He was exhausted. It was nearly four o'clock in the morning.

Roger resolved that the first thing he would do when he got into his office later that morning was call Rosalyn and beg for Jasmine Rakoczi's St. Francis record. He didn't care about the consequences. He found himself wondering how much the general nursing shortage had to do with the fact that Jasmine Rakoczi was employed. The overwhelming chances were that she was not a serial killer. That would be too easy. But the fact that she was employed as a nurse with her attitude was a travesty as far as he was concerned, and he intended to do something about it.

Roger pressed the elevator's down button and hazarded a glance back toward the surgical nurses' station. It was only for a split second, but he thought he caught a glimpse of Jazz eyeing him from around the edge of the door to the utility room. Roger wasn't so sure, and as tired as he suddenly felt, it could have been his imagination.The woman made him uneasy. He hated the thought of being a patient under her care.

The elevator came, and he boarded. Just before the doors closed, he looked back at the utility-room doorway. For the second time, he didn't know if it was his eyes or his brain that was tricking him, because he thought he saw her again.

He took the elevator down to the basement level, where he'd never been. In contrast with the rest of the hospital it was completely utilitarian. The walls were unadorned stained concrete, and myriad exposed pipes—some insulated, some not—ran along the ceiling. The lighting fixtures were simple porcelain sockets with wire cages. Just beyond the elevators, an old sign composed of peeling paint applied directly onto the concrete wall said "autopsy amphitheater," accompanied by a large red arrow.

The route was labyrinthine, but by following the red arrows, Roger eventually arrived at a set of double leather doors with oval windows set at eye-level height. The glass was covered with a greasy film. Although Roger could tell a light was shining in the room beyond, he couldn't make out any details. He pushed through, then propped the door open with an old brass doorstop.

Inside was an old-fashioned, semicircular two-story medical amphitheater, with rows of tiny seats that rose up on tiers into the shadows. Roger guessed it had been built a hundred years ago, when anatomy and pathology were kingpins in the academic medical curriculum. There was a lot of old, scraped, and pitted dark varnished wood, and the lighting came from a single, large, hooded lamp that hung on a long cord from the ceiling. The light was centered on an antiquated metal autopsy table that occupied the center of the pit. Against the back wall was a glass-fronted cabinet with a collection of stainless-steel autopsy tools. Roger wondered when they'd last been used. Outside the medical examiners' office, few autopsies were now done, particularly in managed-care hospitals like the Manhattan General.

Standing within the pit, along with the autopsy table, there were several shrouded hospital gurneys, obviously supporting corpses. Roger started forward, not knowing which was Patricia Pruit. As he approached the first body, he questioned, as he'd done in the past, why Laurie had chosen forensic pathology as her career. It seemed so contrary to her vibrant personality. With a shrug, he grabbed the edge of the sheet and lifted.

Roger grimaced. He was looking at the remains of an individual who had been involved in some kind of accident. The man's head was horribly distorted and crushed such that one eye was completely exposed. Roger replaced the sheet. His legs felt weak. As a medical student, he'd not liked pathology, particularly forensic pathology, and this victim reminded him of that fact in an uncomfortably brutal fashion.

Roger took a few breaths before stepping over to the second gurney. He reached for the edge of the sheet, but his hand didn't make it. Instead, he was propelled forward off his feet, having been hit smack in the middle of his back with what felt like a two-by-four. He knew he was falling, and his arms reflexively flew out to cushion himself, but before he hit the tiled floor, the board hit him again, taking his breath away.

Roger collided with the floor and skidded forward on the glazed tile. His head thumped up against the wall that separated the pit from the tiers of seats. He tried to move, but blackness descended over him like a heavy, suffocating blanket.

seventeen

When Laurie's alarm shattered the silence early Saturday morning, she felt about the same way she had Friday morning. Once again, she hadn't slept well, and what sleep she did get was marred by anxious dreams.

The first thing she did after getting out of bed was repeat the pregnancy test with a new kit. As a doctor, she was well aware of the necessity to repeat tests to rule out false readings. When she returned to check the results, she was aware of a definite ambivalence. But again, it was clearly positive. There could be little doubt that she was pregnant.

Adding credence to the test results was the morning nausea, which seemed a little worse than it had been the previous days, but after eating some dry raisin bran, she felt better. The accompanying right lower quadrant discomfort was another thing. Luckily, it wasn't anything like she'd experienced the prior evening on her way home from her rendezvous with Jack. Then it had been frank pain, strong enough to make her writhe. It had come on suddenly in the taxicab like severe intestinal cramps. For a few seconds, she thought she'd have to put in a call to Laura Riley, but then, as suddenly as it appeared, it vanished. As intense as it was, Laurie was convinced it was related to her digestive system. Its quality was much sharper than a menstrual cramp, which made her think it couldn't have anything to do with her being pregnant. The only confusion was that in the mornings, it appeared along with the nausea, suggesting it was related.

Laurie put her empty cereal bowl down

on the countertop. Concerned about the lingering discomfort, she gingerly pressed in on her abdomen in the general area of the pain with her index finger, trying to determine if there was any pinpoint pain. There wasn't, and curiously enough, the palpation alone seemed to be beneficial. When Laurie took her hand away, the discomfort had vanished, suggesting to her once again that the problem was intestinal, perhaps gas.

Relieved that the sensation had vanished, Laurie quickly dressed. She was on call for the weekend, which meant that of all the medical examiners at the OCME, it was her turn to go in and see what kind of cases had arrived during the night. She knew that she would probably be doing a few autopsies, unless they all could be put off until Monday, which in her experience had never happened. There was a person on second call in case of a flood of urgent cases, but in Laurie's experience that never happened, either.

The weather was typical for New York in March—drizzling and cold. Laurie huddled under her umbrella as she trudged north on First Avenue. She had briefly searched for a taxi, but whenever the weather turned sour, they were hard to find.

As she walked, Laurie thought more about her conversation with Jack. In hindsight, she realized how her emotions had understandably been careening from one extreme to another. Although she now felt self-conscious about her reaction to Jack asking who the father was, since it was, in the final analysis, a reasonable question, she gave herself credit in general for having admirably maintained her composure. Considering the stakes involved, it might have been one of the most important conversations in her life. All she could do now was pray Jack would respond as she hoped. Given Jack's track record, she imagined the chances were only about fifty-fifty.

On the street outside the OCME were several TV media trucks, suggesting that something newsworthy had happened overnight, and Laurie's guard went up. Dealing with the media was not her favorite part of being a medical examiner. She'd had some unfortunate experiences with journalists in the past, to the extent of putting her job in jeopardy.

For a moment, Laurie hesitated and debated if she should head around to the 30th Street morgue entrance. She glanced back at the TV trucks. There were only three, and their antennae were not extended, suggesting that they were not anticipating breaking news. Guessing that whatever had drawn them to the OCME was not front-page news, Laurie climbed the steps and entered. A dozen or so journalists and three cameramen were making themselves at home in the lobby.

Waving a greeting to Marlene, who came in for a few hours every Saturday morning, Laurie tried to walk across the lobby to be buzzed in. Almost immediately, a journalist who recognized her blocked her way by thrusting a microphone in her face. Several bright lights switched on, bathing the lobby in stark illumination as cameramen hoisted their equipment to their shoulders.

"Doctor, do you care to comment on the accident?" the journalist questioned. Others crowded around, extending their own microphones. "In your opinion, was it a double suicide, or were the two boys pushed?"

Laurie shoved the microphone out of the way. "I have no idea what you are talking about, and any information coming from this office has to be cleared by the chief, the deputy chief, or the public relations office. You people know that."

Laurie pushed her way toward the ID room while ignoring a welter of further questions. To her relief, Robert was visible through the central glass pane. With his help, she got inside and closed the door behind her with the journalists stranded out in the lobby.

"Thanks, Robert," Laurie said, peeling off her coat.

"They're like a bunch of wolves," Robert responded.

"What's this is all about?" Laurie asked.

"A couple of thirteen-year-old boys were run over by a subway train."

Laurie winced. Such a scenario was going to be emotionally taxing for her, and she was surprised she'd not been called during the night. Luckily, the current batch of tour doctors was particularly competent, and they had significant experience under their belts to handle all but the most critical cases. The tour doctors were mostly senior pathology residents earning a bit of money by moonlighting.

"Have the IDs been done?"

"Yup! That was all taken care of during the night."

Laurie was glad that was out of the way. For her, the ID process was especially trying with children, as it invariably meant dealing with the bereaved parents.

Laurie continued into the ID office, delighted to see Marvin's weekend call coincided with hers. He'd already made the coffee and had laid out the folders of the cases that had come in, with one of them in front of him.

Laurie and Marvin exchanged greetings as she helped herself to a mug of coffee. "Looks like we're going to be busy," she said, eyeing the folders.

"I'm afraid so," Marvin agreed. He tapped the folder in front of him with his knuckle. "We got another of these confusing postoperative cases from the General."

"No kidding!"

"There's a note from Janice on the front."

Laurie read the note quickly. It outlined the details on Patricia Pruit, answering all the usual pertinent questions. Laurie sucked in a deep breath. Providing she found no significant cardiac pathology, her series was now up to fourteen, with eight at the Manhattan General alone. It couldn't go on.

"Let's do Pruit first," Laurie said.

"Before the two boys?" Marvin questioned. "Did you see all the newspeople waiting out in the lobby?"

"I did, and they can wait some more," Laurie said. She wanted to confirm as soon as possible that Pruit was part of her series and let Roger know. Something had to be done. They couldn't stand on the sidelines any longer.

"Okay, I'll go down and get set up."

"Anything else of note?"

"Most seem routine to me. I think you'll want to pass on the majority of them. My guess is that we are looking at doing four cases, but you may have other ideas."

While Marvin went down to the autopsy room, Laurie went through all the folders. As she had anticipated, Marvin was right. They'd do the four cases and call it a day, unless anything of note came in while they were working. With that decided, Laurie went up to her office to stash her coat. She was glad she had, because sitting on her desk was a stack of hospital charts. To her amazement, the PAs had somehow managed the impressive feat of getting Lewis and Sobczyk's charts from the Manhattan General and the six charts from St. Francis, all in record time.

The chart on the top of the pile was Rowena Sobczyk's. Laurie flipped it open and shuffled through some of the pages, glancing at the OR notes and the anesthesia record. As with McGillin and Morgan, there was nothing out of the ordinary. She was about to put the chart down when a short strip of abnormal EKG flopped out. It was about two feet long, having been folded, accordion-style, into the chart with just the first six inches glued to the page.

Laurie opened the chart to the location. It was a note written by the resident in charge of the resuscitation attempt. Laurie quickly read it and found it unenlightening. She then extended the EKG tracing and studied it. The complexes were stretched out, suggesting that they represented ineffectual heartbeats, if they had been heartbeats at all. They could have been merely poorly coordinated cardiac electrical activity that didn't cause any muscular contraction. As the sequence continued, the complexes became progressively more distorted, then rapidly flattened out to a straight line. On the border, scribbled in pencil, was the message: "Short EKG segment from the outset of the resuscitation attempt, after which no further electrical activity was obtained."

She'd never had a strong background in reading EKGs, and this short segment didn't suggest anything to her. Yet she couldn't help but think it might be significant, since there had been no similar tracings on either McGillin or Morgan, who'd had no electrical activity on EKG whatsoever, and she thought she might show it to someone more knowledgeable than she. She marked the spot in the chart with her ruler, and even scribbled on a Post-it note to remind herself to show the tracing to a cardiologist.

Her phone rang, and the sound made her jump. She eyed it, hoping and wondering if it could be Jack. She put her hand on it and allowed it to ring again, feeling the vibration through her skin in a vain attempt to influence the identity of the caller. Her efforts notwithstanding, it was Marvin, and the message was simple: All was ready downstairs in the autopsy room.

Laurie returned Sobczyk's chart to the top of the pile, with the ruler sticking out of the side. She was looking forward to going over them later that afternoon, particularly those from Queens, to make sure the cases mirrored those from the General. She then looked back at the phone, and for a brief moment contemplated calling Jack. In the process, she noticed the small light on the side of the phone indicating she had voicemail. Confused by who would have left her a voicemail during the night, she picked up the receiver again and checked her messages.

Laurie was surprised first by the time of the message and then by the sound of Roger's voice. She was impressed that he had taken her suggestion so seriously that he'd been working nonstop until two o'clock in the morning. She was even more impressed that he had managed to come up with what he considered a list of suspects, including an anesthesiologist by the name of Najah who'd recently transferred from St. Francis to the Manhattan General. As she continued to listen to the message, she felt a definite sense of satisfaction and an eagerness to hear the details, although when was another matter. As she headed back toward the elevators to the basement, she wondered if and when Jack might call. You never knew with Jack.

As Laurie had anticipated, the post on Patricia Pruit was strikingly similar to the others in the series, with absolutely no pathology to account for her sudden demise. True to form, the operative site was without any excessive bleeding, without signs of infection, and there were no clots in the major vessels of the legs, abdomen, or chest. The heart, lungs, and brain were all entirely normal.

At the end of the procedure, Laurie helped Marvin move the corpse back onto a gurney.

"Which one of the kids do you want to do first?" Marvin asked as he unlocked the gurney's wheels.

"It doesn't matter," Laurie said. She had opened the two folders on a neighboring autopsy table and was searching for the forensic investigator's reports. Then, getting a second thoughts, she said, "In fact, why not put them both up at the same time."

"Fine with me," Marvin said agreeably.

He pushed the gurney with Pruit's corpse out through the main door.

A few years ago, Laurie would have taken the folders up to the lunchroom between cases, but now that she had on her moon suit, it was too much trouble, so she read the investigative reports standing up, with her ventilation fan as a backdrop. She could immediately see why some journalists would be interested. The tragic episode had the kind of lurid appeal that the tabloids loved. The accident had happened at three o'clock in the morning at the 59th Street station. The uptown train had thundered in and run over the two kids.

Conflicting stories were the problem. The engineer claimed that the kids had waited until the last minute to jump, so there was nothing he could do. Such a scenario suggested a double suicide, but the engineer failed a Breathalyzer test, casting severe doubt on his reliability. The other story came from the conductor, who claimed he was between car one and car two, looking out at the station, as the train came in. He said he didn't see any kids on the platform, and he passed the Breathalyzer test. The third story was from the agent in the token booth, who claimed that a suspicious man had gone through the turnstile right after the kids but disappeared.

The door to the hall burst open and Marvin pushed in another gurney. “This is not pretty,” he said.

“I can imagine,” Laurie said. She continued reading the investigative reports. No suicide notes were found, either on the platform or on the victims. Conversations with both sets of parents did not confirm any episodes of depression. In the words of one of the parents, the kids were “wild and full of the devil but would never kill themselves.”

“I’m going to get the other one,” Marvin called out.

Laurie waved over her shoulder as she continued to read. Once again, she was impressed with Janice’s work. How Janice could pack as much as she did into a single night, Laurie had no idea.

When Laurie was finished with her reading, she took out the sheets for the autopsy notes from the two folders and turned around to face the first of the two corpses. As she did so, Marvin came back in with the second one.

"Good Lord," Laurie murmured as she looked down at the first boy's remains. Teenagers weren't as difficult emotionally for Laurie as younger children, but they were still tough.

Being run over by a train was at the upper end of traumatic experiences. The boy's arm had been severed at the shoulder and it lay alongside the torso. The head and the face had been reduced to a pulp. There was no way things could have been cleaned up for the parents' benefit.

Laurie began the external examination by detailing the all-too-visual trauma. It was obvious that the body had tumbled along beneath the train until it had been brought to a stop.

"There's the second one," Marvin said as he wheeled the empty gurney over to the side of the room.

Laurie waved over her shoulder without turning around. She found something unexpected on the boy's penis, which made her move down and look at the soles of his feet. Marvin joined her on the opposite side of the table.

"I noticed that," Marvin said, following Laurie's line of sight. "What do you make of it?" In addition to the abrasions, there was a bit of charring.

"Where are the shoes?" Laurie asked.

"In a plastic bag in the walk-in."

"Bring them in," Laurie said. She was preoccupied and immediately stepped over to the second child.

By the time Marvin was back with the clothing from both cases, Laurie felt she had solved the mystery by the external exam alone. Marvin brought over the sneakers that the kids had been wearing. Like the bodies themselves, they were a sorry sight. Laurie picked them up and looked at the soles. "Seems pretty clear to me what happened."

"Oh?" Marvin questioned. "Fill me in."

At that moment, the door to the hall banged open, surprising both Laurie and Marvin. It was Sal D'Ambrosio, one of the other mortuary techs. He was more animated than his usual indifferent self. "We got a headless, handless male corpse that just arrived, along with some cops. What should I do?"

"Did you x-ray it, weigh it, and photograph it like you're supposed to do?" Laurie questioned. In sharp contrast with Marvin, who needed little direction, Sal's apathy often grated on Laurie's nerves. There was a protocol to be followed with every body arriving at the OCME.

"All right already," Sal said, sensing Laurie's impatience. "I thought with the cops here, it might be a different story." He ducked back out and the door closed.

Laurie paused for a minute. Hearing that a headless, handless body had arrived created a sense of déjà vu that took her back seven years, when a similar corpse had been brought in after floating around in the East River. With some effort, identification had been made. The man's name turned out to have been Franconi, and Mr. Franconi posthumously had taken her and Jack on a wild adventure to Equatorial Guinea in West Africa.

"Hey!" Marvin interrupted Laurie's brief reverie. "Come on! You got me curious here. What's with these two kids?"

Laurie again started to explain, but the door to the hall reopened. A gowned, hooded, and masked figure walked in, much to Laurie and Marvin's surprise.

"I'm sorry, but no one is allowed in here," Laurie called out, holding up her hand like a traffic cop. For a moment, she thought the intruder might have been a particularly adventuresome journalist who'd somehow managed to infiltrate OCME security. "It's dangerous, and full protective gear is mandatory."

"Oh, come on, Laur!" the man said while stopping in his tracks. "Jack told me on the weekends things weren't so hard-nosed around here and that this is the way he dresses unless it's an infectious case."

"Lou?" Laurie questioned.

"Yeah, it's me. You're not going to make me get into one of those suits, are you? They drive me crazy."

"If Calvin comes in, you'll be banned for life."

"Realistically, what are the chances of him coming in?"

"Nil, I suppose."

"Well, there you go," Lou said. He walked over to Laurie and glanced down at the two boys, then quickly looked back up at Laurie. "Yuck! What a sight! How you do this for a living?"

"It does have its downside," Laurie agreed. "What brings you in here so early on a Saturday?"

"The headless horseman I came in with. It's caused another stir over at the Manhattan General. I tell you, that place is going to be the bane of me."

"I think you'd better fill me in."

"I got called at the crack of dawn this morning. Seems that the guy who takes care of the bodies over at the General came in to work as usual and then found a body that wasn't supposed to be there." Lou laughed. "I mean, there's some humor here, finding an extra body in a morgue. I've heard about bodies being misplaced or missing, but finding an extra one is a bit out of the ordinary."

"Why were you called? Why wasn't it just taken care of by the local precinct?"

"My captain got word of it subsequent to his sister-in-law's murder over there yesterday morning. He practically has an open line to the hospital. So he calls me right off the bat and tells me to get my ass over there. The problem is that there haven't been any breaks in his in-laws' case, so he's got the thumbscrews to me. Also, there are some similarities. This new corpse has what look like two bullet holes, just like his sister-in-law."

"No ID?"

"Nope, not a clue. And there's no one missing at the hospital, like patients or staff."

"And what about the head and the hands?"

"Gone. They're nowhere to be found."

"So your captain thinks this new corpse relates somehow to his wife's sister's case."

"He didn't say so in so many words, but that was obviously what was on his mind. It is weird. The corpse was as clean as a whistle when the guy found it in the back of their old anatomy cooler. No blood, no gore, no nothing, as if the guy just got out of the shower. The whole thing is kind of eerie if you ask me, and I've seen a lot of weird stuff in my career."

"How were the head and the hands cut off?"

"What do you mean?"

"Was it clean, or were they hacked off?"

"Clean. Very clean."

"Like maybe the way a doctor might do it?"

"I suppose. I hadn't thought about it like that, but yes."

"Sounds like an intriguing case."

"Will you do it right away? The captain said he wants to hear from me ASAP."

"I'll be happy to do the case, but not until I finish with these two boys."

Lou glanced around Laurie and took another look at the remains. "What's the story here?"

"Two kids run over by an A train."

Lou grimaced. "Is this what attracted the media types up in the lobby?"

"I'm afraid so. Just the idea of being hit by a train is gruesome enough, but to make it even more appealing to the tabloids is the question whether it's a double suicide or a double homicide."

"Yeah," Marvin said, speaking up for the first time. "I was just about to hear the answer the moment you came in."

"Really?" Lou questioned. He overcame his hesitancy and stepped nearer. "These guys look like they went through a meat grinder. What was it, suicide or homicide?"

"Neither," Laurie said. "It was accidental."

With obvious surprise, both Lou and Marvin looked up at Laurie.

"How can you be so sure?" Lou questioned.

"I'm confident that when I do the posts, I'll find evidence the children were dead when the train struck them. Look at the slight charring on the feet." Laurie picked up a foot from each child in turn and pointed to the darkened, scorched areas.

"What am I looking at?" Lou questioned.

"Burns," Laurie said. Then she pointed to the children's penises. "Just like those on the tip of their glandes."

"What the hell are glandes?" Lou asked.

"It's plural for glans, or head of the penis."

"Ouch," Lou said, making a grimace of pain.

"I think these two boys made the fatal mistake of peeing in tandem on the third rail while standing either on the steel edge of the platform or on the rails themselves. There was such a good ground, the electricity arced up their urine streams and simultaneously electrocuted them."

"My good God!" Lou said, straightening up. "Remind me never to do that."

Lou stayed for the posts on the two boys, which went quickly. As Laurie had anticipated, there was visible evidence that the massive trauma the boys received occurred after their hearts had ceased to beat. While Laurie worked, she told Lou about the first case they had done, Patricia Pruit, and that as a consequence, her series of mysterious, inexplicable, unexpected deaths at the Manhattan General had risen to eight.

"Good grief," Lou responded. "Jack told me yesterday you had seven, and that he was coming around to your idea about a serial killer, but that the front office wasn't buying as of yet. What's Calvin's reaction now? Is the OCME willing to take a public stand?"

"Calvin doesn't know about the one this morning," Laurie said. "I don't know what his reaction will be, but I'm not optimistic. I'm afraid it's going to take some momentous event to get him to see the light, since no help has come from toxicology. When it concerns the Manhattan General, he has blinders on. He still thinks of it as the old, venerated academic center where he trained. The last thing he'd want to do is tarnish its reputation."

"If healthy people keep dying over there,

its reputation is going to suffer, one way or the other. But let me know if he comes around to your way of thinking. Like I told Jack, with everything else that's happening at the moment, my hands are tied, at least officially. I'm up to my eyeballs with this Chapman case. If I don't come up with a suspect, I might be out selling pencils."

"Actually, I'm working with Dr. Roger Rousseau to generate some legitimate suspects, and he left me a voice message last night, saying he'd made some progress."

"I hate to hear you are 'working' with that guy, for obvious reasons. But if you and he can come up with some names, I can do something, even if it's not official."

"I think we already have one," Laurie said. She finished sewing up the last of the two boys and handed the instruments to Marvin. "Let's go ahead and put up the headless John Doe before the tourist." The tourist was the fourth case they planned on posting. He was a college student who had presumably died from acute alcohol toxicity. The level in his blood had already been shown to be off the charts. He'd been found in Central Park by an early-morning jogger.

While Marvin went out to get Sal to help him with the corpses of the two boys, Laurie continued to talk to Lou about her series. She explained her idea about the potential killer apparently moving from St. Francis to the Manhattan General, and that Roger was going to look into transferees, among other people, and might even have talked to some of them, including the anesthesiologist Najah.

"Wait a second!" He held up his hand. "Hold it right there. Are you telling me this boyfriend of yours is planning on approaching Najah and some of these other so-called suspects himself?"

"I believe so, yes," Laurie responded. She was caught off guard. She hadn't expected such a negative reaction from Lou.

"This is nuts," Lou said. "You know how I feel about amateur detective shenanigans. It's one thing to come up with some names as part of an armchair game, but it's something else entirely when it comes to actually approaching anybody."

"Why? You'd have to narrow it down to find out which ones could truly be suspects. Otherwise, it's pure conjecture."

"Jesus H. Christ! Laurie, I hate to hear

you talking like this. Let's suppose for a second there really is a serial killer behind your so-called series. If there is and if he's not absolutely bonkers, then he could be extremely dangerous. The slightest provocation could push him over the edge."

Marvin and Sal came back into the autopsy room. While they moved the teenagers' corpses onto the waiting gurneys, Laurie and Lou stood silently. They were both self-conscious about Lou's sudden vehemence. When the door closed behind the techs pushing their gurneys, Lou cleared his throat.

"Sorry," he said. "I didn't mean to come on that strong. It's just that amateur sleuthing scares the bejesus out of me. The last thing I want you doing is risking your life like you did playing detective back during that Paul Cerino cocaine affair. Dealing with psychopaths is not for novices."

"I think I get your point," Laurie said.

"On a lighter note," Lou said, eager to change the subject, "I've been dying to ask about your dinner date with Jack last night. How'd it go? Are you guys going to bury the hatchet or what?"

Laurie didn't answer right away, and

when she did, all she said was that the jury was still out. Lou was hardly satisfied, but his intuition told him to let it go.

Marvin and Sal returned with a single gurney, Marvin pulling, Sal pushing. After Marvin placed an X-ray he had under his arm on a neighboring surface, the two techs expertly transferred the headless and handless male corpse.

"I see what you mean," Laurie said after taking one look at the body. "It is remarkably clean." In sharp contrast to the teenagers' mangled bodies, there was no blood, even at the severed neck and wrists, which were cut off so sharply as to look like illustrations in an anatomy book. Sal took the gurney back out into the hall while Marvin put up the X-ray.

The two bullets stood out as pure white blotches in the gray-to-black field. One was a flattened irregular shape and the other normal. Laurie pointed to the misshapen slug in the middle of the torso. "My guess is that this one hit the spine." She then pointed to the defect in one of the vertebrae. "I'd say it ended up in the liver. The other one is in the mediastinum, in the center of the chest, and I wouldn't be surprised if we find it penetrated the aortic arch. That was the fatal shot."

"Looks like a nine-millimeter," Lou said.

"We'll see," Laurie said.

She went back to the body to start the external exam. While standing on the corpse's right with Marvin on the opposite side, Laurie asked the tech to roll the body toward him. She wanted to view the entrance wounds as well as photograph them. But when Marvin did as she asked, she caught sight of a small, intricate tattoo of an octopus in the small of the corpse's back.

Laurie staggered and sucked in a lungful of air. She reached out and grasped the table's edge to keep herself erect. Her eyes were fixated on the tattoo.

"Dr. Montgomery, are you okay?" Marvin asked.

Laurie didn't move. Although she had initially staggered, now she seemed frozen.

"Laurie, what's up?" Lou asked. He bent forward to try to see through her plastic face mask.

Laurie shook her head to break her momentary trance. She took a step back from the table. "I need a break," she said in a high, breathless voice. "This autopsy is going to have to wait." She turned on her heel, and headed for the door.

Both Marvin and Lou looked after her. Lou called her name, but she didn't answer. When the doors closed behind her, Lou looked at Marvin. "What's going on?"

"Beats me," Marvin said. He eased the corpse back to a supine position. He gave a short, mirthless laugh. "This has never happened before. Maybe she's sick."

"I think I'd better check," Lou said, and he started for the door.

Expecting Laurie to be in the corridor, Lou was surprised when he didn't see anyone. From where he was standing he could see all the way down to the security office. There didn't seem to be anyone in there, either. Confused as to what was going on, he walked down the length of the bank of small, refrigerated compartments where the bodies were stored prior to autopsy. When he reached the end, where there was a large walk-in cooler to his left, he was able to see to his right down into the supply room where the moon suits were stored. Although she was partly out of view, he was able to catch a glimpse of Laurie climbing out of her gear. When he got down there, Laurie was plugging her battery pack into the charger.

"What's going on?" Lou asked. "Are you okay? Aren't you going to do the case?"

Laurie turned and faced her friend. Her eyes were brimming with tears.

"Hey," Lou said. "What is with you?" He pulled off his mask, peeled off the gown covering his street clothes, and enveloped her in a sustained hug. She didn't resist.

After several minutes, Lou leaned back to see Laurie's face, still keeping his arms around her. She worked her arm up between them and wiped her eyes with her hand, then dried it on the front of her scrub shirt.

"Are you ready to talk?" Lou asked softly.

Laurie nodded but made no attempt to free herself from Lou's embrace. She took a deep breath, started to talk, stuttered, and then stopped to wipe her eyes again.

"Take your time," Lou urged.

"I'm afraid I know the identity of the headless body," Laurie said finally in a halting voice. "It's Roger Rousseau, my friend from the Manhattan General."

"Good God!" Lou said, half in sympathy

and half in irritation. "Now you see why I said amateur sleuthing is dangerous."

"I don't need a lecture," Laurie said. She pushed herself out of Lou's arms.

"I'm sorry, I know you don't, but this is a disaster."

"Tell me about it," Laurie challenged. "This person was someone important in my life, and I'm the one who put him up to what he did. Oh, God, what a mess!" Laurie cradled her head in both hands.

"Excuse me, Dr. Montgomery, but that's not what happened. You made a suggestion for him to come up with some names. Unless I'm off base, you didn't put him up to going around talking to people. That was his idea."

"At the moment, that seems like an academic distinction," Laurie said while letting her hands fall to her sides.

"Are you going to do the case?" Lou asked.

"No, I'm not going to do the case," Laurie snapped.

"Okay, okay. You don't have to get mad at me. I'm on your side."

"Sorry," Laurie said with a shake of her head.

Robert Harper, the head of security, passed by Laurie's line of sight down near the walk-in cooler. After disappearing in the direction of the autopsy room, he did a double take and returned to view. He quickly approached.

"The media people are getting restless," Robert reported. "They've heard about the headless corpse and now insist on getting details."

"How did they hear about the new arrival?" Laurie demanded.

Robert made a questioning gesture with his hands. "I've no idea. Marlene just called me to come up there to calm them down."

Laurie looked at Lou. Lou put up his hands. "I didn't tell them."

Laurie shook her head dejectedly. "This is a circus."

"What should I tell them?" Robert asked.

"Tell them that I'm calling the deputy chief."

"I doubt that will satisfy them."

"It's going to have to," Laurie said. She pushed between both men and walked out of the storeroom on her way back to the autopsy room.

Robert and Lou exchanged a quick

glance before Robert headed back upstairs. Lou went after Laurie. By quickening his step, he caught up with her. "Rousseau's got to be posted," he said.

"You don't have to tell me what I already know," Laurie said. She pushed open the autopsy door, leaned in, and told Marvin to take a break and that she would be back to him in a little while. She then headed for the back elevator. Lou followed.

As they rode up in the elevator cab, Lou looked at Laurie, who stared back. For the moment, her shock and sadness had turned to anger.

"Maybe this is the wake-up call," Laurie said. "Maybe now all you naysayers will think a bit more seriously about this series of mine."

"I beg to differ," Lou corrected. "Rousseau's death does not unequivocally validate that the deaths of the patients in your series are homicides. All it does is confirm that we have a killer at the Manhattan General who is targeting doctors and nurses. Maybe this individual is killing patients, maybe he's not. Avoid jumping to conclusions."

"I don't care what you say, I think they are related."

"Maybe so," Lou said. "Did Rousseau leave any other name besides Dr. Najah?"

"No, that was the only one."

"But you suspect he had more."

"There's no doubt he had more. He said as much."

"Do you think he might have written the names down?"

"I do. He mentioned he had lists."

"Well, thank the good Lord for small favors."

They arrived at Laurie's floor. Lou hurried after Laurie, who bolted out of the elevator and headed down to her office. When Laurie sat down at her desk and picked up her phone, Lou did the same at Riva's desk. With some hesitation, Laurie dialed Jack's number. She prayed he'd be in his apartment and not out playing basketball. To her relief, he picked up on the second ring.

"I hate to bother you," Laurie began.

"Bother? It's no bother. It's good to hear from you."

"I know I said I'd wait for your call, but something has come up. Jack, I need you here at the OCME."

"Are the cases so uninteresting that you need comic relief?" Jack suggested. He started to say more, but Laurie cut him off.

"Please, hold the sarcastic humor! Roger Rousseau was brought in this morning as an unidentified homicide victim. He was shot last night at the Manhattan General Hospital."

"I'll be right there," Jack said and hung up.

After slowly replacing the receiver, Laurie put her elbows on her desk, cradled her head with her hands, and rubbed her eyes. Ever since that fateful night in Jack's apartment when she couldn't sleep, it was as if her life had spun out of control. She seemed to be hurled from one upheaval to another. Behind her, she could hear Lou talking with some of his men over at the Manhattan General. He was telling them to seal Dr. Roger Rousseau's office until he got over there and to run a background check on a doctor named Najah.

An involuntary moan escaped Laurie's lips as she straightened herself up and took her hands away from her face. She would need to grieve for Roger, but it would have to be later. She picked up the phone and dialed Calvin's number. After she spoke briefly with his wife, Calvin came on the line.

"What's up?" Calvin asked in an impatient tone. He did not like to be bothered at home without good reason.

"I'm afraid a number of things. First things first, but I'm not sure how to say this."

"I'm not in the mood for games, Laurie. Just tell me what you have to tell me."

"All right. I'm ninety-nine percent sure that the chief of the medical staff at the Manhattan General, the doctor friend with whom I have been confiding about my series, is at this moment lying on a table in the autopsy room, waiting to be posted. He'd been shot last night in the hospital and found this morning in the anatomy cooler."

For a moment, Calvin didn't say anything. Laurie might have thought they'd been disconnected if she couldn't hear his breathing.

"Why aren't you one hundred percent sure?" Calvin finally asked.

"The corpse is headless and handless. Whoever did this to him didn't want him identified."

"So he was brought in as a John Doe?"

"That's correct."

"And how did you make the ninety-nine percent identification?"

"I recognized a rather unique tattoo."

"So, I suppose it's safe to say this individual was more than a friend."

"He was a friend," Laurie persisted. "A good friend."

"Okay," Calvin said, willing to change the subject. "Knowing you as I do, I assume you take this episode as further support to your serial-killer idea in regard to your series."

"It stands to reason. It was just yesterday morning that I told the victim about the Queens cases and suggested he look into employees who had transferred from Saint Francis to the General. He left me a voice message during the night, saying that he'd come up with some potential suspects, whom he was going to approach."

"Are the police actively involved?"

"Most definitely. Detective Lou Soldano is here right at this moment, talking to his people over at the hospital."

"I think it would be inappropriate for you to do the post."

"It never crossed my mind. Jack is on his way in."

"Jack's not on second call."

"I know. I thought that not only could he do the autopsy, but he could lend me some needed moral support."

"Okay, that's fine," Calvin said. "Are you sure you want to stay? I could have someone take your place for the weekend. I imagine this is rather a shock."

"It's a shock, but I prefer to stay."

"That's your call, Laurie, and I won't force the issue. At the same time, I have to be clear about the stand of the OCME in regard to your series. As I said before, we are not in the speculation business. There's no proof any of these patients of yours are homicides. Are we on the same page, Laurie? I have to be sure, because I don't want you going to the media. There's too much at stake here."

"There was another case for my series this morning," Laurie said. "A healthy thirty-seven-year-old woman. That makes eight at the Manhattan General alone."

"Numbers are not going to sway me, Laurie, and they shouldn't sway you. What would sway me is if John came up with something toxicological. I'll see if I can put some pressure on him on Monday to redouble his efforts."

A lot of good that is going to do, Laurie thought dejectedly, knowing how much effort had already been expended.

"What else is going on?" Calvin asked. "You implied there was something more."

"There is," Laurie admitted. "I wouldn't have bothered you about it, but since I have you on the line, I might as well inform you." Laurie went on to tell the story about the two teenage boys. When she got to the end, she mentioned the media people in the lobby and then added, "I would like permission to inform them about my findings on these two cases. I believe it is in the public interest for this information to get out sooner rather than later, in hopes of discouraging kids from doing it again in the future."

"Are the media people aware of the headless corpse?"

"Unfortunately, yes."

"If you talk with them, will you be able to restrain yourself from talking about the headless corpse or your series? They'll undoubtedly ask you."

"I believe so."

"Laurie, it's either yes or no."

"Okay, yes!" Laurie voiced with some impatience.

"Don't get testy with me, Laurie, or I'm not going to allow you to talk with any media."

"Sorry! I'm a little stressed."

"You can talk to the media about the subway incident, provided you emphasize your findings are a preliminary impression pending further study. I want you to say that specifically."

"Yes, fine, okay," Laurie said, eager to get off the line. Suddenly, she was tired of talking with Calvin, as he was a constant reminder of the political side of being a medical examiner.

When Laurie finally hung up, she turned around to face Lou, who'd also completed his calls. She inwardly winced with a sudden sharp pain in her lower right abdomen. Luckily, it was a far cry from what she had experienced in the taxi the evening before, but it got her attention nonetheless.

"Jack's coming in," Laurie said. She changed her position to relieve the pain. It did to some degree, but not completely. "He'll do the post on the headless corpse."

Lou nodded. "I overheard. It's a good call, because there's no way you should do it. I also overheard about your plan to talk to the newsmen downstairs. I can help you out by talking to them about the headless corpse while you stick to the subway accident. That way, you'll stay out of trouble with Calvin."

"Sounds like a good plan," Laurie said. She stood up, and the pain lessened.

"And I have to tell you that I already found out something very interesting. This Dr. Najah has a sheet. He was arrested four years ago trying to board a plane to Florida with a pistol in his briefcase. Of course, he claimed it was an accident and that he had forgotten it was in there, and he did have a license for it."

"Was it a nine-millimeter?"

"It was."

"Interesting!" Laurie placed her hand on her hip so that she could use her fingers to surreptitiously massage her abdomen. Similar to that morning, the maneuver was almost immediately curative.

"And something else," Lou said. "Before

he retrained as an anesthesiologist, he'd been a surgeon."

"My word," Laurie said while picturing the neatly cut ends on the corpse where the head and hands had been removed.

"We're going to pull him in for a few days and have a couple of our more experienced interrogators have a crack at him. We're also going to get a search warrant and see if we can't come up with that nine-millimeter he was trying to take to Florida."

"Sounds like a very good idea to me," Laurie agreed.

eighteen

It wasn't long after Laurie and Lou had gone down to face the media that Jack arrived, much to Laurie's surprise. She had suspected he had taken a cab, but Jack had corrected her. He had explained that at that hour of morning, his bike was the vehicle of choice for any crosstown travel when time was of the essence.

For Laurie and Lou, dealing with the journalists had been taxing from the start. Just getting them to quiet down had been difficult, since they had worked themselves into a minor frenzy. The story possibilities of a nameless, headless, handless corpse discovered by accident in the anatomy cooler of a major hospital were in some respects better than those of the two male teenagers getting run over by the A train. With characteristic imagination, some truly lurid scenarios had been envisioned.

Laurie had addressed the journalists first. The idea that the kids had been electrocuted while peeing on the third rail had raised a few eyebrows but no abiding interest. The group had been much more attentive, as well as rowdy, when Lou talked about the unidentified corpse, despite his cleverly not saying anything of substance.

Jack autopsied Rousseau a little while later, working with Marvin while Lou observed. Laurie made it a point not to even watch. Instead, she teamed up with Sal to post the college student found in the park. The cases were finished at about the same time.

Up in the lunchroom, over vending-machine sandwiches and drinks, Jack gave a thumbnail sketch of the findings on Rousseau. He explained that the first bullet had severed the man's spinal cord so that the victim would have been a paraplegic, had it not been for the second bullet. Jack described the second projectile as the coup de grâce, since it pierced the heart after grazing a rib, ending up in the left ventricular wall.

During the short monologue, Laurie struggled to maintain a calm exterior, actively suppressing that the details of what she was hearing concerned someone who was dear to her. To maintain the charade, she actually asked a few technical questions, which Jack was happy to answer. He said there was absolutely no doubt in his mind that the hands and the head had been removed well after the heart had stopped beating. It was also his opinion that the man had not suffered, as death had been almost instantaneous. As far as the bullets were concerned, they were definitely nine-millimeter.

After Lou had called his captain to fill him in on the details of the autopsy, he suggested that Laurie come over to the Manhattan General Hospital with him to help locate and identify whatever kind of lists could be found in Rousseau's office. Laurie agreed immediately. Not to be left out, Jack had asked to tag along. He said he wouldn't miss an opportunity to participate in AmeriCare's deserved comeuppance, certain the media was going to have a field day once they got a whiff of what was going on behind the scenes. Particularly after hearing about Patricia Pruit, he was now firmly in Laurie's camp.

Before leaving the OCME, Laurie took a detour into the communications room behind the ID office to let the operator know she was leaving. She made sure the operator had her cell phone number on hand. As the medical examiner on call, Laurie had to keep in touch.

To get over to the Manhattan General, they all climbed into Lou's Chevrolet Caprice. Laurie got in the front while Jack sat in the back. The morning drizzle had slowed to more of a mist. Still, both Jack and Laurie preferred to have their respective windows open and deal with the moisture rather than breathe the car's interior air. While they rode, Laurie brought Jack up to speed on the phone message Roger had left for her.

"This Najah sounds like a good candidate," Jack said. "Maybe too good. Having an anesthesiologist behind this mystery would go a long way to explain why toxicology has failed to come up with anything. There could be some kind of extremely volatile gas involved."

Lou told Jack what he'd already learned about Najah, specifically regarding his nine-millimeter handgun. He added that the handgun would be tested by ballistics, if they were lucky enough to get their hands on it.

Except for a rather obviously increased uniformed police presence, the hospital appeared to be functioning in its normal, bustling fashion, with people coming and going, and patients in wheelchairs being discharged. A long line of visitors snaked from the information booth, and doctors in white coats and nurses in scrubs criss-crossed the lobby.

Lou excused himself for a moment to talk to one of the policemen. Laurie and Jack stepped to the side.

"How are you holding up?" Jack asked.

"Better than I would have expected," Laurie responded.

"I'm impressed," Jack admitted. "I don't

know how you can concentrate with everything that's on your mind."

"Actually, trying to figure out what is going on over here is helpful," Laurie said. "It keeps me from dwelling on my own problems." At the moment, Laurie was referring to the abdominal discomfort she'd been experiencing. It seemed that the jarring she'd experienced in the ride over in Lou's car had aggravated it to a degree. It wasn't as sharp as it had been in the cab the night before, but it was pain nonetheless, and Laurie started thinking seriously about it being appendicitis. The location was correct, even if the presentation was irregular. Just when she was thinking about mentioning it to Jack, Lou returned.

"Let's head down to the crime scene before we hit Rousseau's office," Lou said. "Apparently, the CSI boys have made some headway."

They took the elevator down to the basement level and followed the arrows to the old autopsy amphitheater. The aged leather double doors were propped open with their stops, and a length of yellow crime-scene tape stretched across the entrance. A uniformed police officer stood to the side. Lou ducked under the tape, but when Laurie tried to follow, the policeman blocked her way.

"That's okay," Lou said, coming back to Laurie's aid. "They're with me."

Heavy-duty droplights illuminated the semicircular amphitheater's interior, reaching even the top row of the tiered seats. Several crime-scene investigators were still working.

"Word is you've made some progress," Lou said to the lead tech, Phil.

"I think so," Phil said modestly. He waved for them to follow over to the far wall of the pit. He pointed to markings in chalk on the floor. "We've determined that the body initially ended up here, with the victim's head in contact with the baseboard. Even though the area had been superficially cleaned, we were able to clearly delineate blood spatter, which gave us an idea where the victim had been when he'd been shot."

Phil then took the group back toward the ampitheater's entrance and pointed to two neighboring chalk circles. "This is where we found the two nine-millimeter shell casings, which leads us to believe the killer was about twenty feet from the victim at the time of the shooting."

Lou nodded while looking back and forth between where the body had been found and the cartridge casings.

"And finally," Phil said while motioning for them to follow him again. He walked over and put his hand on the old autopsy table. "This is where the dismemberment occurred."

"A regular operating theater," Lou commented. "That was handy for the killer."

"I should say," Phil responded. He pointed toward the cabinet filled with autopsy instruments. "He even had access to the proper tools. We've been able to determine which knives and saws were used."

"Good work," Lou said. He looked at Laurie and Jack. "You guys have any professional questions?"

"How did you determine the autopsy table had been used to take off the head and the hands?" Jack asked.

"We took the drain apart," Phil said. "There was evidence in the trap."

"Let's see where the body was found," Lou asked.

"No problem," Phil said. He led them

back across the pit, beyond where the body had been outlined on the floor, and through a single door into a short hallway. They passed a small, cluttered office, which Phil said was the diener's. At the end of the hall, they came to a stout wooden door that looked as though it belonged in a butcher shop. It made a loud click when Phil opened it. A cool mist that reeked of formaldehyde billowed out to layer itself on the floor.

Both Laurie and Jack were familiar with the style of the room beyond. It was exactly like the anatomy cooler where the cadavers had been stored in medical school before being divvied out for dissection. On either side were rows of naked bodies hanging by tongs inserted into their ear canals and attached to a track in the ceiling.

"The victim's body was on a gurney in the very back, covered by a sheet," Phil said, pointing down the central aisle. "It's a little hard to see the space from here. Want to go back?"

"I think I'll pass," Lou said. He turned around. "Cadaver coolers give me the creeps."

"I'm impressed the body was found so

quickly," Jack said. "It looks to me like these other guys have been hanging around for years."

Laurie rolled her eyes. It always amazed her that Jack found humor everywhere. "The murderer didn't want the body found or identified," she added.

"Let's get up to Rousseau's office," Lou suggested.

Since it was a Saturday, the administration office area was mostly deserted. A uniformed police officer reading a copy of the *Daily News* jumped when he caught sight of the group, particularly Detective Lieutenant Soldano. Behind the officer was the closed door to Roger's office. A piece of yellow crime-scene tape was stretched across the front.

"I trust that no one has been in here," Lou said to the policeman.

"Not since you called this morning, Lieutenant."

Lou nodded and pulled the tape off one side, but before he could open the door, a voice called out his name. Turning around, he saw a tall, lean man with movie-star good looks striding toward him with his hand outstretched. His sandy hair was streaked with gold and his face was tanned, which made his blue eyes seem that much bluer. It appeared as if he'd just returned from the Caribbean. Lou tensed.

"I'm Charles Kelly," the man said, pumping Lou's hand with unnecessary vigor, "president of the Manhattan General Hospital."

Lou had tried to set up a meeting with him the previous day but had been rebuffed, as if it had been beneath the president's dignity. If Lou had felt it had been imperative, he would have insisted, but as it was, he'd had other more pressing things to do.

"Sorry we were unable to connect yesterday," Charles said. "It was a ghastly day, scheduling-wise."

Lou nodded and noticed that Charles was casting a look at Laurie and then at Jack. Lou introduced them.

"I'm afraid I know Dr. Stapleton," Charles said stiffly.

"Good recall!" Jack said. "That must have been a good eight years ago when I helped you guys out when you had all that trouble with those nasty germs."

Charles looked back at Lou. "What are

they doing here?" His tone was anything but hospitable.

"They're helping me with my investigation."

Charles nodded as if pondering Lou's explanation. "I will let Dr. Bingham know they were here on Monday. Meanwhile, I wanted to introduce myself to you, Lieutenant, and say that I will avail you of any help we can provide."

"Thank you," Lou said. "I think we're doing okay at the moment."

"There is something I would like to ask of you."

"Okay, shoot," Lou said.

"With two unfortunate murders in as many days, I would like to ask you to be as discreet as possible, particularly about the gruesome details of the one discovered today. Furthermore, I would like to respectfully request that all information to be released goes through our public relations department. We have to think of the institution and limit the collateral damage."

"I'm afraid a smidgen of the lurid facts have already gotten to the media," Lou admitted. "I have no idea how it was leaked, but I was forced to give a mini-press conference. I can assure you that I did not give them any details. In an investigation like this, it is best not to do so."

"That's my opinion precisely," Charles said, "although I imagine for different reasons. In any event, we appreciate any help that you can give us in this most unfortunate circumstance. Good luck with your investigation."

"Thank you, sir," Lou said.

Charles turned and went back into his office.

"What an ass," Jack commented.

"I bet he went to Harvard," Lou said enviously.

"Come on," Laurie urged. "I've got to get back to the OCME."

Lou opened the door and the three walked into Roger's office.

While Laurie hesitated just over the threshold, Lou and Jack went directly over to Roger's desk. Laurie's eyes slowly traversed the room. Being in Roger's space brought back the enormity of her loss. She'd been acquainted with him for only five weeks, and she knew deep down that she really didn't know him, yet she'd liked him and perhaps even loved him. She'd felt intuitively that he was a good person and had been generous to her at a time when she was needy. In some respects, she might have even taken advantage of him to a degree, which caused her a twinge of guilt.

"Laurie, come over here!" Lou called.

Laurie started across the room, but stopped when her cell phone jangled in her coat pocket. It was the OCME operator with the message that a police custody case had come in. Laurie assured her that she'd be back within the hour and asked the operator to tell Marvin to start setting up. Deaths in police custody were politically notorious, and this was certainly one that she'd have to post rather than wait until Monday.

"Looks like we've got a lot of material here," Lou said when Laurie joined him and Jack. "These sheets might be the most important. They've even got stars next to the names." He handed the sheets to Jack, who scanned them before handing them on to Laurie. They were the credentialing records for Dr. José Cabreo and Dr. Motilal Najah.

Laurie read through both. "The timing of

Najah's transfer and the fact that he apparently favored the night shift are suspicious, to say the least."

"I'm wondering why the record of his arrest isn't on there," Lou questioned. "That's important for someone handling controlled substances. I mean, it would have to have been on his DEA application."

Laurie shrugged.

"Here's another list that Rousseau put on star on," Lou said. "It's people who transferred from Saint Francis to the General between mid-November and mid-January."

Jack glanced at it and handed it to Laurie.

Laurie read down the list of seven names, noting which department in the hospital they worked. "All these people would easily have access to patients, especially on the night shift."

Lou nodded. "We've got our work cut out for us. It's almost too much. Here's a list of eight docs that got kicked off the General's staff over the last six months. I imagine one of them could be a deranged oddball who'd like to get back at AmeriCare somehow."

"That sounds familiar," Jack said. "Maybe you should add me to that list."

"I'm going to have to get a whole team to start working on all this," Lou said. "If Najah isn't our man, then we'll be looking at interviewing the lot. Hmmm. What's this, I wonder?" Lou held up a CD that was on top of several of the lists.

"Let's check it out," Laurie said. She took the CD and booted up Roger's computer by quickly typing in his password, which caused Jack's eyebrows to rise. Laurie caught the reaction but opted to ignore it.

The CD turned out to be the digital hospital records of all the cases in her series, including those from St. Francis. She guessed that Roger had gotten the St. Francis data when he'd gone over to get the employee records. Laurie explained to Lou what it was and asked if she could take it with her back to the OCME. It might help her when she went over the charts.

Lou thought for a moment. "Can you make a copy?"

Laurie located the computer's CD burner and made herself a copy.

"Actually, I wouldn't mind having copies of all this printed material as well," Laurie said after she thought about it. "Later this afternoon, I'll have time to go over it all, and maybe I'll have some helpful ideas. I'm sure there's a copy machine somewhere close by."

"Not a problem," Lou said. "With this much material, we can use all the help we can get."

The copy machine was just outside Roger's office, and Laurie made copies of all Roger's lists. When she was finished, she told Lou and Jack that she was heading back to the OCME.

"Do you want me to go back with you?" Jack asked. "I mean, I'll even take call if you want to go home."

"I'll be fine," Laurie assured him. "I'd rather stay busy than sit around in my apartment. You're welcome to come, but it's up to you."

Jack looked at Lou. "What's your plan?"

"I want to interview the man who found the body," Lou said. "Then I want to meet this Najah, and check to see if we lucked out obtaining his gun. It might be that just reminding him of the science of ballistics might make him spill the beans, and wouldn't that be nice."

"Mind if I hang with you for a while?"

Jack asked. "I'd like to meet Dr. Najah myself."

"Be my guest."

Jack turned to Laurie. "I'll be over. I'll even help you with that police custody case if you'd like."

"It's not going to be a problem," Laurie said. "I'll see you when I see you, but thanks for coming in and doing the case that you did. I really mean that."

Laurie gave each man a hug and lingered a little longer with Jack. She even gave his arm an added squeeze before walking out.

Prior to leaving the hospital administration area, Laurie took a detour into the ladies' room. Balancing Roger's lists and the CD on the edge of the washbasin, Laurie went into the stall. While she relieved herself, her mind flip-flopped from Roger's untimely demise to those of the two teenagers, whose innocent mischief had caused their deaths. It reminded her that humans, like all living organisms large and small, were always precariously poised on the edge of the abyss.

Preoccupied with such thoughts, Laurie used a small, folded wad of toilet tissue to wipe herself. As she was about to drop the paper in the toilet, she noticed something abnormal. There was a tiny bit of blood. She was spotting!

Laurie instinctively recoiled from the implications. It was only a minute amount of blood, yet as far as she could remember, any bleeding wasn't a good sign during a pregnancy, especially so early. At the same time, the limited exposure she'd had to obstetrics as a medical student had long since faded in her memory, so she didn't want to jump to conclusions.

Why does something like this always have to happen on a weekend? Laurie silently lamented. She'd like to ask Laura Riley the significance but was reluctant to call her on a Saturday. Laurie took a fresh piece of toilet tissue and again blotted herself. The blood didn't reappear, which provided a bit of consolation, yet combining the fact that there had been any blood with the right lower quadrant discomfort she'd been having lately seemed inauspicious at best.

Out at the sink, while she was washing her hands, Laurie looked at herself in the mirror. The last few nights of restless sleep had taken their toll. Although hardly in Janice's league, her eyes had dark circles and looked tired, and her face was drawn. She had a bad feeling that she might be facing yet another upheaval and prayed that if it were to happen, she'd find the emotional reserve to deal with it.

nineteen

It didn't take Laurie as long as she'd feared to get back to the OCME, but once again, the ride in the taxi markedly aggravated her abdominal distress. Marvin had been waiting for her, and she immediately posted the police custody case, which turned out to be therapeutic. By the time she finished the autopsy, the pain had vanished and in its stead was a vague sensation of pressure. As she changed out of her scrubs, she pressed the area with her fingers. In contrast to what had happened that morning, palpating the area made it feel worse. As confused as ever, she went into the toilet stall to see if she was spotting, but she wasn't.

Laurie went up to her office and stared at her phone. Once again, she thought about calling Laura Riley but had the same reluctance. She didn't even know the woman, and she hated to start out the relationship by bothering her on a weekend with a problem that could probably wait until Monday. After all, Laurie had been having the symptoms for a number of days. The sudden appearance of the few drops of blood was the only aspect that was truly different, and that seemingly had stopped.

Annoyed with herself for her indecisiveness, Laurie switched to thinking about calling Calvin. She could update him on Roger and give him a heads-up on the police custody case. She'd found extensive trauma to the prisoner's larynx, with the implication that excessive force had been used. Such cases were invariably politically challenging and Calvin would need to be apprised. Yet there was no apparent pressure from the media, and the toxicology had yet to be done. Laurie decided it could all wait until Monday unless Calvin took it upon himself to call.

Instead of making any phone calls, Laurie decided to spend some serious time with the charts from Queens and then Roger's lists. She felt she owed it to him, since he had, in a way, sadly given his life for the cause.

The first thing that she noticed was that the St. Francis charts were significantly different from the General's. Whereas the Manhattan General was a tertiary teaching hospital, St. Francis was a mere community institution. There were no interns or residents writing notes, so the charts were much skimpier. Even the attending doctor's notes and the nurses' notes were shorter, which made them much easier to go through.

As she expected from having read the forensic investigators' reports on each of the cases, the demographics matched those of the General. The victims were all relatively youthful, and had died within twenty-four hours of elective surgery. They were also all healthy, compounding the tragedy.

Laurie then remembered Roger saying that he'd discovered that the General cases were all relatively recent subscribers to AmeriCare. Turning to the biographical data section of the chart she was currently examining, Laurie saw that it was the same. She quickly checked the other five Queens charts. All of the patients had been AmeriCare subscribers for less than a year. Two of them had been subscribers for only two months.

Laurie pondered this curious fact and wondered if it was significant. She didn't know, but she took out a ruled pad of paper and wrote: all victims recent AmeriCare subscribers. Beneath that, she wrote: all victims within twenty-four hours of anesthesia; all victims on IV's; all victims young to middle-aged; all victims healthy.

Laurie looked at her list and tried to think of any other ways the victims had been related. Nothing came to mind, so she put the pad aside and went back to the charts. Although she knew the General cases had occurred in various parts of the hospital with many on the surgical floor, she didn't know about the Queens cases. Quickly, she determined that it was similar, with cases spread around the hospital.

Since the Queens charts were considerably thinner, Laurie was more tempted to look at every page, and with one chart, she found herself even reading the admission orders, which were standardized on a printed form. They described prepping the operative site, proscribing anything by mouth after midnight, and various routine laboratory studies. As Laurie's eyes ran down the list, she stopped on a test she didn't recognize. It was grouped with blood tests, so she assumed it was a blood test. It was called MASNP. She'd never heard of a test called MASNP. She wondered if NP stood for nuclear protein, but if it did, what did MAS stand for? She didn't know, but if she was right about the meaning of NP, then the test might be some kind of immunological screen.

Switching to the back of the chart where all the laboratory test results were appended, Laurie searched for the result. She didn't find it. Although she found all the other test results, there was no MASNP result.

With her curiosity piqued, Laurie looked

in the other Queens charts. Each one had an order for an MASNP, but no result. It was exactly the same with the charts from General: Each chart had the order, but no results.

Laurie reached for her ruled pad and wrote: All victims had an MASNP ordered but no MASNP result; what's an MASNP?

Thinking about laboratory tests reminded Laurie of the short run of EKG in Sobczyk's chart taken by the resuscitation team. She shuffled through the charts until she found the right one. It was easy, since it still had her ruler sticking out. Laurie opened the chart, unfolded the segment, and reread the Post-it note she'd written to herself to show the segment to a cardiologist. Putting Sobczyk's chart aside but open to the EKG, she then checked to make sure none of the other charts had any EKG associated with the resuscitation attempts. She hadn't remembered seeing any, but she wanted to be certain.

"I hope I'm not interrupting anything," a voice said.

Laurie turned around. Jack was standing in the doorway. Instead of his usual mildly sardonic expression, his face reflected concern.

"You look awfully busy," he added.

"It's best I stay busy," Laurie responded. She reached over for Riva's chair and pulled it over next to her desk. "I'm glad to see you. Come on in and sit down."

Jack lowered himself into the seat and scanned Laurie's desk. "What are you doing?"

"I wanted to make certain the Queens cases were the equivalent of those at the General. They are, to a surprising degree. I also found something curious. Are you acquainted with a blood test called MASNP? I assume it is an acronym, but I've never heard of it."

"Me neither," Jack said. "Where did you see it?"

"It's part of the standardized preoperative orders in all these cases," Laurie said. She picked up a chart at random and showed the order form to Jack. "It's in every chart. I guess it's part of AmeriCare's established routine, at least at these two hospitals."

"Interesting," Jack commented. He shook his head. "Did you look in the back to see what kind of units the results are recorded in? That might be a clue."

"I tried that, but I couldn't find any results."

"Not in any one of the charts?"

"Nope. Not one!"

"Well, I'm sure we can clear that up on Monday by asking one of the forensic investigators to look into it."

"Good suggestion," Laurie said. She made herself another Post-it note. "There is something else curious about all these victims. Without exception, every one of them is a relatively new subscriber to AmeriCare, having joined the plan within the last year."

"Now that's a cheery thought, considering that's what we are."

Laurie gave a half laugh. "I hadn't thought of that."

"The plan is growing so fast, I imagine a fair percentage of subscribers falls into that group."

"True, but it still seems odd to me."

"Anything else of note?" Jack asked.

Laurie glanced around at the charts scattered across her desk. "There is one other thing." She picked up Sobczyk's chart with the short run of EKG recording folded out, and handed it to Jack. "Does this tracing ring any bells with you? It was taken by the resuscitation team the moment they got to the patient and just before the patient flatlined."

Jack glanced at the squiggles, too embarrassed to admit he'd never been much good at EKG interpretation in even the best of circumstances. He had decided early in medical school that he was going into ophthalmology, and he didn't pay too much attention to skills that he wasn't going to need.

With a shake of his head, Jack handed the chart back to Laurie. "If I was forced to say something, I'd say that it looks to me as if the conduction system of the heart is failing, but that's obvious with the way the complexes are spread out. But you shouldn't be asking me. My advice would be to show it to a cardiologist."

"That's my plan," Laurie said, taking the chart back and putting it with the others.

"What about Roger's lists?" Jack asked. "Have you had time to go over them?"

"Not yet. I had to do the police custody case first, so I've only been here for half an hour or so. I'll spend some time with the lists when I finish the charts. It's with the charts that I feel I can make the biggest contribution. There's got to be some piece of the pie I'm not seeing."

"You don't think it's random?"

"No. There's something that links these patients together, beyond what we already know."

"I'm not so sure. I think the cases are opportunistic with the victims being at the wrong place at the wrong time."

"Did you guys have any luck with Najah?"

"Yes and no," Jack said. "They picked him up all right, but he's not cooperating. He claims he's being discriminated against and victimized by racial profiling. They've got him in custody, but he won't talk. He's insisting on waiting for his attorney, who'll be up from Florida tomorrow for the arraignment."

"And the gun?"

"It's been sent to ballistics. But results won't be available for a while. In the meantime, I'm sure he'll be given bail."

"What's Lou's take on whether he's the man?"

"He's optimistic, especially given his behavior. Lou says if someone is innocent, they're happy to cooperate. Of course, Lou is only concentrating on who shot the nurse and Rousseau. He's not thinking about your series."

"What about you?"

"As I said, I like the idea he's an anesthesiologist. Given his training, he could be knocking these patients off in a way that would be hard for us to figure out. As for him shooting the nurse and Rousseau, that's equally circumstantial, since it's based merely on knowing he owned a nine-millimeter handgun. The problem is that there are a lot of those weapons out there."

"You don't think that whoever is killing the patients killed the nurse and Roger?"

"I'm not sure."

"I am," Laurie said. "It stands to reason. The nurse probably saw something suspicious. Her death occurred the morning after there were two additions to my series. As for Roger, he'd gone up in the hospital specifically to talk to people he thought were potential suspects. He could have confronted Najah. Maybe he even saw him in Pruit's room."

"Very good points," Jack conceded.

"I'm glad they arrested Najah," Laurie said. "If he's the one, he'll think twice about any more shenanigans while Lou is breathing down his neck, which means I'm going to sleep a little better tonight. In the meantime, I'm going to go over Roger's lists very carefully, in case he doesn't pan out."

Jack nodded several times that he agreed with Laurie's plan. There was a brief pause until Jack said, "I know it's a bit off-topic, but can we pick up where we left off last night?"

Laurie eyed Jack warily. As they had been talking, she'd noticed that his typical sardonic expression had gradually reappeared, which she couldn't help but feel was a bad sign now that he was suggesting turning the conversation to personal issues. Deep down, a combination of frustration and irritation begin to brew. With everything else going on, from guilt about Roger's death to the pressure in her lower abdomen, she was uninterested in weathering any more disappointment.

"What's the matter?" Jack asked, in response to Laurie's silence. Misinterpreting her hesitancy, he raised his eyebrows questioningly and superciliously added, "Is this still not the time or the place?"

"You got that right!" Laurie blurted, struggling for control in the face of Jack's tone. "The city morgue is hardly the place to discuss starting a family. And furthermore, to be honest with you, I suddenly realize I'm finished discussing it. The facts are pretty damn plain. I've made it clear how I feel, up to and including the new development of my pregnancy. What I don't know is how you feel, and I've got to know whether you're interested and capable of abandoning your self-absorbed grieving role. If that is what you want to tell me, then fine! Tell me! I'm sick and tired of discussing it, and I'm sick and tired of waiting for you to make up your mind."

"I can see this is definitely not the time or the place," Jack said with equal irritation. He stood up. "I think I'll wait until a more opportune circumstance."

"You do that," Laurie snapped.

"We'll be in touch," Jack said before walking out the door.

Laurie turned to her desk, cradled her head in her hands, and sighed. For a brief second she considered running after Jack, but even if she did, she wouldn't know what to say when she caught him. It was obvious he wasn't about to tell her what she wanted to hear. At the same time, Laurie questioned if she was being too pushy and demanding, especially since she'd not told him about her latest symptoms and the fear that she had yet to voice even to herself: the fear of a miscarriage, which would change everything all over again.

It was a little after four in the afternoon when David Rosenkrantz turned his car into the parking lot of the small commercial building where Robert Hawthorne had his office. In its previous life, the building had been a warehouse, but like much of the renovation in downtown St. Louis, it had been recycled. It now had an upscale restaurant on the first floor and boutique offices on the second. When Robert Hawthorne—or Mr. Bob, as he was known to his operatives—came to town, first to found a company called Adverse Outcomes and subsequently to set up Operation Winnow, he had found the space and thought it convenient, since it was close to the law offices of Davidson and Faber. David didn't know what the relationship was with the law firm, and he knew he wasn't supposed to ask. What he did know was that Robert was called over there on a fairly regular basis.

It wasn't often that David was in town, since it was his job to travel around to the various cities and check in on the field operatives and deal with them as necessary. This was not an easy job, considering the oddball characters they had functioning as independent contractors. At first David just put out fires, but now that he'd worked for Robert for more than five years, he'd been entrusted with recruitment as well. The recruitment was more fun and challenging. Robert would come up with the names from an old Army buddy who still worked in the Pentagon. They were mostly people who had worked in some sort of medical capacity in the military and who had been discharged less than honorably. David hadn't been in the military himself but could appreciate how the experience could affect people who were trying to return to civilian life, especially those who had seen any sort of combat. With Iraq grinding on, they had plenty of potential recruits. Of course, they also looked for people fired from civilian hospitals. Most of those tips came from people who were already embedded.

The door to the office was unmarked. David rapped on it with his knuckle in case Yvonne, the secretary, who was also Robert's live-in girlfriend, was in the back office. It wasn't a big operation. Robert, Yvonne, and David were the only employees, and for quite a few years, it had been just Robert and Yvonne.

There was a loud click of the locking mechanism as big-busted Yvonne opened the door. With her syrupy, southern-accented voice, she coquettishly invited David to step inside. Her syntax was interspersed with a lot of "honeys" and "dears," but David wasn't fooled. Despite the bleach-blond hair and the floozy affectations like spike heels and a short skirt, he knew that she worked out regularly with Robert and was proficient in tae kwon do. David felt sorry for anyone who might mistakenly decide after a few drinks to take advantage of her flirtatious behavior.

The office was simple. There were two desks, one in the front room and one in Robert's inner office, two computers, a couple of small tables, a few chairs, a file cabinet, and two couches. It was all rented.

"The ugly old boss is in the back room, honey," Yvonne whispered. "Now don't you go off and upset him, you hear?"

David had no intention of upsetting Robert. He knew something was up when Robert called him in. David had arrived back in town the night before, after a number of days on the West Coast, and was supposed to be enjoying some downtime.

"Sit down!" Robert said when David entered. Robert was at his desk with his legs crossed and his feet perched on the corner, hands behind his head. His Brioni jacket was tossed over the arm of the couch.

"You want any coffee, dear?" Yvonne questioned. There was an Italian espresso machine on the table in the front room.

David smiled and thanked Yvonne but declined. He looked at Robert, who had his lips pressed together in an expression of frustration. "I got some bad news a little while ago," Robert said. "It seems that our little Hungarian number in the Big Apple just can't control herself."

"Another shooting?" David asked.

"I'm afraid so," Robert said. "This time, it

was one of the doctor administrators. The woman is a menace. She's good, but she's jeopardizing the whole operation."

"Are you sure she did it?"

"A hundred percent sure? No! Ninety-nine percent sure? Absolutely. Shootings follow her around like flies on a hunk of smelly cheese. Obviously, this kind of thing can't go on, so I'm afraid your little vacation has to be put on hold. Yvonne got you a reservation on a flight that gets in around ten-thirty."

"It's short notice. What about a gun?"

"Yvonne's taken care of that as well. You'll just have to make a detour on your way into the city."

"I don't remember her address."

"Yvonne's got that, too. Don't worry, we've thought of everything."

David got to his feet.

"You don't mind, do you?" Robert asked.

"No, I don't mind. I knew it was going to happen sooner or later."

"Yeah, I guess I did, too."

Outside of Laurie's rather dirty office window the gray day had faded into night as she'd pored over the charts yet another time, hoping to find some hidden piece of critical information. As had been the case on her previous readings, nothing jumped out at her. She had her Post-it notes to show the short strip of EKG to a cardiologist and to get the forensic investigators to clarify the nature of the MASNP test. Other than that, she didn't know what else to do.

She'd also carefully reviewed all of Roger's suspect lists, ranking them in order of their potential relevance. She still thought Najah was the most intriguing and most likely suspect, but the other seven individuals from various hospital departments who worked the night shift and who had transferred from St. Francis to the General around the critical time were almost equally interesting, especially since the entire group had easy access to the patient floors. The next list featured eight physicians whose hospital privileges had been canceled during the immediately preceding six-month period. She'd like to find out if possible what each one had done to warrant the disciplinary action.

Between studying Roger's lists and going over the charts for the final time, Laurie had thought about calling Jack. Although she felt her reaction to him earlier was understandable under the circumstances, she regretted it. She'd been far too precipitous and bitter, and she should have at least given him a chance to speak his mind, even if she suspected he was not going to say what she wanted to hear. At the same time, what she had said to him was unfortunately all too true. She was tired of his indecisiveness, which was the reason she'd moved out of his apartment when she had. Ultimately, Laurie decided not to call. It would have been like throwing salt on a wound. Instead, she decided to wait until morning, and if he hadn't called by then, she would call him.

Laurie stacked the hospital charts into two neat piles. Next to them, she put the notepad with her own list of how all the cases resembled one another. She put the CD with the digital records on top of the pad. She looked at her watch. It was quarter to seven, which she thought would be a good time to head back to her apartment. She would make herself a light supper before bed. Whether she would be able to sleep was another issue entirely. She hadn't wanted to go home earlier, for fear of becoming depressed. It had been better to stay busy all afternoon to keep from thinking about Roger's death, Jack's aggravating behavior, and her own looming problems.

Pushing back from the desk, Laurie was about to get up when she looked back at the CD. Suddenly, the idea occurred to her to look and see if there was a difference between the digital record and the hard-copy hospital chart—specifically, in respect to the unknown blood test. Maybe she could find a result, and if so, maybe she could figure out what the test was.

Pulling herself back to the desk, Laurie booted up her computer and inserted the CD, scrolling through the pages until she arbitrarily found herself at Stephen Lewis's laboratory values. The print was very small, and Laurie used her finger to run down the column on the left side of the page. Near the bottom, she found MASNP. Running her finger horizontally, she saw the result. It was "positive MEF2A."

Laurie absentmindedly scratched her scalp as she stared at the recorded result. There was no explanation. MEF2A didn't make any more sense to her than MASNP. It was like looking up the definition of an unknown word and finding an unknown synonym. Laurie took another Post-it from the dispenser and wrote down the result, followed by a question mark. In order to put the new Post-it with the others, which she had stuck to the wall behind her desk, she scooted her chair back and half stood, leaning forward with her hand outstretched.

A muffled cry of pain escaped from Laurie's lips. Instead of pasting the Post-it to the wall, both her hands went down on the surface of her desk to support her weight. She'd gotten a sudden, strong cramp in her lower abdomen, and for a few seconds, she held her position as well as her breath. Thankfully, the pain began to lessen, and Laurie slowly let herself sink back into her chair. She held herself stiffly, lest she aggravate whatever was going on inside her body.

A continuous low-grade discomfort had persisted in Laurie's abdomen following the autopsy on the police custody case. It had waxed and waned to a degree, but it had never entirely gone away. She had characterized it more as pressure than pain until she'd tried to place the new Post-it with the others.

Once the pain had lessened to the point that Laurie could breathe normally, she allowed herself to adjust her weight in her chair by sitting up straighter. Thankfully, what had now become an ache stayed at the same tolerable level. Perspiration had appeared on her forehead, and she wiped it off with the back of her hand. She knew she was anxious, but she was surprised that she was anxious enough to perspire so freely. She wondered if she could have a fever, but didn't think so. Gingerly, she palpated her abdomen with a single finger. In contrast to previous occasions, there was now an area of definite tenderness, which seemed ominous to her. As she had noted earlier, it was exactly the location where the pain of appendicitis occurred.

With hesitation, Laurie slowly got to her feet. It had been the sudden motion of half standing a few minutes earlier that had brought on the current episode, and she was eager to avoid a repeat. Luckily, there was no reoccurrence. Her perspiration was another matter. That had actually gotten worse.

Cautiously, Laurie took a few steps out of her office and into the hallway while continuing to support herself with her hand against the wall. The pain remained bearable. With gathering confidence, she walked slowly down the length of the corridor to the ladies' room. Inside, she got some toilet tissue and wiped herself. The spotting had reappeared, and there was more blood than there had been earlier. She knew she didn't have appendicitis.

With gathering anxiety, Laurie retraced her steps back to her office and returned to her chair. She eyed the phone. She was still hesitant to call Dr. Riley, though now she felt she had little choice. The spotting ruled out appendicitis, and along with the location of the pain, suggested a possible ectopic pregnancy, which was far more serious than a mere threatened miscarriage. Finally, she reluctantly picked up the phone and called Laura Riley's office number. When the operator answered, Laurie gave her name and direct-dial number. Thinking it might expedite the callback, she included her M.D. title and said she needed to talk with the doctor. She said it was an emergency.

As Laurie put the receiver back down, she noticed a new sensation: vague shoulder discomfort. It was so mild that she wondered if she was imagining it, yet it added to her already considerable anxiety. If it was real, it suggested the ominous development of peritoneal irritation. To test the possibility, Laurie carefully pushed in on her abdomen with her index finger, then suddenly took her hand away. She grimaced with a fleeting stab of pain. What she had felt was called "rebound tenderness," and it also suggested peritoneal irritation, which now made her worry that not only might she have an ectopic pregnancy, but that it might have already ruptured. If so, it was a true medical emergency for which time could be a critical factor. She could be hemorrhaging internally.

The phone's harsh ring interrupted her obsessing, and she snapped the receiver up to her ear. She was relieved when Dr. Riley identified herself. Laurie could tell she was on a cell phone and in a public place. Loud conversation could be heard in the background.

Laurie began by apologizing for calling on a Saturday night and said that she had resisted because she worried it was a bad way to start out a professional relationship, but she believed she truly had no choice. Laurie went on to describe her symptoms in detail, including the rebound tenderness. She admitted she'd had discomfort prior to speaking with her on the phone the previous day, but had forgotten to mention it and had thought it could wait until her scheduled visit the following Friday.

"First of all," Laura said when Laurie had finished, "there's no need to apologize. In fact, I would have preferred you call sooner. I don't want to alarm you, but it we should consider an ectopic pregnancy until we can rule it out. You might be bleeding internally."

"I thought as much," Laurie admitted.

"Are you still diaphoretic?"

Laurie felt her brow. It was damp with perspiration. "I'm afraid so."

"What's your pulse, approximately? Is it fast or normal?"

Using her shoulder to hold the phone, Laurie felt her pulse at her wrist. She knew it had been fast earlier, and she wanted to be certain it had remained so. "It's definitely on the fast side," she admitted. She had hoped the sweating and the rapid heartbeat had been due to her anxiety, but Laura's questions had made her acknowledge that there could be another explanation: She could be going into shock.

"Okay," Laura said in a controlled, businesslike voice. "I want to see you in the emergency room at the Manhattan General Hospital."

Laurie felt a shiver descend her spine at the thought of being a patient at the General. "Could we pick another hospital?" she questioned.

"I'm afraid not," Laura said. "It's the only hospital where I have privileges. Besides, they are fully equipped if we have to be aggressive. Where are you at the moment?"

"I'm in my office at the Office of the Chief Medical Examiner."

"On First Avenue and Thirtieth Street?"

"Yes."

"And where is your office in the building?"

"It's on the fifth floor. Why do you ask?"

"I'm going to send an ambulance."

Good God! Laurie thought. She didn't want to ride in an ambulance. "I can take a taxi," she suggested.

"You are not going to take a taxi," Laura stated unequivocally. "One of the first rules about being a patient in an emergency medical situation, a rule which is particularly hard for doctors to accept, is that you must follow orders. We can argue about the necessity later, but right now we are not taking any chances. I'm going to send an ambulance ASAP, and I will meet you in the ER. Do you know your blood type?"

"O positive," Laurie said.

"See you in the emergency room," Laura said and disconnected.

With a shaking hand, Laurie hung up the phone. She felt shell-shocked. Upheavals were becoming the norm. In a single day she'd been forced to identify a friend's corpse and now face the terrifying prospect of a medical emergency and possibly surgery at a hospital where a suspected serial killer was killing patients like her. The only consolation was that the most likely suspect was in custody.

Laurie snatched up the phone. She'd been reluctant to call Jack for a variety of reasons, but with this new development, her hand was forced. She needed his support, she needed him as an ombudsman or guardian in the hospital if she did end up having emergency surgery.

The phone rang once, then twice. "Come on, Jack!" Laurie urged. "Answer it!" The phone rang again, and Laurie knew he wasn't there. As she suspected, after the next ring, his answering machine picked up. As Laurie waited to leave a message, she felt a wave of resentment wash over her. It seemed uncanny how Jack managed to irritate her in so many different ways. Undoubtedly, he was out on his neighborhood basketball court, pretending he was a teenager. Laurie knew she was being unreasonable, but she couldn't help it. She was actually angry that he wasn't there. Although she knew it was an unfair comparison, she couldn't help but think that had Roger not been killed, he would have been available.

"A major problem has come up," Laurie said when it was time for her to speak. "I need your help again. At the moment, I am waiting for an ambulance to take me to the Manhattan General. Dr. Riley thinks I might have a ruptured ectopic pregnancy. On the plus side, it will mean that the pressure will be off you, but on the negative side, I'll be facing emergency surgery. I need you to be there. I don't want to become part of my own series. Please come!"

After pressing the disconnect button, Laurie dialed Jack's cell phone. She went through the same process, leaving a similar message in hopes he'd get one or the other. Then she pushed away from the desk with the idea of getting her coat before heading down to the basement level, where she expected the ambulance to arrive. As she stood up, she kept her hand pressed against her lower abdomen, hoping to avoid another severe cramp. Instead, she heard ringing in her ears and felt a wave of dizziness.

The next thing Laurie was aware of was voices, particularly the voice of a man seemingly talking on the telephone. He was saying something about the blood pressure being low but steady, the pulse at one hundred, and the abdomen being slightly tense. Laurie realized her eyes were shut, and she opened them. She was on the floor of her office, facing up at the ceiling. A female EMT was busily taping an IV line against her left arm. A male EMT was standing to the side while speaking on his cell phone. Behind him, she recognized Mike Laster. Alongside Laurie was a collapsed gurney with an IV pole.

"What happened?" Laurie asked. She started to get up.

"Easy," the female EMT said, placing her hand on Laurie's chest. "You just had a little fainting episode. But everything is okay. We're going to be getting you out of here in two seconds."

The male EMT snapped his phone shut. "All right, let's go!" He walked around behind Laurie's head and insinuated his hands beneath Laurie's back and into her armpits. The woman went to her ankles. "On three," the man said, and then quickly counted.

Laurie felt herself lifted over onto the gurney. The EMTs quickly secured her with straps, raised the gurney to waist-height, and jockeyed it out into the corridor.

"How long was I unconscious?" Laurie questioned. She'd never fainted before. She had no recollection of falling to the floor.

"It couldn't have been for very long," the woman said. She was at the foot pushing, while the man was at the head, pulling. Mike walked alongside.

"Sorry about this," Laurie said to Mike.

"Don't be silly," Mike responded.

They took the elevator down to the basement level. As they passed the mortuary office, Laurie saw the evening tech, Miguel Sánchez, standing in the doorway. Laurie waved self-consciously. Miguel waved back.

The gurney bumped across the morgue's concrete floor, past the security office, and out onto the loading dock. The ambulance was parked next to one of the Health and Hospital's mortuary vans. Laurie thought of the irony that she was going out the same way the bodies came in.

Once in the ambulance, the female EMT inflated a blood-pressure cuff around Laurie's right upper arm.

"What is it?" Laurie asked.

"It's fine," the woman said, although she reached over and opened the IV a little more.

For Laurie, the ride over to the Manhattan General Hospital was surprisingly rapid. She'd felt detached enough to close her eyes. She could hear the siren, although it seemed as if it were in the distance. The next thing she knew, the doors of the ambulance were flung open, and she was rolled out into bright light.

The emergency room was typically chaotic, but she didn't have to wait. She was whisked into the depths and directly into the acute care section. As she was being transferred onto an examination table, Laurie felt a hand grip her forearm. Laurie turned and found herself gazing up into the face of a youthful woman dressed in scrubs, complete with a hood.

"I'm Dr. Riley. We are going to be taking good care of you. I want you to relax."

"I'm relaxed," Laurie responded.

"Since we've not met before tonight, I need to ask if you have any medical problems, whether you are taking any medication, or whether you have any allergies."

"No to all of those questions. I've been blessed with very good health."

"Good," Laura said.

"Wait a second," Laurie said. "There is something I wanted to mention to you. I've recently been tested positive for the BRCA1 marker."

"Have you seen an oncologist about it?"

"Not yet."

"Well, I don't think that is going to influence what we need to do in this situation. Let me give you the game plan. First, we'll do a rapid culdocentesis, which is to confirm if you have any blood in the space behind your uterus. It's done with a needle through the apex of your vagina. It sounds worse than it is. You'll feel a pinch, but that's about all."

"I understand," Laurie said.

True to her word, Laura quickly did the procedure, with little discomfort to Laurie. The result was positive.

"This pretty much makes the decision about surgery for us," Laura said. "My biggest concern is that you are continuing to hemorrhage into your abdominal cavity. We've got to stop that. We also will need to give you some blood. Do you understand everything that I'm saying?"

"I do," Laurie said.

"I'm sorry you've had to experience a problem like this. I want to make certain you don't think it is your fault. Ectopic pregnancies are more common than people realize."

"There is something in my past that may have contributed. In college, I had an episode of pelvic inflammatory disease associated with an IUD."

"That may or may not have contributed," Laura said. "Meanwhile, is there anyone you would like us to call?"

"I've already called the person I'd like to be here," Laurie said.

"Okay, I'm going up to the surgery floor to make sure everything is ready. I'll see you in a few minutes."

"Thank you again. I'm sorry If I've ruined your Saturday night."

"What are you talking about? Getting you back to normal is going to make my Saturday night."

For a few minutes, Laurie was left by herself. She felt curiously detached, as if the whole episode involved someone else. She could hear telltale evidence of dramas unfolding in neighboring rooms, and saw people dash by the open doorway on various urgent errands.

Laurie felt lucky to have Laura Riley as her doctor, and was indebted to Sue for recommending her. With the kind of confidence and professionalism that Laura projected, Laurie wasn't as fearful about the upcoming surgery as she would have imagined. She knew she needed it, with the growing fullness in her abdomen and the general weakness the blood loss caused. Her only real worry was the fear of being victimized by SADS after the surgery and becoming a member of her own series, but she put the thought out of her mind. Instead, she thought about Jack and wondered when he would get her message. There was some concern that he was upset enough at her not to come in. If that were to happen, Laurie had no idea what she would do, so she put that thought out of her mind as well.

twenty

Jack had managed to fool Flash with a head fake and clever use of a pick, and for a moment, Flash had no idea where Jack was. By the time Flash had figured out what had happened, Jack had snaked his way in under the basket. Warren had seen the move out of the corner of his eye and shot a perfect pass into Jack's waiting hands. Jack twisted around and was poised to make a simple layup to win the tied game. Unfortunately, that was not what happened.

By some inexplicable miscalculation on Jack's part, the ball didn't glance off the backboard and drop through the basket as he intended. Instead, it fell far short, lodged between the basket's rim and the backboard, and stayed there.

Play ground to a halt. Totally embarrassed to have missed such an easy shot, Jack had to leap up to knock the ball free. Then, as the final indignity, a player on the opposing team grabbed the ball, stepped out of bounds, then let loose with a long pass down the court to Flash, who'd taken advantage of Jack being under the basket to break free. Jack was supposed to be guarding him. Instead, Jack had to watch impotently while Flash went in to make a layup at the opposite end, and, unlike Jack, he didn't miss. The game was over. Flash's team had won.

Jack slunk off the court, wishing he could disappear. He dodged some of the puddles along the sidelines. With his back pressed against the chain-link fence in a dry area, he sank to a sitting position with his knees up in the air. Warren sauntered over, hands on his hips and a mocking, wry smile on his face. Warren was fifteen years

Jack's junior, with a body that would have made a men's underwear model jealous. As the best basketball player in the neighborhood, and as a keen competitor, he hated to lose, and not just because it meant he might have to sit out a game or two. For him, it was a personal affront.

"What the hell's the matter with you?" Warren questioned. "How could you miss that shot? I thought you had recovered, but that has to go down as one of your more pitiful exhibitions."

"Sorry, man," Jack said. "I guess I wasn't concentrating."

Warren gave a short, derisive laugh as if that was the understatement of the year before taking a seat next to Jack with his knees angled up in a similar fashion. In front of them, a new group of five was getting ready to take on Flash and his team. Despite the crummy weather and the fact that it was Saturday night, there had been a big turnout.

Jack's basketball had recovered to a degree over the last several weeks, but that afternoon, Laurie's pushiness and her playing the victim role had provoked him to no end. He could sympathize with her about what she was facing lately, but from his perspective, she had no idea what being a victim was really like. On top of that he couldn't believe she kept harping on him about his use of humor, which he felt was his only defense against the harsh reality that fate and AmeriCare had thrown at him. And, worse yet, he couldn't comprehend that she wouldn't listen to what he'd been thinking about this new curveball of her being pregnant. After she'd broken the news, he'd thought of nothing else and had been looking forward to sharing his feelings, both pro and con. The news had forced him to face the idea of a second family as a reality, and he'd come around to believing he might not be quite as scared of the situation as he thought . . . at least until that afternoon, when she acted so demanding and victimized. When he thought about the conversation again, he couldn't believe she was "sick and tired" of discussing having a family, because, prior to her moving out, he couldn't remember that last time she'd even brought up the subject.

"Hell!" Jack exclaimed suddenly, snapping his headband off his forehead and throwing it to the pavement.

Warren looked at him questioningly. "Man, you're in bad shape! Let me guess! Laurie's still acting up."

"You've no idea," Jack said scornfully. He was going to elaborate when he heard a distant muffled beeping. Grabbing his backpack, he opened the zipper and took out his cell phone, which he normally didn't bring out onto the court unless he was on call. But that evening after the fracas with Laurie, he wanted to stay in touch in case she came to her senses. When he flipped the lid and saw that he had a message, he checked caller ID.

"It's her," Jack said with a touch of exasperation. With no idea what to expect and scant hope for a miracle, he called his voicemail. As he began to listen to the message, he stood up. As he continued to listen, his jaw slowly dropped, then he disconnected and looked down at Warren, momentarily paralyzed. "Good God! She's been taken by ambulance to the Manhattan General for emergency surgery."

Breaking free from his brief, stunned immobility, Jack bent down and snatched up his gear. "I got to change and get the hell over there!" He turned and started at a run toward the playground exit.

"Hold up!" Warren called after him.

Jack didn't stop or slow down, knowing full well the seriousness of a ruptured ectopic pregnancy. When he was held up by traffic on the street, Warren caught up to him.

"How about I give you a lift," Warren said. "My ride's just around the corner."

"Fantastic," Jack responded.

"By the time you get your ass back down, I'll be sitting out here waiting on you," Warren said.

Jack waved acquiescence before sprinting across the street. He took the stairs in his apartment building by twos and started pulling off his clothes on the final flight. The rest of his basketball outfit came off as he traversed his apartment, anxious to get to the hospital before Laurie was taken up to the OR. He didn't like the idea of her having surgery, and he didn't like the idea of her being at the Manhattan General.

As he thundered down the stairs, Jack struggled into the same clothes he'd worn that day. True to his word, Warren was sitting in his black SUV when Jack emerged from his building. Jack jumped in and Warren took off with a screech.

"Is this surgery serious?" Warren asked.

"You'd better believe it," Jack answered. While he tied his tie, he chastised himself for reacting so emotionally to Laurie's mini-outburst that afternoon. What he should have done was just let her rant without getting his dander up, but he'd not been in control. He'd not been in control since she walked out of his apartment.

"How serious?" Warren asked.

"Let me put it this way; people have died from the problem she has."

"No shit!" Warren murmured as he pressed his foot down on the accelerator.

Jack grabbed the handhold above the passenger-side door to steady himself as Warren's SUV surged forward to make the traffic light at the 97th Street traverse. A few minutes later, Warren had the Manhattan General in his sights.

"Where do you want to be dropped off?" Warren asked.

"Follow the signs for the emergency department," Jack said.

Warren ended up nosing in between two ambulances at the receiving dock, and

Jack jumped out. "Thanks, man," Jack called.

"Let me hear how things go!" Warren shouted out his window.

Jack waved over his shoulder, then vaulted up onto the platform and ran inside. The waiting area was packed with people. Jack headed directly for the double doors that led into the emergency room proper, but he was barred by a beefy, red-faced, uniformed policeman. The man had been standing to the side, but stepped in front of the doors as Jack neared.

"You gotta sign in at the desk," the officer said, pointing over Jack's shoulder.

With a bit of effort, Jack got out his wallet and flipped it open. Attached was his formal medical-examiner badge. The policeman drew Jack's hand closer to examine it. "Sorry, doc," he said when he recognized what it was.

After glancing into a few of the cubicles and having no luck finding Laurie, Jack stopped one of the nurses, who was scurrying down the corridor with a clutch of blood-sample tubes in her hands. When Jack asked for Laurie by name, she squinted as if she were slightly myopic at a dry-erase board that Jack had not seen back near the entrance doors. “She’s in the acute-care area,” the woman said. She pointed into the depths of the complex. “Room 22.”

Jack found her alone in the room, surrounded by all sorts of acute-care equipment. Behind her was a flat LCD screen with real-time tracings of her blood pressure and pulse. Her eyes were closed, and her hands were folded on her chest with her fingers intertwined. Except for her pallor, she looked the picture of contented repose. Behind her and hanging from an IV pole were a cluster of bottles and a plastic pouch of blood, which ran into her left arm.

A few steps brought Jack to Laurie’s side. He put his hand on her forearm, reluctant to wake her from her peaceful slumber but afraid not to. “Laurie?” he called softly.

Laurie’s heavily lidded eyes opened. She smiled when she saw Jack. “Thank goodness you’re here.”

“How do you feel?”

“Considering everything, I feel pretty good. Anesthesia came down and gave me some kind of preop. I’m about to go up to surgery. I was hoping you'd get here before I went in."

"Is it a ruptured ectopic pregnancy?"

"All indications point to it."

"I'm so sorry you're going through this."

"Aren't you a little relieved? I mean, be honest!"

"No, I'm not relieved. In fact, I'm worried. Can't we get you over to another hospital? What about your father's hospital?"

Laurie smiled with drug-induced serenity. She shook her head. "My doctor only has privileges here. I asked about going someplace else right off, but I'm afraid I'm stuck. She's pretty sure I'm still bleeding internally, so we don't have the benefit of a lot of time." Laurie detached her forearm from Jack and gripped his. "I know what you are thinking, but I'm okay with being here, and more so now that you've come. Although theoretically I'm at risk of being a victim of my series, I don't think it's that high. The odds are in my favor, especially with Najah away from the scene."

Jack nodded. He knew she was right statistically, but it was hardly consolation, particularly with the case against Najah so circumstantial. The fact was, he didn't like Laurie being there period, yet he resigned himself to there being little choice. She could exsanguinate during a transfer.

"I'm okay, really," Laurie added. "I like my doctor. I've great confidence in her. And I asked her what was going to happen to me tonight. She said that after the surgery, I'd go to the PACU."

"What the devil is the PACU?"

"Postanesthesia care unit."

"What happened to the recovery room?"

Laurie smiled and shrugged. "I don't know. Now it's called the PACU. Anyway, she told me that I'd probably stay in the PACU all night, and if I were to leave, she wants me in an acute-care unit because of how much blood I've lost. None of the cases in my series happened in intensive care, only on hospital floors. I feel safe until tomorrow, when I'm sure we can arrange for a transfer. My father can get me over to the University Hospital, and even if my doctor can't follow me over there, my old GYN would fill in, I'm certain."

Jack nodded. He still wasn't happy, but he could see her point. Besides, in terms of emergency surgery, the Manhattan General was right up there with the best.

"Are you as comfortable as I am?" Laurie asked.

"I guess so," he admitted.

"Good," Laurie said. "And remember, all this is in addition to the fact that the prime suspect is safely in custody."

"I'm not willing to rely on that," Jack said.

"Nor am I, if it were the only thing," Laurie said. "But it adds to my peace of mind."

"Good," Jack responded. "And your peace of mind is the most important. For me, I like the idea you'll be in the PACU. That's real security. The case against Najah is pure supposition."

"Without a doubt," Laurie agreed. "Which leads me to a suggestion. There's no reason for you to hang around here doing nothing while I'm up in surgery. Why don't you go back to the OCME and take a look at the material on my desk, particularly Roger's lists. You could even bring them back here. I've written down some of my ideas, but it would be good to get your take, especially if Najah turns out to be a dead end, pardon the pun."

"Sorry!" Jack asserted forcibly. "I ain't leaving here while you're in surgery. No way!"

"Okay, don't get huffy. It was just a suggestion."

"Thanks but no thanks," Jack reiterated.

There was a pause in the conversation. Jack glanced up at the LCD screen. He was mildly concerned that Laurie's blood pressure was low and her pulse was high, but he was pleased to see that they were staying steady.

"Jack," Laurie said, gripping his arm tighter. "I'm sorry I was so irritable this afternoon. It was wrong of me not to let you talk. I apologize."

"Apology accepted," Jack said, directing his eyes back down at Laurie. "And I'm sorry I was so damn sensitive. You've had plenty of reasons to be distraught. The problem is I've been pretty upset myself. Of course, that's hardly an excuse."

"Okay, Laurie!" a cheerful voice said. Laura Riley bounded into the room, along with an orderly. "The operating room is ready, and all we need is you."

Laurie introduced Laura to Jack and was careful to mention that Jack was a fellow medical examiner. Laura was gracious but cut the conversation short, saying she really wanted to get things under way. There had already been a little delay waiting for one of the operating rooms to free up.

"Would it be okay if I observe?" Jack asked.

"No, I don't think that is a good idea," Laura said without hesitation. "But since it's the evening shift, I can probably take you up to the surgical lounge, and you can wait there. That's bending the rules a bit, but you are a physician. Then, as soon as we've gotten Laurie taken care of, I can give you an update. That is, of course, if it's all okay with Laurie."

"It's okay with me," Laurie said.

"I'll take you up on the surgical lounge offer," Jack said. "But first, maybe it would be a good idea if I gave blood. Laurie and I are the same blood type, and if she needs another unit, I'd like to be the donor."

"That's very generous," Laura said. "Chances are we'll use it." Turning to Laurie she said: "Now let's get you up to the OR and get you fixed up." She nodded to the orderly who unlocked the wheels of the gurney and began angling it toward the hallway.

Excuse me," an accented voice called out in a peremptory tone.

Jazz stopped and turned around. It was the owner of the sundry store on Columbus Avenue that she frequented. He had also tapped her on the arm at the same time he had spoken.

"You forgot to pay," the man said, pointing to her canvas bag, which was slung over her shoulder.

A wry smile appeared on Jazz's face. She estimated that this anemic-looking guy weighed less than ninety pounds when he was wet, yet here he was, accosting her in the middle of the sidewalk on Columbus Avenue. It was amazing the nerve some people had, despite having no way to back up their behavior. Of course, he could be packing, but Jazz seriously doubted it. He had on a snug white apron tied around his middle, precluding access to any pockets.

"You took milk, bread, and eggs but no pay," the man elaborated. He then bunched his lips into a tight ball and thrust out his chin. From Jazz's perspective, there was no doubt he was pissed, and he acted as if he was ready to fight, which didn't make sense unless he was gazillion-level black belt in some exotic martial art. She was bigger than he, invariably in better shape, and had her right hand holding her Glock in her coat pocket.

"You come back to the store!" the man ordered.

Jazz instinctively glanced around. No one seemed to be paying them any attention, yet that would undoubtedly change if she created a scene. Still, she was tempted. She looked back at her heckler. But before she could speak, her Blackberry in her left coat pocket beeped and vibrated in her hand. She usually left it on when she was out walking around.

"One second," Jazz said to the store proprietor as she pulled her Blackberry out in the open. A larger, more genuine smile took over her face as she noticed it was a message from Mr. Bob. After getting three names in the last two days, she wasn't expecting another, but why else would he be contacting her at the time of day when she got names? She quickly opened the message.

"All right!" Jazz exclaimed. There on her screen was the name Laurie Montgomery. Taking her right hand out of her pocket, she gave the storekeeper a thumbs-up sign. She couldn't have been more pleased. Another five thousand dollars was coming her way, meaning that in three nights, she'd earned a whopping twenty thousand dollars!

"My wife will call the police if you don't come back and pay," the man insisted.

With the windfall addition of five thousand dollars to her net worth, Jazz experienced a flush of uncharacteristic magnanimity and largesse. "You know, now that you mention it, I think I did walk out without paying. Why don't we wander back and settle up."

The airplane's wheels thudded against the runway, and the fuselage shook from the impact. The noise and vibration yanked David Rosenkrantz from the depths of sleep. Momentarily disoriented, it took him a moment to get his bearings. Turning his head to the side, he looked out the rain-streaked window. He had landed at La-Guardia Airport, the terminal's lights barely visible through the misty air.

"A good night for ducks," a voice said. "They said it was going to start raining again around ten, and for once they were right."

David turned to the man sitting next to him. He was a prim, late-middle-aged fellow with rimless glasses, dressed like David in a shirt and tie. Robert insisted David wear business clothes. He explained it lent an aura of legitimacy to their operation. David liked it because he felt he blended in better. With all the flying he had to do, he looked like just another businessman.

David's fellow passenger was leaning forward to see out of David's window. "Are you coming home, or are you on business here in New York?" the man asked. Throughout the entire flight he'd not uttered a word. He'd had his nose in his laptop the whole time.

"Business," David said without elaborating. He didn't like talking too much with his fellow travelers; conversations inevitably worked their way around to what kind of business David was in. In the past, if forced, David had said he was in healthcare consulting. That had worked until the day he found himself chatting with a fellow passenger who was legitimately in the field. The remainder of the conversation had been rather dicey, and David had been saved by the opportunity to deplane.

"I'm in business, too," the prim man said. "Computer software. By the way, where are you staying? If you're staying in Manhattan, maybe we could share a taxi. When it rains in New York, they're like hen's teeth."

"That's very generous," David said, "but I've yet to make arrangements. This trip was put together at the last minute."

"I can recommend the Marriott," the man persisted. "They almost always have availability on the weekend, and it's a good central location."

David smiled as best he could. "I'll keep that in mind, but I'm not going directly into town. I have to make a stop here in Queens." He planned to take a taxi to Long Island City, where he'd have the cab wait while he picked up the arranged gun.

"Remember, this hellcat is usually packing," Robert had advised. "So don't give her much breathing room. In fact, don't give her any breathing room at all. The whole problem is that she has no compunction whatsoever about using her piece."

David had nodded at this unsolicited advice, but he didn't need to be told any such thing. He was a professional and had been doing this for years. He reached into his jacket pocket and pulled out a piece of paper. The address was 1421 Vernon Avenue, Long Island City. He wondered what kind of place it would turn out to be. He also wondered if getting the gun would go smoothly. On a recent trip to Chicago, the gun source had been picked up the day before on unrelated charges, throwing off the whole operation and forcing David to stay in the windy city for five days. He hoped the same snafu wouldn't happen in New York, since he was anxious to be on his way back to St. Louis in twenty-four hours or so.

David looked at the other addresses he had written down on the paper. They were Jasmine Rakoczi's apartment and her health club, both on the Upper West Side.

"Where is that Marriott?" David asked the prim man, who was busy packing his laptop into its carrying case.

"Times Square," the man said.

"Is that on the West Side?"

"It sure is, right near the theater district."

He thought he'd keep the Marriott in mind. His general plan was to get the gun and then find a hotel. He was exhausted from having spent a number of long nights out on the West Coast, and he was looking forward to a good, long sleep. Then he'd figure out the best way to deal with the Rakoczi woman. The nicest part of the whole affair was remembering what she looked like. Robert had even said she had one of the best bodies he'd ever seen, and Robert definitely had good taste. David fully planned to see for himself, which meant her apartment would be the best bet.

twenty-one

With a backhanded motion, Jack tossed the *Cosmopolitan* magazine back onto the surgical lounge's coffee table. He was desperate for something to read, but that particular magazine wasn't going to do it for him. He'd been through just about everything else, including old copies of *Time, People, National Geographic,* and *Newsweek,* plus Saturday's papers. He'd even tried to watch CNN for a while, but he couldn't concentrate on the TV, especially after the two cups of coffee he'd drunk. It was a quarter to twelve, and Laurie was still in surgery, which made him progressively antsy.

Jack had gone up to the third floor with Laurie, Dr. Riley, and the orderly. He had given Laurie's hand a final, reassuring squeeze before she and the others disappeared into the OR. With the hope that Laura might reconsider his watching the procedure, he'd gone into the men's locker room and changed into scrubs, using an empty locker with no lock for his clothes.

But Laura was steadfast in her insistence that he remain in the surgical lounge, saying that she'd be in as soon as the procedure was over. Jack trled to entertain himself to keep from obsessing about what was taking so long. While he waited, the hospital shift had changed, with an entirely new group manning the OR and rotating in and out of the lounge. No one bothered Jack, which he appreciated. He was in no mood for socializing.

Just before midnight, Dr. Riley finally appeared at the lounge's arched entranceway. When she spotted Jack, she walked over.

Jack stood up. She appeared exhausted, but to his relief, she was smiling.

"I'm sorry to keep you in suspense," Laura said. "It took a little longer than we expected, but everything is okay."

"Thank goodness," Jack said. "What was the problem?"

"Continued bleeding. She'd lost a lot of blood, and her clotting wasn't what we would have liked. She's now in the PACU, where I want her to stay so they can follow her clotting status and blood pressure."

"Sounds like a good plan."

"I see you changed into scrubs."

"I was hoping you'd relent and allow me to observe."

"Sorry," Laura said. "I know from Laurie that your association with her isn't just professional. With births, I'm happy to have actual participation of partners, but with operations like this, I'm not."

"You don't have to apologize," Jack said. "She's okay, and that's all that matters."

"Actually, it's good you're in scrubs. I got approval for you to come in and have a quick visit, provided you're okay with the idea."

"I'd love to come in," Jack said. "But tell me, was it an ectopic pregnancy?"

"Yes," Laura said. "In the isthmus of the oviduct, fairly close to the uterine wall, which might be why there was so much bleeding. The oviduct itself was visibly abnormal, and we ended up removing it along with the right ovary. On the positive side, the left oviduct and ovary appear entirely normal, so her fertility shouldn't be significantly affected."

"She'll be pleased to hear that," Jack said. Now that he knew Laurie was on the road to recovery, he allowed himself to think about the lost conceptus, surprised at his emotion. He was saddened, even though he'd anticipated being relieved that the pressure was off, as Laurie had suggested. Although mourning on any level wasn't pleasant, in this situation, he felt there was a positive side, since it lent further credence that he might be more capable of having a child than he would have thought only a few days earlier.

With a wave for him to follow, Laura led him into the main portion of the operating room. Several women were at the main OR desk, bent over paperwork. On the opposite wall was a large dry-erase board scribed like graph paper. On the left were the numbers of all the operating rooms. Across the top, forming columns, were spaces for patient name, anesthesiologist, surgeon, circulating nurse, scrub nurse, and procedure. Jack could see that there were eight cases under way. He saw Laurie's name with a line drawn through it.

The PACU was located just beyond the desk. It was a large, starkly white room with sixteen beds, eight on a side. Each backed up into an array of anesthesia equipment, including banks of monitors for blood pressure and pulse, an EKG lead, and blood oxygenation. Only four of the sixteen beds were occupied. All the patients appeared to be sleeping, despite the bright ambient light and the sense of frenetic activity. Each patient had his or her own nurse, who constantly checked everything, from vital signs to urine output, from respiratory status to core body temperature, writing the results on a clipboard attached to the bed. In between these activities, they were adjusting IV rates, checking surgical drains, or running into a supply closet for IV fluids or medications. A no-nonsense-appearing female charge nurse with frizzed blond hair and a stocky, bulldog habitus manned a centralized main desk. She exuded a drill sergeant's sense of control. Laura introduced Jack. Her name was Thea Papparis.

"I hope you understand you can only stay a few minutes," Thea said. Her voice was as commanding as her physical presence.

"I appreciate you letting me come in at all," Jack said, showing uncharacteristic respect for the rules. Under more normal circumstances, he viewed bureaucratic edicts as mere guidelines, but with Laurie's potential care possibly dependent on his behavior, he was being particularly circumspect, as evidenced by his restraint in not having run down to Laurie's OR when her case had dragged on.

"You got a fine wife there, doctor," Thea said. "She's a charmer, even under the influence of the anesthesia." For a second, her attention switched to a monitor built in over the desk. One of the patients had had an extra heartbeat with a compensatory pause. Jack used the opportunity to glance at Laura, who flashed him an exaggerated expression of guilt, meaning she'd fibbed about marital status to get Jack invited into the PACU.

Thea redirected her attention back to the visitors. "What was I saying? Oh, yeah! Your wife is one amiable individual. Most of the people we see in here are just out of it, although some can be uncooperative and even belligerent. Not your wife. She's just as nice as pie."

"Thank you," Jack said. "I appreciate the attention you've given her."

"That's our job," Thea said.

Laura motioned for Jack to follow her, and they walked over to the bed farthest against the wall. A male nurse with an impressive tattoo of a mermaid on his left upper arm was adjusting Laurie's IV. She was also getting another unit of blood.

"How's she doing, Pete?" Laura asked. She glanced briefly at the clipboard before walking up along the right side of the bed.

"Smooth as silk," Pete said. "Blood pressure and pulse hanging in there just fine. She's putting out urine, and nothing has come out of the drain."

"Good," Laura said. She grasped Laurie's forearm, gave it a little shake, and called her name.

Laurie's eyes popped open, but only about halfway. Her forehead was wrinkled as if she was struggling keep them open. She looked at Laura, then over at Jack, who'd come up along the left side. She smiled placidly and reached out and laid a limp hand in Jack's.

"Do you remember me telling you that your operation is over?" Laura asked.

"Not really," Laurie admitted without taking her eyes off Jack.

"Well, it is," Laura said. "You're doing fine. The bleeding has been stopped. I'd tell you to relax, but you are already doing that."

Laurie turned her head slowly toward Laura. "Thank you for all you have done, and I'm sorry about your Saturday night."

"Don't you worry," Laura said. "It's been a blast."

"Am I in the PACU at the moment?"

"Yes, you are."

"And I'm going to stay here overnight."

"That's affirmative. I've asked for them to keep you here and monitor you until I come in and make my rounds. The intensive care unit happens to be full, but this is just as good and maybe better. I hope you don't mind. It might be hard to sleep with all the activity."

"I don't mind in the slightest," Laurie said, giving Jack's hand a squeeze.

"Now," Laura added. "I'm going to leave you two, and, Laurie, I'll see you in the morning at seven. I'm sure everything will be fine, and we can move you to a room on the OB-GYN floor, provided they have a bed. I know they are overbooked tonight, but we'll worry about that tomorrow. Okay?"

"Okay," Laurie responded.

With a final wave, Laura walked away.

Laurie turned back toward Jack. "What time is it?"

"Around midnight," Jack said.

"My gosh! Where did the evening go? Time really does fly when you're having fun."

Jack smiled. "It's good to hear you haven't lost your sense of humor. How do you feel?"

"Great. I know that sounds ridiculous, but I've got no discomfort whatsoever. The worst thing is a dry mouth. Whatever they gave me has me on cloud nine. And now that it's over, I can admit I was pretty darn scared. I was foolish to let the problem get out of hand."

"I don't think you should be blaming yourself."

"I do. My not reacting to incriminating symptoms is a prime example of one of my not-so-wonderful character traits: namely, putting out of my mind anything potentially unpleasant, physically or emotionally. I'm more of my mother's daughter than I'd ever cared to admit."

"You're starting to scare me with this kind of insight under the influence of anesthesia," Jack joked. "What did they give you, some kind of truth serum? Don't answer! Let's talk about something a bit more topical. Did they tell you had a ruptured ectopic pregnancy?"

"I'm sure they did, but my short-term memory is not up to speed."

"As soon as I heard you were all right, I felt a curious emotion."

"Now, that's a weird thing to say," Laurie said with a slight smile on her lips. "What were you, disappointed I was going to pull through?"

"That didn't come out right. What I meant to say was that when I didn't have to worry about you, I felt sad that we had lost a child."

Laurie didn't say anything for a moment, and her smile faded. She stared at Jack with a look of disbelief.

"Hello!" Jack called. "Are you still with me?"

In slow motion, Laurie lifted her free hand to her face and used a finger to wipe away a tear. She shook her head as if she still couldn't believe what Jack had said. "If I heard correctly, under the circumstances that might have been the dearest thing you've ever said to me. You're going to make me cry."

"Don't cry!" Jack said nervously as he noticed Laurie's pulse rate quicken on the LCD screen behind her bed. He certainly didn't want to be disturbing her in her fragile state. "Let's talk about something less emotional, provided we have time." He glanced first at Pete, who pretended he wasn't listening, and then back at Thea at the central desk to make sure she hadn't caught Laurie's reaction. Luckily, the charge nurse was momentarily preoccupied with another problem. With a sense of reprieve, Jack redirected his attention to

Laurie. "I'm not going to be able to stay in here very long, and I might not be able to come back. Normally, I wouldn't be so restrained, but they have you as a hostage. I'm afraid if I step out of line, they'll take it out on you in some way. I know it's a ridiculous idea, but it seems to me this place is run by the Gestapo."

"What did you do with yourself for three hours?" Laurie asked.

"I had a ball," Jack said. "I . . ." He tried to think of something witty, but nothing came to mind. Embarrassed, he gave a short laugh. "I can't believe it. My sense of humor has abandoned me."

"You're bored and exhausted. Why don't you go home and get some sleep."

"Sleep?" Jack questioned. "That's out of the question. I had several cups of coffee in the surgical lounge. I'm not going to sleep until about Tuesday."

"You can't just sit here in the hospital," Laurie said. "If you really think you can't sleep, why don't you do what I suggested earlier and go back to my office? If you have to be awake, you might as well make use of the time."

"You know, I might just do that," Jack

said. It crossed his mind that he could bring all that material back to the surgical lounge. After all, the night shift was in the hospital. It might help to pass the time if he tried to talk to a couple of the people on Roger's lists, although, when he thought about it again, he had to admit that Roger's fate took away some of his enthusiasm for the idea.

"Sorry to interrupt here," Thea said. She had appeared at the foot of the bed. "You people are going to have to wind things up. We've got a couple of cases coming in imminently."

"Just a moment longer," Jack said to Thea, who nodded and retreated back to her command post.

"Listen," Jack said to Laurie, bending over to be close to her ear. "Before I go, I want to be absolutely sure you feel comfortable here. Be honest! Otherwise, I'll just park myself right outside the door and refuse to budge."

"Perfectly comfortable. You should get some sleep."

"I'm telling you, I'm not going to sleep! I'm charged up, ready to do a triathlon."

"Okay! Calm down! Then go back to my

office so you can at least keep yourself busy. Bring everything back here."

"You're sure you're comfortable?"

"I'm very sure."

"Okay," Jack said, giving Laurie's forehead a kiss before straightening up. "You can get some sleep for both of us. I'll be back and try to come in here in a few hours if that Brunnhilde lets me." He hooked a thumb over his shoulder.

"I'll be fine," Laurie said. "Don't worry!"

With a final squeeze of Laurie's hand, Jack walked back to the central desk. While Thea was on the phone, standing behind her desk chair, Jack wrote down his name and cell phone number.

"Thanks again for letting me come in here," Jack said when she hung up and looked at him.

"Don't mention it," Thea said. She went up on her tiptoes, looking at something over Jack's shoulder, and shouted: "You got it, Claire. That's the line I was talking about. I don't think it's running right." She looked back at Jack. "Sorry! Don't worry about your wife. We'll take good care of her."

"I've written down my cell phone number," Jack said. He handed the paper to Thea. "If there is any change in her status in any way or form, I'd appreciate hearing about it."

"We'll do our best," Thea said. She glanced at the paper, then tossed it onto the desk in front of her. She flashed Jack a brief smile and a quick wave, then turned to one of the nurses who'd approached with a question.

With a final look in Laurie's direction, Jack walked out of the PACU. He crossed through the surgical lounge. The faces had changed, but the scene hadn't. Inside the men's locker room, he quickly changed out of the scrubs and put on his clothes.

The main lobby of the hospital was eerily quiet and a far cry from its daytime bustle. As he exited through the front door, he was pleased to see that a few taxis were patiently waiting in the taxi line. The rain that had been forecasted had started.

The cab dropped Jack off at the morgue's loading dock, and he walked in past the security office. Carl Novak, the night security officer, bounded out of his chair as if caught unawares, causing the paperback book he was reading to fall to the floor. He leaned out his door and called after Jack, "Is something up that I should know about, Dr. Stapleton?"

"Nope," Jack called over his shoulder.

The night mortuary tech, Mike Passano, had a similar reaction when he heard Jack's voice echo about the tiled morgue and Jack passed the mortuary office. While Jack waited for the elevator, Mike's head appeared. "Is a case coming in that we'll be posting?" he asked.

"Nope," Jack said. "I just love this place so much, I can't stay away."

The fifth floor was barely illuminated, such that the orange office doors appeared a muddy gray-brown. Once inside Laurie's office, Jack flipped on the overhead light and squinted in its relative glare. He sat down in Laurie's chair and surveyed all the series material on her desk. There were two neat piles of hospital charts. Next to them were Roger's lists and a ruled notepad. On the pad was a list of the ways Laurie had determined that the cases were related. On the wall above the desk were two Post-it notes: one a reminder to show Sobczyk's

EKG segment to a cardiologist, and the other questioning what kind of lab test an MASNP was. Looking down on the desk was another Post-it wrinkled enough to make it hard to read. Jack spread out the wrinkles. On it was written in Laurie's handwriting: "positive MEF2A," followed by a large question mark. Jack had no idea what MEF2A stood for.

What Jack didn't see was the CD that he remembered Laurie making in Roger's office, and he briefly looked under the charts and under Roger's lists. He even opened Laurie's desk drawers, which were extraordinarily neat, in sharp contrast to his. There was no CD. He scratched his head. Where would she have put it? Then he glanced at his watch. It was almost one-thirty in the morning.

After taking a deep breath, Jack tried to organize his thoughts. His heart was racing from the coffee and his mind was going a mile a minute. It was hard to concentrate on anything. He didn't like being away from the Manhattan General Hospital with Laurie in such a vulnerable state, yet it truly would have driven him crazy to sit in the surgical lounge hour after hour, staring at the clock.

As Laurie had suggested, he had it in his mind to take all the material on her desk back to the surgical lounge. But before he did that, he had another idea. He thought he could take the time to possibly get answers to the three Post-it questions. With several hospitals literally next door, it would be a quick errand and might have some significance.

Getting to his feet, Jack shuffled through the charts until he found Sobczyk's. The EKG segment was easy to find, since Laurie had it marked with a ruler. He looked at it again, and again admitted that it made no sense to him. In fact, it was his opinion that no one would be able to make any sense of it. It was essentially the serendipitous recording of cardiac conduction cells in the throes of cellular death. Carefully, he extracted the page with the recording from the rest of the chart. Taking it and the other two Post-it notes, he stepped out of Laurie's office, leaving the light on, and walked back to the elevator. When he pressed the button, the door immediately opened. That never happened in the daytime. It was as if he was the only person in the building.

As he rode down to the basement level,

he mapped out his strategy, despite his mind jumping all over creation. He thought he'd run over to the NYU Bellevue medical center, pop in to the ER, and have the on-call cardiology resident paged. Jack couldn't imagine that that would take too long, as the resident might very well be in the emergency unit already. Then Jack thought he'd head to the laboratory and see if he could find the night supervisor. If anybody could tell him what kind of test an MASNP was and what a positive MEF2A meant, it would be a hospital laboratory supervisor. Vaguely, he wondered if the two unknowns were related.

It was still sprinkling outside, so Jack literally ran up First Avenue with the page from Sobsczyk's chart protected under his coat. The emergency room looked pretty much the same as Manhattan General's had looked when Jack had gone in to see Laurie. The crowds generally didn't thin out until after three in the morning. Jack went to the main desk and caught the attention of one of the nurses, who looked like he could have been a bouncer in a club. His name was Salvador, and he had on what looked like a dozen gold chain necklaces nestled on a remarkably hairy chest.

"I'm Dr. Stapleton," Jack said. "Do you happen to know who the on-call cardiology resident is?"

"I don't, but I'll find out," he said before bellowing the question to a colleague within the treatment area, which the main desk opened onto on its opposite side. He put his hand behind his ear to catch the response. The other individual was out of Jack's line of sight.

"Dr. Shirley Mayrand," the nurse said, redirecting his attention to Jack.

"Do you know if Dr. Mayrand is in the emergency room at the moment?"

The nurse shrugged his shoulders. "No idea."

"How can I page her?"

"I can do it for you." Salvador said. He picked up the phone and dialed the page operator. "Should I page her for the emergency room?"

Jack nodded. "I'll wait right here." He turned around and gazed at the scene. If nothing else, it was visually entertaining. Spread out in front of him and filling the vinyl waiting-room chairs was an egalitarian slice of New York City life in both its glory and banality. From crying infants to the tottering aged, from homeless bums to folks in fancy clothes, from the drunks to the mentally anguished, from the injured to the sick, they were all there, waiting to be seen.

Hold your horses," Thea shouted at her jangling phone. She was trying to fill out a supply requisition form. Giving up, she picked up the phone. It was the night shift OR supervisor, Helen Garvey.

"What's your bed count?" Helen demanded without mincing words.

"Occupied or empty?" Thea questioned.

"Now, that's one of the dumber questions I've heard tonight!"

"You're in a bad mood."

"I have a right to be. According to the ER, we're about to be inundated with trauma cases, and the first wave is on its way up. There was a head-on collision with a bus and a van, and the bus went over a guardrail. As I understand it, they distributed the victims, but we got the lion's share. I've contacted all the on-call people so we can be running up to twenty ORs. It's going to be a long night."

"I've got thirteen patients with only three empty beds."

"That's not encouraging. What are the patients' statuses?"

Thea let her eyes roam around her domain while she mentally reviewed each case. "Everybody is in good shape except for an abdominal aneurysm re-bleed. He's got to stay, because he might have to be opened up yet again. He's still losing blood out of his drain."

"So the others are stable?"

"At the moment."

"Then clean house, because you're next for this tidal wave."

Thea hung up the phone. She was psyched. Challenges like this were her forte. "Listen up!" she called out to her troops. "We're switching to disaster mode, and this is no drill."

The release of the wheels jolted Laurie from her drugged slumber to a semiwakefulness. Her eyes squinted against the bright overhead fluorescent lights, and for a moment, she was disoriented to time and place. There was another jolt when the bed began to move, and the jostling brought a brief but sharp reminder that she had had intra-abdominal surgery. All at once, Laurie knew where she was, and the large clock over the PACU room's door, which she was approaching, told her the time: It was twenty-five minutes past two.

Turning her head to the side in response to a babble of voices, Laurie caught a glimpse of the flurry of activity at the central desk. Bending her head back so she could see behind her, she looked up at the face of the orderly pushing her. He was a rail-thin, light-skinned African-American with a pencil-line mustache and graying hair. The muscles of his neck stood out as he strained to angle Laurie's bed toward the swinging doors.

"What's happening?" Laurie questioned.

The orderly didn't answer, focusing instead on stopping the bed's forward motion before backing it up a few steps. The PACU's doors had burst open. Another bed was coming into the room with a patient fresh from surgery. There was a person at the foot of the bed, pulling, and another at the head, pushing. An anesthesiologist walked alongside, maintaining the patient's airway patent by holding the individual's chin back. All three seemed to be talking at the same time.

Laurie repeated her question to the orderly behind her. She felt the stirrings of apprehension in the pit of her stomach. Something was up. Her understanding was that she was not be moved until Laura Riley came in to see her in the morning.

"You're going to your room," the orderly said, preoccupied with maneuvering Laurie's bed to allow the incoming patient to get by.

"I was supposed to stay here in the PACU," Laurie said with building alarm.

"Here we go," the orderly said as if he'd not heard Laurie. He grunted as he managed to get the bed rolling forward again.

"Wait!" Laurie yelled. The effort of her outcry made her wince with pain from her incision.

Shocked by Laurie's outburst, the orderly halted the bed yet again. He looked down at her with concern. "What's the matter?"

"I'm not supposed to be leaving here," Laurie stated. She had to talk loudly to be heard over the general level of conversation in the room. To keep the pain to a minimum, she had to press her hand gently over the upper part of her abdomen to avoid jostling the lower part. Earlier, when Jack had visited, she'd had very little discomfort from the operation. Unfortunately, that had changed.

"I got strict orders to take you to your room," the orderly said. His expression was half defiant, half confused. He took a piece of paper out of his pocket and glanced at it. "You're Laurie Montgomery, aren't you?"

Ignoring the orderly's question, Laurie lifted her head off her pillow and looked over at the central desk, which was a beehive of activity. Ahead, the doors to the hall burst open again and another patient, fresh from surgery, was whisked into the room. Once again, the orderly had to back Laurie's bed up to allow them to pass.

"I want to talk to the charge nurse," Laurie demanded.

With obvious indecision, the orderly looked back and forth between Laurie and the central desk. He shook his head with frustration.

"You're not taking me anywhere," Laurie

stated. "I'm supposed to stay here. I need to talk with a supervisor. Anyone in control."

Shrugging his shoulders in resignation, the orderly walked over to the counter, leaving Laurie and her bed stranded in the middle of the room. He was holding in his hand the piece of paper he'd taken from his pocket. Laurie watched as he tried vainly to get someone's attention. When he did, the person pointed out a square-built woman with a helmet of blond hair. Laurie watched as the orderly showed Thea his paper then pointed in Laurie's direction.

Thea bounced her palm off her forehead as if dealing with this new problem was the last thing she needed. She rounded the edge of the central desk and walked directly up to Laurie, the orderly a few steps behind.

"What's your problem?" Thea demanded. She had her hands on her hips.

"I was supposed to stay in the PACU until Dr. Riley saw me," Laurie said as she struggled to think what to say. Coupled with having been just awakened by such an urgent situation, the lingering effects of the drugs and anesthesia were causing her mind to work in slow motion.

"Let me reassure you that you are doing just fine. You're as stable as the rock of Gibraltar. You don't need the PACU, and unfortunately, we have a slew of patients who do. We'd love to entertain you all night, but we have work to do. So, until next time, be well!" With a final reassuring squeeze of Laurie's forearm, she turned back to the central desk, immediately barking orders about another patient to one of the other nurses.

"Excuse me!" Laurie called after her vainly. "Can you call my doctor, or can you let me make a call?"

Thea didn't even turn around. She was already immersed in the next problem.

The orderly returned to his position behind Laurie's head and once again got her bed rolling. He aimed it at the PACU double doors, and the bed collided with them and pushed them open. Out in the hall, he struggled to orient the bed parallel with the corridor before getting it to move forward. Laurie noticed several gurneys parked against the wall, with patients waiting to be taken down to operating rooms.

"I need to make a phone call," Laurie said as they passed the surgical desk.

"You're going to have to wait until you get in your room," the orderly said. He aimed the bed at the doors leading from the operating room.

A sense of desperation gripped Laurie as they reached the bank of elevators. She was being rudely removed from her promised sanctuary and thrust out in harm's way, and she was powerless to prevent it. Suffering the double whammy of weakness from blood loss and pain with the slightest movement made it hard for her to imagine herself any more vulnerable. And remembering her list of how the patients in her series had been related, she knew she fit the profile. She was the right age, she was healthy, she was on an IV, she'd had surgery, and she was a relatively new subscriber to AmeriCare. Her only consolation was in statistics and the fact that Najah had been arrested.

"Where am I going?" Laurie asked, trying to find a ray of hope. "To ob-gyn?"

The orderly consulted his piece of paper. "No! They're full in OB-GYN. You're going to room 609 on the general surgical floor."

Laurie closed her eyes as she felt a shudder pass through her.

twenty-two

"Dr. Stapleton! Hey, Dr. Stapleton!"

Hearing his voice over the buzz of conversation and the sound of crying infants, Jack looked back at the emergency-room desk. With all the caffeine on board, he'd been pacing back and forth from the desk to the front doors, intermittently staring outside at the rain falling on the cement of the wheelchair ramp. As the time had passed, he had begun to think of switching to plan B, which was to give up on the Post-it quest, run back to the OCME, grab the material in Laurie's desk, and beat it back to the Manhattan General. It was two-thirty in the morning and he'd already been away for an hour and a half.

Jack could see Salvador waving for Jack to come back to the desk. Next to him was a girl who looked as if she were fifteen. She had straight, shoulder-length, light brown hair, parted in the middle and swept back on either side behind conveniently large ears. Her eyes were huge and separated by a narrow, upturned nose.

"This is Dr. Shirley Mayrand," Salvador said, motioning toward the cardiology resident as Jack quickly returned to the counter.

Jack was momentarily mesmerized by the woman's youthfulness. For the first time in his life, he felt old. Although he was pushing fifty, playing basketball with kids half his age made him forget how old he really was. As the cardiology resident on call, this woman in front of him had to have been through college, medical school, and a significant number of years as a resident.

"What can I do for you?" Shirley asked.

To Jack, even her voice sounded prepubescent.

After Jack introduced himself, he fumbled with the page from Sobczyk's chart, placed it on the countertop, and folded out the electrocardiograph tracing.

"I'll leave you two," Salvador said and walked away.

"I know this is not much," Jack said, pointing to the strip of EKG, "but I was wondering if you could comment on it."

"It's awfully short," Shirley complained while bending over the tracing.

"Yeah, well, it's all we have," Jack said. He noticed that the part in Shirley's hair meandered around as it made its way from her forehead over the crown of her head.

"What lead is it?"

"Good question. I have no idea. It was a strip taken at the outset of an unsuccessful cardiac resuscitation."

"Probably one of the standard leads," Shirley remarked.

"Maybe so," Jack said.

The resident looked up. Jack realized one of the reasons her eyes appeared so big was that he could see the whites all the way around her corneas. It gave her the look of continuous, innocent surprise.

"I don't know what I can say," Shirley said. "You'd really have to show me more for me to be able to comment with any confidence."

"I assumed as much," Jack said. "But this tracing is from a patient who unfortunately is already dead, which you know since I said it was taken at an unsuccessful resuscitation attempt. My point is, it's not going to be to the patient's detriment if you take a wild guess, say, if you were forced to come up with some opinion. Anything."

Shirley looked back at the tracing. "Well, as you certainly have already noticed, it does suggest a widening of both the PR interval and the QRS complex, while the QTRS seems to have been fused with the T wave."

Jack gritted his teeth. Somehow, it seemed unfair that this petite, youthful woman made him feel both old and stupid. "Maybe," Jack suggested, "it would be best if you could limit your comments to something that I can understand. I mean, you could tell me your impression without telling me how you came to it."

"Well, it does suggest something to me," Shirley said, looking up at Jack. "But I have an idea."

"Okay! What is it?"

"Dr. Henry Wo, one of my attendings, happens to be here in the ER at the moment. He'd been called in to do an angiogram on a suspected acute myocardial infarction. Why don't we show it to him."

Jack was pleased. The possibility of getting an attending's opinion in the wee hours of the morning hadn't even occurred to him.

"Come on around into the ER proper!" Shirley said while leaning over the counter to point out the route Jack would have to take. "I'll meet you and take you back to the cath room, where he is working."

The elevator doors opened, and with a grunt, the orderly got Laurie's bed to roll out into the lobby on the sixth floor. Since there was a slight discrepancy between the level of the floor of the elevator and the lobby floor, there was a jolt, and Laurie grimaced from the pain it caused. It was apparent that whatever she'd been given for pain had all but worn off.

Although Laurie felt just as panicky as she had when she'd first left the PACU, she'd at least reconciled herself to the reality that there was little she could do until she got to use a phone. She'd asked the orderly where her belongings were, with the idea of getting a hold of her cell phone. Unfortunately, he'd said he had no idea.

The orderly pushed her down the short corridor from the elevator lobby toward the nurse's station, which loomed like a beacon of bright light in the dimmed and mostly sleeping hospital. The recessed nightlights with frosted glass were spaced at intervals along the walls, about two feet off the floor.

After getting the bed up to the speed of a brisk walk, the orderly had to struggle to get it to stop abreast of the nurse's station. Once he did, he engaged the foot brake before leaving Laurie and approaching the counter over the nurses' station desk. Laurie could see the tops of two female heads—one with cropped hair, the other with a ponytail. Both women looked up when the orderly plopped Laurie's metal-covered hospital chart on the countertop.

"Got a patient for you people," the orderly said.

Laurie saw the woman with the cropped hair take the chart and read the name emblazoned on the front. She immediately stood up. "Well, well, Miss Montgomery. I must say, we have been wondering where you were."

The two nurses came around from behind the desk while the orderly walked back toward the elevators.

Laurie watched as the women approached her bed, each going to a separate side. Both were dressed in hospital scrubs. The one with the cropped hair had dark skin, almond-shaped eyes, and a narrow, aquiline nose. The other's complexion was paler, with broader features that gave a hint of an Asian mix. Since both faces were illuminated from below by the nightlights, only the bony prominences were clearly visible. The rest of their faces was lost in relative shadow. To Laurie, who was already anxious, they looked decidedly creepy.

"I need to use a phone," Laurie said, looking from one to the other, unsure if one was more senior than the other.

"Jazz, I'll take her down to the room and

get her settled," the Asian-appearing woman said, ignoring Laurie's comment.

"That's good of you, Elizabeth," Jazz said, "but I think I'll take care of Miss Montgomery personally."

"Really?" Elizabeth questioned. She was obviously surprised.

"Hello!" Laurie said with some annoyance. "I need to use a phone!"

"Suit yourself," Elizabeth said to her colleague and walked back toward the nurses' station.

Jazz tossed Laurie's chart onto the foot of Laurie's bed and went behind to start pushing.

"Excuse me!" Laurie said, rolling her head back to keep Jazz in view. "It is very important for me to use the phone." She grimaced as the bed's brake was released, and again when the bed lurched forward down the long, dark hall.

"I heard you the first time," Jazz said. Her voice reflected the strain of pushing the bed. "I think I should remind you it's two-thirty in the morning."

"I know what time it is," Laurie snapped. "I have to call my doctor. I'm not supposed to be here. I was supposed to stay in the

PACU until she came in to do her rounds in the morning."

"I hate to break this news to you," Jazz said. "But your doctor, like all the other doctors, is fast asleep. She doesn't want to be disturbed about some logistics problem."

"Stop this bed at once," Laurie commanded. "I'm not going to this room."

"Oh?" Jazz questioned, but she didn't so much as hesitate. She continued pushing Laurie's bed at a speed significantly quicker than the orderly. She was eager to get Laurie to her room. Earlier that evening, when Jazz had first come into the hospital, she had trouble locating Laurie. At first she thought perhaps Mr. Bob had made a mistake about the name of the hospital, but it turned out the problem was only a delay in Laurie's name being entered into the hospital computer system. Jazz had figured that out when she'd checked the ER log while getting the potassium ampoule.

"I demand that you stop," Laurie cried when Jazz ignored her. Laurie was forced to press her hand against her upper abdomen to control the pain. Yelling jarred her incision.

"I can see you are going to be a difficult patient," Jazz said with a short laugh. Actually, she felt the opposite. Laurie was going to be one of her easier sanctions, thanks to OB-GYN being full. Having Laurie on her floor while she was acting charge nurse made everything a snap.

At room 609, Jazz rapidly rotated Laurie a hundred and eighty degrees to push her bed into the room headfirst. As they crossed the threshold, Jazz flipped on the room's overhead light, making both women squint. Jazz maneuvered Laurie over next to the regular hospital bed, which was significantly wider than the gurney-like bed that Laurie currently occupied.

Laurie glared at the nurse, whose attitude she couldn't fathom. She blanched when she caught sight of the woman's nametag: Jasmine Rakoczi. Despite the drugs still in her system, Laurie remembered it instantly as one of the names on Roger's list of people who had transferred from the night shift at St. Francis to the night shift of the Manhattan General!

"What's the matter?" Jazz questioned as she lowered the guardrail on the appropriate side. She couldn't help but notice Laurie's startled reaction. "Something amiss?"

Without waiting for an answer, Jazz pushed Laurie alongside the hospital bed. She grabbed the top edge of Laurie's blanket and whipped it off with a flick of her wrist, catching Laurie by surprise and exposing her to the world. She was clad only in a hospital Johnny, with her bare knees, lower legs, and feet sticking out. A bulge over the right lower part of her abdomen covered the dressing applied to her incision, and a surgical drain snaked out from under the edge of the gown and entered a plastic device that maintained a negative pressure. A streaking of blood was evident within the tubing.

"Okay," Jazz said dispassionately. "Scoot over there, and we'll get you nice and comfortable." She then went to the head of the bed and transferred Laurie's IV bottle to the pole on the hospital bed.

Laurie didn't move. The panic she'd felt from being taken from the PACU had ratcheted up a notch after seeing Jazz's nametag. She was paralyzed with fear. For all she knew, Jazz could be the serial killer.

"Come on, sister," Jazz said. She stepped

back around to Laurie's side and looked down at her. "Let's move your butt over onto the bed."

Laurie stared back with the most defiant look she could manage. It was all she could think of doing.

"If you want to be uncooperative, I'll have to get Elizabeth down here, and we'll move you one way or the other. This isn't a negotiation."

"I want to speak to the charge nurse," Laurie blurted.

"Well, isn't that convenient," Jazz laughed. "You're already talking to her. I am the charge nurse. At least the acting charge nurse, which is the same thing."

Laurie's sense of desperation went up yet another notch. She felt progressively snared in a treacherous web of terrifying circumstance.

"Now, why don't you want to move?" Jazz questioned with obvious frustration. She extended her hand over Laurie to point out the room's amenities. "Check out that comfortable bed with all its controls. You can crank yourself into just about every position you can imagine and then some. You've got a TV, a pitcher for water with no water since you're still NPO, a call button for us slaves . . . all the comforts of home. What else can you ask for?"

Laurie's eyes involuntarily took in what Jazz described and did a double take. Sitting on the nightstand was a telephone! She questioned why she had not thought about it until that second. The orderly had even mentioned it. It would be her lifeline. Gritting her teeth, Laurie rose up on her elbows and began moving her backside over toward the hospital bed. Then she repositioned her legs and repeated the maneuver, inching herself across the divide.

"Very good," Jazz said. "I see you've decided to be cooperative. I'm pleased for both of us."

As soon as Laurie was in the hospital bed, Jazz moved across the suction device for Laurie's drain. She pulled up the cover that had been positioned across the foot of the bed and let it settle across Laurie's chest. She then took Laurie's blood pressure and pulse. As she did this, Laurie watched her intently. Jazz avoided eye contact.

"Okay," Jazz said, finally making eye contact as she lifted up the guardrail with a jolt. "Everything seems in order other than your pulse is a little on the high side. I'll mosey on back to the desk and go over your orders. I'm sure you have something ordered for pain on an as-needed basis. Are you in need, or are you fine at the moment?"

Laurie was amazed at the lack of normal human warmth in Jazz's voice and actions. Ostensibly, there wasn't anything specific that Laurie could complain about other than her requests being ignored, yet there was a worrisome detachment that seemed incredibly out of place, and as such, it added to her already considerable unease. There was something definitely strange about Jasmine Rakoczi.

"Cat got your tongue?" Jazz questioned with a wry smile. She spread her hands waist-height. "That's okay with me. You don't have to talk if you don't want to. Frankly, it makes my job that much easier if you don't. But if you change your mind, you've got your call button. Of course, when you get around to pressing it, I might be involved with someone a bit more communicative."

With a final smile that Laurie interpreted

.s brazenly indifferent, Jazz walked out of the room.

Being careful not to move too quickly, Laurie reached out over the bed's side rail and lifted the phone. The effort required her to tighten her abdominal muscles, which caused significant discomfort. Gritting her teeth in the face of the pain, she managed to move the phone from the night table to the bed. She put it next to her, and then struggled to remember Jack's cell phone number in the face of her anxiety and the drugs she'd had. It took her a moment, but then it reassuringly popped into her mind. She then snatched up the phone receiver and put it to her ear.

Laurie's heart skipped a beat. There was no dial tone! Frantically, she pressed the disconnect button, hoping for the familiar sound. There was nothing. The phone was dead. Just as frantically, she grabbed the nurse's call button and pressed it, not once but several times in a row.

Although getting an attending's opinion on Sobczyk's short segment of EKG tracing seemed like a great idea, Jack hadn't factored in the attending's availability. When Jack and Shirley got back to the cath room, Jack found out that Dr. Henry Wo was in the middle of his catheterization. Jack was forced to resort to additional caffeine-driven pacing in the corridor, punctuated by frequent glances at his watch. Shirley stood by stoically. If she was aware of Jack's restless agitation, she didn't mention it.

It wasn't until almost three A.M. that Henry came out of the room, snapped off his latex gloves, and removed his mask. He was a rotund Asian man with flawless skin and dark, closely cropped hair. He snapped up Jack's hand and pumped it enthusiastically as Shirley introduced them. Shirley mentioned the quandary about the short EKG segment, and Jack handed over the page from Sobczyk's chart with the tracing attached.

"I see, I see," Henry said, nodding his head and smiling as he glanced at the EGK strip. "Very interesting. Is this all we have?"

"I'm afraid so," Jack said. He recounted the brief story, as he knew it, concerning the failed resuscitation attempt. He added why he thought that even a guess on their part might be helpful.

"It's dangerous to say too much with so little," Henry said while again studying the tracing. He then looked up at Shirley. "Dr. Mayrand, perhaps you could tell us what you were thinking?"

Shirley reiterated what she had said to Jack about the various waves, intervals, and complexes while Henry continued to nod. When Shirley had finished, Henry asked her if she had any idea of what might have accounted for such alterations.

"The conduction system seems to be failing," Shirley said. "Perhaps that means the sodium pumps within the cells of the bundle of His are not functioning or perhaps overwhelmed, resulting in a deleterious alteration in membrane potentials."

Jack again gritted his teeth. He had a sudden urge to throw a tantrum. Shirley's short monologue painfully reminded him of the academic gibberish he'd endured in medical school. In the grip of coffee-enhanced anxiety, Jack had little tolerance for such didactic mumbo jumbo and was about to make his impatience known when Henry took the words out of his mouth.

"I think Dr. Stapleton is interested in some particular agent that might account for what we are seeing on this short strip of EKG. Am I correct, Dr. Stapleton?"

Jack nodded enthusiastically.

"Well," Shirley said, visibly uncomfortable in being put on the spot, "I'm sure there are a number of drugs that could create this type of picture, including toxic amounts of most of the arrhythmia drugs. But I think it could have possibly been caused by a sudden electrolyte imbalance, particularly potassium or calcium. But that's about all one could say."

"Well said," Henry complimented. He handed the page from Sobczyk's chart with the EKG tracing back to Jack.

Jack took the paper from Henry, mulling over what Shirley had said. She hadn't added anything new, but the words "sudden electrolyte imbalance" gave him an idea. The reason he and others had dismissed the possible role of potassium was because the lab had reported that the victims' potassium levels had all been normal. Now that Jack thought about it, what the lab was saying specifically was that the postmortem potassium levels were normal. As everyone knew, potassium levels soar after death because the body's vast potassium store is intracellular and is maintained by an active transport system. After death, the transport system stops and the potassium immediately leaks out. Any sudden increase in potassium in an individual by an injected bolus prior to death would be effectively masked. Jack had to admit that if someone wanted to kill off patients, it would be an insidiously clever way to do it.

"If you happen to find any additional EKG recordings, let us know," Henry was saying. "Perhaps we could be more definitive with more leads. Just let us know."

"One other thing," Jack said, catching sight of Laurie's two Post-its attached to the back of the page. "Do either of you know what this laboratory test is?" He pulled off the Post-it with "MASNP" written on it and handed it to Henry. Henry glanced at it, shook his head, and looked at Shirley. Shirley shook her head as well.

"No idea," Henry said. He handed the piece of yellow paper back to Jack. "But I know someone who probably would: David Hancock, the night lab supervisor. The lab's conveniently right down the hall." Henry pointed to a door no more than twenty feet away. "I know he's here tonight, because he helped me earlier."

Jack took back the Post-it and reattached it to the page next to the other one. With the lab so close, he thought it would be worth taking the time to duck in and see if David Hancock was available.

"I don't know what kind of test an MASNP is, but I do know what MEF2A is," Henry said, catching sight of the second slightly wrinkled Post-it.

"Oh?" Jack questioned. He wasn't even sure where Laurie had come up with the acronym.

"That's a gene," Henry said. "It produces a protein that controls the cascade of events that assures the health of the coronary arteries' inner lining."

"Interesting," Jack said vaguely, wondering how it could be associated with Laurie's series, or if it was associated at all. "What would a positive MEF2A mean?"

"Now, that's a bit misleading," Henry admitted. "When they write 'positive MEF2A' in the literature, what they really mean is positive for the marker for the mutated form of MEF2A. In that case, it is someone who produces a defective protein and, as a consequence, will have a high probability of experiencing coronary artery disease, such as my patient tonight. He's positive for the MEF2A marker, and here he is, having had an acute myocardial infarction, even though we've tried to avoid it by keeping his LDL cholesterol as low as possible."

"Well, I'm sure this will all be helpful," Jack said, although in reality he had no idea. When he got back to the Manhattan General and got to see Laurie, he'd have to ask her about where she'd found the acronym and then, if appropriate, tell her what he'd learned.

Jack thanked both Henry and Shirley, and quickly headed down toward the laboratory door, hoping David Hancock would be conveniently available. As he entered the lab, he glanced at his watch, and his level of anxiety inched upward. It was twenty-two after three.

Laurie pressed the nurse's call button several more times. She had lost count of how many times she had pressed it since Jazz had left, and the fact that no one responded made her feel even more vulnerable. It occurred to her that Rakoczi was being purposefully passive-aggressive, as she had suggested she might be when she'd left. Laurie looked down at her hand holding the call button. She was shaking.

To add to her anxiety, Laurie's pain from her surgery had gotten worse, particularly after moving herself from the gurney to the bed and then lifting the telephone. Earlier, she felt it only when she moved, but now it was constant. There was no doubt that she needed some analgesia, but she was reluctant to ask for it because of the inevitable hypnotic effects. Under the circumstances, Laurie didn't want to be any more obtunded than she was already. She had to keep her wits if she was to have any chance of protecting herself until Jack got there.

Just when Laurie had decided to see what it would be like for her to get out of bed and stand up, someone came sweeping into the room. It wasn't Jazz or Elizabeth. It was another woman even more swarthy than Jazz, with long, straight, black hair held back with a clip. She carried a large tray by its handle. The tray was divided into numerous cubbies filled with blood tubes, syringes, and the like.

"Laurie Montgomery?" the woman questioned while glancing at a requisition form.

"Yes," Laurie said.

"I need to draw some blood for some clotting studies." The woman put her tray on the foot of Laurie's bed, took out the proper color-coded stoppered tubes, and came alongside Laurie, dangling a tourniquet.

"I need a telephone," Laurie said as the woman picked up Laurie's arm and began searching for veins and patting those she saw to check if they'd be appropriate for venipuncture. "The one here by my bedside doesn't have a dial tone."

"I can't help you with your telephone," the woman said in a high, singsong voice. "I'm just a laboratory tech." She found a vein that she thought was promising and applied the tourniquet.

Laurie was about to explain at least a part of her dilemma when she caught sight of the woman's laboratory nametag. It said Kathleen Chaudhry. Like Rakoczi, it was a rather unique name. Also like Rakoczi, it was a name on Roger's list of people who had transferred from St. Francis during the suspect period. And like Rakoczi, Laurie thought she too could be the serial killer.

Laurie yanked her arm away from Kathleen such that the lab tech took a shocked step back. Kathleen quickly regained her equilibrium. “Calm down!” she said. “I’m just going to draw a little blood.”

“I don’t want my blood drawn,” Laurie stated. She was adamant and her voice reflected it. She felt paranoid but for good reason. It was as if she was being tormented, surrounded by potential serial killers.

“Your doctor has ordered these tests,” Kathleen said. “It is for your own good. It will just take a second. You’ll barely feel it, I promise.”

“I’m not having any blood drawn,” Laurie said unequivocally. “I’m sorry. There’s no use in trying to talk me into it.”

“Okay, have it your way,” Kathleen said, throwing up her hands. “Fine with me. I’ll just have to let the nurses know.”

“You do that,” Laurie said. “And while you’re at it, tell one of the nurses to come back down here immediately.”

After making it a point to express her frustration by literally tossing the blood tubes haphazardly into her tray, Kathleen walked out of the room.

Once again, the heavy silence of the sleeping hospital closed in around Laurie. She was now beginning to question her sanity. Had those names really been on Roger's lists, or was her overwrought mind making it all up? Laurie wasn't sure, but she knew one thing without a shred of doubt: She wanted Jack to come in and get her the hell out of there.

Steeling herself against the pain, which was made worse with any movement of her abdominal muscles, Laurie began to inch herself down toward the foot of the bed. She wanted to get beyond the side rails and try standing. She'd only gotten halfway when Jazz breezed in.

"Hold on there, girl," Jazz said. "Where do you think you're going?"

Laurie stared at her with uncamouflaged scorn. "I need to find some nurses who will respond to the call button."

"Let me tell you something, dearie," Jazz said. "You are not the only patient on the floor, and you are hardly the sickest. We have to prioritize, which I'm sure you'd understand if you stopped to think for one lousy minute. What is it you want, pain meds?"

"I want a telephone," Laurie said. "The one on the night table has no dial tone."

"Getting your phone functioning is the mission of the day-staff communications department. This is the nursing night shift. We don't have time for that kind of stuff."

"Where are my belongings?" Laurie demanded. Everything could be solved if she could get her hands on her cell phone.

"Surgery must still have them."

"I want them down here this minute."

"You do have a lot of demands," Jazz ridiculed. "I have to give you that. But listen, sweetheart! Surgery happens to be very busy tonight, which means we're going to be busy. They will get to your crap when they have the time. Now, if you'll excuse me, I've got patients to see."

"Wait!" Laurie cried, before Jazz ducked out the door. When Jazz turned back to her, she added: "I want this IV out."

"Sorry," Jazz said with a shake of her head. She came back into the room, and coming alongside Laurie, she hooked a hand under Laurie's armpit. Without warning, she pulled Laurie back to where she had been in the bed. Laurie winced with the pain. She was also impressed with Jazz's strength. "You were in shock when you came into the emergency room," Jazz continued. "You need that IV in case you relapse. You need fluid, and you might need more blood."

"Another IV can be put in," Laurie contended. "I want this one out. If you don't take it out, I'll pull it out myself."

Jazz stared at Laurie for a beat. "You are a feisty one, aren't you? Well, you might have some trouble pulling that baby out. It's a peripheral central line, which sounds a bit contradictory, but it's a long catheter that's been stitched under that little bandage covering the entry point. You'd be pulling away a sizable hunk of tissue if you were to yank it out."

"I want my doctor called," Laurie said. "Otherwise, I'm going to take out this IV no matter what, get myself out of this bed, and walk out of here."

Jazz's wry, brazen smile that she had left with earlier reappeared. "You are too much. Seriously! I read that you practically bled out this evening, and now a few hours later, you're giving orders. I'll tell you what I'll do.

I'll call the doctor and explain exactly what you just told me. How does that sound?"

"It would be better if I told her myself."

"Maybe, but that is problematic, since your phone is not yet set up. Anyway, I'll make the call, explain the situation exactly, including your refusal to have blood drawn for a clotting study, and then I'll be right back. How is that?"

"It's a start," Laurie conceded.

As Jazz walked out of the room, Laurie let her head fall back against the pillow. Her bed was cranked up about thirty degrees. Her heart was pounding in her temples, and the pain in her incision site was worse, and she now had the new concern that she might have torn a few stitches. Yet she felt as if her panic had peaked. She took a deep breath and let it out, trying to relax a degree. She even closed her eyes. Having Jazz get in touch with Laura Riley wasn't as good as getting Jack on the line, but as she had said to Jazz, it was a start.

twenty-three

Once again, events didn't progress as Jack would have preferred. David Hancock was at lunch but due back any minute. At first, Jack thought this news was someone's idea of a joke, since it was in the middle of the night. That was before he remembered that people who worked the night shift lived in a completely opposite world time-wise, and for them, their middle-of-the-shift meal was lunch, no matter what the clock said.

Jack paced the room until David Hancock appeared. He was a slight man of indeterminate genealogy. As if in compensation for the scant hair on the top of his head, he wore a scraggly, graying goatee and mustache, giving him a decidedly devilish look. He listened to Jack's request without comment before taking the Post-it. While he looked at it, he noisily sucked his teeth.

"Are you sure this is a laboratory test?" David asked, raising his eyes to Jack.

Jack's optimism about getting an answer took a nosedive. "Reasonably sure," he said as he reached out to retrieve the note.

David moved the Post-it from Jack's reach as he continued to stare at it. "What made you think it was a laboratory test?"

"It was part of the preoperative orders on a number of patients," Jack said while looking over his shoulder at the door.

"It wasn't a preoperative order in this hospital," David said.

"No," Jack agreed, nervously shifting his weight, trying to make up his mind if he should just turn around and leave. "It was at the Manhattan General and at the Saint Francis out in Queens."

"Pshaw," David voiced disparagingly. "Two AmeriCare institutions."

Caught off guard by the lab supervisor's comment, Jack leaned forward to get a better look at the man's expression. "Do I detect a value judgment in your voice?"

"You'd better believe it," David said. "I've got a sister in Staten Island who works for the city, and she's had some medical problems. AmeriCare has given her the run-around. It's all a business with those people, and taking care of patients is the last thing on their mind."

"I've had my differences with them as well," Jack admitted. "Maybe someday we could share war stories. But right now I'm interested in learning what kind of test an MASNP is."

"Well, I have to admit I don't know what it is with a hundred percent surety," David began, "but my guess would be it is a medical genomics test."

Jack was taken aback. A half hour earlier Shirley Mayrand had made him feel old. Now he was afraid David was about to do the same thing in terms of knowledge. Jack was acquainted with the science of medical genomics, but his knowledge was limited to identity markers used in forensics. He knew the relatively new field, spurred by the decipherment of the entire human genome, was racing ahead at an exponential rate.

"My guess would be that the MA stands for microarray, which is a high-throughput technology generally used for gene expression."

"Is it now?" Jack questioned innocently. He was already over his head and was embarrassed to admit it, although what David was saying was now relating to what Henry had said about the "positive MEF2A" on the other Post-it note.

"You've got a funny expression, doctor. I mean, you do know what a microarray is, don't you?"

"Well, not exactly," Jack admitted.

"Then let me explain. Microarrays are a grid or checkerboard of minute spots of a mixture of varying but known DNA sequences usually affixed to the surface of a microscope slide. And we're talking about a lot of spots. I mean thousands, such that they can give information on the expression of thousands of genes at any given moment."

"Really!" Jack said and then wished he hadn't. He knew he was sounding stupid.

"But I doubt the test you are questioning about is a test for gene expression."

"No?" Jack voiced meekly.

"No, I don't think so. My guess is that the SNP stands for single nucleotide polymorphism, which I'm sure you know is a point mutation in the human genome. Also as you know, thousands of SNPs have now been mapped so exactly throughout the human genome that they can be linked to specific mutated genes that are passed from generation to generation. Those SNPs that are so linked are called markers. They're markers for the bad, mutated gene."

It was as if the proverbial lightbulb lit up in Jack's mind. He hadn't followed everything David was saying, but it didn't matter. With trembling fingers, he hastened to get out the page from Sobczyk's chart. When he did he pulled off the other wrinkled Post-it. He showed it to David. "Could this possibly be a result of an MASNP?"

David took the second Post-it and scratched his head. "Positive MEF2A," he read out loud. "Does that ring a bell?

Hmmm." He looked away and tapped his baldpate with a knuckle. Then he looked back at the Post-it. "Yes! I remember MEF2A. If I'm not mistaken, it's a gene somehow associated with coronary arteries. I don't know exactly how it is related, but I recall that if someone gets the mutated form of the gene, then the individual has a high probability of getting coronary artery disease. So to answer your question, 'positive MEF2A' could be the result of an MASNP test, meaning the test determined the individual had the specific SNP that was a marker for the mutated MEF2A gene."

Jack suddenly reached out and grabbed David's hand and gave it a rapid, sincere shake. "Let's get together some time! And thanks! I believe you might have solved a mystery."

"What kind of mystery?" David asked, but Jack was already running for the door.

Having come into the lab through the emergency department, Jack used the same route on his way out. He guessed that there was another exit that might have been more convenient, but he didn't want to take the time to inquire. The Post-it quest, as he called it, had turned out to be more successful than he'd imagined. He now thought he had both a possible motive and a possible, although unprovable, method for the deaths that Laurie had been so clairvoyantly documenting. All that he needed was to find out where Laurie had come up with the "positive MEF2A" to see if there were other markers with other patients.

Jack burst through the double doors that separated the emergency department from its waiting room and partially collided with a man in a wheelchair who was being brought in for treatment. The man was wheezing, and his wheezing got worse with the fright of the near collision. Apologizing, Jack wished the man well and ran across the waiting room and out into the night. The rain had picked up, but he didn't care. If what he was thinking was correct, AmeriCare was even more shockingly amoral and venal than he had imagined. And he was even gladder that Laurie was being held in the PACU and not allowed out on the hospital floors.

Reaching First Avenue, Jack turned south. He squinted as he ran into the rain, and he could feel rivulets running down his face. He had a definite idea of where Laurie had come across the "positive MEF2A." He just had to find it as the clincher. He thought he'd give himself fifteen minutes in Laurie's office. If he was unsuccessful after fifteen minutes, he'd put it off until a later time and beat a retreat over to the Manhattan General. Even if Brunnhilde wouldn't let him back into the PACU, he'd be content to park himself outside the door.

Laurie woke up with a start. The fact that she had fallen asleep in the face of her anxiety scared her as much as the commotion that had awakened her. It was Jazz and Elizabeth, both of whom had breezed into the room, talking about another patient. Jazz came over to Laurie's right, while Elizabeth rounded the foot of the bed and ended up on Laurie's left.

With effort, Laurie straightened herself upright. While sleeping, she had sagged over to the point that her shoulder was resting against the bed's guardrail. She glared at both women in turn. She had a constant low-grade pain in her abdomen, and her mouth was bone-dry. Up in the PACU, she had been given ice chips, whereas in her current room, she'd been given nothing.

"My gosh!" Jazz said with surprise, looking down at Laurie. "If we'd known you'd fallen asleep, we could have saved ourselves some trouble."

"Did you talk with my doctor?" Laurie demanded.

"Let's say I talked with one of them," Jazz answered. Her brash smile reappeared as if she was enjoying teasing Laurie.

"What do you mean, one of my doctors?" Laurie questioned.

"I talked with Dr. José Cabreo," Jazz said. "He happens to be available, whereas your Dr. Riley is undoubtedly sleeping."

Laurie felt her pulse quicken. She also remembered Dr. José Cabreo's name from Roger's lists. In fact, she had read the man's credentialing record and had learned about his malpractice and addiction problems. There was no way she wanted anything to do with the anesthesiologist.

"He was very upset to hear you were acting up," Jazz continued. "He reminded me under no uncertain terms that the clotting study ordered for you must be done. He was also very disturbed about your threats to yank out your IV and climb out of your bed, drain and all."

"I don't care what Dr. Cabreo thinks," Laurie snapped. "You said you were going to call my doctor. I want to talk with Dr. Laura Riley."

"Correction," Jazz said, holding up her index finger. "I said I would call *the* doctor, not *your* doctor. I should remind you that the anesthesia department still feels that they have responsibility for you to a large degree. You are technically in a postanesthesia state."

"I want my doctor!" Laurie growled through clenched teeth.

"She's a pistol, isn't she?" Jazz said to Elizabeth.

Elizabeth smiled and nodded.

Jazz looked back down at Laurie and said, "Since it's almost four A.M., you should be getting your wish in just a few more hours. Meanwhile, we intend to strictly follow Dr. Cabreo's orders that he has been nice enough to communicate to us for your own protection." Jazz nodded to Elizabeth.

Laurie started to reiterate her feelings about Dr. Cabreo, but before she could complete a sentence, Jazz and Elizabeth simultaneously lunged for her forearms, pinning them to the bed. Shocked by this sudden, unexpected assault, Laurie struggled to free herself, but a combination of her pain and the nurses' strength made it impossible. The next thing she knew, her wrists were secured in Velcro restraints, which were in turn affixed to the undercarriage of the bed. It had all happened so quickly, Laurie was dumbfounded.

"There! Mission accomplished!" Jazz said to Elizabeth as she straightened up. "We can now relax with the confidence the IV will stay put and this uncooperative patient will not go wandering off."

"This is an outrage," Laurie sputtered. She yanked ineffectually against the restraints, which only made the guardrail rattle. The restraints held firmly.

"Dr. Cabreo doesn't think so," Jazz said with a smile. "The stress of surgery does disorient some people, and they need to be protected from themselves. At the same time, he was concerned you might be a little upset, so he ordered a nice, strong, quick-acting sedative." From her pocket, she produced a syringe that was already prepared for an injection. She took off the needle cap with her teeth and held the syringe up to the light, tapping it gently with the nail of her right index finger.

"I don't want any sedative," Laurie shrieked. She tried again to free her hands.

"That's just the kind of response the sedative is to prevent," Jazz said. "Elizabeth, would you mind holding Miss Montgomery while I do the honors."

With a smile not too dissimilar from Jazz's, Elizabeth grasped Laurie's shoulders and leaned her considerable weight over her. Laurie tried to squirm, but it was to no avail. She felt the cold alcohol pledget swipe across the skin of her upper arm, followed by a pinch and a short, sharp pain. Jazz straightened up, replacing the cap on the used needle.

"Sleep tight!" Jazz said. She waved to Elizabeth, and the two women walked out of the room.

A helpless moan escaped from Laurie's lips as she settled back onto the pillow. Earlier, with her pain and the effects of the drugs she'd been given, she had believed it would have been impossible for her to feel more helpless than she already had, but she was wrong. She was now literally tied to the bed like a potential sacrificial victim. She had no idea what kind of injection she'd been given. For all she knew, it was a poison and the struggle was already over. If it was a sedative, as Jazz had claimed, then soon she was destined to be that much more vulnerable.

Although Jack was in superb aerobic shape from both basketball and biking, he was out of breath when he skidded to a stop in front of the elevators in the OCME. He'd heard Carl Novak yell out his name as Jack ran past the security office, but Jack didn't slow down. No one was in the mortuary office. Jack struck the elevator button repeatedly, as if doing so would speed up its arrival.

As he waited, he tried to think of what Laurie could have possibly done with the CD she'd burned in Roger's office. It had to have been on the CD that Laurie had come across the MEF2A reference. The elevator arrived and Jack jumped on. The CD hadn't been with the charts or the lists, and he hadn't seen it in her desk drawers. The only place he hadn't looked was the four-drawer file cabinet. He glanced at his watch. It was five minutes past four. He'd now been gone from the Manhattan General a little more than three hours, which he felt was the upper limit of what he was comfortable with. As he had decided, he was going to hold himself to fifteen minutes for the CD search.

The elevator bumped to a stop, and it seemed to take an inordinately long time for the door to open. Impatiently, Jack hammered at it with the base of his fist. In its own time it slid open, and Jack took off down the darkened hallway. Like a cartoon character, he almost missed the door into Laurie's office because of how quickly he was running. He had to grab the jamb to keep from sliding past on the heavily waxed floor. Once inside Laurie's office, he started with the top drawer of the file cabinet.

After five minutes of vain searching, Jack slid the bottom drawer closed and stood up. He scratched his head, puzzling over where on earth she would have put the damn CD. He glanced at Riva's desk but dismissed it as a possibility. There would be no reason for her to store it there. A better possibility was that he had missed it when he'd gone through Laurie's desk, so he sat down and searched all her drawers again. This time he was particularly thorough, believing the CD had to be in there somewhere.

Jack sat up again after closing the last drawer. "Damn," he voiced out loud. He looked at his watch. He had less than five minutes of his allotted time left. As he looked back up at the desk surface with the idea of going through the stack of charts to see if the CD had inadvertently gotten into one, his eyes noticed the tiny yellow light on the frame of Laurie's computer monitor. Although the screen was dark, the light suggested that the computer was booted but the monitor had powered itself down.

With his right index finger, Jack hit one of the keys on the keyboard. Instantly, the screen illuminated, and Jack found himself looking at a page of Stephen Lewis's record, listing the results of all his laboratory tests. The print was small, and Jack had to fumble with the reading glasses he'd secretly gotten. With the glasses on, he was able to read the print, and his eye went down the column on the left-hand side of the page. Eventually, he came to "MASNP," and running his finger along horizontally, he found "positive MEF2A."

With a shake of his head at his stupidity of not looking for the CD in Laurie's CD drive, Jack took hold of Laurie's mouse and spent the next several minutes scrolling through the digital record of various patients in Laurie's series. What he found didn't surprise him. With every case that he looked at from both the Manhattan General and St. Francis, he found that the MASNP test was positive for a marker for any one of a number of deleterious gene mutations. Some he recognized, but others he did not. When he got to Darlene Morgan's chart, he got a particularly chilling wake-up call. Her MASNP was positive for the BRCA1 gene!

For a split second, Jack stared frozen at the screen. Up until that very minute, he'd thought of Laurie's risk as a potential target for whoever was killing these patients as relatively low, since statistics were on her side. Suddenly, that was no longer the case. Whoever was doing the killing was seemingly targeting people with inherited deleterious genes, and he remembered that Laurie, like Darlene Morgan, had BRCA1.

As if propelled by a rocket, Jack leaped up, dashed out of Laurie's office, and rushed headlong back down the corridor to the elevator. Luckily, the car was still there when he pressed the down button. As he descended, he fumbled for his cell phone in his coat pocket. He looked at his watch. It was sixteen minutes after four. Quickly, he dialed the Manhattan General Hospital, but he didn't try to put the call through. He had no signal.

The moment the doors opened on the basement level, Jack ran the length of the hall, passing a surprised Carl Novak for the second time just going in the opposite direction. Again, Jack ignored the man. He had his cell phone plastered to his ear after having pressed the call button the moment he'd emerged from the elevator. The hospital operator answered as he thundered down the short run of stairs from the morgue's loading dock to the pavement. After identifying himself as a doctor and without slowing down, Jack breathlessly asked to be put through to the PACU. What he wanted was reassurance that Laurie would not be moved until Dr. Riley made rounds. Running full tilt, Jack reached 30th Street and turned west.

Just as he reached First Avenue the PACU phone was picked up. He recognized the charge nurse's authoritative voice and Jack pulled himself to a stop. It wasn't raining as hard as it had been a quarter hour earlier when he'd dashed back to the OCME, but it was still raining just the same, such that he felt he had to shield his phone with his free hand. In front of him, relatively infrequent cars raced northward.

Between breaths, Jack identified himself to Thea.

"Wait a second," Thea said. Then, off the line, Jack could hear her yelling directions about which bed a new patient should be put in. Then she came back on the line. "Sorry, we're kind of busy here. What can I do for you, Dr. Stapleton?"

"I don't mean to be a bother," Jack said. While he was talking, he was looking for a taxi. He'd not seen any. "I wanted to check on Laurie Montgomery's status." He finally saw a cab in the distance with its vacant light illuminated. He was about to step off the curb and raise his hand when Thea shocked him with her response.

"We don't have a Laurie Montgomery."

"What do you mean?" Jack questioned with a start. "She's in the bed against the opposite wall. I was in there tonight. You even told me she was a charmer."

"Oh, that Laurie Montgomery. I beg your pardon. Over the last few hours, we've had a revolving-door situation with a bunch of trauma victims. Laurie Montgomery left the PACU. She was doing just fine, and we needed the bed."

Jack's mouth went suddenly dry. "When did this happen?"

"Right after I got the disaster call from the OR supervisor. My guess would be about two-fifteen."

"I left you with my cell phone number," Jack sputtered. "You were supposed to call me if there was any change in her status."

"There wasn't any change. Her vitals were rock-solid. We wouldn't have let her go if there had been any trouble whatsoever, believe me!"

"Where did she go?" Jack managed, desperately trying to control the anger and dismay in his voice. "To the ICU?"

"Nope! She didn't need the ICU, and it was full anyway. So was OB-GYN. She went to room 609 on the surgical floor."

Jack snapped his phone shut and desperately looked out into the mostly empty, dark, wet avenue. The cab he'd seen earlier had gone by during his preoccupation with the shocking, disastrous conversation with Thea Papparis. The idea that Laurie had been out of the PACU in her vulnerable state for two hours while he'd been out running around on his stupid errands was almost too horrible for him to contemplate. The question *What have I been thinking?* reverberated around inside his mind like clashing cymbals. Overwhelmed with panic, Jack began running northward up First Avenue, mindless of the puddles that appeared like pools of black crude oil. He knew it would take him much too long to run all the way to the Manhattan General, but also knew he couldn't just stand there.

twenty-four

It had been a busy night, maybe one of the busiest Jazz could remember at her present place of employment. They'd been inundated with trauma patients coming up from the PACU and filling all the empty beds. As the self-appointed acting charge nurse, a status that was soon to change, according to rumor, with the hiring of a new, senior night-shift RN, it had fallen to Jazz by default to divvy the patients up among the current night-shift nurses and the nurse's aides. There hadn't been too much complaining, since Jazz had made it a point to take her share. More important, she'd also made it a point to add Laurie Montgomery to her patient roster. Once that had been established and accepted, Jazz relaxed. She knew she'd be able to carry out her Operation Winnow responsibility at her whim.

Jazz stretched her arms over her head and rotated her head a few times to loosen up her neck muscles. She was tense. She'd just finished the last of some paperwork and was looking at some well-earned downtime from patient care, which she intended to put to good use. Even the lunch break had been truncated for everyone because of patient demand, forcing Jazz to skip eating altogether. Instead, she used the time to disappear into the ladies' room outside the cafeteria to load a syringe with the potassium chloride she'd pilfered from the ER stock and to dispose of the empty ampoule. From her perspective, the preparation for a sanction had become routine.

It was four-forty A.M., and all was ready. She had been waiting for the right moment, and it had arrived. Elizabeth, who had been sitting there with Jazz two seconds earlier, doing her own paperwork, had been called to help a patient in room 637 and had just disappeared from view. At the same time, all the other nurses and aides were likewise out of sight, tending to their assigned patients. The dimly lit corridors had that peaceful nighttime tranquility that Jazz had come to appreciate. She looked up one corridor and down the other. It was a perfect opportunity.

Pushing back from the desk, Jazz stood up. Her hand went into her right jacket pocket for a reassuring fondle of the full syringe. Taking a deep breath to control her excitement, she set off. With quickening steps, she silently hastened down to room 609. Pausing outside the door, she cast yet another glance up and down the long corridor. Once she'd started a mission, she preferred not to be seen to avoid any talk after the fact.

Conveniently, no one was in sight. The only sound was the quiet, metronomic beeping of a monitor in a nearby room. Jazz smiled. Sanctioning Laurie Montgomery was possibly going to be the most effortless assignment she'd done, both because she'd been able to pick the time and because the target was sedated and in restraints. *What could be easier?* Jazz questioned under her breath.

Jazz stepped into the room. A half hour earlier, when she had found herself passing by on her way back to the nurses' station after tending another patient, she'd ducked in to make certain the sedative had taken effect. It had. While she was there, she'd lowered the back of Laurie's bed so she was horizontal. She had also turned off the overhead fluorescent lights. Now, similar to the corridor, the room was bathed in a gentle incandescent glow from the recessed nightlights positioned just above the baseboard.

Without a sound, Jazz moved over to Laurie's bedside. Laurie was in a deep, drug-induced sleep. Her mouth was slightly open, and Jazz could see that her lips and tongue were dry and crusted. "Oh, poor dear," Jazz whispered scornfully. Jazz was enjoying herself. Of all the patients Jazz had so far sanctioned, she felt Laurie deserved it the most, with all her demands and poor attitude. For Jazz, Laurie was the quintessentially entitled, rich bitch who was the female equivalent of all the Mr. Ivy Leagues Jazz had to endure. And on top of that, she was a doctor who was still ordering Jazz around while she was a patient! From Jazz's perspective, Laurie Montgomery with her silver-spoon past "had it coming to her" to be taken down one big, ultimate peg.

Jazz eyed the restraints binding Laurie's wrists and felt a shiver of pleasure. There was no doubt that the restraints made the mission easier, and she was confident that Laurie wouldn't be scratching her arm like that bastard Stephen Lewis. But beyond the practical, she thought the restraints had an appeal similar to what she felt when she watched the collection of bondage movies she had downloaded off the Web. For her, it was a control issue.

Gently, Jazz lifted Laurie's head and slipped out the pillow. She was confident with the sedative she'd given her that Laurie wouldn't stir, and she didn't. Jazz tucked the pillow under her arm. She wanted it handy to slap over Laurie's face in the eventuality that Laurie made any untoward noises like pain-in-the-neck Sobczyk. She didn't expect Laurie would; the IV was a central line, meaning the concentrated potassium would be dumped into a major vein and would be less painful than a superficial one, but Jazz wanted to be prepared. She prided herself in being a quick learner, and the fewer the surprises, the better.

Reaching up, Jazz grasped the IV line and opened it so it flowed freely. She waited for a few minutes, to be sure it was running well. When she was certain the IV was functioning perfectly, she got out the syringe with the potassium. Using her teeth to take off the needle cap, she inserted the needle deep into the IV port.

After looking back at the door to the corridor and listening for a moment for any suspicious sounds, Jazz made the injection with strong, sustained pressure. It only took five seconds. She knew that the more the potassium arrived at the heart in a concentrated bolus, the more effective it would be. As usual, as she injected, she saw the fluid level rise in the micropore chamber below the IV fluid bag.

As soon as the syringe was empty, Jazz withdrew the needle and replaced the cap. She then pulled the pillow from under her arm as Laurie stirred, moaned, and popped open her eyes.

"Bon voyage!" Jazz whispered. With the pillow in her right hand poised for action and the syringe in her left, Jazz then bent over Laurie because she thought Laurie had mumbled something. Jazz started to ask her to repeat herself when Jazz recoiled in shocked surprise at the sound of the door to the room being slammed against its doorstop. In the next instant, an apparent maniac dashed into the room. Jazz was momentarily dumbfounded by the sudden, whirlwind arrival in the silent and dimly lit environment, particularly because she was tense and engrossed in what she was doing, and also because she thought she'd been so careful to avoid surprises. Except for taking a reflexive defensive step back, Jazz was momentarily paralyzed.

"How is she?" Jack barked as he rushed to the foot of Laurie's bed. His breaths were coming in noisy heaves. His hair was dripping and plastered to his forehead. He appeared like a wild man with an unshaven face, red eyes, wet clothes, and soggy shoes. He leaned with both hands on the metal foot of the bed as if exhausted but quickly revived. It was apparent he immediately didn't like what he saw. His eyes darted to Jazz, who had not answered him. He saw the pillow and the syringe in her hands. His attention reverted back to Laurie, who was softly moaning and fighting weakly and futilely against the wrist restraints.

"What's going on?" Jack demanded. He rushed around the side of the bed to Laurie's right, across from Jazz. "Laurie!" Jack yelled. His hand briefly clutched Laurie's wrist, but then shot up and gripped Laurie's forehead to keep her from moving her head from side to side. "What the hell are the restraints for?" Jack cried, but he didn't wait for an answer. On closer inspection, it was apparent Laurie was in a worsening, desperate state and possibly agonal. Her face reflected a mixture of terror, confusion, and pain.

"Hit the lights!" Jack yelled. "Call a code!"

Jazz still didn't respond other than to take yet another step back, stunned by the unexpected events.

"Fuck!" Jack screamed at the nurse's paralysis. His voice reverberated off the sleeping hospital's walls. He needed help fast, but he didn't want to leave Laurie alone even for a few seconds.

In frantic, desperate frustration, Jack yanked the bed away from the wall. Its locked wheels made a screeching sound on the composite flooring. After pushing the night table to the side, causing the collection of objects on its surface to crash to the floor in a clatter, Jack squeezed himself between the head of the bed and the wall. With his foot, Jack released the wheel locks. Gritting his teeth and allowing a battle-like yell to escape from his lips, he pushed the bed farther from the wall, yanking out its power cables in the process. With a grunt, he angled the rolling bed toward the door. It picked up speed, and although it hit the door and then the opposite jamb, they were glancing collisions and didn't interrupt his forward progress. In seconds, he was out in the hall, and using all his strength, he got the bed rolling at a good clip down the hallway toward the bright lights of the nurses' station.

"Call a code!" Jack shouted at the top of his lungs as he pushed. An unfortunate housekeeping cart loomed in the way, but Jack ignored it. The bed with Laurie in it had considerably more inertia, and the hapless cart was bowled over with a crash, spilling its supply of individual hand soaps and other material out onto the floor. Next came a walker, which was nearly crushed by the bed's momentum. "Call a code!" Jack yelled again. Nurses, nurse's aides, and even ambulatory patients began appearing in doorways to see Jack streak by.

Jack tried to slow the bed down as he closed in on the nurses' station with only partial success. The bed caromed off the counter, taking with it all the charts that had been left on the top, as well as a vase of cut flowers that had yet to be delivered to one of the patients. In the bright light, Jack could see how bad Laurie looked. She was ghostly pale and unmoving. Her eyes, with dilated pupils, blankly stared up at the ceiling.

Stripping off his wet coat and jacket and letting them fall to the floor, Jack moved to Laurie's side. After quickly determining that she was definitely not breathing and had no pulse, he pulled Laurie's chin back, pinched her nose and sealed his mouth over hers. He breathed into her several good breaths, then vaulted up onto the bed and began closed-chest cardiac massage. Seconds later, several nurses were at his side. One produced an Ambu bag and began respiring Laurie, carefully pacing herself with Jack's compressions. She inflated Laurie's lungs after Jack had applied five compressions. Another nurse wheeled over a bottle of oxygen and connected it to the Ambu bag.

"Has a code been called?" Jack yelled out.

"Yes," the nurse said who was breathing for Laurie.

"Well, where the hell are they?" Jack demanded.

"It's been less than a minute since they've been called."

"Damn, damn, damn," Jack sputtered through clenched teeth. He was out of breath from the running, the pushing, and now the compressions. Silently, he lambasted himself for having left Laurie, even if it had been her suggestion. He should have parked himself outside the PACU as he had threatened. From his position looming over her, he could tell her color was a tiny bit better prior to starting the CPR, so they were making a little progress. "What are her pupils doing?" Jack asked the nurse who was bagging her.

"Not a lot of change."

Jack shook his head in frustration. "How long does it usually take for the resuscitation team to get here?" he yelled between compressions. If what he had suspected had happened to Laurie, her life was clearly in the balance until resuscitation team arrived, and even then, he didn't know what the chances were. One thing he was dead certain of: CPR alone wasn't going to hack it. She had to be treated.

As if an answer to a prayer, an elevator door opened out in the lobby and a cardiac crash cart rattled out. Accompanying it were four medical residents, two women and two men who came running. The leader of the pack was Caitlin Burroughs, who looked as if she had been in Shirley Mayrand's medical-school class for gifted toddlers. If Jack had seen her on the street, he would have thought she was a high-school senior, not a senior medical resident. The men looked young, too, but not nearly in Shirley or Caitlin's league.

One of the residents immediately took over the Ambu bag from the nurse. Two of the others started attaching EKG leads. They obviously knew how to work as a team.

"What's the story here?" Caitlin barked, checking Laurie's pupils.

"Hyperkalemia," Jack shot back.

"That's a rather specific diagnosis," Caitlin exclaimed. She spoke in a rapid, staccato fashion. She might have looked young to Jack, but she exuded confidence that could only have come from experience. "How do you know her potassium is too high? Is she a renal patient?"

"No renal disease," Jack snapped back. He wasn't one hundred percent sure Laurie was suffering from high potassium, but he was a hundred percent sure that if they didn't act immediately, and it turned out that she was hyperkalemic as he suspected, they'd lose her for certain, and she'd end up a statistic in her own series. "It would take too long right this minute for me to tell you how I know, but I know," Jack continued emphatically. "We have to treat for high serum potassium, and we have to do it now! This second."

"How come you're so sure? And, by the way, who are you?"

"I'm Dr. Jack Stapleton," Jack blurted. "I'm a medical examiner here in the city. Listen! You've had a series of unexpected cardiac deaths in this hospital since January. All have been unsuccessful resuscitation attempts on young healthy people just like this patient. A red flag has gone up over at the OCME. We think it's purposeful, iatrogenic hyperkalemia."

"We've got almost nothing on EKG," one of the residents announced, standing by the machine mounted on the crash cart. EKG tape was spewing out the side, tracing poorly formed complexes.

Caitlin grabbed a quick look. Whatever she saw pushed her over the edge into Jack's camp, and she began barking out orders that had the nurses scurrying. She wanted calcium gluconate; she wanted twenty units of regular insulin along with a fifty-gram dose of glucose; she wanted sodium bicarbonate; she wanted cation-exchange resin set up for a retention enema; she wanted blood sent for stat electrolytes; and, most important from Jack's perspective, she wanted a surgical resident paged to help with emergency peritoneal dialysis. In Jack's mind, it was the dialysis that could potentially save the day.

While the nurses were busy carrying out the orders and obtaining and drawing up all the medication, one of the male residents climbed up on the bed and relieved a reluctant Jack, but as soon as the man started his compressions, Jack acknowledged the resident was probably doing a better job. As an ophthalmologist-turned-medical examiner, Jack was out of practice when it came to CPR. He was also exhausted, but it was hard for him to stand there at the foot of the bed and do nothing while Laurie's life hung in the balance. While concentrating on doing the chest compressions, he'd been less able to think about the potential tragedy of what he was witnessing.

Jack hadn't run all the way from the OCME to the Manhattan General Hospital, but he had run quite far just the same. He'd run almost ten blocks up First Avenue without seeing an empty taxi. A number of cars had passed him and sprayed him with water, but none had stopped. Then his luck changed. Near the UN headquarters, a police patrol car had pulled over in front of him, apparently thinking he was fleeing from a crime. When Jack flashed his medical examiner badge and breathlessly said he was on an emergency run to the Manhattan General, the police had told him to jump in. They took him nonstop with their siren blaring. If it had crossed their minds why a medical examiner who deals with dead bodies had an emergency in the middle of the night requiring him to sprint up First Avenue, they hadn't let on.

As Laurie's hyperkalemic treatment began to bring down the high potassium that Jack feared was coursing around in her blood, an anesthesiologist showed up. He proceeded to deftly intubate Laurie so she could be respired with more certainty. When he straightened up after finishing the procedure, Jack caught his name. It was José Cabreo, and Jack did a double take. He remembered the man's name from Roger's lists. Jack found himself watching José's every move and was relieved when the anesthesiologist quickly left.

The peritoneal dialysis was started percutaneously without a hitch, using a large bore trocar. Jack averted his eyes as the trocar was punched through Laurie's abdominal wall, but he was close enough to hear the popping sound it made as it went through the fascia, and he winced. A moment later, he watched as isotonic fluid free of potassium was then run into her abdomen. Jack secretly crossed his fingers and prayed that the procedure would help. He was aware that with the extensive surface area within the abdomen as a result of the loops of intestine combined with the rich plexus of blood vessels, peritoneal dialysis was the most efficient even if passive way to lower potassium or any other elevated electrolyte in the blood.

Unfortunately, after ten minutes of the aggressive therapy, there was disappointingly little change in Laurie's status. Caitlin ordered more calcium gluconate and injected it herself. Jack heard this from afar, as he'd begun pacing between Laurie's bed in front of the nurses' station and the elevator lobby. It wasn't the caffeine that was propelling him now, it was his mounting fear and guilt. His nagging concern was that this episode might be another instance of his being a jinx to those he loved. The thought haunted him mercilessly. In one night, he already had lost a potential child; now he was on the verge of losing the person he loved. To make matters worse, he knew he was at least partially to blame.

When the stat bloodwork came back, Caitlin brought it over to Jack. "Well, you were absolutely right," she said while pointing to the highlighted abnormally high potassium level. "That's about as high as I've ever seen it. After this is all over, I'd like to hear how you knew."

"I'll be happy to tell you," Jack said, "provided Miss Montgomery pulls through." If Laurie didn't make it, he didn't know if he'd be willing to talk to anybody.

"We're doing our best," Caitlin said. "At least her color is good and her pupils have definitely come down."

As the minutes inexorably passed, Jack kept his distance. As a bystander, it was progressively upsetting to him to see Laurie splayed out on the bed with a stranger pounding on her chest and another dispassionately squeezing the breathing bag. The ambulatory patients who had earlier come to their respective doors to watch the unfolding drama had gone back to their beds. Most of the floor nurses had also been called away by the needs of their own patients.

It was twenty minutes to six when the first truly optimistic sign occurred, and it was Caitlin who noticed it. "Hey! Gang!" she shouted. "We're getting some electrical activity in the heart!" The medical resident who was not currently doing either the closed chest massage or the breathing-bag compression rushed over to the EKG machine to look over Caitlin's shoulder. "Send off another stat potassium level," Caitlin yelled to the nurse who was assisting them.

"Wow! Those complexes are starting to look quite normal," the resident said to Caitlin, who nodded in agreement. "And they are getting better."

"Hold up on the compressions!" Caitlin called out to the resident, who was kneeling on the bed over Laurie. "See if she's got a pulse!"

The resident who had been breathing for Laurie also stopped long enough to feel along Laurie's neck for a pulse. "She's got a pulse! And, my gosh, she's breathing on her own!" He took the mask away from the end of the endotracheal tube. With his palm, he could feel the amount of air she was breathing in and out. "She's breathing pretty darn normally, and she's bucking the endotracheal tube."

"Deflate it and pull it out!" Caitlin ordered. "Her EKG now looks completely normal."

The resident quickly followed orders and slipped the tube out of Laurie's mouth but still held her chin back to make sure her airway stayed open. Laurie coughed several times.

Hearing these exchanges, Jack rushed back from where he was pacing in the darkened elevator lobby and went behind the nurses' station desk. Laurie had been connected to one of the monitors built in over the desk, but to see it, one had to be on the opposite side of the counter from where the action was. A half hour earlier when he'd looked at it, the blips for the blood pressure and pulse had been tracing straight lines across the screen. It was different now, and his heart leaped in his chest. Laurie had both a pulse and blood pressure!

"Hold up on the peritoneal dialysis!" Caitlin ordered. "And drain out the cation exchange resin. We don't want to overshoot and then have to worry about too low a potassium level."

Jack rounded the nurses' station counter. There was once again a flurry around Laurie as Caitlin's latest orders were carried out. Jack didn't want to get in the way, but as hopeful as these developments were, he wanted to be close to her.

"Hallelujah!" said the resident who had been most recently breathing for Laurie. "She's waking up!"

Unable to hold himself back, Jack crowded in at the head of Laurie's bed that had been backed up against the nurses' station countertop. He looked down and saw what he thought was a miracle. Laurie's eyes were open, and they were moving from one face poised over her to another and reflected not a little confusion and fear. Unexpectedly, Jack burst into tears such that it was hard for him to see. All he could do was shake his head when he tried to talk.

"Release her wrists," ordered Caitlin, who had pushed in across from Jack. The restraints had been left in place during the ordeal. Caitlin bent over Laurie and gave her shoulder a reassuring squeeze. "Everything is okay. Just relax. We've got things under control. You're going to be all right."

Laurie tried to speak, but her voice was barely audible. Caitlin had to bend down to put her ear next to Laurie's mouth. "You're in the Manhattan General Hospital," Caitlin said. "Do you know your name and what year it is?" Caitlin listened, and then straightened up. She looked across at Jack, who had calmed enough to control his crying and wipe away the tears. "This is looking very good indeed. She's oriented. I have to say your rapid diagnosis undoubtedly saved the day. With as high as her potassium was when we started, she surely wouldn't have been able to be resuscitated."

Jack nodded. He still couldn't talk. Instead, he bent down and put his forehead on Laurie's. Now that her hands were free, Laurie reached up and patted the side of his head and whispered in a scratchy voice: "Why are you so upset? What's going on?"

Laurie's questions unleashed another wave of tears. All he could do for the moment was squeeze Laurie's hand.

A nurse at the nurses' station desk stood up behind the counter. She'd just answered the phone. "Dr. Burroughs," she called.

"The stat potassium on Montgomery is four milli-equivalents."

"My word," Caitlin exclaimed. "That's darn near perfect." She turned to her three resident underlings. "Okay, here's what we are going to do! While I call the attending physician and give her an update, you three get the patient down to the cardiac care unit and get her set up on the monitor. I'll want another potassium level as soon as you get there, and I'll be there as soon as I finish here so we can decide on her fluids."

As the preparations were quickly made to move Laurie, Jack found his voice. "I'm not upset," he whispered in Laurie's ear. "I'm happy you're okay. You gave us a scare."

"I did?" Laurie questioned. Her voice was returning as well, but it hurt her to talk.

"You were unconscious for a while," Jack said. "What was the last thing you remember?"

"I remember leaving the PACU, but nothing after that. What happened?"

"I'll explain everything I know at the first opportunity," Jack promised as the bed started to move.

"Are you coming?" Laurie asked, holding on to Jack's arm.

"You'd better believe it," Jack said as he walked alongside. A nurse ran up and handed Jack his damp coat and jacket.

They used a patient elevator to take Laurie down to the third floor, where the CCU was located. At the door to the CCU, there was a holdup. The charge nurse would not let Jack come in, although he would be able to visit once she was situated. At first Jack had balked at the idea. He wanted to stay by Laurie's side, considering what had transpired when he hadn't. Eventually, Jack relented, convinced that Laurie would be in good hands. The resuscitation residents assured him that one of them would be at the bedside continually.

"I'll be right here," Jack assured Laurie, pointing out a small waiting room just opposite the CCU door.

Laurie nodded, preoccupied with her physical symptoms, which had become progressively more bothersome as her mind had cleared. What she wanted at the moment was some ice chips for her dry mouth and sore throat, as well as something for the pain she felt at her incision site and in her chest. As far as her memory was concerned, it was still a blank after leaving the PACU.

Jack went into the waiting room, which was empty of visitors. A clock on the wall indicated it was six-fifteen in the morning. There were several couches and a number of chairs. A mixture of old magazines littered a coffee table. Complimentary coffee was available in a corner. Jack tossed his coat and jacket on the arm of one of the sofas and sat down, letting out a heavy groan in the process. He leaned back, put his hands behind his head, and closed his eyes. He felt shell-shocked. He'd never had such stress combined with such physical exertion and wide swings of emotion. Making matters worse were the residual effects of the caffeine, which were enough to make him sick.

The process of closing his eyes made it possible for Jack to think about the sheer criminality of what Laurie had luckily endured. With the immediacy of taking care of her, he hadn't thought about it until that moment. In his mind's eye, he could see the tanned nurse in Laurie's room when he'd barged in. In the dim light, she'd appeared almost gaunt, with dark, short hair, deeply set eyes, and startling white teeth. What he remembered the most was the pillow in one hand and the large syringe in the other. He knew there could be many explanations for why she had been holding such things, just as there could be an explanation for her apparent paralysis in the face of what was obviously a life-and-death emergency. Jack had seen others freeze like that when he was a resident. In fact, he had done essentially the same thing on his first cardiac arrest after graduating from medical school. Yet under the circumstances, Jack couldn't help but think of her actions as being suspicious. He'd seen her again during the nerve-wracking resuscitation, but only for brief glimpses when she'd appeared at the nurses' station to go into the drug room to use the computerized dispenser. She'd not participated in the resuscitation. Jack had asked one of the nurses who had helped what the tanned nurse's name was. When she told him, Jack was even more suspicious. It was another name on Roger's lists.

Jack's eyes popped open. He fumbled in this coat pocket for his cell phone. Knowing Lou Soldano's private home number in

SoHo, and despite the hour, he quickly put in a call to him. After what he had witnessed, Lou had to get involved. There could be no more excuses. The phone rang six times before Lou picked up. His voice was gravelly, and Jack had to wait through a coughing jag on the detective's part.

"Are you going to live?" Jack questioned when Lou finally fell silent.

"Cut the humor," Lou growled. "This better be important."

"It's more than important," Jack said. "Laurie had to have emergency surgery last night at the Manhattan General. Then a couple of hours ago, someone put her on the edge of the abyss and gave her a good shove. She came as close to dying and not dying as you can get. In fact, for a few seconds or maybe even minutes, she was dead."

"My God!" Lou blurted, which initiated another fit of coughing.

"Do you cough like this every morning?" Jack asked when Lou came back on the line.

"Where is she now?" Lou asked, ignoring Jack's question.

"She's in the cardiac care unit on the

third floor," Jack said. "I'm sitting in a visitor's room just opposite the door."

"Is she in any danger?"

"Medically or otherwise?"

"Both."

"Medically, I think they have things pretty much in hand. She lucked out with a particularly sharp cardiology resident who looks like she belongs in middle school. She's the second person tonight that has made me feel over the hill. As far as the person who tried to kill Laurie getting another crack at it, I don't think that's a problem. Not in the cardiac care unit—there are too many people around, and I'm sitting outside the only door."

"Do you have any idea who did it?"

"There's one person, a nurse actually, who I'd be willing to put some money on, but it's circumstantial. I'll tell you the details when you get here. We've also got Roger's lists, so your work is cut out for you. But the idea of Laurie's series being hypothetical is no longer tenable. She almost became a statistic herself."

"Do you know the name of this nurse?"

"Rakoczi."

"What kind of name is that?"

"Beats me."

"Does this Rakoczi know you suspect her?"

"I imagine," Jack said. "She's steered clear of me during Laurie's resuscitation. She was in Laurie's room when I got to Laurie and found her moribund." Jack went on to briefly describe the scene as he remembered it.

"Well, she'll be the first person I want to talk to," Lou said. "I'll be there as soon as possible, which will realistically be about a half hour. Meanwhile, I'll call the local precinct and have a couple of uniformed officers over there to stand outside the cardiac care unit door, in case you have to go to the can or something."

"Sounds like a good plan."

"Have you been up all night?"

"I have," Jack admitted.

"All right, hang in there, and I'll see you shortly."

Jack was about to hang up when he heard Lou add, "One other thing. Don't be a hero, okay! Just stay put."

"Don't worry," Jack said. "After what I've been through already, I'm having trouble breathing in and out. I'm staying right here."

Jack disconnected, put his phone away, and closed his eyes again. He felt a certain relief after having talked with Lou Soldano. The burden of the criminality of what had happened to Laurie and the other victims in Laurie's series was off his shoulders. For Jack, it was a little like passing the baton in a relay race, meaning his contribution was over. What he didn't know was how much he was going to regret not following his own advice.

twenty-five

"Excuse me," Caitlin said after giving Jack's shoulder a nudge.

Jack blinked and pulled himself from the depths of sleep. He felt like death warmed over, but as his vision cleared and he became oriented to time, place, and person, he quickly straightened up. He was surprised and frankly aghast that he had fallen asleep.

"What's the matter?" he sputtered. "Is she okay?"

"She's fine," Caitlin said. "Her repeat potassium was normal, and her vital signs have stayed rock-solid. She's even had some fluid by mouth, which was ordered by Dr. Riley. The drain from her incision has also been removed, so she's doing very well."

"Fantastic," Jack said as he slid forward to stand up.

Caitlin reached out and gently pushed against his shoulder, keeping him sitting on the couch. "I know you want to visit, but I think it might be better to leave her be for now. She's exhausted, and she's sleeping."

Jack sat back and nodded. "I'm sure you're right. Actually, I'm more concerned about her safety at this point. Needless to say, as I'm sure you have surmised, someone deliberately gave her the potassium."

"I gathered as much," Caitlin said. "But rest assured! I'm confident the CCU is safe, but to be one hundred percent sure, I've asked one of my residents to stay at the bedside continually. He'll watch everything like a hawk. No one without his authorization will get near her."

"Perfect," Jack said.

"I suppose I shouldn't ask about who you think might have done this to her."

"Probably the less talk the better until it is resolved," Jack agreed. "I know that's difficult in a hospital where gossip spreads like wildfire, but it will probably be best for everyone if you and your colleagues don't say anything about what happened for a day or so. A homicide detective will be here shortly, and I hope he can get to the bottom of things."

At that moment, two uniformed policemen appeared at the doorway. One was a beefy African-American male whose bulging muscles stretched the limits of the fabric of his uniform. His name was Kevin Fletcher. The other was a comparatively slight Hispanic woman named Toya Sanchez. Both acted self-conscious about being in the hospital. They introduced themselves to Jack, speaking in no more than a whisper. They said that their orders were merely to check in with him. Then they acted as if they didn't know what to do.

"Why don't you take a couple of chairs out and sit by the cardiac care unit door," Jack suggested. "Make sure that everyone going in is legitimately supposed to go in."

Then, looking at Caitlin, he said, "I'm assuming that is the only door."

"It is the only door," Caitlin assured him.

Glad to have some direction, the two policemen took Jack's advice and were soon sitting on either side of the unit's double doors. Jack felt their presence was imposing, if nothing else. It was the busy CCU itself that provided the safety.

"I've got rounds to do," Caitlin said. "So I'll leave you here on your vigil."

"Thanks for all you did," Jack said as sincerely as he could. "You were terrific."

"Your tip about potassium was key," Caitlin said. "Maybe you should think about taking a cardiology residency. We'd make a good team."

Jack laughed and wondered if the youthful woman was flirting with him. Then he smiled at his own vanity, thinking he was trying to compensate for how old she made him feel. He waved as the woman walked out of the waiting room.

After Caitlin left, Jack settled back in the sofa. He wasn't about to fall asleep again, since he'd gotten a shot of adrenaline when she'd awakened him. Instead, he began musing about what it really meant for someone to be killing patients who had positive markers for bad genes. It was immediately obvious to him that the explanation for such an unspeakable villainy couldn't simply be a person with an antisocial personality disorder, although the person who was actually injecting the potassium surely had to have such an affliction. Jack knew intuitively that it had to be a more extensive conspiracy, with the involvement of some higher-ups in the AmeriCare organization. In his mind, it was a horrid example of how the practice of medicine could be distorted from having evolved into big business with business interests in the ascendancy. He was personally aware that there were people hidden in the top-heavy administrations of these huge, sprawling managed-care and hospital-management companies similar to AmeriCare that were so far removed bureaucratically and often geographically from the professed primary mission of the organization that they could easily be blinded by the needs of the bottom line, and ultimately, the share price.

A commotion in the hall interrupted Jack's thoughts. A group of nurses had arrived, and there was a great titter about the presence of the police, who were checking IDs before letting them into the CCU. Jack watched them laugh and joke, and he wondered if they would be carrying on as they were if they knew what was going on behind the scenes in their hospital. Even more than the doctors, the nurses were in the trenches on a daily basis, involved in hand-to-hand combat with disease and disability. He was certain they would be outraged if they heard that one of their own was suspected of such treachery.

Such thinking brought Jack's mind back to Jasmine Rakoczi. If she was the culprit, as he thought was possible, then she surely had to be severely antisocial. Jack couldn't help but think he had to be wrong about her. How could someone who is antisocial be a nurse? It seemed an oxymoron to him. But, in the unlikely case she was antisocial, how could she have gotten a nursing job at such a prestigious hospital? It didn't make any sense, especially with the idea that some bean counter buried deep in the fabric of AmeriCare's organizational structure had to tell her who to pump full of potassium.

The door to the CCU burst open and another group of both male and female nurses emerged. They were equally surprised and curious about the uniformed police. The police were polite but noncommittal, and within a few minutes, the nurses' voices trailed off as they disappeared down the hallway.

Jack's eyes wandered up to the wall clock. It was a little after seven in the morning. All of a sudden, it dawned on his tired mind why the group of nurses had come in and another group had gone out. It was the shift change. The day people were taking over from the night people.

Jack leaped off the sofa. It hadn't even occurred to him that Jasmine Rakoczi would be getting off before Lou got there. If she was the culprit and if she sensed that Jack knew it, she might disappear for good. Several strides took him out into the hall, where he quickly told the two police officers that he was going up to the sixth floor. He said that if Detective Lieutenant Soldano came in while he was away, they should tell him where he had gone and send him up there.

Then Jack rushed down to the elevator lobby, where it was apparent that the hospital had transformed itself: The busy day had begun. There were at least a dozen people waiting for an elevator, which included a number of orderlies with gurneys on their way to fetch patients for their scheduled surgeries.

The first up elevator that arrived appeared full when its door opened. Several people boarded just the same, and, not to be deterred, Jack literally pushed on as well. He could sense people's indignation as the door was barely able to close. Pressed cheek to jowl, no one spoke as the car rose.

To Jack's chagrin, the ascent was frustratingly slow. The elevator stopped on every floor and disgorged passengers, more often than not, from the rear, making Jack and a few others step out at each successive elevator lobby. By the time the elevator got to the sixth floor, Jack was having trouble controlling his impatience, and when the door opened, he was the first one out. His plan was to rush to the nurses' desk to inquire about Jasmine Rakoczi. He hoped by chance she'd been delayed so he could catch her before she left.

Directly opposite from Jack's elevator

was another whose door was in the process of closing. Out of the corner of his eye, Jack thought he caught a glimpse of the nurse with her rather striking features. It had been a fleeting image, and by the time he had jerked his head around to look again, the elevator doors had closed.

For a second, Jack debated what to do. If he ran down the stairs, he had a good chance of beating the elevator. But what if he was wrong, and it hadn't been Rakoczi? After several false starts, Jack impulsively reverted to plan A and ran toward the nurses' station. There were a number of nurses in sight, some of whom he recognized, which he thought was encouraging. There was also a ward clerk who had just come on duty. He was busy straightening up the litter on the desk, a lot of which had resulted from Laurie's resuscitation.

In a rapid-fire manner, Jack introduced himself as Dr. Stapleton and asked for Jasmine Rakoczi. The ward clerk, who was a slightly built blond fellow with a ponytail, told him that Jazz Rakoczi had just left two seconds ago. He tried to look around Jack to see if he could see her in the elevator lobby.

"Do you know where she goes?" Jack demanded quickly, guessing that it had indeed been her in the elevator. "I mean which door she goes out or which direction she walks. I need to talk to her. It's important."

"She doesn't walk home," the clerk said. "She's got a cool, black H2 Hummer, which she actually showed me once. It's got a sound system you wouldn't believe. It's always parked on the second floor of the garage across from the door to the pedestrian bridge."

"What floor do you get off the elevator for the pedestrian bridge?" Jack hurriedly asked.

"The second floor, of course," the clerk said, making a face as if it had been the stupidest question he'd ever heard.

Jack took off at a run for the stairs. Earlier, he thought he could have beat Rakoczi's elevator, but now, having spent the time going to the nurses' station, he knew it was out of the question. But he didn't regret his decision, since he would have missed her anyway. He would have run all the way down to the first floor to try to catch her going out the front door. As things turned out, he felt he still had a chance of catching her; she had to walk across the pedestrian bridge and then start her car. Knowing what kind of car she drove might turn out to be key.

The stairwell was painted gunmetal gray. The stairs themselves were steel, and each step sounded like a drum as his shoe thumped against it. The repetitive booming reverberated around the enclosed space. There were two flights for each floor, causing Jack to continually turn as he spiraled down clockwise. He was dizzy by the time he reached the second-floor door, and he staggered a bit when he entered the hallway.

As unshaven and disheveled as he appeared, coupled with his momentary careening, people gave him a wide berth as he hurriedly tried to get directions for the pedestrian bridge. Finally, someone took pity and responded by pointing, and Jack took off, moving as quickly as he could. While saying "excuse me" over and over, he pushed his way ahead in the stream of hospital personnel heading toward the parking garage. After a pair of doors, he could tell he was on the pedestrian bridge, as he could suddenly see up and down Madison Avenue. There was another pair of doors on the garage side that led into a small lobby area, which was crowded with people waiting for an elevator. Jack was reduced to squeezing through until he could push open the heavy door out into the garage's second level. The garage was alive with cars coming and going with their headlights crisscrossing in the exhaust-filled dim light. Outside, the dawn was just bleaching the night sky, whereas infrequent fluorescent lights poorly illuminated the interior of the garage.

Knowing the make of Jazz's vehicle was indeed key, and he was able to pick it out from all the others immediately. As the ward clerk had said, it was parked directly opposite the door to the connecting pedestrian bridge. Elevating himself on his tiptoes so he could see over the cars passing between him and the Hummer, Jack saw Rakoczi! She'd just made it across to her car. Jack could even make out what he guessed was a remote in her hand, which she was aiming at the car as she squeezed along its driver's side. It was separated by a little more than two feet from the neighboring vehicle.

"Miss Rakoczi!" Jack yelled over the sound of the car engines. He saw her turn and look in his direction. "Hold up a second! I need to talk with you!" For an instant, Jack's tired mind questioned the rationale for approaching a woman he suspected might be a serial killer. Yet his desire to keep her from leaving trumped his concerns. With all the commotion of people and cars, he felt reasonably safe, especially since he had no intention of being confrontational in any way or form, just firm.

Jack looked left and right, gauging his crossing with the comings and goings of the traffic. The exhaust as well as noise was unpleasant. Jack got over to the opposite side. Jazz was standing by her car with the driver's-side door ajar. The remote was gone and apparently in her pocket. She was dressed in an oversized, olive-drab coat over her scrubs. Her right hand was in her pocket. Her expression was haughty to the point of being challenging.

Slipping between Jazz's car and the one right next to it, Jack walked right up to the nurse, whose eyes narrowed the closer he got. Jack sensed that there wasn't a lot of human warmth in this person.

"You're needed back in the hospital," Jack said, speaking loud enough to be heard over the roar of the traffic. He tried to sound authoritative to avoid an argument. He even pointed over his shoulder with his thumb. "There are some people who want to talk with you."

"I'm off duty," Jazz sneered. "I'm going home."

Jazz turned and put a foot up into her SUV, with the obvious intention of swinging herself up behind the steering wheel. Jack caught her right arm just above the elbow and gripped it hard enough to keep her where she was.

"It's important you talk with these people," Jack said. He started to say something else about coming with him, but he never got it out. With totally unexpected swiftness, Jazz used a karate-like blow to free her arm and practically simultaneously kneed Jack in the groin. Jack doubled over, clutching his genitals while an involuntary groan escaped from his lips. The next thing he knew, the cold barrel of a gun was pressed against the back of his neck.

"Stand up, asshole," Jazz scoffed loud enough to be heard. "And get in the damn car."

Jack raised his head. He was squinting with pain and wasn't entirely sure he could walk.

"This gun's going to go off if you don't get the hell in there," Jazz hissed.

Jack moved forward as Jazz backed up a step. Still supporting his genitals with his right hand, he used his left to help him get up behind the steering wheel. The pain was like nothing else he'd ever experienced. It made him feel weak, as though he were made out of rubber.

"Climb over into the passenger seat," Jazz ordered as she took a quick glimpse around to see if anyone had noticed what had happened. With all the confusion and noise in the garage, no one paid the slightest heed. "Come on!" Jazz snapped. As an added incentive, she poked the side of Jack's head with the tip of the gun's suppressor.

With the vehicle's gear box in the way, Jack wasn't sure he could physically do what Jazz was ordering, but he felt as if he had no choice but to try. He sagged over the median console into the passenger seat, rotated onto his back, and with his knees bent, brought his feet over. He was now in a tight ball, more or less on his back.

Jazz quickly climbed in behind the steering wheel and pulled the driver's-side door shut, eliminating most of the garage's noise. She kept her gun pointed at Jack's face, just inches from his forehead. "And what do these people want to talk to me about?" Jazz demanded with obvious derision.

Jack started to answer, but Jazz cut him off. "Don't bother answering, because it doesn't matter. What matters is that you've managed to get yourself killed."

The sound of the gun going off despite its suppressor was loud enough within the confines of the vehicle's cab to cause ears to ring. Jack's eyes, which had reflexly blinked closed at the noise, popped open in time to see Jazz's head sag forward and bump against the steering wheel. A rivulet of blood appeared and ran down the nape of her neck. To add to his confusion, Jazz's gun fell onto his chest.

"Excuse me," a male voice said from the dark depths of the backseat. "Would you mind handing Miss Rakoczi's Glock back to me? I prefer that you do it by holding on to the suppressor, not the butt."

Jack picked up the gun as he was directed, and then, by wiggling himself backward, he was able to partially right himself so that he could raise his head high enough to see over the back of the passenger seat. The view was limited because of the heavily tinted windows. All Jack could see was the mere outline of a figure sitting in the backseat directly behind the driver's seat. There was a heavy smell of cordite in the air.

"I'm waiting for the gun," the shadowy man said. "If you don't do as I say, there will be dire consequences. I would think you would be eager to help, since I obviously saved your life."

Bewildered at these unexpected and shocking developments, Jack was in no condition to question the man's request, and he started to extend the gun through the separation between the two front seats. It was at that instance that the driver's-side door was yanked open, and Jazz's limp body tumbled out onto the concrete. Surprised anew, Jack caught sight of an equally surprised Lou. “In the backseat!” Jack yelled. “Watch out!”

Lou disappeared at the same instant the shadowy backseat figure discharged his pistol yet again, followed by the noise of shattering glass. Without thinking, Jack flipped the gun he was holding around so that his index finger slipped into the trigger guard. Still crouching behind the back of the passenger seat, he raised the gun, and aiming blindly in the direction of the shadowy person, pulled off three shots in rapid succession. To Jack, the sound of the weapon was a loud hissing thud like a combination of a fist hitting a punching bag and air being let out of a tire. The expended shell casings clanked down between the front seats. Although his ears were ringing, silence returned. Again, the smell of cordite permeated the vehicle’s cab.

Jack’s heart was pounding. As he huddled against the back of his seat, he heard a gurgling sound from the rear seat. He was afraid to move and half expected the man in the back to loom up and shoot him like he had shot Rakoczi.

“Lou?” Jack called. He was afraid to

move, and he was afraid Lou might have gotten shot.

"Yeah!" Lou's voice sounded from someplace outside the car.

"Are you all right?"

"Yeah, I'm fine. Who fired those last three shots?"

"I did. I shot blindly."

"Who is it you shot at?"

"I haven't the slightest idea."

"Is this the nurse you were talking about on the phone lying next to me on the pavement out here?"

"It is," Jack said. He switched positions. His back was killing him the way it was pressed up against the passenger-side door.

"I thought you promised you weren't going to be a hero," Lou complained. "Did you shoot her, too, or what?"

"I didn't shoot her," Jack exclaimed. "It was the guy in the backseat."

"Whoever the guy is shot at me," Lou said. "I don't like that."

In addition to the gurgling, Jack now heard definite wheezing. At that moment, he caught sight of Lou's eyes between the open driver's side door and the doorframe.

He was now squatting next to the driver's-side front wheel, holding his pistol up alongside his head.

Jack managed to get his legs down where they belonged under the dash so that he could move his head and cautiously look into the backseat between the front seats. In the dim light and limited view he could see a flaccid hand lying on the back-seat with its index finger still within the trigger guard of a pistol. At that point, Jack heard stertorous breathing.

Gaining courage, Jack raised his head and peered over the top of the front seat. He could just make out a man sitting upright but with his head back and arms splayed out to the sides. With his head back, Jack could see that he was wearing a ski mask. His breathing was labored.

"I guess I shot him," Jack said.

Lou stood up, walked along the side of the car, and stuck his pistol through the back window that had been blown out. He was holding his gun in both hands and pointing it at the stricken individual. "Can you hit the lights?" Lou asked.

Jack spun around and briefly searched for the interior lights. When he found them, he switched them on. He looked into the backseat at the man. An expanding stain of blood was on the man's chest.

"Can you reach his gun?" Lou asked. He kept his gun trained on the apparently unconscious stranger.

Jack extended his hand warily toward the gun as if the man would suddenly wake up like in a thriller movie for one more desperate struggle.

"Just touch the barrel, not the butt," Lou directed. "And put it on the front seat."

Jack did as he was told, then quickly got out the passenger-side door. He opened up the back door and leaned in to get a closer look at the man. Up close it was more apparent how labored the individual's breathing was. Jack pulled off the ski mask in hopes it would help the man breathe. Lou opened the door on the man's other side.

"Do you recognize him?" Lou asked.

"Not at all," Jack said.

While Jack felt for a pulse, Lou grabbed the fabric on the front of the man's shirt, and with a sudden lateral tear, ripped the shirt wide open. Buttons popped off. Three entrance wounds were apparent in the man's chest.

"I'll say you shot him," Lou remarked with admiration.

"His pulse is thready and rapid," Jack said. "He's not long for this world unless we act fast. On the positive side, he's already at the hospital."

"You check the nurse!" Lou said. "I'll start getting him out of the car."

Jack ducked back out of the vehicle and ran around to the other side. Bending down, it took him only a second to ascertain that Jazz had been shot execution-style through the back of the head at very close range. The bullet had undoubtedly passed through the brainstem. She was clearly moribund.

Jack stood back up and stepped over the woman. He could see that Lou had the injured individual half out of the car.

"What's the situation with the woman?" Lou grunted.

"She's gone. Let's concentrate on the guy."

With the back door open against the neighboring vehicle, Jack had to reverse directions, step back over Rakoczi, and run all the way around the SUV to lend a hand with the man. Lou had his hands under the individual's armpits. Jack squeezed by and grasped the man around the thighs.

"God! He weighs a ton!" Lou complained as they managed to get out from between the parked cars. They were immediately caught in the headlights of a car attempting to exit the garage. The driver had the nerve to beep the horn.

"Only in New York," Lou complained at the impatient driver through clenched teeth. He struggled with the injured man. "What the hell is this guy anyway, a professional football player?"

As they approached the doors to the pedestrian bridge, a few of the departing hospital workers stopped to gawk, unsure of what they were witnessing. At least one had the sense to reverse direction and reach back to hold open the door.

Halfway across the bridge, Lou staggered. "I got to stop," he said while panting.

"Let's switch," Jack suggested. They put the man down on the concrete floor of the bridge, quickly changed places, and then picked up the man again.

"You certainly picked a good time to show up," Jack said and grunted.

"Apparently, I just missed you outside the CCU," Lou said. "Then I just missed you on the sixth floor. It was a good thing the clerk told me to look for a black Hummer."

In the better light, it was apparent that the stains on the man's shirt were blood, and people were now willing to help. By the time they got across the bridge, two male nurses had pitched in. One was at the head with Jack, while the other had a leg with Lou.

"The ER is on the floor below," one of the nurses said between breaths. "Should we wait for an elevator or try the stairs?"

"The elevator," Jack answered. He was aware the man was no longer breathing. "But we're going up, not down. He needs a thoracic surgeon, and he needs him now."

The two nurses looked at each other in consternation but didn't say anything. Rather than put the man down, Jack backed up against the wall and hit the elevator button with his free hand. Luckily, a car arrived almost immediately. Unfortunately, it was full.

"Coming in!" Jack yelled. He was not to be deterred, and he backed right into people who momentarily had not moved. Recognizing the degree of the emergency, a number of people got off, creating the necessary space. The door closed.

The four people holding the injured man looked at one another while the people in the elevator stared at the wounded individual. No one said anything as the elevator rose up a floor.

When the doors opened on the third floor, they carried the man out and then pushed through the double doors. As they passed the arched opening into the surgical lounge, Jack cried out that they had a man who had been shot in the chest three times. By the time they got to the doors leading into the OR itself, a number of surgeons who had been waiting for their cases to start were walking alongside. Several of them were thoracic surgeons, and they started to assess the man's condition, as evidenced by the position of the entrance wounds. Although there was some disagreement about the nature of the injuries, all thought that the only chance the patient had for survival was to be put on cardiopulmonary bypass immediately.

As the group came abreast of the OR

desk, several of the nurses were aghast that people had entered their sterile domain in street clothes. Their indignation was shortlived when they realized that a patient with a mortal wound was being rushed in.

"Room 8 is being set up for open-heart surgery," one of the nurses behind the desk yelled.

The group hustled down to room 8 where they put the man directly onto the operating table. The surgeons wasted no time. They cut off the man's clothes. An anesthesiologist appeared and yelled that the man was no longer breathing and had no pulse. He quickly intubated the patient and started respiring him with one hundred percent oxygen. Another anesthesiologist started several large-bore IVs and began running fluid into the man as fast as possible. He also called for blood to be typed and cross-matched stat.

Jack and Lou stepped back as the surgeons crowded around. One of the thoracic surgeons barked for a scalpel, and one was quickly slapped into his waiting palm. With no hesitation and without even bothering to glove, the surgeon cut through the man's chest with a decisive swipe. Then, using his bare hands, he cracked open the ribs only, to be faced with an enormous amount of blood. At that point, Lou decided he'd wait out in the surgical lounge.

"Suction," the surgeon yelled.

Jack tried to see as best he could from the head of the table. It was a spectacle the likes of which he had never seen. None of the surgeons had on gloves, masks, or gowns, and they had blood up to their elbows. It had all happened so quickly that no one had had a chance to follow the normal presurgical protocol. Jack listened intently to the banter, which only underlined something that he had already known: namely, that surgeons were a breed unto themselves. Despite the unorthodox nature of the event and the gore, they were enjoying themselves. It was as if the episode served to conveniently validate their enormous curative powers.

It was quickly determined that the man had suffered what would have been a mortal wound, except for the fact that it had happened at a major hospital. Two of the bullets had gone through the lungs. For the surgeons, that was a pedestrian problem. It was the third bullet that presented the challenge. It had, among other things, pierced the great vessels.

Quickly, the damaged vessels were clamped off, and the patient was put on the heart-lung machine. At that point, some of the surgeons left to start their own scheduled cases while the two thoracic surgeons stopped long enough to scrub and don the usual operating-room apparel. Jack moved over to chat with the anesthesiologist about what she thought the chances were the man would survive, but the nursing supervisor tapped him on the shoulder.

"I'm sorry," the supervisor said, "but we're trying to reclaim sterility here. You'll have to leave and put on scrubs if you want to observe." She handed him a pair of booties to cover his street shoes.

"Okay," Jack said agreeably. He'd been amazed that he hadn't been kicked out earlier.

As Jack walked back down the long operating-room corridor, the events of the long night began to take their toll. He was exhausted to the point that his legs and feet felt as if he had weights strapped to them. As he passed the operating-room desk he shivered through a bout of discomfort akin to nausea. He found Lou sitting in the crowded surgical lounge, talking on his cell phone. In front of him on the coffee table were a wallet and a driver's license.

Jack sat down heavily in a chair facing Lou. Lou pointed to the driver's license without interrupting his conversation. Jack leaned forward and picked up the license. The name was David Rosenkrantz. Holding the card closer, Jack studied the laminated picture. The individual appeared like an all-American football player with a thick neck and a broad, toothy smile. He was a handsome man.

After flipping his phone shut, Lou looked over at Jack. Then he leaned forward with his elbows on his knees. "At the moment, I don't want a long explanation how this all happened," he said in a tired voice. "But I'd just like to know why. The last thing you promised me was that you were going to sit outside the CCU."

"I meant to," Jack said. "Then I realized the shift was changing, and I was suddenly worried the Rakoczi woman would disappear. I just wanted to make sure she hung around until you got here."

Lou rubbed his face briskly with both

hands and groaned. When he took his hands away, his eyes were red. He looked almost as bad as Jack. "Amateurs! I hate them," he remarked rhetorically.

"It never dawned on me she'd have a gun," Jack said.

"What about the other two recent gun-shot-wound deaths over here? Didn't they at least go through your pea brain?"

"No," Jack admitted. "I was really worried we wouldn't see her again. I thought I'd just ask her to stay. I wasn't going to accuse her of anything."

"Bad decision," Lou said. "That's the way people like you get killed."

Jack shrugged. In retrospect, he knew Lou was right.

"Did you look at the license of the man you shot?"

Jack nodded. He didn't like to think he'd actually shot somebody.

"Well, who is David Rosenkrantz?"

Jack shook his head. "I haven't the slightest idea. I've never seen him before nor heard his name."

"Is he going to live?"

"I don't know. I was about to ask the anesthesiologist's opinion, but I was told to leave. I think the surgeons are pretty optimistic, the way they have been talking. If he does make it, it proves that if you are going to get shot, make sure you get shot in a decent hospital."

"Very funny," Lou said without laughing. "What's Laurie's status?"

"Good! Very good! Or at least it was when I left. Let's walk down and check in with the CCU. I didn't expect to be gone this long. It's just down the hall."

"Fine with me," Lou said, getting to his feet.

The CCU charge nurse came out of the unit and told Jack and Lou that Laurie was doing fine, she was sleeping, and that her doctor had been in to see her. She also said that there were plans afoot to move her to the University Hospital, where her father was on staff.

"Sounds good," Jack said. He looked at Lou.

"Sounds good to me, too," Lou said.

After the CCU, Lou wanted Jack to come with him down to the emergency room. He wanted Jack to identify for the record that the dead woman was the nurse who Jack had seen in Laurie's room. He explained that when he'd left the OR earlier, he'd called police headquarters about setting up the Hummer as a crime scene and bringing the body inside the hospital. He was particularly interested in having the Glock checked by ballistics.

As they walked back toward the elevator, Lou cleared his throat. "I know you're exhausted, and for good reason, but I'm afraid I have to know what happened from the moment you got down to the garage."

"I caught the nurse just as she was about to get into her car," Jack said. "She already had the door open, so I yelled and ran up to her. Obviously, she wasn't cooperative, which is an understatement. When I grabbed her arm to keep her from getting in the vehicle, she kneed me in the balls."

"Ouch!" Lou commiserated.

"That was when she pulled out the gun and ordered me into the car."

"Take this as a lesson," Lou said. "Never get into a car with an armed felon."

"I didn't think I had a lot of choice," Jack said.

They reached the elevator lobby, where there was a smattering of people waiting. They lowered their voices.

"That's when I appeared on the scene," Lou said. "I saw you get into the car. I could even see the woman's gun. Unfortunately, I had to wait for a few cars before I ran over. What went on in the car?"

"It all happened so fast. The guy was obviously already in there, apparently waiting for Rakoczi. Just when she was about to shoot me, he shot her. God . . ." Jack's voice trailed off as he thought of how close he had come to one last trip over to the OCME.

"You crazy ass," Lou complained. He gave Jack's shoulder a light smack and then shook his head. "You have this weird penchant for getting into the damnedest situations. You walked right into the middle of an execution-style hit. Are you aware of that?"

"I am now," Jack admitted.

The elevator arrived and they boarded. They moved to the back of the car.

"Okay," Lou said. "The question is why? Do you have any ideas?"

"I do," Jack said. "But let me backtrack. First of all, Laurie was almost killed with a sudden overwhelming dose of potassium, which is a clever way to kill someone.

There's no way to document it, thanks to the physiology of potassium in the human body, but don't get hung up on that. The point is that I think all the patients in Laurie's series were killed in this shrewd fashion, but they weren't random targets. All of them, including Laurie, had tested positive for the genetic markers of serious medical illnesses."

The elevator arrived on the first floor, and Lou and Jack got off. The hospital was crowded with people, and they kept their voices down.

"So how does all this add up to a gangland-style hit on the nurse?" Lou questioned.

"I think it is evidence that there is a major conspiracy here," Jack said. "I think if you are lucky, you're going to learn the nurse was working for someone in some tangled web which will eventually lead back to an actuarial type within the AmeriCare administration."

"Wait a second!" Lou said, pulling Jack to a stop. "Are you suggesting that a major healthcare provider like AmeriCare might be involved with killing their own patients? That's crazy!"

"Is it?" Jack questioned. "In any geographical area where these healthcare giants actually compete with each other, something they try to avoid by choking off competition or buying out the opposition if they are big enough, they compete with the cost of premiums. How do they determine their premiums? Well, the old-fashioned, actuarial way was to pool risk, figure out how much it is going to cost to take care of a group of people by essentially guessing, then add on profit, divide by the number of people, and bingo, there's the premium. Suddenly, under everybody's noses, the rules have changed. With the decipherment of the human genome, the old concept of health insurance is bound for the trash heap. Using single, easily performed tests, people who are destined to cost them significant money can be recognized. The problem is that the large healthcare companies cannot show discrimination, so they have to take them. At that juncture, from a purely business perspective, they should be eliminated."

"You mean to tell me that you think some AmeriCare administrators are capable of committing murder?"

"Actually, no!" Jack said. "The actual killing has to be done by severely screwed-up individuals, which I'm quite certain you'll be learning about Miss Rakoczi if she is indeed the culprit. What I'm talking about is a horrid variant of white-collar crime with varying levels of complicity. At the top, I'm talking about some person who might have been recruited from the automobile industry or any other business, who sits in an office, far removed from patients, and thinks about the bottom line exclusively. Unfortunately, that's the way business works and why some level of government oversight is necessary as a general rule in a free-market economy. I might sound like a misanthrope, but human beings tend to be basically self-interested and often function as if they are wearing blinders."

Lou shook his head. He was disgusted. "I can't believe you're saying all this. Hospitals for me have always been the place you go to be taken care of."

"Sorry," Jack said. "Times are changing. The deciphering of the human genome has been a monumental event. It has briefly dropped off everyone's radar, but it is coming back big-time. It is going to change everything we know about medicine in the not-too-distant future. Most changes are going to be for the good, but some are going to be for the bad. It's always that way with technological advances. Maybe we shouldn't label them 'advances.' Maybe a less value-laden word like 'changes' would be better."

Lou stared at Jack. Jack stared back. Jack thought the detective's expression hovered somewhere between frustration and irritation.

"Are you pulling my leg about all this?" Lou questioned.

"No," Jack said with a short laugh. "I'm being serious."

Lou meditated for a moment and then said moodily, "I don't know if I want to live in your world. But screw it! Come on! Let's make this ID on Rakoczi."

They entered the ER, which was already overflowing with patients. Several uniformed policemen were in evidence. Lou sought out the ER director, Dr. Robert Springer. Dr. Springer took Lou and Jack back to a trauma room, the door of which was closed. Inside, they found Jasmine Rakoczi. She was lying naked on an ER bed. An endotracheal tube had been inserted and then attached to a respirator. Her chest was intermittently rising and falling. Behind her, on a flat-screen monitor, blips recorded her pulse and blood pressure. The blood pressure was low, but the pulse was normal.

"Well?" Lou asked. "Is this the lady you saw in Laurie's room?"

"It is," Jack said. Then he looked at Dr. Springer. "Why are you respiring her?"

"We want to keep her oxygenated," Dr. Springer said while he adjusted the respirator's rate.

"Don't you suspect her brainstem was destroyed?" Jack questioned. He was surprised that they were making such an effort in such a clearly moribund situation.

"Without doubt," Dr. Springer said, straightening up. "The organ people are trying to locate any next of kin. They want to salvage the internal organs."

Lou looked up at Jack. "Now that is going to be ironic," he said. "She might save a handful of people."

"Ironic isn't a strong enough word," Jack replied. "I'd lean toward mordantly satirical."

To Dr. Springer's surprise, the detective then cuffed the medical examiner on the head, accused him of being a pompous ass, and then the two walked out, laughing.

epilogue

6 WEEKS LATER

Detective Lieutenant Lou Soldano nosed his departmental Chevy over to the curb next to a fire hydrant and tossed onto the dash the plastic-laminated card that spelled out who he was and who owned the vehicle. He then reached over, got out his breath spray from the glove compartment, and gave himself a few good squirts to hide the Marlboros he'd inhaled en route. Tipping his rearview mirror down, he looked as his reflection. He needed a shave, but he always needed a shave, especially at a quarter after eight in the evening. Since he couldn't do anything about his stubble, he used his fingers to get his hair all going in the same direction. Satisfied with his appearance, he opened the door and stepped out onto the street.

The air had the silky feel of a spring night. Thanks to daylight savings, the sky was a light rose color that faded to silvery violet to the east. Lou walked up Second Avenue with a spring to his step. He'd called Jack and Laurie that afternoon in the hope of meeting up with them to bring them up to speed on the AmeriCare case, and they had invited him to join them for dinner at their favorite restaurant, Elios.

Lou had already had a few meals with Jack and Laurie at Elios—some good, some not so good. In the latter category was the evening Laurie announced that she was a marrying the twerp she had dragged along. Lucky for everyone, it was a false alarm and the memory of the evening brought a smile to Lou's face. It was also lucky that he and Jack didn't shoot themselves right there in the restaurant. They both had been devastated.

Lou paused outside. Directly in front of the door was Jack's mountain bike, secured to a parking meter with a panoply of locks. Lou shook his head. Neither he nor Laurie could talk Jack out of using the damn thing. Lou smiled wryly about Jack constantly ragging on him about his smoking being dangerous for his health, since the danger of riding a bike in the city, particularly the way Jack rode, was a thousand times greater.

Inside the restaurant, the evening's festivities were in full swing. People were clustered about the bar to the point of impinging on the diners occupying the coveted front tables. Lou felt decidedly self-conscious, as he always did around such high rollers, particularly the glitterati who seemed to laugh and talk a bit louder than everybody else.

After making his way through the bar crowd, Lou was faced with the jam-packed dining room. Slowly, his eyes made the circuit, looking for a familiar face. With relief, he spied Jack and Laurie at a table in the far right-hand corner.

With as many tables and chairs packed into the room as humanly possible, it took

Lou some time to worm his way over to his friends. En route he knocked one man's arm, causing him to spill his wine. When Lou turned around to apologize, he dragged the belt of his raincoat, which was over his arm, through another person's soup. Despite these travails, he eventually made it.

"Sorry I'm late," Lou said as he gave Laurie's cheek a peck and shook hands with Jack across the table. He made sure he didn't knock over their fluted glasses with his arm or his coat.

"No matter," Laurie said. She pulled a bottle of champagne from the ice bucket and filled the glass in front of Lou.

Lou tried to drape his coat over the curved back of his chair, but his antics quickly brought an attentive waiter, who took the coat. Lou sat down and used his napkin to blot the line of perspiration that had appeared along his hairline. To him, it felt as though it was 90° inside the restaurant. He quickly undid the top button on his shirt, loosened his tie, and then fanned himself. "Next time, we'll meet down in Little Italy with my people," he said.

"You're on," Laurie said cheerfully.

After a few pleasantries, Jack said, "I'm

really curious about the AmeriCare investigation. What's the news?"

"Me, too," Laurie said.

Lou eyed his friends. When he thought about their friendship, he was always a little amazed. He wasn't even friendly with his own doctor, nor his kids' doctor, for that matter. Most of Lou's friends were other police officers, although there were a couple of firemen who he played cards with on a regular basis. But Jack and Laurie were different than the other doctors Lou had encountered. They didn't look down on him for his education or what he did for a living. In fact, he felt it was just the opposite.

"Okay," Lou said. "Business before pleasure, but let's see! Where shall I begin? First off, I have to say that what Jack told me the morning Jasmine Rakoczi got shot has turned out to be prophetic. Jack, my boy, you were on the money."

Jack smiled and gave Lou a thumbs-up sign.

"However," Lou continued. "The lion's share of the kudos goes to Laurie for being persistent in the face of universal ignorance on everybody else's part, including Jack's, and for finding Rakoczi's tissue under Stephen Lewis's fingernails."

"I'll drink to that," Laurie said. She raised her flute and clicked glasses with the others.

"Now," Lou continued after putting his glass down. "Ballistics are back, and they indicate that Rakoczi's gun killed both my captain's sister-in-law and Roger Rousseau." Lou reached over and gave Laurie's forearm a squeeze. "Sorry to bring up a painful subject."

Laurie smiled and nodded acknowledgment of Lou's sensitiveness.

"Ballistics also indicate that David Rosenkrantz's gun killed Rakoczi, so that gets Jack off the hook."

"Very funny," Jack said.

"Now, I know you guys are familiar with Rousseau's head and hands being found in Rakoczi's refrigerator, since they were brought over to the OCME, so I won't go into that."

"Please don't," Laurie said.

"Since David Rosenkrantz was from out of state, the FBI jumped into the ring from day one, and lo and behold, there have been similar deaths in AmeriCare hospitals across the country. And now in each location, there is an ongoing investigation as to the perpetrator."

"Good grief!" Jack blurted. "When I suggested a conspiracy, I was thinking of one or two higher-ups and Rakoczi—certainly nothing on a national scale."

"Well, let me get to the juicy part," Lou said. He pulled his chair closer to the table and leaned forward. "Our saving that dirtbag Rosenkrantz has turned out to be key. He's copped a plea and has cooperated by implicating his immediate boss, Robert Hawthorne. Hawthorne has turned out to be one interesting dude, and the lynchpin of the whole operation. He's a retired Army Special Forces officer and maintains contact with the military through a network of buddies. He's had an ongoing interest in dissatisfied military medical personnel. Whether he was recruited or had just cleverly created a niche for himself, we don't know. What we do know is that he has been acting like an independent contractor secretly in the employ of a big Saint Louis law firm, which specializes in plaintiff malpractice work. This firm is extremely active, carrying on simultaneous cases all over the country. As near as can be determined, Hawthorne recruited and ran a group of mostly disgruntled nurses, some of whom had been in the military, who were paid to communicate episodes of adverse outcomes from their respective hospitals, and who got bonuses if the case went to trial."

"I've heard about that," Jack said.

"Me, too," Laurie said. "It's mostly OB and anesthesia cases. It's the modern equivalent of the ambulance chasers of old."

"Well, I don't know about those details," Lou said. "But here comes the most interesting part. Over the last few years, there has been movement to make managed-care companies liable for malpractice, which, as an aside, seems reasonable to me."

"What's reasonable and what isn't has little to do with decisions about healthcare in this country," Jack interjected. "Everything is decided according to vested interests."

"By a strange twist of fate," Lou continued, "managed-care companies and malpractice plaintiff attorneys suddenly found themselves in the same bed in their desire to keep any malpractice-reform legislation from happening. I mean, the goals were slightly different in that the managed-care companies didn't want things changed so they could be sued, and the malpractice attorneys didn't want changes that would cap pain-and-suffering awards or eliminate contingency fees, among other things. Both groups employed lobbyists to make sure malpractice law did not change, which brought them together. So, essentially, their waking up in the same bed spawned a weird marriage between the two groups. How it happened is anybody's guess, but someone in AmeriCare must have realized they could use the shady services of Robert Hawthorne, since at least some of his contacts were . . . what should we say? Psychopaths or sociopaths capable of murder without pangs of conscience."

"The newest term is 'antisocial disorder,'" Laurie chimed in.

"Okay, whatever," Lou said. "Anyway, some AmeriCare bureaucrat—or bureaucrats, as the case may be—became interested in tapping into the law firm's cast of unsavory medical insiders, which the law firm had formed to drum up business, in order to set up an elimination scheme for high-risk subscribers. These were the subscribers who they knew would be costing them millions of dollars in specialized care and thereby put upward pressure on premium rates. I mean, it makes some sort of sick sense."

"Good grief!" Jack reiterated. "This is close to what I feared, but on a larger scale."

"Let me finish!" Lou said after making sure no one was overhearing. "Whether there was any further cooperation in the works, such that the malpractice lawyers would then take advantage of the deaths by appealing to the next of kin to sue the doctors involved, we don't know. So far, we are only aware of one suit involving a doctor at Saint Francis Hospital."

"But that suit will surely be dropped now that homicide is suspected," Jack said.

"Maybe so," Lou said, "But I wouldn't count on it, since the perpetrator was in the hospital's employ."

"So, what's the state of the investigation at this point?" Laurie asked.

"There's a very active hunt for the Jasmine Rakoczis at these other institutions where a similar pattern of deaths has occurred. The hope is to nab one and have that individual turn state's evidence. If that happens, maybe the whole house of cards will tumble down."

"Have there been any indictments so far from the hit man's testimony?" Laurie asked.

"Only Robert Hawthorne, who isn't talking and is in fact out on sizable bail," Lou said. "Unfortunately, the hit man was not really apprised of the whole operation. All he knew was that his boss, Robert, was a frequent visitor to the law firm. He didn't know whom he saw or what was ever talked about."

"Nobody in the AmeriCare hierarchy has been indicted?" Jack asked plaintively.

"Not yet," Lou admitted. "But we have our fingers crossed."

"What a nightmare," Laurie said with a shudder, remembering something of her ordeal in the hospital.

"Hey!" Lou said, eyeing the bubbles rising in the flute next to his water glass as if it were the first time he'd seen them. "This is champagne." He reached out and lifted the bottle from the ice bucket. "I don't know why I'm looking at this. I wouldn't know one brand from the next." He nestled the bottle back into the ice. "What is this, some kind of celebration?"

"Sort of," Laurie said with a smile. She looked at Jack, who raised his eyebrows as if there was a secret.

"Okay, out with it!" Lou commanded. He looked from one to the other.

"Well, it's not that big a deal," Laurie said. "I had a medical test today, which wasn't very pleasant I must say, but the result was reassuring. Apparently, the reason I had an ectopic pregnancy was because I had an abnormal or damaged oviduct. The test I had today showed my remaining oviduct is perfectly normal."

"That's great!" Lou said. He nodded a few times. He again looked back and forth between his two friends, both of whom were avoiding eye contact by looking down and swirling their drinks. "Well," Lou added. "Does this favorable result mean you two are planning to put this oviduct to the real test?"

Laurie looked up at Jack and said, "Unfortunately, at the moment, it just means it could be put to the real test."

"Too bad," Lou commented. "Well, if you need any volunteers to test that duct, I'm available."

Jack laughed and looked up at Lou and then Laurie. "Why do I have the feeling you two are ganging up on me?"

"Hey, I'm just trying to be a good friend," Lou said while raising both hands to profess his innocence.

"Well, good friend," Jack said, putting his arm around Laurie. "In the oviduct-testing business, I think Laurie and I can manage just fine."

"I'll drink to that," Lou said, raising his glass.

"Me, too," Laurie said.

author's note

The announcement of the completion of the first draft of the human genome's 3.2 billion base pairs was made with great fanfare in June of 2000, and included the participation of two heads of state, President Bill Clinton and Prime Minister Tony Blair. Although the media's excitement could be measured by coverage on both the network evening news as well as prominent front-page space in all the major newspapers on the following day, the public greeted the event with vague interest, a touch of bewilderment, and varying degrees of ennui, then quickly forgot about it. Despite glowing promises of future benefits, the subject apparently was too esoteric. Perhaps because of the public's reaction, the mass media soon forgot about it as well, except for a few follow-up articles on the colorful personalities of the leading scientists of the two competing organizations that carried out the painstaking work and the almost soap opera-like race to the finish.

The public's disregard for this landmark achievement has continued, even though the involved science and technology have been charging ahead, and reporting startling discoveries, such as the surprising fact that we humans have only about twenty-five thousand or so genes—a far cry from the hundred thousand experts had predicted not too long ago—and not that many more than an organism as comparatively simple as a roundworm! (This discovery is a blow to humanity's hubris equivalent to the Copernican revelation that the earth revolved around the sun, instead of vice versa.) In short, the decipherment of the human genome and the avalanche of research cascading from it has disappeared from most everyone's radar except for those working in the two new and related endeavors of Genomics and Bioinformatics. Genomics, in simple terms, is the study of the flow of information in a cell, while Bioinformatics is the application of computers to make sense of the enormous amount of data coming from Genomics.

In my mind, this lack of interest or apathy or whatever it might be called is startling; I believe the decipherment of the human genome might be the most important milestone in the history of medical science to date. After all, it gives us all the letters of the "book of life" in the right order, despite our having, as of yet, imperfect understanding of the language or the punctuation. In other words, in a cryptic form that is now being decoded with gathering speed, we have access to all the information nature has amassed to make and run a human being! As a consequence, the knowledge of the human genome will change just about everything we know about medicine, and some of the changes are going to happen sooner rather than later.

Like every major discovery/milestone in science, this one will have both good and bad consequences. Consider the consequences stemming from research into the inner structure and workings of the atom. We didn't do so well in that instance, as evidenced by current events, and we have to do better with the decipherment of the human genome, since it behooves society to consider all consequences of major leaps in science and technology and deal with them in a proactive manner rather than on a reactive, ad hoc basis.

Marker deals with one of the negative consequences—i.e., the negative impact of the ability to predict illness when confidentiality is breached and the information is obtained by or otherwise falls into the wrong hands. Unfortunately, the chances of this occurring will be high, since microarrays as described in *Marker* already exist, with the ability to test with ease for literally thousands of markers linked to deleterious genes with a single drop of blood. (A marker is a point alteration in the sequence of nucleotide bases forming the rungs of the ladder of the DNA molecule. Markers have been mapped throughout the human genome.) The microarray slides are read automatically by laser scanners, and the results, thanks to Bioinformatics, are fed directly into computers armed with appropriate software such that risk and hence cost can be predicted with rapidly advancing speed and accuracy. The end result will be that the concept of health insurance, which is based on pooling risk within specified groups, will become obsolete. In other words, risk cannot be pooled if it can be determined.

From my perspective, the implications of this developing state of affairs are prodigious. As a physician, I have always been against health insurance except for catastrophic care and for those financially unable to pay. The doctor-patient relationship is the most personal and rewarding for both the patient and the physician when a clear, direct fiduciary relationship exists. In such a circumstance, in my experience, both individuals value the encounter more, which invariably leads to more time, more attention to potentially important detail, and a higher level of compliance—all of which invariably results in a better outcome and a more rewarding experience.

With the power of Genomics and Bioinformatics obviating the pooling of risk within defined groups, I have had to revamp my position, which has resulted in my switching from one extreme to the other. I now feel that there is only one solution to the problem of paying for healthcare in the United States, indeed for all developed countries in this global economy: to pool risk for the entire nation. (Under the rubric of healthcare I mean preventive care, acute care, and catastrophic care.) Although I never thought I'd be advocating this, I now believe that the sooner we as a nation move to a government-sponsored, obviously nonprofit, tax-supported single-payer plan, the better off we will be. Only then will we be able to pool risk for the entire country, as well as decide rationally how much we should spend on healthcare in general. One of the other effects of Genomics on healthcare will be the opportunity to individualize care. The entire pharmacological basis of therapeutics will be changing, thanks to another new field: Pharmacogenics, which will tailor-make drugs for individual patients according to their unique genomic makeup. The benefits of such care will be enormous, but so will the costs. Since we already spend over 15 percent of our GDP on healthcare, this has to be an important consideration.

There are other compelling arguments for a national, single-payer plan for healthcare, but to my mind none of them is nearly as persuasive as the developing power of Genomics. But change will not come easily. As Jack Stapleton comments in *Marker:* "What's reasonable and what isn't has little to do with decisions about healthcare in this country. . . . Everything is decided according to vested interests." Difficulties aside, it is my fervent belief that the sooner we move to such a plan, the better off the country will be. Luckily, we have the experiences of a number of other industrialized countries that have already enacted single-payer systems to learn from.

I would like to add just a few words about how a nurse as antisocial as Jasmine Rakoczi could get—and keep—a nursing job. Quite simply, there is a severe nursing shortage in the United States, and our hospitals, even our premier academic centers, are forced to continuously recruit nurses. As mentioned in *Marker,* this recruitment extends to other countries, including undeveloped nations. The combination of low compensation and the pressure to increase productivity (translated into forcing individual nurses to take on more patients than they can reasonably handle) has created enough of an adverse working environment that experienced nurses seek alternate employment, and young men and women are reluctant to begin the long, arduous, and expensive training. What makes this particularly unfortunate is that we all know (at least those who have experienced hospitalization) that the onus of care is not on the doctors who write the orders and leave to go back to their busy offices or cozy homes but on the nurses who stay and carry them out. And for those people who have suffered a major problem in the hospital, it's more likely than not that it was a nurse who recognized it, called the physicians, and instituted lifesaving care. In my opinion and experience we need less high-priced administration, and better pay and optimum working conditions for our beleaguered nurses, who are, as Jasmine Rakoczi herself said, in the trenches, actually taking care of people.

—Robin Cook,
March 2005